Alien Land

ALIEN LAND

By Willard Savoy

With a foreword by Robert B. Stepto

NORTHEASTERN UNIVERSITY PRESS • BOSTON
Published by University Press of New England
Hanover and London

NORTHEASTERN UNIVERSITY PRESS
Published by University Press of New England
One Court Street, Lebanon, NH 03766
www.upne.com

Printed in the United States of America 5 4 3 2 1

Library of Congress Control Number: 2006933924
ISBN–13: 978–1–55553–657–2
ISBN–10: 1–55553–657–3

*All of the characters, all of the events, and all of the places in
this book are fictitious. Any resemblance to persons, living or
dead, is purely coincidental.*

DEDICATION

To my wife, with deepest affection, for without her patient endurance of the many tribulations known only to writers and to their wives, this book could never have been written—

To the child which my wife and I may someday have—and to the children of each American—in the fervent hope that at least one shall be brought to see more clearly the enduring need for simple humanity; that at least one shall because of its pages meet his fellows free of jaundice which twists the mind and hardens the heart against the importunities of the soul; in the hope too, that these shall understand that the importance of this story is not that a man went to live in an alien land, but that something fearful drove him to make the journey in the face of every instinct which was his.

In this hope, and to these, this book is dedicated.

WILLARD SAVOY

FOREWORD

THE PUBLICATION in early 1949 of *Alien Land*, written by "the newest Negro novelist," as Willard Savoy was dubbed by the New York *Herald Tribune*, met with immediate attention and considerable fanfare. Within weeks, the novel was reviewed in newspapers including the *Christian Science Monitor*, Chicago *Sun-Times*, Cleveland *Plain Dealer*, Pittsburgh *Courier*, Hartford *Courant*, San Francisco *Chronicle*, New York *Times*, and Washington *Post* as well as journals such as *Commonweal* and the *Saturday Review of Books*. The reviewers included estimable writers of the day, notably Nelson Algren, Arna Bontemps, and Ann Petry. Often referred to in the commentaries as Lt. Savoy of the U.S. Air Force (no doubt in response to the striking photograph of him in uniform on the dust jacket), Savoy was swiftly scheduled for book events ranging from high-publicity book signings at big-name bookstores such as Brentano's in Washington, D.C., to academic events including a seminar on "The Role of the Writer in Building One World" at Fisk University. The Book Shop division of *The Crisis* (the journal of the NAACP) offered *Alien Land* from the very moment of its publication; it is striking to see it in the same select fiction list for April 1949 that promotes Dorothy West's *The Living Is Easy*, Willard Motley's *Knock on Any Door*, William G. Smith's *Last of the Conquerors*, and Zora Neale Hurston's *Seraph on the Sewanee*.

Alien Land garnered this kind of attention in great part because Dutton, the major New York publishing house, believed in Savoy and his novel and marshaled the resources to provide a proper and hopefully profitable debut in public for author and book alike. The correspondence between Savoy and Dutton (copies of which have been generously shared with me by Lauret Savoy, Willard Savoy's daughter) reveals a publisher placing trade advertisements, planning sales conferences, and even musing about seeking blurbs from Sinclair Lewis and Eleanor Roosevelt! On the eve of *Alien Land*'s publication, Nicholas Wreden, a Vice President for Dutton, wrote Savoy declaring that "everything connected with the publication of *Alien Land* is progressing beautifully." He went on to remind Savoy that Dutton was planning to print 15,000 copies (3,000 more than originally intended) and to spend $5000 on the initial advertising.

Curiously enough, also on the eve of the novel's publication, Savoy received a quite different letter from J. R. de la Torre Bueno ("Bill B") in Dutton's publicity department about a "basic problem . . . a question." I must quote from the letter at length.

> When interviewers or others say to us, Is Willard Savoy himself of Negro extraction?—what shall our answer be? It will have to be direct and unequivocal—we will have to say No or Yes. We must be ready with our answer ahead of time—the same answer agreed to by both parties.

"Bill B" is not entirely happy bringing this matter up; he soon attempts to address it purely as a business matter (". . .I don't believe that either answer will have a marked effect on the sale of ALIEN LAND"). But then he returns to speaking heart-to-heart:

> . . . the answer could have a profound and lasting effect on your whole life and career. Your social life, your Army career, what else you can guess better than I. In thinking through to your answer, you must bear all possible ramifications in mind; and they are considerably more important to your happiness than to the success or failure of ALIEN LAND. That's why the question is yours to decide about, rather than ours. No doubt you have been thinking of it continuously . . .

"Bill B" adds that "we'll" need to know the answer in about three weeks.

What does one make of this? Many people at Dutton knew that Savoy was a Negro; Savoy himself was always forthright about this. Even so, was "Bill B" nevertheless considering being coy or evasive about Savoy's race for publicity purposes? Might it be that "Bill B" assumed that the story of *Alien Land's* "half-white" Kern Roberts is Savoy's story? Does this confusion tell us anything about Savoy's short-lived literary career or about his later reluctance to admit (to his daughter at least) that a literary career or first novel ever existed?

o   o   o

Willard Wilson Savoy was born in September 1916 (Kern Roberts, the novel's hero, is born the same year) in Washington, D.C., a city that is more a charged field than an urban backdrop in *Alien Land* and in a number of pieces he began but never published. His father, Alfred Kiger Savoy, was a principal and later assistant superintendent of the colored division of the District's public schools. Little is recorded of Savoy's mother, Laura Wilson Savoy; Savoy himself enters her in one document merely as "Laura W., housewife." But there seems to be much more to be said about her in terms of the forging of Savoy's identity and the making of *Alien Land*. For one thing, if Laura Wilson Savoy wasn't white, she was certainly white enough in appearance for her son to imagine, or perhaps more exactly to *experience*, what it was like for young Kern Roberts to grow up with a white mother in black Washington. (Photographs can be deceiving, but to see the photo taken at the Brentano's book party of Laura Savoy *and* her sister Margaret—two white matrons if you ever saw any—hovering above a sheepish looking Willard is to be convinced that this "black boy" must have had some childhood!).

The omnipresence for Savoy and for his young Kern of both their paternal and maternal surnames also begs attention. Early on in *Alien Land*, a mark of Kern's disavowal of the Negro race is his name change: "He was not Kern Roberts now. Not any more. He was Kern Adams—another, an entirely different person." "Adams" is not a name out of the blue; it is his mother's maiden name; Kern has decided he'd rather be his (white maternal) grandmother's ward than be his (black) father's son. Arguably, Willard Savoy could imagine Kern choosing between "Roberts" and "Adams" because he himself was both a "Wilson" and a "Savoy." He knew well how living within two names could signify living within a confused—or conflicted—racial identity.

But of central interest here is Savoy's selection of his mother's name, Laura, as Kern's mother's name. Of course, *Alien Land* is fiction, but what are we to make of the fact that the young white woman—who marries Kern's (near white) father, births Kern, willingly moves to Washington, "becomes a Negro," and tries to protect her son from the "twisting, tearing forces" awaiting in the District's Negro schools—bears the same name as Savoy's mother? Even more remarkable, what unbridled act of imagination might we be encountering when Savoy has young Kern witness the murder of his mother, Laura, by a brutish black man—in chapter one no less? One can only wonder what Laura Savoy thought of all this.

In the world of real events, Willard Savoy did attend Washington's Negro schools including the famed Dunbar High School, noted for a faculty as well credentialed as that of many colleges. On the subject of this esteemed faculty, Savoy would later in life be quite caustic: "It would seem now that the tiresome rantings of teachers equipped with dusty Masters degrees won on some minor variation of an oft repeated thesis, harked through the years with scant attention to the changes in the world, had a thin virtue." This grudging praise hardly masks the fact that the young Savoy, not unlike his young Kern Roberts, was contemptuous of the Washington "bona fide Café du Lait society" (which Kern terms the "Association of Oldest Inhabitants") and of the clubs, schools and churches that supported its aspirations and prejudices. Even so, despite whatever Savoy thought of Dunbar and his fellow black bourgeoisie classmates, he managed a record there that earned him matriculation at Howard University.

Savoy spent most of the 1930s attending college: six years were spent at premier historically black institutions, Howard and Fisk, and he was also a year at the University of Wisconsin. Curiously enough, given the writing and communications careers he later pursued, Savoy was a science student, majoring in organic chemistry. It appears that he did not earn a degree. One is tempted to assume that Savoy was a restless, independent soul in those days, as critical of certain prevailing modes of "striving" campus culture (especially at Howard and Fisk) as he had been of the milieu at Dunbar High. One can even imagine him majoring in chemistry in order to be "responsible" (to himself, to the race) in his studies, as "race men" like Charles Roberts, Kern's father, would insist he be, only to realize that he (like Kern) could not play out that role.

When the United States entered World War II in 1941, Savoy joined the U.S. Army Air Corps. By the end of the war, he was a First Lieutenant and Lead Navigator in the 618th Bombardment Squadron. After the war, he remained in the Air Force until 1949, assigned as a Lieutenant to the Press Branch, Air Information Division, U.S. Air Force, with offices in the Pentagon. In the years immediately before the publication of *Alien Land*, Savoy managed the Special Interest Unit of the Air Force's Public Relations Division. His work involved preparing copy on the activities of Negro military personnel worldwide for "use in media types ranging from TIME Inc., to SEP [Saturday Evening Post], Reader's Digest, Encyclopedia Brittanica [*sic*] . . . AP,

UP, and total range of Negro print." This is the "day job" that made the completion of *Alien Land* possible.

The Air Force enabled *Alien Land*; *Alien Land* was to enable for Savoy a new life beyond the military. What Savoy sought was something nearly impossible to find: relief from the daily reminders of being Negro in 1940s America. As he poignantly put the matter in a September 1949 letter to Arna Bontemps:

> I do know that I am looking for several things . . . One of them is a respite from the day to day, actively fighting-the-fight which has been my occupation for the past five years. Another, and certainly related, is the flight to a breathing spell in which personal dignity may be a thing accorded as a mere matter of course, rather than given with the grain of condescension one finds here.

Savoy's "flight" would take him to France and to "all of Asia," where he wrote speeches and news copy for the "Marshall Plan" Economic Cooperation Administration. By 1953, Savoy was in Los Angeles, breaking into the "TV game." Television was to be his "bread and butter" while he finished a new novel about a Negro artist from a Washington middle-class family.

○   ○   ○

African American fictions and other narratives often are set in carefully constructed geographies: freedom and oppression are mapped; each has a landscape and a climate; each has exterior and interior spaces to be negotiated. Though there is some suggestion in *Alien Land* that Negroes can be alien, and alienated, in all of America's geographies, the alien land referenced in the novel's title is most specifically the American South.

In passages reminiscent of W. E. B. Du Bois's descriptions in *The Souls of Black Folk* of traveling South ("If you wish to ride with me you must come into the Jim Crow Car"), Savoy first introduces the region by way of portraying Kern Roberts's journey "as a Negro traveler" southward from Cincinnati, then southward still from Nashville to Valley View, the small Alabama town where he will live with his Aunt Paula and Uncle Jake and attend the local black college. The Jim Crow car is a venue where the Negro is "in his place," where "if his spirit feels the vise of shame drawing in upon it it is helpless." The Jim Crow car, though in motion, denies freedom of movement. How ironic, as Savoy knows full well, that the only trains in *Alien Land* providing

Jim Crow cars south of Nashville are the *Dixie Flyer* and the *Comet*. (The names of the trains are like the names of slave ships; "bright" and "ironical," as the poet Robert Hayden claimed in "Middle Passage.") Savoy is also attentive to signage: "Kern's mood changed with . . . the first 'For Colored' sign he had seen." While Kern had doubtless seen such signs when growing up in Washington, these signs signify that "the land through which he rode was alien and hating." Kern discovers that there are more signs to come, including the big one greeting him at the Valley View train station.

And the land: "Beyond Nashville . . . the rolling, green hills gave way to a broken, rutted land on the face of which long, ragged, narrowing gashes showing red earth, ran upward and out of sight into the hillsides." Once in Alabama, Kern is at first hopeful; the "softness of the night" suggests that Valley View "might not be so bad." But the road out to Paula and Jake's prim and tidy home is a "short grayish strip . . . deeply rutted"; it pitches Jake's little car back and forth. There are railroad tracks to cross and a steep hill to climb. Little wonder that the air seems to Kern "filled with something strange." Little wonder, too, that something awful is about to happen.

The North in *Alien Land* includes New York City, the principal site of the "Interlude" chapters which take place in the 1940s and which depict Kern's struggle with his racial identity as he begins to write (personally as well as professionally) and attempts to be truthful with Marianne, the white woman he comes to love. Kern's New York is familiar to readers of modern African American "passing" novels. His "dangerous" irresistible trips up to Harlem recall those of Nella Larsen's Claire Kendry in *Passing* (though not with the same fatal result). Moreover, like James Weldon Johnson's Ex-Colored Man, Kern, once in New York, is not merely racially ambiguous but a white man who has made a little money—who is *also* a black man a white woman is willing to marry. Uncannily, when both the Ex-Colored Man and Kern muse at the end of their respective stories about what it might have been like, in Savoy's words, to be "one with that tiny band of men—the Whites and Washingtons, Du Bois and Wilkins and Douglass—men who gave their whole lives to the fight for a race," we sense that both protagonists can make the gesture of such sentiment because they are at peace with the "bargain with Life" each has forged.

Life in New York may have created the ingredients for such peace but the site for future happiness is "Home" in Vermont, with

Marianne and daughter Margaret (named in memory of Kern's mother's mother—note, too, that *Savoy's* mother's mother and sister were named Margaret!). Though not without its own occasions for disappointment, Vermont is *Alien Land*'s upper North and moral high ground precisely as Alabama is the novel's lower South and moral abyss. Vermont is the land of Kern's mother's people, the Adamses. When Kern flees Alabama and the violence that destroys the lives of Paula and Jake, he seeks out Vermont, his grandmother, and close proximity to his mother's grave (Kern's grandparents do not get to raise him in Vermont, but they do get to bury their daughter there; Charles, his father, doesn't dare stand in the way of that). When Kern changes his surname to Adams, it is as if he seeks not only to reclaim New England for himself but to reenter the Garden, to begin again in an Adamic sense. Vermont may be where a distraught Kern rehearses being a white boy snarling "Nigger" after fleeing Alabama at age nineteen (what might the therapists tell us about Kern landing upon *this* definition of how to become a white boy?), but it is also where he eventually becomes the best person he can be: a "self-realized" man who figures out how to reconcile with his father at the same time that he refuses to be his father's version of a near-white black man.

Kern's reconciliation with Charles—after nine years of acrimony and absence—occurs in Washington, D.C. This is in keeping with Savoy accentuating the fact that so much that happens to Kern and to his family occurs in the nation's capital. Not unlike William Wells Brown and other earlier African American narrativists who limn images of slave markets cheek to jowl with the District's halls of legislation and justice, Savoy repeatedly creates courtroom scenes, including a final one in which Charles argues before the Supreme Court, dramatizing how elusive justice is for the Negro even in a venue like the capital where one would hope it would be most accessible. At the other end of the spectrum from the High Court, at least in terms of solemnity, is a District Negro barber shop—The Tuxedo Tonsorial Parlor—which Savoy (with considerable ethnographic prowess) also fills with speech. A mark of Savoy's talent and his politics is that the "dozens" boomed by the barber shop patrons are as witty and soulful as the court orations by the Negro lawyers are sonorous and eloquent. In either venue, the ur-text is the narrative of being, as one barber shop brother puts it, "Jim Crowed in the Capitol."

Above all, one must note what befalls the Roberts family personally because Charles has chosen the capital as the site of his family's new "Negro" life. Washington, D.C., is a charged field in *Alien Land* in great part because it is a stage. Charles outwardly rails against acting and the theatre when son Kern shows an adolescent's passion for it, little realizing that he himself is playing a highly-scripted role as a light-skinned civil rights lawyer who has suddenly discovered his blackness. Moreover, Charles is hardly prepared to accept that in coercing his white Vermonter spouse to play the role of a Washington Negro wife and mother he may well have imposed the circumstances that led to her violent death.

In chapter one, Laura Roberts is fatally in the wrong place at the wrong time because she is desperate to see her one childhood friend residing in Washington, Dorcas Kuydendahl, to explain her despair over Charles's determination to send Kern to the Negro schools (in essence, she fears that her son will become as much as stranger to her as her race-absorbed husband has become). While on her way home, traversing that part of the park (Rock Creek Park, no doubt) that leads to the streetcar that makes "the rattling journey down the long winding hill along 'You' Street, teeming with Negroes," Laura and Kern are separated and Laura is accosted, groped, and stabbed. Dorcas, who had walked part way with them, hears Laura's cries and is soon on the scene. Taking charge, she orders that Laura be transported to her home, the Netherlands Embassy where her husband is secretary.

This in itself is an extraordinary "geographical" expression of the situation. Best friend Dorcas determines that Laura, in what remains of her life, doesn't need to be in a white hospital with her husband screaming at her for "passing," or in a Negro hospital futilely playing the Negro mother right to the end. Dorcas's arrangements for her dear friend are a gift: an opportunity to let Laura live her last hours in what is in effect another country, a small space in small remove from the race wars decimating the nation, the nation's capital, and Laura's family.

Laura Roberts's death occurs specifically in 1927. Why that date, we might ask? One reason is so that we might understand that the preceding seven years of racial turmoil afflicting Washington and the Roberts family in particular are those that erupted right at the end of World War I, especially once the black troops returned. Willard Savoy would have been especially mindful of such tensions, having just recently served in—and returned from—World War II. Another reason for the date is so that we can know quite specifically that Kern is age ten or eleven when he witnesses the assault of his mother, is cuffed by the assailant, is brutalized at school for identifying a black man as the assailant (however true), and when he begins the sorry remaining years of his childhood being raised by an absent father and Nettie, a spiteful colored housekeeper who seems to have transferred her contempt for Kern's mother to Kern. (A key moment in the story thread concerning Kern's fascination with the theatre involves Nettie saving and mischievously presenting to Charles a playbill that "convicts" Kern of "passing" at a "white" theatre in order to see a production of Hamlet. Shortly thereafter, Kern assaults Nettie's boyfriend, when he surely wants to beat her, for every intrusion including sitting in his mother's chair.)

Savoy may also have chosen 1927 because no year more epitomizes the successes of the Harlem Renaissance. And so, if you are Savoy, an aspiring African American writer in the 1940s, determined like Richard Wright and Chester Himes among others to declare a new project well removed from what you deem the tepid aesthetic of the Renaissance 1920s, you might well begin *Alien Land* with a killing in Washington instead of a gay Harlem party. (A related matter is that *Alien Land*, like many of its contemporary texts, is a swing-era novel virtually bereft of music: it seems beholden to the concept that even a whisper of music will entertain, not edify, and hence dilute the message.) The 1940s-style aesthetic project to which Savoy aspires is well expressed when the barber at the Tuxedo Tonsorial Parlor supports Kern's desire to become a writer by declaring, "We need writers. Need people to tell our story to the world. To tell the truth—tell when we right and when we wrong. . . . Every people need that. Too few of us do it. Dunbar and Johnson and those—good enough for their time. But things are changing now and we need to tell today's story. Got a few men like Hughes and Cullen and such telling it in poems. But that ain't good enough. We still need the cold facts told in writing."

This opinion clearly privileges prose over poetry and "cold facts" over whatever might be construed in writing as warm and less than factual—feelings like sentiment or compassion. If this is indeed Savoy's own opinion, too, it confirms that he was, in his own way, to be numbered among writers like Richard Wright and Franz Fanon, writers whom he studied and admired. And it explains why Savoy, like Wright and Fanon, would write of the anger and madness besetting the Negro in what are often clinical terms. There is more than one instance in *Alien Land* when a black man's rage at his circumstances, often expressed in the most poignant personal vernacular ("You take 'n take 'til you feel murder build up 'n you gotta go—or die"), reads like something coldly impersonal—like clinical transcription. This is because Savoy, like Wright and others, believes that there is fundamentally nothing in the Negro's individual experience that does not bespeak a larger, national American malaise. Even what seems unique in the life of Kern Roberts is, Savoy would argue, a story that could have been anticipated, given the race rituals of the national culture.

While *Alien Land* shares features with the African American fictions (and nonfictions) of its time, it does possess its own singular attributes, which invariably challenge one protocol or another. For one thing, the novel is in its own way at times frankly sexual or erotic. In one of the Interlude chapters, for example, the evening gets late and Kern ends up spending the night at Marianne's apartment. The episode, including the "morning after," is tastefully offered; when Marianne whispers "You are home," she expresses the love in both their hearts. But still, the fact is that two unmarried people have just bedded each other; one is white and the other, Kern, is a quadroon Negro. The episode is challenging in its time, notably in insisting that interracial sex may be simply and disarmingly human, and not inevitably violent or criminal.

More extraordinary, however, are those moments in *Alien Land* when Savoy's gorgeous women of color parade through, like a bevy of 1940s pin-ups in a lonely soldier's calendar. Kern expects his Aunt Paula to be "a dour old maid"; imagine his astonishment when he discovers her to be "a willowy, tall girl, with a wealth of shining black hair . . . a golden brown girl . . . an unusually beautiful young woman." The element of repetition in this passage in itself expresses Kern's wonder. And there are more intoxicating young ladies to come, including the demure Adoriah (note the name!) whose eyelashes, olive skin, flowing hair, "Indianlike" cheekbones, and beguiling smile are mesmerizing. She becomes Kern's steady date at Valley View College.

The most remarkable colored beauty of them all is Samuella "Sammy" Thompson. On the one hand, Savoy emphasizes her rage and boldness in frankly relating how she and two other Valley View coeds were accosted by some local Alabama rednecks. On the other hand, for reasons not entirely clear, Savoy also wants us to admire how sexy Sammy is when she is angry. Not to be overlooked in Savoy's rendering of this performance, which pointedly takes place in the college's Playhouse theatre, is Sammy's mixed-race heritage ("Hagar has contributed to Sammy's blood"), her connection to economic power ("I am going home to my daddy's lumber company, and every goddam Southerner he has working there is going to get the boot"), and her mobility ("[T]his child of Hagar is leaving here as soon as money comes by wire"). All this, combined with certain natural endowments, makes Sammy the "hottest" woman in the novel: "Pushing her flaming red hair angrily back from her ears, green eyes flashing, her full figure tense with excitement and anger, she seemed older and more mature than her listeners—as mature as she actually was."

Later, after her account of wrestling free from the "ragged peckerwoods," we are told that Sammy "pressed her clenched fists tight against her hips, her breasts rising and falling with her deep stormy breathing." Mac Rodgers, the drama coach, chastises Sammy for not acting more ladylike, but that doesn't seem to be the point. The point is that Sammy is neither a lady nor a girl (even African American literature is full of both) but a (newly created albeit fantasized) Woman. Hence, when she gets right up in Rodgers's face and tells him that she is a "big girl" who is absolutely certain that leaving Alabama isn't running away but *leaving*, Kern Roberts listens carefully. This is the very thing he should be able to say to his father, but can't manage to say, when he determines on his own flight from the South.

Most central to *Alien Land*—and to African American literary history—is how Savoy advances the modern fictive project (that we first associate with James Weldon Johnson and his Ex-Colored Man) of presenting a mixed-race protagonist who is male, not female. Much of what is new in the novel is generated by one simple reversal of expectations: in Savoy's plot the white parent is the mother and the black parent the father. What this means, at the very least, is that the maternal ties that indelibly bind the protagonist to his colored mother and her race in so many other preceding fictions function here to explain Kern's loyalty to his white mother and forebears. *Alien Land* ends with Kern, Marianne, and daughter Margaret (named in memory of Kern's *maternal* white grandmother) residing in Vermont, the ancestral land of Laura Roberts, his mother. One senses that Kern had been journeying there ever since his mother died and he discovered that he could only find peace in his father's house when he retreated to his mother's private rooms.

Charles Roberts is the black parent—the black father—but neither phrase neatly sums him up, in part because he is also a mixed-race protagonist. Indeed, one way to think of Charles (with literary history as a guide) is to see him as the familiar mixed-race character (white father/black mother) who, in Savoy's novel, does two extraordinary things: he chooses to be a black man and a race man and to align himself with race men (Douglass, Du Bois, et al.) while helping to found the Freedom League (to be likened to the NAACP); and he fathers Kern, the new mixed-race character (black father/white mother). According to the preferred narrative among African Americans, Charles has made the right, heroic choice in becoming a race man. However, for Savoy, ever the modernist, this does not mean that Charles is flawless. He is distant as a husband, cold and nearly violent as a father, and devoted to his work to a dangerous degree. Charles is, as the New York *Times* review opined, "self-righteous." At times, his self-righteousness is a form of insanity. In a novel full of angry, maddened, plebian black men, Charles is the educated colored crazy. That in itself renders the reconciliation at the end between Charles and Kern difficult to applaud. In part, we worry about Kern and his family: *which* Charles is about to visit them in Vermont?

Willard Savoy continued writing after the publication of *Alien Land* and completed a novel, entitled at least for a time *Michael Gordon,* which was summarily rejected in 1954 and 1955. According to Savoy's records, his novel was unacceptable because it "'attacked' a then 'sacred cow'—Washington D.C. in the earliest stages of desegregation and school integration." Savoy was also told that he had written "an angry, bitter, hopeless and untrue story." Timing is everything, and the rejection of Savoy's *Michael Gordon* in the mid-1950s may well have had more to do with McCarthyism, the Cold War, and the *Brown v. Board of Education* decision than with anything inherently wrong with Savoy's new novel. Then, too, it may well be that Savoy was still writing in the 1950s a certain kind of angry, protest, 1940s novel that seemed particularly out of date, especially after Ralph Ellison's *Invisible Man* was published to widespread acclaim in 1952. Who can be sure?

What we do know is that *Alien Land,* the novel Willard Savoy did publish, is remarkable as a mid-twentieth-century reinvention of the "passing" novel. Moreover, it is also remarkable as a mid-century protest novel, complete with portraits of how fatal violence and freighted courtroom deliberations, North and South, affect the lives of complex, racially mixed people. Savoy was always thinking forward, convinced that the next book would prove to kith and kin what he was worth. He should have been more satisfied with *Alien Land* than he seemed to be: it is a gift to his parents, to his wife and daughter, and certainly a fascination for students of American literature.

ROBERT B. STEPTO

Acknowledgments
I thank Richard Yarborough, series editor, and Ellen Wicklum of the University Press of New England for their considerable help and generosity. I thank Lauret Savoy for urging the republication of her father's novel, and for trusting me to play a role in making that happen. Lauret Savoy also shared with me all sorts of documents related to the first publication of *Alien Land*, including announcements, reviews, her father's correspondence, and his private journal entries. These remarkable materials greatly assisted my work on the foreword.

Alien Land

PROLOGUE

NEW ENGLAND—1935

THE AUTUMN WIND sifted down from the high hill-locked bowl that held the cold waters of Lake Cabojan. Small smickers of it made their separate ways through thick-clustered pines and spruce and, scarcely disturbing the needled branches, came to the thin barrier of alders that lined the edge of the pool. There the wind ruffled the surface of the water and crossed to the pool's far side to tug at the boy's shirt where he sprawled out on a granite ledge. Then the separate smickers joined forces behind him and went tumbling over the brim of the hill to rush with gathering force, like the water of the pool itself, past his grandmother's house and down to Northport in the lower hills. It was at first a gentle wind with something of Cabojan's chill in its breath.

Outstretched, Kern gazed over the edge of the stone into the water below him, poking jerkily at the reflection of his face with a length of willow switch. Now and then the wind-ruffled surface hid the face from his sight. When this happened, he waited with a studied patience until the pool became smooth and his face showed clear again. Moody and serious, it stared back at him. One curling lock of dark hair fell across a temple, shadowing the already serious eyes and adding to the expression of worry they held. Tight-drawn lips added to its strained appearance. It was a boy's face with the mark of manhood already upon it. A young face with too much of age.

Nigger!

The word was a thought—a compulsion—deep buried in him.

Flat-stretched on the rock-ledge, he felt it start to life. The thought that he must say this word caught at his throat with tight fingers, and hot waves of shame ran through him

But he must say it!

He must! He knew that.

He must say it over and over again. Until it fell easily from his lips. Until it was hard with scorn and hot with contempt. Until it had the sound and shape "Nigger" would have coming from the lips

11

of a white man. Until it was charged with tearing hate and malice such as it could never find on the lips of a Negro. Until then he must say it. In this quiet place and in his room—in the aloneness of himself he must repeat it. It must become a part of him—and he of it. Until it became real—it and the rest of his new self—and set him apart forever from suspicion, he must say it. It was to be brick and mortar in the wall which he was building—the wall that must shut out any possible suspicion that he could be anything other than what he appeared to be—until he could never be mistaken for a Negro.

He must never slip back.

Never! Never again must he know the sick shame of being a half-man in the eyes of other men.

Nigger!

A hated word. A fighting word—a killing word. Except that one never killed. Except that one lived instead with the stifling, frightening angers the word had wrought. A word to make madness boil in the brain. A word that *was* madness—that went brutally to the quick core of the soul and tore and rended with hopelessness and anger, shame and despair. That turned the eyes and the mute lips and the pain-quivering heart to God asking——

"Why?"

—and reminded that "—in His own image God created man—"

Just a word that he must say.

Nigger!

It did not come easily. Though every muscle and tendon went taut as he willed the word into being—though each separate plasm of his brain shaped the word and urged his tongue and throat to give it sound—it did not come easily. The learned lessons of nine-teen years were reluctant to loose their grasp. But then—that word never came easily—not, at least, the first time. The syllables shaped and joined, swelled large in his throat and finally, stiffly, took shape under his awkward tongue. His body went rigid. His arms straightened, rodlike, against the unyielding granite and thrust his body up from the ledge. Each muscle struggled to obey his mind's determination that the word be spoken. His hands tightened fiercely on the supple switch and bruised away its thin bark.

"Nigger!"

There! It was said—blurted out in the silence.

The second time and the third—all the other times would be easier.

"Nigger!" A hoarse-spoken denial of what heritage there was for him of race. Shame lumped and stuck in his throat. Slowly the stiffness went out of his arms and he sank back to the rock. For a sickening instant he saw his eyes in the water below him. They were wide and filled with unconcealed scorn. Anger blossomed in him at the thing which forced him to this act. Anger at the final act of cruelty which had brought him to this moment. At the act which had been but another in the day-by-day train of acts, small and large, which had led inevitably to flight. Writhing anger at this final act which had, before his very eyes, twisted two kind and gentle people into inhuman shapes which he had not been able to recognize. Anger. Twisting in him now. Twisting as it had during all of the past years. And a puzzled, not-yet understanding why this thing had to be.

For no reason he could recognize it was suddenly important that he destroy that face. The switch whistled as he cut savagely down. Untouched, safe, feet below the water's surface, the face mocked the impotent switch. Deliberately he inched forward and poised the switch above the reflection. Spearlike it darted through the brief space into the image. For an instant the face was totally destroyed; then, as the switch bobbed back to the surface and drifted inward under the ledge, it began to take form again. Fascinated, he watched as it took shape inside the outspreading circles. Under the rock on which he lay the switch lodged in a hidden crevice and moved gently back and forth in time to the suck and gurgle of water against the rocks.

He turned his head aside and his cheek felt, and did not feel at all, the stone's warm, weathered smoothness.

Later, when he had mustered strength, he would look at his face again. He would say the word again. When the waves of sickness had gone and he had gathered enough strength to turn his head and force his eyes to meet his own face in the water, he would try again. He would try again because he had to—because the fear of the past was in him, stronger than any shame, stronger even than his dread of the unknown future before him.

He could not go back. His decision was made and there was no way to retrace his steps. He was not Kern Roberts now. Not any more. He was Kern Adams—another, an entirely different person. He was his grandmother's ward. Charles Roberts had settled that— his own father—had bluntly renounced him and branded him as a coward.

Nor was he a Negro any more. He was a white man now. He himself had settled that the day, the night, he had fled the South. He himself had settled that.

Or so, at least, he thought.

❈ ❈ ❈

The past was not long ago—little more than a month and a half gone by. Its memories were still vividly clear.

The nearest of the past was of flight, of the terrifying fear that had driven him to run from all that he had ever known or heard of. To run from the completely familiar, to a way of life for whose members he had learned only fear and anger and hate. Afraid for his very life, cowering, willing to submit to any humiliation in order to escape, he had run from the South. He understood dimly that the fear that had been in him as he fled the South had deep roots. Understood that it had lived in him for days and years before. Had been in him for so long that he could not remember when it had not filled him. He remembered fear and the need for anger, for hatred, swelling in him, crowding out everything else. Coming, in the end, to threaten the one ambition he cherished.

Jake and Paula too were in the foreground of memory—they were close enough to tear at his heart—close enough in memory to numb and hurt with their nearness.

Side by side with Paula and Jake were "Tige," Sheriff Bill Noble and Tom Meeker, reminding him of blind anger and godless cruelty. Jake and Paula—and Bill Noble—were dead now. And "Tige" was doomed to the living death he would know in the South.

With these in the past were "Old Henderson" and his own father, so much alike yet so completely different. Each of them had helped to shape his point of view. Kern realized dimly that he was standing at the crossroads to which "Old Henderson" had said he would someday come. The old headmaster had said, "A man can die from the lack of self-realization—just as a man will starve for want of food. Someday you will come to a crossroad in your life—" And at that crossroads, confused and frightened, there had been his father's voice, snarling, bitterly angry. "You are a coward—you can't run from this. You have a responsibility to your race." His mind's center had echoed unspoken answer to his father's contemptuous words. "I have a responsibility to the realization of what I am or may be."

Becky and 'Doriah—part of the past. Both of them, in some strange way, held the sweetness of first love. Lips and eyes and girl

14

forms and first breathlessness, begrudging the heart its right to beat. Brown-faced 'Doriah and white-faced Becky.

"Blondie" and Rollie were boyhood and school days. "Blondie" and Rollie were something hard and angry, directed squarely at him. Something that coiled and lashed out—that struck him and hurt. Something that he did not even now entirely understand. Something he hated in return for its hurt. "Blondie" and Rollie were dark-skinned and he—well, he was a "no-nation nigger."

His mother was the beginning of memory. She was everything he remembered as a child, of laughter and happiness and hope. About her were gathered other memories—stormy memories. A race riot's rattling gunfire. Confused shouting. His first awareness that the color of a man's skin was important. The sex fiend who attacked his mother. The turbulent courtroom in which the man was brought to trial.

First anger grew during those years. First anger that never entirely died out, that had as its target the Freedom League, the organization that held so much of hope for an entire race.

The past held many memories. Confused. Jumbled.

Black man. White man.

Hope. Despair. Ambition. Fear.

Doctor. Lawyer. Negro doctor. Negro lawyer.

One short life to live. One dream to make come true in one short life.

He shuddered as one will shudder at cold or in fear.

I can't go back! I won't lose this last chance to write—to be myself. I won't go back! The vehemence of the thought shook him.

* * *

Later he turned his head and looked at his face in the water. He used the word again. It grated from his lips harshly and many other words followed it. All of them were cutting, slurring words. All of them were filled with learned contempt—forced out of him by fear. They were a part of his new self, those words.

Kern Roberts would never have used them. For Kern Adams, they must become second nature.

Each time he used them, they came more easily. This he had planned.

Each time he used them, he hated a little more deeply. This he had not known would happen.

* * *

15

He went carefully down the slope, picking his way along the needle-matted path, wary of the slippery bayberry bushes that sprawled lank across his way.

Tomorrow—or the next day—he would come back again and he would say the words again. Over and over. The same words. Until they were learned. Until they could never be forgotten. Until there was an anger in him that would forever deny the tide of sympathy that came with remembering.

At the turn he stopped and leaned against the face of Settlement Rock where, a decade before the first Continental Congress met, his great-great-grandfather Caleb Adams had parleyed with Indian warriors and made a lasting peace.

Caleb's house was before him now, tall and white. There was certainty in its shape and something of the uncompromising, taciturn Yankee in its simple façade. Under the late-afternoon sun, the house took on new color, as if it drew from the light itself something of coral and flesh tone and sky blue, until it was no longer white but another—an entirely different—color. Kern saw the house with a keen sense of pleasure. As always, it brought him calmness —steadied him and made him more sure of himself and of what he was doing.

Beyond the house, the hills rolled easily down to where Northport's two church spires reared up above gathered elms that marked the village square. Patches of red clover dotted the open spaces of field, and blended before his eyes into the water-paint colors of early fall that stained the trees. The white blossoms and orange-red seed berries of second-flowering hawthorn danced together in the wind. Farther down the hillside, beyond Caleb's house, the laden boughs of Jason Bridges' plum orchard were a purple haze against the snakelike line of trees that marked the tortuous path of Crazy River to Miller's Bend at the eastern edge of town. At Miller's Bend, the river bent sharply and ran with quickening speed out of sight toward the blue line of distance at the southern end of the valley. Toward the South, Kern thought, toward the terror he'd left behind him. Toward all he'd known of life. Dead now, that way of life. Dead. Dead, and a new way of life begun. A new and alien way. A lone crow cawed at the silence in ill-tempered voice, interrupting his thoughts.

Kern's eyes came back to the house. His grandmother would be waiting for him to come back. He knew that, knew too that she understood his solitary trips into the hills were a part of his struggle to find an answer to his problem. He could think of no way to explain these trips to Margaret Adams. He could imagine the tiny frown lines that would come to her forehead if he tried to tell her. And the impatient way she would run her hand over her already smooth, white hair. In imagination he could see even the faint lines of her face tighten as they did when she was deeply displeased. His grandmother would not understand his desperate effort to shut out everything that he had ever known, even though it meant he must hurt other people.

She would not understand.

He stepped away from the face of the Rock, and started down the hill.

He was no longer Kern Roberts.

He was Kern Adams.

He was no longer a Negro.

He was white.

✿   ✿   ✿

His grandmother stood at the corner of the porch, arranging the basket of cut flowers that hung from one arm. A pair of cutting shears swung loosely by a string from her waist, just fallen from one gloved hand. Under a wide-brimmed hat, her face was framed softly by white hair. Kern called to her as he came toward the house and broke into a run. The cheeriness in his voice when he called was forced.

"Hi, Gran'."

He bounded onto the porch and swept her into his arms, holding her tightly. Over her shoulder he looked at the green hills.

"I can't go back—I can't!"

"I won't!"

NEW YORK—OCTOBER, 1940

KERN sat there and dabbled at his dinner and tried to tell himself that it was not so—that he was not going.

But he was. He knew that he was.

He was going to Harlem. No matter how he tried not to, he knew in the end he would go. Twice before he had gone. He remembered those times. He had fought against going then. But he had gone.

The impulse that had made him go before—that was about to make him go again—was a curious thing. He had speculated on those impulses before. He did so now with an intensity that pushed an awareness of the restaurant and the diners about him out of mind.

The impulse to go to Harlem was a strange one. An unwanted urge. An urge that was more than a little frightening. It was, Kern thought, a part of something else. Vaguely he linked it with his restlessness. He *was* restless, he reflected, and dissatisfied. He'd been dissatisfied with each job he held.

Continuity and trash. That was all he'd written since he left school. Each day he went down to the Dowd Newspaper Office and rode upward twenty-six stories. Each day, except Saturday and Sunday, he walked down the main corridor of the twenty-sixth floor of the Dowd Building to the lettered glass door at the end of the hall. The letters on the door never changed. Their slim, modern lines always said, "The Dowd Radio Station—WQAM." At the end of the hall he turned to the left each morning. The second door on the left-hand side of the hall opened into his cubicle-like office. It had been a long time since he had opened that door with any pleasure, since he had whistled as he hung up his coat and rolled his shirt sleeves up. It seemed to him now that he hadn't whistled since the first week he'd begun to work there.

Going through the heavy revolving doors of the Dowd Building had become a chore. Riding the packed elevator was a moment in time when he was imprisoned, unable to move, able only to torture himself with his restless dissatisfaction. With the knowledge that he would be sitting at his desk in a few moments—sitting there, staring down at the comic pages, ready to play the role of the "Comic-man." Twice a day for fifteen minutes each day, for more than nineteen months, he'd broadcast as the Comic-man. In between the quarter hours, he clipped comics and wrote continuity.

And muzzled his growing anger at Dan Croom.

Twice he'd almost lost control of himself and given way to the goad of anger. Bill Gabel had stopped him both times. He knew he should be grateful to Bill, but try as he might, he was not. He wanted to tell Dan Croom off. But he knew Bill was right. He couldn't expect to tell a program director off and get away with it. The Dowd chain would take care of that. He would be blacklisted. He thought of the Dowd chain as a great spider whose legs sprawled all over the nation. There were few places to which he could go and escape a Dowd black list. Kern grimaced at the thought of being fired by Dan Croom.

Dan Croom was deliberately needling him. He knew that. Croom had needled him since the very first week when Kern had tried to sell him on a special program idea. This "Comic-man" thing was just a part of Croom's needling. He hated Dan Croom, his smooth voice, his supercilious attitude. A thousand times he'd looked at Croom's carefully clipped little moustache and wanted to slug him just beneath it. And tell him in detail what he could do with his job.

Kern could see Croom clearly as he had been that morning he outlined the comic program idea. He could hear Croom's voice too, as he rocked back in his chair and dandled a letter opener from his finger tips.

"This is your big chance, Adams. We want this comic thing worked up for our family audience. We want to reach the kids with snappy quarter-hour programs. You'll do them twice a day. Get plenty of power and punch into it. D'you understand, Adams?"

"Yes, Mr. Croom." Kern remembered that was what he had said. He had thought, "power and punch" and wanted to laugh but he had not. He'd simply said, "Yes, Mr. Croom."

"Frankly, Adams, I was against your selection for this. Can't quite seem to see enough imagination in you. Bill Gabel insisted you could do it tiptop." Kern had felt a wave of gratitude for Bill and

20

at the same time made note to cuss him roundly. Comics! Bill knew he wanted to do serious writing.

"At any rate, I decided to give you a try. We're shorthanded." Kern looked at the little moustache and thought, "Once, just once, right under—" Dan Croom had turned around in his chair and Kern knew he was dismissed. Outside, in the hall, he had laughed. Loud. Long.

Power and punch! A comic program. And he, Kern Adams, who had his heart set on giving something new to radio—he was to be the Comic-man.

He walked down the hall laughing and stood in his slitlike office and stared out of his window. And his laughter died out.

He thought of the world on fire. Of anti-Fascists fighting for life. Of the heart-folk of Spain and Ethiopia rotting under tyrants. Of Blackshirts and Falangists. Of Nazis, of Guernica, Munich, Rotterdam. Of Compiègne. Of Plymouth and of Coventry. Of whole nations facing death each morning—more horrible death than they had ever imagined. And of the battlefield dead, in stinking, obscene postures not like any statue ever raised to those who died in battle.

He stopped laughing. He had not been able to convince Dan Croom that it would be worth the effort to tell this—to try to tell America something of all this. Instead, Dan Croom wanted power and punch—in a comic program.

Kern wrenched his mind back to the present, to the tables that were rapidly filling about him, to the almost darkness beyond the rain-spattered wide window. To the certainty that he was going to Harlem. Again. Somewhere below the cafeteria, the Interborough rumbled by with a deep guttural voice and was gone.

❂   ❂   ❂

At Penn Station, city-wise travelers flow down wide flights of stairs to a ramp that leads to the subway turnstile. In jostling, hurried impatience, they swirl along the tile-walled ramp to a brief slope, where, with scraping feet, they descend in seemingly endless flow to the turnstiles. Here, as thick-greased cogs count the minting of money at a dime for each quarter-revolution of the stiles, the hurrying travelers slow for a moment, as their width constricts, push impatiently through the turnstile and hurry on again to the uptown and downtown ramps, each in accord with the direction of his travel.

The "A" train goes to Harlem. It goes rocketing north under the

21

bed of the city, stopping first below 42nd Street and again below 57th, before lurching forward to race and sway along its underground passageway west of Central Park to 125th Street, almost seventy-five blocks away. And all the way, its passengers crowd its seats. Fill the aisles. Stand and sit. Some sleep. Some merely close their eyes. Others sway at the ends of their straps and stare into space. Standing. Sitting. Swaying. Expression seldom touches their faces.

❀   ❀   ❀

Kern's eyes were on a flame-touched girl in a white bathing suit who arched through space, advertising sunburn cream. His mind was centered on a question he could almost see.

"Why am I going to Harlem?"

Twice before he had gone. Twice he had risked everything it had cost him to gain security as a white man. He remembered those first years of college with sharp clarity. They had been months of agony in which he had begun to live as a white man. Months during each day of which he had been on constant guard, eternally vigilant against making a slip, against saying or doing something that would mark him as a Negro. Each one of those days he had lived in dreadful fear of exposure—of being discovered and cast into some outer world in which both white man and black would reject him. He had learned anger at Negroes to erect a barrier between them and himself—to mark himself as anti-Negro. He'd learned to say "nigger"—and, almost, he had learned to hear it said without anger. Almost. Not quite.

"Well," he thought, "I've found security. I am white. I have a job. *Why* am I going to Harlem? Why am I rearousing old memories, sympathies, suspicions, that cannot possibly fit into my life." It was senseless.

❀   ❀   ❀

The train slid into 57th Street station. He did not move.

❀   ❀   ❀

Bits of life as a Negro flashed through his mind in a shocking kaleidoscope and he asked himself, "Were I exposed, if I had to— go back—could I take it? Would I lose my mind?"

The first time, Kern could almost understand. There had been something he could point to—call a reason. A news story in an

22

evening daily that had caught his eye months ago. A bold-faced head announced that the Freedom League was holding its annual national convention in New York. As he read the story, Kern had consciously and actively thought of the League and of Negroes for the first time since he had been a senior in college. Even now, fragments of that story came back to him. "Civic and organizational leaders to appear at Mass Meeting." "Twentieth anniversary speaker—to be introduced by Attorney Charles Roberts." Kern had read that story and remembered many things.

His mother and Charles Roberts, his father. The League, as it had been during those early days of its birth, when he had often heard his father say, ". . . this League must fight bigotry forever— for all minorities," and he had not understood.

That had been his reason the first time. Maybe it wasn't actually a reason. Maybe it was a compulsion, a hunger for something once known. Whatever it was, it had been large enough to make him go to Harlem. Automatically Kern noticed a flashing station sign, 110th Street. He crossed his legs. His eyes stayed on the girl in the sign before him.

The first time, he thought, he could understand. The second time puzzled him. Just as now, there had been no reason for his going there that he could put his finger on. He had—just gone. Suddenly, in the course of a normal day's work, the knowledge that he would go had been plain in his mind. That evening he had gone. He went and walked and looked, going north and east until he became tired, and then he retraced his steps. Just as now. The train slowed and the first station lights flashed by the windows before him.

❊ ❊ ❊

Harlem's faces were all about him. Few were like his own. Few were white. Mostly they were dark faces, in shades of sepia and tan and brown and black. A sea of faces burrowed, most of them, into upturned collars against the cold wind that angled down St. Nicholas Avenue from the northeast. Kern looked up at the low scud that raced before the wind, and made a mental note that it was through raining for a while. His thoughts came back to the faces about him.

Faces in a ghetto. Of every color. Tired and lined. Not tired or lined. Faces dull with hopelessness and twisted with an inner, as yet unrecognized, anger. Faces laughing and those marked with "Let the devil pay the cost." Faces sober, tired, determined. Emi-

23

grant faces. Emigrants, Kern thought, most of whom had, as had he, fled the hated South. Emigrants who had found the northland "Green—but not as fruitful as had been promised."

Kern watched curiously as his mind moved toward new questions and toward answers.

What force is it, he wondered, that moves these people? What above all else is strong enough to make them feel life is worth living when covenants herd them into this jungle—when bare subsistence wages keep them in slavery? In a corner of his mind he filed away the certainty that—whatever it was—it was larger than the mere unwillingness of living flesh to die—that such a force must have a spiritual quality.

At 7th Avenue, he turned north and walked into the full force of the wind. Kern raised his coat collar and walked on. The store fronts were thinner now, having given way to the entrances of tenements and apartment dwellings. At 127th Street a man and a woman stood arm-locked in a doorway that shielded them against the wind. They did not notice Kern. Between 129th and 130th, he broke his stride as a chattering group of men and women crossed the sidewalk and piled into a luxurious Cadillac at the curb. He watched as the car slid away with a high-powered, expensive purr and was lost in the breakneck rush of traffic. A passer-by greeted him with a flat stare and went on without slowing his steps. At 133rd Street, a woman with a shawl about her shoulders swore in a shrill voice as she followed a man down the dark maw of the street.

Beyond 137th, light flooded the sidewalk. A sign proclaimed that the entrance led to "Fred's Place" and the huge pictures of a smiling piano player advertised that Rachel Thompson was "Swinging Symphony" inside.

Kern stared at the sign indecisively. He'd been here once before. The second time he had come to Harlem. He wanted to go in again. He snapped his collar down and went in. From behind doors on the far side of the lounge, there came the boogied strains of a prelude: Bach, he thought.

A glittering pyramid of chrome and glass stood in the center of an oval bar, its shelves filled with close-lined bottles of various brands and quartered by four shining cash registers. Only one bartender was working when he stepped up to the bar. Jerry was his name, Kern remembered. He smiled as the man came toward him, flipping the towel he held in greeting.

24

"Hi yah?"

"Hi."

"Whiskey?"

"Yep." Kern settled one elbow against the bar and slowly unbelted his coat. Jerry reached for bourbon on the rack behind him and held the bottle up for Kern's approval.

"Bourbon. Right?"

"That's right." The amber liquid rushed up to the brim of the shot glass and stopped with neat precision. Jerry filled a glass half full of cracked ice.

"Water, isn't it?"

Kern nodded.

The bourbon became heat in the pit of Kern's stomach and spread its fingers out through his body. Kern widened his coat and slouched more comfortably against the bar. A quick glance told him that there were two men across the bar from him, almost hidden by the register. They were drinking beer. Down the bar from him, a heavy-set man in early middle age stood beside a young woman. She was obviously young and he was marked in middle age by gray hair and deep graven lines in his dark face, by the pouches under his eyes. Kern looked from the man to find the girl's eyes on him. An amused smile seemed to touch the corners of her mouth. Kern switched his glance to where Jerry stood polishing glasses with an automatic motion, placing each one on a shelf behind him.

"Stopped raining outside?"

"Yep. Street's almost dry now."

"Good thing. This weather's bad on business. Keeps everyone home." Kern nodded again.

"Jerry—" Jerry turned, "how about another round?" It was, Kern saw, the man with the young girl. Kern watched them as Jerry mixed their drinks. The girl didn't quite seem to fit in with the man. From the show floor at the rear of the club, Rachel Thompson started something by Korsakoff. It didn't fit in with the bar-room—not any more than the man went with the girl.

The girl was the color of new ivory with flashing dark eyes. She wore a black dress that was chic and a small hat that slanted down from her up-done hair to shade one eye. She was smiling at something Jerry was saying. The man beside her watched her face. Kern didn't blame him. Wherever the man's eyes went in the room, they came back to her face. The way he looked at her was as plain as words. "This is mine. Mine!"

25

He looked at the diamond he wore in the same way. Just as often and in the same way. Nothing was wrong with the man. His clothes were in good taste. His voice was even and controlled. But he just didn't seem to go with the girl. Jerry came toward him, pitching his bar towel over his shoulder. His eyes went to Kern's empty glass.

" 'Nother one?" Kern nodded. "I guess so." Jerry followed his eyes.

"She's a looker, ain't she?" Kern agreed.

"Name's Green. That's her husband with her. Doc Green."

"Doctor?"

"Yep. One of them baby doctors." As an afterthought, Jerry added, "He's pretty sporty, though."

"Sort of—sort of old though, isn't he?" Kern ventured.

Jerry shrugged his shoulders.

"Yeah, he's pretty old. But he's got it like dirt. Plenty of moolah. They on'y been married a few months." He went back to polishing his glasses. Kern thought he understood how a girl like that would have married a guy like Doc Green. With what she had—color, looks, poise—she could take her pick of the Negro marriage market —and probably had. As for the doctor, she represented a lot of things he'd probably always wanted—some of the things he'd probably never consciously realized that he wanted.

"Makes a lot of dough, huh?"

"Oh, yeah. Ol' Doc can buy 'bout anything he wants." Kern thought immediately of some things Doc couldn't buy.

"Where you say you from?"

"Chicago." Kern lied without hesitation.

"Oh. Knowed you wasn't no New York man. Everybody 'roun' Harlem knows Doc. He delivered 'bout half uh the babies in Harlem." Kern tried to estimate the obvious exaggeration.

"Where you workin'?"

"Down at the Dowd Building—Radio Section."

"Yeah? Porter, huh?"

Kern inclined his head and Jerry was satisfied. "Good pay?"

"Not bad—odd jobs 'n everything. I make ends meet." Jerry smiled with understanding.

"Me, I'm from the South." Kern marked the way Jerry's voice emphasized the "from."

"Yes siree," Jerry said. "I'm 'from' down South and I ain't goin' back." His deadly serious face contradicted any joking mood that his words might have held. "Drink up." He gestured to Kern's

26

glass with a bottle and poured a sloshing drink up to the brim of the shot glass he held. "The lushes'll pay for it 'fore the night's over." Replacing the bottle in its place on the rack behind him, he leaned confidentially against the bar. His eyes were moody and dark and Kern recalled sharply the fearful urgency with which the talk of Negroes always turned to "the problem" no matter with what subject they began. It was only a matter of time, of minutes, he reflected, before their thoughts and their words swiveled to this thing. In a far recess of Kern's mind, an idea came to life and he rejected it at once as too fantastic—too insane—for consideration.

"—you don't know!" He forced himself to listen to Jerry's words. "It's really hell down there for a nigger. Things happen'd make your hair curl. It's all right if'n you're dumb. Blind dumb. You don't mind too much, I guess."

His words began to match the thought in the back of Kern's mind.

"But you can't stay dumb. You fin' out what's happenin' to you. Even in the fourth grade, you learn there's a better life to be had than the one you got 'n then your trouble starts."

Bill Noble had said, "School ain't for niggers! Jes' give 'em a lotta damn fool notions an' ruins 'em." Kern saw that Jerry's eyes were fixed soberly on his square-fingered wide hands.

"Then you start to get hungry for somethin' better. You take 'n take 'til you feel murder build up 'n you gotta go—or die."

Jake had said that. The night he stood in the kitchen. That night in far-off, long-ago Valley View, Jake had said the same thing. In other words—but the same thing. To have made good his threat would have meant the death Jerry spoke of.

"—I kill him, with these two hands. An' You, God—I believe in You these years. I say You do the right thing always. Hah! You don' like my killin' him? Then, damn You—You come down here an' stop me. You so great—You stop these two han's." Jake to whom God had meant even more than Paula. Jake had said that. The memory shook Kern. Jerry's voice was like a dirge.

"Detroit, L.A., Philly. They's all the same. Jim Crow. Not bad as the South. Not as open. But when it gets you, some sly dig, it's worse 'n the South 'cause you ain't lookin' for it. You know what I mean?" His eyes searched Kern's face for accord. He found it.

"Made up my min' finally, I don't want no part of no pecker-woods." He turned and took a glass in his hands and began to polish it. It had already been polished. A rumbling undertone of despair was in his voice. Kern recognized that despairing voice—it was the voice of the Freedom League. The individual voice. The collective voice. It was a voice that had a kinship with the fantastic idea in the back of his head. The voice of Negroes.

"Tough for a nigger everywhere. You get treated like you ain't got no heart or soul. That's what gets a man. Like your color means you ain't got no feelings." Jerry shrugged his shoulders expressively.

Kern knew why he had come to Harlem. Suddenly, he knew the reason. For this time and the time before. He had it now. The answer to the restlessness that gnawed at him. He tossed off his drink and placed his glass on the bar.

* * *

Heat rattled thinly in the radiators as Kern let himself into his apartment and tossed his coat onto the davenport halfway across the living room. In the darkness he dropped into the big easy chair and draped his legs over one chair arm. His thoughts almost made pictures on the screen of darkness before him. Bit by bit the full impact of what he was thinking broke on him. It was so simple and urgent that it astonished him. It was so big that it dwarfed anything else he had ever thought of. It was so honest that it frightened him.

Jerry had given him the real thing.

Man's inhumanity to man. An inhumanity which, as practiced against the American Negro by his fellow man, was as harrowing as any exquisitely refined medieval torture.

That was the thing in Kern's mind. His thoughts took the shape of little words on the screen of darkness before him.

Man's most criminal act is his simple inhumanity to other men— his unreasoning refusal to acknowledge in other men the existence of heart and soul and dreams such as his own. A barbaric conceit is at the core of this inhumanity, basing its denial of these simplest of dignities on the color of a face. Fear too, whether admitted or not, is at the core of the thing. Fear that a wrong done may be avenged. And guilt, that struggles, with righteously spoken catchwords, to justify its wrongdoing.

No act of man to man is more totally damning than this—none more ruinously destructive to the doer and to the victim. No deed of men denies so completely as does this one the teachings of all ages and all faiths. Nothing else assails with such brutal directness —assails and questions and denies—the ultimate worth of men on

28

earth in the handful of years they shall know in the long light-years in which space and a cosmos shall be. Nothing else tears so cruelly at the taproot of mankind's existence as does this inhumanity. Tears and hurts and leaves jagged-edged wounds that are covered over with angry scar tissue—and that fester underneath.

Nowhere else was this so true as in America. Kern saw that too. Saw that the destructive quality of American inhumanity began and ended with hypocrisy which, in one breath, preached the doctrine that all men were created free and equal and, in the very next breath, denied to millions the simple respect which should naturally go with such a belief. Carefully, he measured his own small success and found that it was not success at all—that he had achieved nothing more than should be expected of any white man who had been given the opportunities which had been his. He looked with a new and a fierce anger at the force which had driven him to flight from the Negro race and realized, dispassionately, that he would never have run, had it not been for the "thing"—for the fearful, in-pressing, bruising tensions of life as a Negro.

Kern looked at the white way of life—his chosen way—as he had not looked at it before. He saw its callous disregard for the blunting inhumanity it practiced.

He thought of Negroes. Of the ever-present despair that clouded the mainstream of tenderness and blotted out majestic emotion, postponing beyond the sight of men perhaps, the time when among Negroes the virtues which made great peoples might be passed on from generation to generation, free of the tearing, twisting hates and suspicions which white America had taught.

He thought too of the Negro's daily preoccupation with his lot, of the tremendous outpouring of time and thought that went into his each day's brooding, angry consideration of "the problem." He thought of the energy that white men gave to fostering the discrimination and segregation of the Negro—of the countless devices shaped to "keep him in his place." Then he tried to picture this total force, multiplied many millions of times over. He could not imagine such a total force.

Then, in the simplest words he knew, Kern sat before his typewriter and began to describe this force—imagining the returns it might have brought to men had such energy been poured into deeds of simple kindness.

He wrote feverishly after that, night after night. Some nights the pages piled one atop the other on the end of his desk in a steady flow. Other nights, he wrote more slowly and his work left him with a feeling of frustrated dissatisfaction.

There were nights, many of them, when his clattering typewriter would stop abruptly in the middle of a page. Without warning. When he would stare into space, or light a cigarette and lean back to gaze at the ceiling through the shifting, blue-gray clouds of smoke. Or pace restlessly through the apartment.

When this happened, he was searching for a word. For *the* word. Or for words with which to capture a thought. Words that would describe something seen or felt or done. Many, many nights he knew the agony of trying to put an elusive thought into words. Many times he found the right words. Often he did not, and when this was so he felt baffled helplessness.

There were nights—and days—when he could write nothing. When the whole story fled from him and stopped just beyond the reach of his mind, tantalizing him with its nearness. Days and nights when he almost believed he could not write—could not finish what he had begun. Days and nights that held a kind of madness for him. And often, very often, a deep contentment.

All of that started with the first words Kern typed that night.

CHAPTER I

WASHINGTON—1927

I

Dorcas Kuykendahl sat on the terrace halfway down the slope and watched them go and the lengthening evening shadows sharpened the somberness of thought that was in her eyes.

Beyond the clearing and the wide stairs below her, at the edge of the thin file of trees that bordered the footpath that ran between the bridle run and the creek, they turned and waved to her. Then they disappeared from sight and the sound of their voices was lost in the silence.

Her gaze wandered along the floor of the Park, touched for a moment on the footbridge that spanned the creek midway its length, reached to the stairs that climbed the eastern slope at the farthest end, then turned inward upon the images of her thoughts.

Leaning against the tree at her back, she lifted the heavy coils of hair away from her neck and found pleasure in the coolness that came. Tiny furrows of concentration showed between her brows; and her eyes, following the idle pattern of her fingers in the grass about her, were reflective. Restlessly, almost impatiently, she clasped her hands in her lap. "I won't have my son a Negro!" The words had been spoken with hysterical quietness. She had listened to Laura, her dearest friend, and thought her almost a stranger. That had been a short hour ago and the words still dinned in her ears.

With shapeless foreboding Dorcas thought, "It's too late for that now—much too late!" She had thought that when Laura spoke, but she had remained silent as her thoughts ran backward almost twelve years through time to the days in Vermont when she and Laura were growing into womanhood.

Twelve years ago. This had begun then—with an introduction at a college dance, with casual words that had run like quicksilver into a pattern from which there had been no escape. And now this!

"I've tried, Dorcas—Heaven knows I have. But I just cannot make a go of it. Charles is determined that Kern shall enter public school this fall and you know what that means. He'll find out that—"

31

Laura's voice rose and her eyes asked Dorcas to understand. "I simply cannot face his learning that he is a Negro. I won't have it!"

And Dorcas, listening, had been able to say nothing. "I—we—knew years ago," she had thought, "that it wouldn't work." She had looked to where Kern lay on his back under a shade tree, busy with the thoughts of youth, and thought, happily, that he had no idea of the storm that was brewing about him. If only Charles had—even now Dorcas could scarcely believe it true—if only he had not been a Negro. None of them had wanted to believe it.

Laura's hurt that day had been dark in her eyes and in the trembling set of her chin, as she had burst into Dorcas' house. Disbelief was as sharp now, Dorcas found, as it had been when she had listened to Laura's halting voice.

"He just told me—a little while ago. He can't—he says he shouldn't—ask me to marry him!" For a moment, relieved, she had thought, "A lovers' quarrel—only that. Nothing more." But it had been more than that. Laura's dull voice told her, "Charles is a Negro!"

"A Negro! That's impossible— Why he—" But Laura had smiled wanly, "That's what I told him, darling, but he said it was—quite—possible." Laura's self-control had given way to gasping sobs. Through her tears, her words had been jumbled. "Oh, Dorcas—Dorcas—what am I to do? I love him so much— What am I going to do?"

Trembling now herself, Dorcas had held her and thought, "This must be a mistake! Not Charles!" Negroes were black and wore bandannas. They—they ate watermelons. Fay said so and she should know. She came from Florida and she "knew niggers." She had even danced with Charles—dated him! Besides, what man in his right senses would damn himself with the label of Negro birth unless he were mad, unless—she had come unwittingly on the answer—unless he spoke the truth.

The news had broken like a bombshell in the Adams' household. They had gathered in the tall living room. Dorcas and Laura and Mrs. Adams sitting close together on the davenport before the wide-mouthed hearth, as if by their nearness they would muster up protection against fear—hoping that Charles would somehow tell them that this was all a ghastly joke. The Judge stood in front of them, short, stocky-figured, his Irish underlip prominent, with his hands thrust deep in the pockets of an old smoking jacket. He peered up anxiously at his young law clerk from under gathered brows.

"I'm sorry, sir," Charles' words had dashed their hopes. "I should have told you first." His voice was level and his searching gray eyes fixed on the Judge. It seemed to Dorcas that he squared his shoulders and raised his head a bit before his next words.

"I am a Negro. My mother was a Negro. My father was a white man. We—my sister and I—were born in Tennessee. When we were quite young, our neighbors—white neighbors—forced us to leave. You see, my father—mother told me—loved my mother. We moved to Washington where mother taught school. She died before I finished college. My father died shortly afterward. I had to tell Laura before things went any further. I—I—" He ran his fingers quickly through his thick black hair. "I came to work with you only because——"

Caleb Adams lowered his head before the words, "—because I am called the 'great liberal.' Is that why?" He looked up to see Charles' nodded assent, then turned to stand before the open hearth absently toeing the foot of an andiron. His shoulders slumped. His hands stayed deep in his pockets. A mirthless smile quirked his lips. Now and then, in the dead silence of the room, he murmured to himself, "The great liberal."

All of them had watched him wrestle for the first time with the need to apply to his own life and loved ones the code which had won him greatness.

Dorcas had watched Charles, searching his face and bearing for some sign that would mark him as a Negro, and as she had, Laura slipped from between them and went to stand beside Charles, finding his hand with hers.

The quickening run of shadow touched Dorcas' face, and she stirred, realizing that her husband would soon be home. That she could stay here on this terrace only a little longer if she was to meet Kurt at home.

Her thoughts went back to Laura. Even after they had married, it could have worked. Charles was accepted by the citizens of Northport. He fitted in. His work as Judge Adams' clerk won increasing attention with each term of court. The matter of what he had been and where he had come from had been pushed into the background of their thinking. It was a secret the five of them shared, something they never mentioned—nor found need to—lest the mention alone awaken unpredictable currents.

For a year and a half the pattern of Charles' and Laura's life together had differed in no way from the ordinary. They had been, if anything, a little more happy, a little more successful than were most young couples. Taciturn and quiet-spoken by nature, Charles was given to long silences and to brief, considered speech. Judge Adams took special pride in his logical attack upon the problems he met, and began to outline in detail the course which "the most promising young jurist I have ever known" was to follow.

The nation went to war. It was 1918. Charles went early and willingly and at home they followed him, by his letters, through the brief months of training camp and officers' training school. Once, before sailing overseas, he came home on a brief leave. When he wrote again from France, he had been assigned to the Judge Advocate General's section. He had been gone a little more than six months when Kern was born. A sturdy, bawling youngster, Kern was the image of his grandfather and from the moment of his birth he was ruler—and often tyrannical—of the household.

Those days at Northport sped quickly and smoothly and the future spread its promise before them with no warning that it would continue in its untroubled path for but little longer.

Whatever had changed Charles, Dorcas mused, must have happened in France. Exactly what it was, they never learned. But Charles had changed. The taciturn manner and the considered word were still there. And the brief moments of humor. But to these had been added an edge of bitterness, something felt rather than seen.

Charles folded his uniform and boxed it, and confided to Laura, a heresy among New Englanders, that he would "never wear one of those again." He turned aside questions about his service with something less than his usual grace. "Just a desk job," he would say. "I was with the Judge Advocate General's office—Department of the Seine." Then his thin lips would close tightly. Later, and by chance, they learned odds and ends about him, not enough to tell when or exactly why he had changed—but enough to warn them against the pursuit of the mystery.

"Something about nigra troops—"

In time they studiously avoided any question which might lead to embarrassing disclosures.

Charles came home from the war in May and by Christmas he seemed almost his old self and they forgot their first cold fear. Then it happened at dinner on Christmas Day. Dorcas shuddered, remembering that Christmas Day eight years ago.

Certainly neither Dorcas nor the family could have had an inkling

34

of what was in his mind when he rose and tapped on his wineglass for attention. Ringed about the table, their chairs pushed back, a family and its dearest friend, they smiled up at him, tall before them, and waited. His smile faded.

"I toast," he lifted his glass high, "this Christmas we have spent together and I hope," a sardonic smile edged his mouth, "it will not be our last Christmas together." They raised their glasses. He had stood above them, glass in hand, unsmiling, and anxiousness had crept into them. "I find that I do poorly at practicing deceits." His voice was almost harsh, and in the room only Kern did not know what he meant. "Therefore it is my decision," his words had been slow and distinct, "to return to my home and to my race and to the work that is there to be done." He drained his glass. Then in the shocked silence, he walked quickly from the room.

Not even the revelation of his mixed bloods could compare with the thunderclap of this announced determination. Judge Adams had stared incredulously at his wife and she at him. Dorcas had drawn line after precise line on the old linen cloth with her knife. Had she cut it to strips, no one would have noticed. Laura spoke gently to Kern, quieting his restlessness, her whisper loud in the room. They sat and mustered up their arguments against this decision, and knew as they did so, that nothing would change his mind.

Charles had gone to Washington—in spite of the storm of protest, the welter of tears, the threats of legal action to stay him—and Laura and Kern had gone with him. Uncertainty and determination were in Laura as she had faced the strange prospect of life as a Negro. She confided to Dorcas, "I can't give him up now—and I can't lose my baby. If there is no other way, I will become a Negro." Kern slept in his cradle. One tiny fist was clenched tightly.

More than seven years had passed since that day. For the first year Laura's letters had come close together, gay and cheerful, filled with news about the quiet old house to which Charles had taken her, about the life she led, Charles' position in the community and, always, with page after page of Kern. For that year, their fears had been dulled. Toward the middle of the second year, however, her letters became more brief, and held an intangible something which told them that all was not going well with Laura.

Finally her letters arrived at long intervals, and said nothing beyond bare statements that Kern was well and growing, that her life was happy—this latter statement was never convincing—and that she "missed" them. This declaration ran through all of her letters and more than anything else told them that she was finding life as a Negro more difficult than she had thought it would be. More than once Caleb Adams talked of "going down there" to bring his daughter and grandson home. Always, when reasoning moments reminded him of the futility of such a course, he vowed, "The next time!"

One spring Laura brought Kern home to Vermont. The first rush of green she loved so well had been on the land. They saw she was not the same Laura who had gone away. Tiny lines edged her mouth, and a strained expression had crept into her eyes. These and her constant reserve combined to make her almost a stranger. During the month they stayed, she scarcely mentioned Washington. Most of the time she sat about the porch and the house in brooding silence. Twice, reproaching herself for selfishness, she had packed lunch and taken Kern by the hand, to go tramping off into the hills. She had, too, a chance to renew her acquaintance with the familiar things that filled the house, moving from room to room to stand for minutes on end before the wide-manteled fireplace, the tall clock at the bend of the stairs, her grandfather's picture, the polychrome candlesticks on the long dining-room table. Often she would reach out and touch them gently with her finger tips before passing on.

Many times Kern stood beside her as she told him the special history that made each object an important part of the house. Only when it came time to leave did a quick rush of tears reveal how miserable she was. Their hearts ached for her.

But if Laura had been their despair, Kern was their delight. He was six that spring and living for the first time in the dream world about which his mother had told him a thousand stories. He listened eagerly to what she said about the house and breathlessly repeated it to his grandparents at his earliest opportunity, prefacing each narrative with "Do you know what?" Once, in a disappointed tone, he remarked to his Grandfather Caleb—"Our house in Washington doesn't have a history," and was puzzled when the old man made no reply. Kern filled out that spring, and when it came time to leave he was bronzed and healthy as his mother was pale and listless.

That was the summer Dorcas remembered so well, when she met Kurt Kuykendahl. In December they had been married. She had come to Washington to live in the rambling Netherlands Embassy

36

house on the avenue where Kurt performed his secretarial duties. With her had come the Adamses' plea, "Keep in touch with her, Dorcas."

Bit by bit after coming to Washington, Dorcas learned from Laura things which explained the gaps that had been in her letters. She understood in the end why Laura's lips had been bound. She learned enough to understand the hopelessness which had filled her voice only an hour or two ago. Part of Laura's despair was seven years old, the impact of a race riot during her first month in Washington. Caught on a downtown street with Kern when fighting began between whites and Negroes, she had found two days of sanctuary in a white hotel. In the harsh aftermath of emotion, Negroes had thoughtlessly accused her of "passing" for white when the acid test of principle had come. "But, Charles," she had tried to explain, "I had a baby in my arms. What could I have done? I couldn't come home. It wasn't safe for any white to—" Laura had learned at bitter first hand the contempt in which Negroes were held. The sneering change of expression on the face of a formerly courteous shopgirl as Laura gave her home address— in a Negro section—had been her first lesson. Another was the crawling recollection of a white taxi driver's insulting proposal as he stopped before her house—and her frantic fear when his fingers had pawed at the joining of her thighs as she left the cab—reminded her beyond forgetting. Laura had told her those things. Dorcas knew, too, of Laura's sick knowledge that she could go neither where she wanted to nor when she wanted. Word by word, Laura had recounted Charles' reasons for insisting that she patronize neither the downtown (white) theaters nor dining places to which she had at first, infrequently, gone. "You're white, you must remember—" "It's only natural that Negroes should be suspicious of you at first—" "After all—I do have to make my living here"— Reasons which, Dorcas saw, pruned to nothing what little opportunity Laura had had to find relief from the unaccustomed pressures of living as a Negro. Laura finally came to hate the "places to which she could go" because she was unable to go elsewhere. Dorcas understood that too.

On every hand Laura had been met with thinly guised tolerance in the Negro community. The "Association of Oldest Inhabitants" treated her as an interloper, a white woman, who had caused an eligible bachelor to by-pass women of his own race.

None of this could have mattered if only Charles had helped

37

her. But he had not. Instead, from the formation of the Freedom League shortly after the race riot, Charles had begun to change. He became almost a stranger. Instead of comfort and understanding, he gave her the Freedom League—and a daily consciousness of its fight to protect Negroes against prejudice and discrimination. Laura could and did understand the need for the fight. She applauded its goal. But the never-ending absorption with "the problem" in all its varied forms, the constant impulse to hate which she felt about her, were sickening. No corner of her daily life was safe from the intrusion of these violent emotions. "The problem" was everywhere—touching everything.

Through Laura, Dorcas had begun to understand that this unceasing preoccupation with hate engendered hatred in a Negro; that the insistent emotional stress, the constant outpouring of energies sorely needed in more fruitful endeavors; that mere existence as a Negro, all combined to twist and warp the personality until, in the end, the essentials of what one might have been and thought and loved were unrecognizable in the shape of what one had become.

Charles' insistence that Kern enter Washington's Negro schools brought Laura face to face with the possibility that her son would grow up subject to these twisting, tearing forces.

Dorcas' eyes were troubled as she came back to the present and searched for Kern and Laura along the line of trees. She could not find them. The pulse in her temples became heavier and she bent her head backwards to ease the throbbing. She should, she chided herself, be home. She thought, "In a moment," and rose from the terrace. "I'll walk along the creek a ways."

II

They were mother and son. A stranger, passing them as they hurried along the footpath, would have known that in the moment of passing. Though Laura was sapling-slim with a mass of shining chestnut hair and Kern was a blocky, sturdy lad, with an unruly black mop that forever fell across his face, their eyes were the same odd, smoky color of blue. The curve of their mouths and the bones that shaped their faces were beyond question of one blood, and the oneness of inflection which marked their speech and gesture was too singular to have had another explanation.

Thin threads of an early evening breeze touched their faces and

38

at intervals stirred the branches above them to tentative life that crowded out the splashing creek and subsided to silence again. The bridle path was empty of riders, and the picnic places, the stone tables and benches along the edge of the creek, were empty of their usual throng. The park was poised in silence, waiting for the chattering, laughing voices that would shortly, with the passing of the heat, be sounding back and forth throughout its length.

Not even the caretaker, whom they had always seen at one or another of the brick ovens with his cart and brooms, was to be seen at his routine of cleaning. The place was deserted.

Above them, one itinerant cloud shared the wide, blue expanse of sky with the looming shape of Calvert Street Bridge, as it reached out and across to span the park. Its shadow issued dark and immobile from the heavily wooded western slope and lay across the floor of the park. Its outer edge embraced the footbridge that hurdled the creek, and bent at the foot of the eastern hill to run upwards and curved to the top where it joined again with the bridge itself.

At the footbridge, out of breath, Laura paused for a moment as Kern turned to gaze toward the place where they had left Dorcas. He could not see her and disappointment filled his voice. "Has she gone, Mama?" Laura saw no sign of her friend on the slope.

"I suppose so, darling. She had to get home too." They clasped hands and hurried on, scarcely noticing the creek as it boiled along below them. Beyond the bridge, at the first bend of the curving path, they heard the faint, insistent clanging of a bell. The streetcar! They stopped short.

The bell announced that in five minutes the car would swing out from the loop that circled the covered waiting stall on the hill above and begin its rattling journey down the long winding hill along "You" Street, teeming with Negroes, to meet with Florida Avenue and continue, at halting pace, to the farthest edge of town. A quarter hour would pass before another car left the loop. "We'll be late!" Kern knew why happiness faded so abruptly from her face. His father would be waiting at home when they arrived, coldly angry that they had visited Dorcas. Charles always knew when they saw Dorcas, even when they conspired to make their journeys secret. Nettie, the "girl of all work," saw to that. To go was bad enough, but to be late—!

For days afterward the house would be tense with his anger. They quickened their pace and hurried along the path. Ahead of them the steps climbed out of the park. "Kern," his mother caught at her side, "Kern, run on ahead. See if you can catch the car. Ask the conductor to wait a minute."

Kern's flying legs covered the distance in moments, and, short of breath, he began to climb the steep stairs. Above him, the motorman and the conductor leaned against the rail, smoking. As he climbed, one of them turned and flicked away a spent cigarette, head turning to follow its curving, downward path.

Kern shouted, "Mr. Conductor, Mama's coming. Wait for us." He waved his arms and gathered himself to shout again. He could not understand what they were calling to him. Both men had turned to stare down at him and he knew that he must make them understand.

✿　✿　✿

The first scream shattered the silence and became an echo. "Help—Kern!" A frantic, terrified scream.

"Mama!" Kern recognized the voice. He stood stock-still with shock, then went hurtling back down the steps toward her voice, slipping, heedless of scrapes, not knowing that the motorman and the conductor were rushing down behind him. Near the foot of the stairs, he saw his mother struggling with a man. She saw him and screamed in terror.

"Kern! Go back!" Her blouse had been ripped away from one shoulder and her waist was awry. Kern covered the last few steps as the man dragged her into the towering, bloomless forsythia at the foot of the stairs. Kern thrashed into the hollow circle of bushes and saw her still struggling, tearing at the man's thick figure with her free hand. His grasp circled her body and pinioned an arm at her side, while his free hand clawed at her clothing. His bent head seemed to lean against her shoulder and neck. Crying, Kern fell on the broad, blue-shirted back, kicking, pounding, biting, the saltiness of sweat in his mouth and in his nostrils.

"Let my mother go! You let my mother alone!" The man shrugged around and struck viciously.

The caretaker!

Kern recognized the caretaker as the man's hand caught him a glancing blow on the side of the head and threw him backward against the heavy bushes. He lay there, dazed, wanting to move and unable to do so; unable to utter a sound; wide-eyed, as his mother went limp in the man's arms. Suddenly, the man raised

40

his head and looked wildly about him. His grasp on Laura loosened and she slipped to the ground as he, fumbling in a hip pocket, drew out a heavy clasp knife. Opening it, he bent and stabbed her. Once in the side and again in the shoulder. Kern screamed in terror and pressed back against the wall of stems as the man turned on him. Voices and heavy steps sounded beyond the circle and the caretaker stopped in his whirl toward the boy.

"Went in there, Joe. Come on!"

The man dropped his knife and went thrashing through the bushes up the wooded hillside. Kern fainted. When he regained consciousness, he lay on his back near the foot of the stairs. Low voices sounded about him. He turned his head on a side and saw his mother. Her blouse had been pulled up to cover her shoulder. It was marked at the shoulder with a red stain that spread slowly outward to join the brighter red that was at her side.

About him, the calls of searchers sounded as they cast back and forth across the park, looking for the caretaker. Kern recognized the conductor and the motorman in the crowd about him, and when he found that he could not understand their questions he began to cry.

Looking down and beyond Kern, the motorman had seen the caretaker leap from the heavy bushes and seize Kern's mother as she came along the path. Kern had mistaken the warning he had shouted to her as an answer to his call. Angry mutters ran through the crowd, mostly men, as he talked. Newcomers pressed in, eager to learn what had happened, and the tale was retold with, at first, minor additions.

Among the first women to arrive was Dorcas. She pushed forward to stoop beside them.

"Laura, oh Laura!" She turned to Kern. "What happened, Kern? Are you all right?"

He knuckled the tears from his eyes. "I guess so—Mama's hurt though. She can't talk to me."

"I knew it was Laura when I heard the scream," Dorcas spoke almost to herself as she took his mother's wrist between her fingers. She listened until her fingers told her there was still life, then she looked up at the faces about her. "Here," she gestured to two men, "lift her carefully—we'll get a car at the top of the hill and take her to my house."

Eager volunteers lifted Laura and carried her up the stairs. A stranger took Kern easily in his arms and followed a pace or two

41

behind them. Mutters ran through the curious onlookers who halted their descent on the stairs and parted for them as they climbed toward the crowd that lined the edge of the bridge.

"—a nigger done it——"

"—get the goddamned sonofabitch——"

"—thought we'd taught them bastards something with that last riot——"

Kern sat in the front seat of the commandeered auto, half turned, staring at his mother. She lay outstretched on the seat, her legs bent against the door, her head resting in Dorcas' lap. Her eyes were closed. She did not move.

❈   ❈   ❈

In the upper sitting room, Kern stared blankly at the door beyond which his mother lay. Dorcas had taken complete charge. Her call had summoned the doctor. Her brief conversation with Judge Adams had served to start him and Mrs. Adams on their way to Washington. Failing to reach Charles at either his home or his office, she had listed several telephone numbers and placed a maid on the phone with orders to continue calling each ten minutes until Attorney Roberts was contacted.

Now she sat with Kern, trying to lessen his fears, hiding, she hoped, the hopelessness that was in her. When the door opened and the doctor came toward them, they started forward.

"I don't think you had better let him see her yet. She is in shock." He shook his head in a slow negative to the question in Dorcas' eyes. "Perhaps four, five hours. Perhaps less. There is nothing—" He went back into the sickroom and Kern knew that something terrible was happening. A light tapping sounded from the hallway, and Dorcas crossed the room to open the door. She talked briefly to the man who stood there, then closed the door and came to Kern. Her eyes were brimming with tears.

"Are you sure it was the caretaker, Kern? Very sure? You would know him if you saw him again?" Kern nodded over the lump in his throat.

"I am sure it was him."

"Let's go downstairs and talk to the lieutenant, Kern."

❈   ❈   ❈

Men crowded about the lounge where they sat. Scratching pencils, the rustle of turned pages and the restless shift of feet were the only sounds as Kern answered the lieutenant's questions.

42

"How do you know it was this caretaker, son?"

"I—I just know." He thought, then added, as if it explained exactly "how" he knew. "Mamma and I always waved to him in the park, but he never waved back. He just looked at us."

"Then what happened?" The questions led him through the entire afternoon, from the moment they had left Dorcas to that last instant. Omitting not the smallest detail, he told them in a halting voice how the man had struck him—how he had stabbed his mother and then run away. A policeman on the fringe of the group spoke up.

"His story checks with what the motorman and the conductor said, Lieutenant. They saw the whole thing from the street level."

"You have their names?"

"Yes, sir. Right here." He held his pad up. "They are coming down to headquarters after they finish this run."

"Good."

"What did he look like?" One of the reporters shot at Kern, watching him closely.

Kern thought carefully. "Well—he was very dark—" he remembered his father's caution, "Call no one black!"—"and he had a gold tooth in front." The flying pencils took each word of his reply. "And he had a white spot on one hand."

A nurse beckoned to Dorcas from near the door and she rose and went quickly to where the woman stood. They talked briefly and Dorcas came back to where Kern sat. The men waited, sensing a new turn to things.

"Kern," she stifled a sob, "let's go upstairs and see your mother." The ring of men was quiet as she led Kern to the door. There she stopped and spoke half over her shoulder, "I offer one thousand dollars for this man's capture, gentlemen, preferably dead." Her voice gritted in the silence.

❂   ❂   ❂

Laura turned her head as they entered the room. She raised one hand weakly from the coverlet and began to speak in a rapid, slurred voice. Kern understood only a word here and there of what she was saying. He stood beside her, not knowing what to do. Afraid. When his fingers touched hers, he was close to tears. Beside him, Dorcas spoke quietly. "Laura, Kern is here." Beyond the bed, the doctor looked across at Dorcas. "Only a little longer——"

His mother smiled at his name, a tiny smile that touched the corners of her mouth and was gone. Her eyes opened, and her fingers tightened anxiously about his.

"I won't be away long, son."

So she *was* going away!

Kern fell to his knees beside her and buried his face in the cloud of her hair on the pillow. Laura bit her lip as tears pressed from under her lids. "Grow up as we had planned, darling. Don't be afraid." Her speech grew swift and slurred and then she was silent. The doctor looked down at the boy, then went slowly into the hall. After a while, Dorcas bent and raised him. He did not cry.

III

"All of it, Kern. You'll feel better." He drained the glass and handed it back to Dorcas. She crossed quietly to the door and pulled it to behind her as she stepped into the hall. Drowsiness came to Kern almost at once. He was dimly aware of the half-light of dusk that outlined the windows and shadowed the ceiling and walls. He heard Dorcas talking to the doctor in a low voice. The murmur of their voices was faint as he drifted off to sleep.

"The sedative will help him. No telling what form shock will take with a youngster. Better to be safe."

"I'll look in on him later on, Doctor," Dorcas promised.

"Good. If he's awake then, you might give him the other powder. It won't hurt. Have you located his father?"

"Not yet. We are searching high and low. I don't know where he could be." The doctor's "Humph!" was contemptuous.

❂ ❂ ❂

Kern slept the dreamless sleep of those in whom emotion has plowed so deep a channel that, for the moment, the mind is insensible to further feeling. He awoke to the sound of voices in the hall, and listened intently, wondering if Dorcas was still talking to the doctor. Slowly he understood that the darkness in the room meant night. That hours had passed, that he had slept. He recognized the man's voice in the hall. It was his father's. The edges of sleep unraveled more quickly.

"What should I have done?" This was Dorcas, irritated and edgy.

"You might have called me first."

"Oh, I might, might I?" Her voice was scornful. "And just what do you think I have been trying to do all night long?" She hurried on,

44

not waiting for an answer. "If you hadn't been tied up with that 'hate league' of yours, you would have known." His father sounded tired.

"When are they coming?"

"They?"

"The Judge and Mrs. Adams."

"They will be here around noon tomorrow." The "they" sounded sharply.

"Here?" The search for words to express his thoughts was an effort.

"Here. This is my house. I trust you will find no objection to my receiving old friends."

"I—I didn't mean that." He heard his father's breath go out in a long, gusty sigh. "Did Kern really see this man? *Really* see him?"

Dorcas' voice scoffed at him. "Not only did he see him—he was struck by him."

"But the attacks in the newspapers—Kern said those things about—" Charles' legal mind groped for facts on which to hang its conclusions.

"Of course not. Kern is a child. He merely identified the man. The rest—the newsmen did themselves."

"But the reward——"

"That was *my* idea, Charles. I did that."

"You—" Charles was incredulous. "But you don't hunt a man down in this day and age. Why, he's not been proven guilty. You're helping to brand a whole community for what we don't even *know* this man did."

Dorcas' laugh was short and bitter.

"I intend to see that reward paid."

"But——"

She cut him off abruptly. "You listen to me, Charles. I had nothing to do with your marriage to Laura. It was not my affair. But you will remember that I saw it develop from the very start. I didn't think then that it would work. Neither did the Judge—nor Mrs. Adams. But all of us prayed for the best. It needn't have come to this miserable end had you given it a decent chance. You didn't—you dogged it. That's water under the bridge. Your motherless son is in that room. Let me see you make that up to him if you can! Get your precious Freedom League to help you now. I tell you that he will grow up a stranger to you. Wait!" Wide awake now, Kern could almost see the imperious gesture with which Dorcas halted his father's objection.

"Hear me out. I'll have no more to say after this. I have no feeling against Negroes. I have none for them. But I do hate a dog, what-

45

ever his extraction. And I intend to see this one dead. If money will help, I have plenty." Her footsteps ran quickly down the hall out of earshot, and Kern listening, suddenly hoped that his father would not come into the room. He lay tense and straight on the bed, and hoped in the moment before the door swung open that he would not touch him or speak to him.

His father came and stood beside the bed. Kern squeezed his eyes tight shut as the man bent and lifted him from the bed, and lay unresponsive in his arms as Charles rocked back and forth in the darkness. Kern knew that the quivering and the strange noises in his father's throat were grief. That night, Charles Roberts was frightening and more of a stranger to his son than he had ever been. Kern was relieved when, without warning, the door opened and Dorcas came in.

She switched on a lamp and stood watching them with a glass of milk in her hands. Her face was impassive as Charles looked at her, then put Kern on the bed. When he stepped away, Dorcas sat beside Kern.

"Drink this, Kern. It's nice and cool. It will help you go back to sleep." Her eyes stayed on Kern as he sipped the drink. "I've had the middle room fixed, Charles. You'd better try to get some sleep." Her voice was softer than it had been in the hallway. She took the empty glass from Kern and, turning the lamp out, she left the room. Kern watched his father's outline as he dropped into the chair before the window. Minutes after Dorcas had gone, he was surprised to hear him say, "Thank you." The sheer curtains stirred restlessly before the windows, and somewhere beyond the house a cricket took possession of the silence.

Kern's second sleep was filled with dreams. The tortured images of nightmare after nightmare made him a curious-eyed watcher of himself as he was pursued through sleep by a huge hand that clutched a knife. Kern fled before the hand, but each desperately chosen avenue of escape came to an abrupt end at a tall, branchy wall. Each time at the last terrifying moment, the wall parted and allowed him to run again. Over and over the chase was repeated until, in the curious, inexplicable way of dreams, the fabric of his nightmare altered. The hand was gone, and he raced blindly across a wide space toward a great pool of light and the sound of his name. There was a rattling noise and the glare of light disappeared. When Kern opened his eyes, he saw Dorcas lowering the blinds, cutting off the sunlight. His father still sat in the chair before the window. Kern brushed his hand across his forehead and stared at the beads of perspiration that clung

46

to his fingers. Dorcas bent beside him and together they watched his father.

Charles slouched deep in the chair's cushions, chin lowered on his chest. His eyes were unblinking. His hands gripped the chair arms, and the heavy veins that ridged their backs stood out sharply under the webwork of hair. Sleepless, red-rimmed eyes were sunk in their sockets. His hair was in shaggy disarray and a heavy stubble of beard covered his jowls and darkened the lines in his face. Dorcas was shocked at his appearance. Kern, frightened, wished that he could tell him how much he missed his mother.

"Charles," Dorcas hesitated. "Charles, you'd better straighten up a bit, don't you think?" He did not answer. "You'll find everything you need in the bath—then breakfast. Afterwards," she paused, "if you wish, I'll help you with—with funeral arrangements." She bit her lip.

"No." His answer was neither ungrateful nor resentful. It was only a word. The effort of turning his head to look at them told them how tired he was.

"Thanks. I'll go alone. I'd rather—if you don't mind." His eyes asked her to understand. He stood and looked down at them as if they were strangers. Without a word he turned and walked from the room. Dorcas shook Kern's head impulsively.

"Get dressed, young fellow. Then you can go to the station with me."

IV

They were in the upstairs sitting room when Charles returned. The storm of grief which had shaken them all on seeing his mother had passed. Kern lay with his legs curled under him, and his head in his grandmother's lap. She idly stroked his temples and watched her husband as Dorcas told them all she knew of the tragedy. She spoke gently, chose her words with care, trying to spare them what she could of brutality. They listened, Judge Adams and Margaret his wife, and Dorcas saw how fearful a blow this tragedy struck them. They seemed to shrink under its pain, as if the core of their world had died, and with it all reason for life. Caleb Adams said nothing when Dorcas finished. Nor when Charles entered the room, did he turn his head. Only when Charles crossed to the center of the room and stood before them, did Caleb take notice of him. Anger was plain in him and in the abrupt nod with which he accepted Charles' "Good morning, sir."

47

"I've made the necessary arrangements." Fire ran back into the old man's spare frame as Charles spoke.

"We are, of course, taking her home with us." The Judge did not raise his head, and Charles stiffened at his arbitrary tone. "You know," Judge Adams straightened in his chair, "that you have handled this —this whole marriage badly." His wife patted Kern's shoulder.

"Now, Caleb—" cautioning him against temper. Dorcas averted her eyes and said nothing.

"Each of us must act according to what we believe to be right." Charles made an obvious effort at restraint.

"I am doubling Dorcas' reward," the old man baited him. "I want that Negro caught!" His inflection was sharp.

"I, too."

Hands locked behind his back, Charles rocked on his toes. He seemed about to add something to what he had said, and Caleb Adams leaned forward as though to meet the words before they reached him. There were no words. Only a brief, negative headshake as Charles looked at them.

"I'd like to thank you, Dorcas. I'm more grateful than I can say for all you have done."

"I am sorry, Charles," her voice was quite kind, "so terribly sorry."

V

At dinner, the last evening before they took Laura back to Vermont, Margaret Adams asked Charles about Kern. She straightened decisively in her chair and looked quickly about at the dining room over which her daughter had presided as mistress for almost seven years and then she began to speak.

"Charles," it was the first thing that had been said since they had gathered at the table. Charles and Caleb, Kern, and Nettie, standing near the buffet, turned to look at her, as she went on, "Charles, I'll come to the point. What about Kern?"

Nettie, turning kitchenward with a serving tray, almost collided with the door in her eagerness to listen. Charles politely raised his eyes.

"Kern? What about him?" His eyebrows rose slightly with his question and he looked down as his fingers aligned his silver beside his plate.

"We'd like to take him with us, Charles. There are advantages——"

"Oh—" Charles gave no hint of his thoughts. His fingers were busy with his silver.

48

"It's not an entirely selfish wish, Charles. We need him—yes. But he needs us, too. He needs a mother." She pleaded with him to understand what she was trying to say. "We would like to raise him as a——"

"As a white boy?" The words ground themselves out deliberately. They were brutal, sprung from Charles' need to hurt as he was hurt. Across the table, Caleb Adams' face blazed with anger. His wife continued in her patient voice.

"No—no, Charles, just as a boy. A boy with school and home and careful attention. With someone to be a mother to him." Margaret studied Charles' face. What she could see of it told her nothing. "What race he may be of is not important, is it, Charles? Is not the important thing that he is your son and that he deserves a chance to live a healthy, normal life?"

Charles looked at her then and his answer was in his face. "You know that a man can't live a lie. We tried it, Laura and I, to the sorrow of us all."

"But you were a man, Charles, grown, with a man's conditioning behind you. Kern is a boy. He's not grown, not shaped. Why not give him this chance——?"

Charles listened with respectful attention, and all of them, even Kern and Nettie, back and forth between dining room and kitchen, understood that he would not change his mind.

"Charles, you know that I have never held any personal anger. Think now. How will Kern fit into the life which you are decided to live? What will that life do to him? Is it really a normal life?"

Kern knew, with a boy's understanding, that his father's mind was made up. He knew, too, that he wanted to go back to Vermont and stay with his grandparents. With a slow, negative headshake his father pushed away from the table and, excusing himself, left the room. His words hung in the room after he had climbed the stairs and gone into his study.

"It's not as easy as that. Kern must learn life for what it is—for what he is. He must learn that the last thing to do of all is to run away."

❊   ❊   ❊

Kern and his father went with them to Vermont. Two days later, when his mother had been buried in the little green plot that shouldered against the church and the first slope of the hill that climbed away behind it, he stood at the door of his grandmother's house and waited for his father, looking down the yard to where the car waited for them at the gate.

49

CHAPTER II

THE BEGINNING OF ANGER

I

ONE moment Kern was curled loosely on the window seat, absorbed in his book. The next, he was staring apprehensively over his shoulder at the door behind him, as if he expected it would open suddenly and he would find someone standing there—someone whom he did not want to see. Without realizing it, he had fallen into the habit of that sudden backward look and into the habit of keeping to himself.

The children who lived along the block, Melvin and Eddie and Avis, were more conscious of this latter practice than he was. Shyness had always been a part of Kern and they accepted it now as they had when his mother lived. Their games of "Red Light" and "Rover" never included him. Charles, keenly aware of Kern's withdrawal into himself, had searched without success for some means of stirring new interests in him—of bridging the gap between himself and Kern. His sister Paula had written from Valley View to say that she had accepted a teaching position at the college and would not be able to come and live with them. Kern, imagining Paula to be a shrewish combination of his father and Nettie, had been secretly relieved at this, and Charles had no choice other than to divide the responsibility for overseeing Kern between himself and Nettie. She, thus loosely vested with authority, interpreted Kern's habit of seeking his own company as a studied expression of superiority and accordingly transferred to him the antagonism which she had held for his mother.

Kern stared at the door until he was satisfied that it would not open, then turned back to the window before him. The book which he had been reading slipped from his knees and lay unnoticed on the window seat as he stared out into the darkness. Above his head the half-lowered splint blinds slatted gently back and forth at the ends of their drop cords. The cool air flowing through the slitted opening beneath the window brought with it the smell of clean-washed, leafy things. Rain beat against the wide bay window in a ragged patter and made a flat, leaden sound as it sheeted down on the gray slate porch roof outside the window. Wind harried the twisted oak that towered upward beyond the window and threatened, in passing, to snuff out the flickering street light. Kern glued his eyes to the open space between window and sill and intently watched the miniature cascade of water that washed down the sloping roof to swirl along the gutter out of sight. Now and then a hurrying pedestrian moved from darkness to darkness across the dull-orange circle of the gas lamp's wavering light and he invented strange, romantic missions to account for their being out on such a miserable night.

Shortly he grew tired of this game and sprawled at length, hooking his stockinged feet over the end of the seat. He came often to this room which had been his mother's. Nowhere else in the house was he so much at ease. Not even in his own room. His eyes wandered over the room. Everything he saw, the maple furniture, the pictures they had bought on an excursion to the "Boston House," the many-colored hooked rugs, reminded him of her. Without turning his head, he could see the rocking chair beneath the lamp and the sewing basket on top, open on the table where his mother had left it. Kern even thought he could hear the clicking slither of her knitting needles, darting back and forth.

Below him, from the living room, came the sound of voices, now light, now heavy, to disturb his thoughts. A meeting of the Freedom League was in session. Kern wished angrily that the meeting would end. He could see the people below him clearly. The "Board of Strategy"—the Reverend slumped heavily in his mother's best chair, legs outthrust, a ponderous man with eyes almost hidden in the puffy flesh of his face. The Reverend reminded Kern of a huge mud doll. He would, Kern knew, listen. Now and then he would gravely nod his head in approval. Sitting on the edge of her chair beside him would be fidgeting, spinsterish Miss Carey. Countless times before, Kern had wondered if she ever fell off onto the floor. Occasionally she would break into the conversation with her heavy, bass-drum voice. When she did, the others would turn and stare at her in amazement—just as they had done a hundred times before— as though they had never been quite so surprised. Miss Carey would flush with embarrassment, clear her throat, and launch out again in determined, booming tones. Mr. Graves, the postman, was the little man whose Adam's apple bobbed up and down so convulsively. Kern could see them plainly, and the others whose names he had never learned.

The undercurrent of anger in their voices reached him. It was, as his mother had remarked, filled with righteousness, as though they were engaged in a divine mission and held a special grant to invoke God, loudly and frequently, as their ally. Now and then the hum of discussion rose and strange new words like "nigger" and Negro and "mean white trash" would spice the air. When Kern found that he could not fit those words into the realm of "what he knew," he filed them away in his mind for future thought.

Tonight their voices aroused the familiar resentments more sharply than they usually did and he wondered why the League could not hold its meetings somewhere else. Always he and his mother had moved to this same upper room to escape the tempest of emotion these meetings brought. Almost always his father and mother had been engaged in quarrels which had left her sick and shaken. Kern remembered clearly the last argument they had, the only one he actually witnessed. He had been about to go to bed that night when the hallway door had opened and his father stood there, his face pale with anger. His mother had been about to kiss him good night and her hand, tightening on his shoulder, had hurt. His father's breath had come heavily.

"Did you have to embarrass me?" His mother had urged him toward the door.

"Kern is here," and he understood that she wanted his father to wait until he had left the room. "Time for bed, son."

His father's lips had curled.

"So he is. And it is past time that he began to understand—this tommyrot you've been teaching him." "Tommyrot!" As he slipped by his father and went down the hall, Kern wondered what "tommyrot" could be. He had never heard of it before. He had sat on the edge of the bed in his dark room at the end of the hall and pulled at the knots in his shoestrings, straining to understand their voices as they sounded in the hall.

"Charles, we've been through this before, and we agreed that Kern was to be kept out of it. We——"

"My God, woman! How can he be kept out of it? He is a Negro. Can't you understand that? It's time he began learning what being a Negro will mean. God knows he will be one long enough."

"Oh, Charles, why can't you give up this fighting, this hating? Why?" Her voice had broken and Kern had been angry at his father and at the Freedom League meetings that always preceded these arguments.

"I'll tell you why. As long as bigots treat other men as animals, someone must fight. Those of us who are able must fight!"

"You're not the same man I married, Charles. You're twisted inside with hate. I'm sorry for you," his mother's voice had echoed back, thin and miserable. She paused for breath. "Well, I'm not one of you—and neither is Kern. And I won't let him be dragged into this—" She stopped. There was a dead silence and the door had slammed shut, cutting off the ray of light in the hall and the sound of their voices. Puzzled with anger and sadness, not understanding, Kern undressed in his dark room and went to bed.

"Negro—nigger—mean white trash!"

"You're not the same man I married—I'm not one of you." He had never forgotten those words, nor did he forget his father angry and his mother in tears. He remembered quarrels that the Freedom League always brought.

Kern sat upright at the window as voices and the sound of moving feet came from the living room. He listened until the last footsteps thumped down the wooden stairs and splattered off up the rain-drenched street into silence. Then the front doors shut heavily, and he heard his father's steps pause in the hallway below as he stopped to speak to Nettie. Kern picked up his book and quickly crossed the room. Turning out the lamp, he hurried down the hall to his own room and slipped out of his clothes. Hanging them on the door he climbed quickly into bed and lay there wiggling his toes. Later, remembering a forgotten part of his nightly ritual, he slipped from the bed and stood before the low dressing table, peering down at his mother's picture. He touched it gently and clambered into bed. That night he completely forgot to kneel and say his prayers. Shortly, he heard his father's steps sound in the hall, come closer and stop outside of his door. The footsteps moved away down the hall and Kern gradually relaxed.

Sleep came slowly that night and its drowsy beginnings were cluttered with thoughts of the three weeks that had passed since he and his father had left Vermont.

❊   ❊   ❊

His father's bitter, parting refusal to entertain any discussion of leaving him with his grandparents had puzzled him as their train had rushed southward from Vermont the day after his mother's

53

funeral. He had lain in the darkened compartment, longing for his mother, afraid of the still, silent man in the berth above him and wondered what lay in store for him. He wished that he could share his questions with someone. If his mother had been there, she would have understood. Or Dorcas—Dorcas could have answered them, he knew. But Dorcas was not there.

❀   ❀   ❀

In another week he would begin school. That much had been decided. What he had seen of school had been disappointing. The drab, red-brick building sprawled in the middle of a bare, black, dirt play yard, and as they had approached it he had lagged a little behind his father. Inside it had been better. The grooved stone steps that seemed to fit his feet, and the shiny handrail smooth in his grasp had combined with the strange smell of the place to stir his interest. Peering from side to side as they reached each floor, he had gotten fleeting glimpses of classrooms with their regular rows of desks; with lined blackboards and pictured windows.

Prim, tall Miss Washburn seemed forbidding when they first entered her office. She had questioned him at length, and now and then had noted his replies on a pad before her. What he knew of English and history erased the lines of doubt which had come to her face as he had stumbled in arithmetic, and Kern had felt a quick pleasure when he was complimented for the simple connections he made between these two subjects.

"Someone's done a good job with this lad," she told his father. "There should be more of this association of ideas in elementary schools and less of teaching so-called facts that are just so much tommyrot." Kern, catching a glimpse of his father's face from the corner of his eye, had the feeling that someone was not quite right about the meaning of "tommyrot." Miss Washburn had started him in the fourth grade.

"He will never be a scholar, Attorney Roberts, but he may be something better. He is a dreamer." She had permitted herself the temporary relaxation of ruffling Kern's hair. "Even so, he is going to have more difficulty making friends than he will have with books." Sorting among papers on her desk, she took up a printed slip and ran her eye over it before handing it to Charles. "Get these books for him. He might run through them before school starts. He has almost three weeks yet. When he comes the first day, bring him here. I will take him to his teacher myself."

54

Kern's dread of school had almost vanished by the time they walked into Maxwell's bookstore. Blinking his eyes to adjust them after the glaring sunlight, Kern followed slowly after his father down the long aisle, past the green-shaded light that swung in the tiny post-office booth, to the rear of the shop. Delightedly he had looked about him at shelves of books that filled the walls and towered to the ceiling and at the cabinets on the counters, filled with paper and books, notebooks with pens and inks and erasers. Here were all the materials of school, the things he had seen older boys and girls carrying when he had been a little boy and they had passed along his street en route to school. Now he would have some of his own.

That day Charles bought him pads, pencils, pens, a pencil box and his first schoolbooks—all of them new. Mr. Maxwell, turning to look down from the shelf where he had climbed to get an English book, had asked, "A new one or a secondhand copy, Counselor?" Kern's father had looked at him for a moment, then answered, "Better make it new, I think," and Kern had been happy. He had touched the book's crisp new pages as they lay on the counter before him, had felt the smooth bindings and had hardly been able to wait to get home so that he could take it to his room and begin reading. He would, he knew, print his name carefully in the square, neat letters his mother had taught him.

Several blocks from home, his father had stopped beside him.

"Kern, do you think you can get home from here?"

He could hardly believe that he was about to be trusted to go through the streets by himself.

"Yes sir." He looked up at his father. "I think so. It's straight ahead until I come to the circle, then it's just around the corner." His father had nodded agreement.

"Be careful crossing the streets."

"Yes, sir."

"And tell Nettie that I will be home about five. I am going to catch a streetcar downtown."

Gulping down his first uncertainty, Kern hurried off down the street. At each corner he stopped to look about him, then settling his precious package under his arm, hurried across.

Had Kern looked behind him, he would have seen his father standing where he had left him, watching until he was out of sight. Concern mingled with other feelings in Charles' eyes, and only when Kern had disappeared, did he cross the street to catch the downtown car to his office.

Now close to home, Kern almost ran. Before him lay the privacy of his room and the prospects of his new books.

❖   ❖   ❖

Charles had barely begun to read through the stack of mail on his desk when the buzzer sounded beside him. Still running his eye over the letter in his hand, he removed the receiver from its cradle.

"Yes?" His clerk's voice advised him, "It's your Nettie, Chief." Nettie was somehow always "your Nettie," Charles knew, his "special prize," when others referred to her.

"Put her on." He dragged his mind from the letter in his hand. What could Nettie want now? Not dinner—they'd decided about that. Money? No. He'd given her money yesterday. Kern? It must be Kern! His spirits fell. What now? Nettie calling him at the——

"H'lo, h'lo, Mistuh Charles? Kern's done gone and—" Nettie's words tumbled, one over the other. Charles sighed. It was Kern!

"Wait a minute, Nettie. Just wait a minute." He brought her to a halt, her gulping excitement audible on the other end. "This must be bad," he thought.

"They's got him, Mistuh Charles. They's got him. Oh, Lawdy!" Nettie wailed distress.

"Who's 'got him'? What do you mean?"

"The p'lice. They come here and got him!"

"Do you mean the police have Kern?"

"Yessuh. Dat's what Ah mean. Two 'tectives took him 'n they done tol' me—" She gasped for breath.

"They told you what, Nettie?"

"If'n you wants to see him, they's gone to headquahtahs to 'dentify da man what hurt his ma." Headquarters? Identify? That meant the line-up room.

"Nettie, you stay there until I call. Answer no questions for anybody. Understand? Absolutely none!" He slammed the receiver on the hook, snatched up his hat and bolted through the outer office past his staring clerk, and into the street.

II

The "line-up room" was in the basement of Police Headquarters. Motionless layers of smoke hung along its length, testifying to the inadequacy of the noisily whirring fans which were intended to provide ventilation. Uneven rows of chairs filled the larger part of

56

the room and their scattered occupants, staring at intervals and with concentrated attention at the platform beyond them at the far end of the room, shifted restlessly in their seats and scuffed wider clean spaces on the trash-littered floor about their feet. Odd-sized "Wanted" and "Reward" runners shared the crowded wall space with red-lettered "No Smoking" signs. Below the raised platform, just outside the glaring spotlights, a police sergeant called out names, descriptions and offenses in a tired voice. With each name a man moved across the platform to stand in the brilliant light until ordered to move on.

Kern sat midway of the room, nervously watching the line-up platform before him. Perspiration burned his eyes as he gazed intently at the board and caused the black lines and numbers marking feet and inches of height to blur and waver. Beside him sat Lieutenant Toomey. Behind him, and to the other side, a round-faced man with a perspiring bald head leaned forward with his chin in his hands. Toomey called him "Chief." They watched Kern keenly as man after man came forward in answer to his name and stood in the hard light. Only once, when Kern sat quickly forward in his seat to stare at a Negro suspected of armed robbery, had the Chief halted the ceaseless champing of his jaws that rolled a burned-out cigar from one corner of his mouth to the other and back again. Then he stopped and glanced quickly at Lieutenant Toomey whose tense face was registering disappointment. When Kern failed to recognize the man and relaxed in his chair, the Chief began to chew his cigar again and Toomey expelled a sigh of relief. Kern noticed neither of these things.

Charles saw them the moment he entered and sat in the rear of the room, watching. He looked from Kern to the line-up board and back again with each new name, watching the boy's reaction. The parade of petty felons was familiar to Charles. The name called out and then the suspect, moving into the light, blinking, sometimes defiantly stalking, surly at having been hauled in on a routine roundup; or innocent and ashamed; or cowering, frightened, fearful of recognition. The flotsam of a city passed over the line-up stage each day. The guilty and the innocent held by law. Charles knew them all.

"Tom Hawks!"

"Tom Hawks!" The bored voice was louder as the officer looked up inquiringly.

"C'mon, Tom, let's go. We ain't got all day."

"Awright. Keep your shirt on." Tom, wearing polished patent shoes and a pin-stripe suit, sauntered toward the center of the platform.

57

Derby pushed back on his head, one hand casually plied a toothpick as he looked about him. The other hand swung a watch chain with a seal-tooth fob in slow, careless circles.

"Time's one thing I got plenty of," he smilingly informed all and sundry.

"Awright. None of your lip." Tom Hawks turned easily and doffed his derby eloquently to the Sergeant.

"Your majesty—" Mock deference flowed from him.

"Tom Hawks—five ten—one seventy—suspected of confidence games." The voice droned on. "Awright, Tom, you can go. But one of these days——"

A snarl replaced Tom's smile. "Yeah—so tell me when, copper!" He smiled quickly and sauntered out of sight, flipping his hand in a good-bye wave to the Sergeant.

"Jeff Mason."

"Jeff Mason," the voice continued its routine. "Five feet eight; one eighty-five; age thirty-nine; race, Negro," the Sergeant's head came up as he looked at Jeff. "Arrested for attempted felonious assault and criminal attack on the persons of——"

Kern's eyes widened as Jeff Mason slouched out upon the platform. Heavy shoulders sagging, head thrust forward, Jeff Mason peered into the darkness before him from under lowered brows. Standing wide-legged, it seemed to Kern that the man looked directly at him and was about to lunge outward toward where they sat. The Sergeant's voice ran on in the background "—Mrs. Anna Kelter and daughter on September 3rd, near Lansdowne, Maryland. All right, boy—stand straight up there."

Kern gulped and stared, brushing at his forehead. He did not notice the intent stares with which Lieutenant Toomey and the Chief watched him. His voice was husky when he spoke as though he could not find words easily.

"That's him—that is the man!" He sat frozen in his chair as Jeff Mason's eyes followed the sound of his voice.

"Are you sure, son?" Toomey pressed him for confirmation, nodding over his shoulder at the Chief with satisfaction. Charles came to where they sat, anxiously watching Kern.

"Yes, sir, I'm sure." Kern spoke with more conviction and was more composed.

"Why do you say *this* is the man, Kern?"

Toomey turned at the father's interruption and the Chief took his cigar from his mouth to study Charles' face. "You his father?"

58

Charles merely nodded. "Why, Kern?"

"Just a minute, Roberts," Toomey broke in. "The boy made an unsolicited identification and it's good enough for us. There ain't no mistake. We're convinced and a Grand Jury will be, too. Right, Chief?"

"Right!"

Toomey bellowed an order. "Hold that nigger on a charge of murder, Sergeant." The Chief smiled at Kern.

"You did all right, kid. S'good somebody in your family wants to see this thing cleared up." His lip curled as he looked at Charles.

"C'mon, Toomey."

Charles blocked his way. "I want to see the man who murdered my wife punished more than anyone else—but this is a serious——"

"Yeah, yeah. But this is a serious charge 'n you want to be sure the right man takes the rap." The Chief laughed and Kern thought that it was not really a laugh at all. "I know, Roberts—I know all about you." They both faced Charles now, truculent and contemptuous. Toomey deliberately spat at his feet.

"All I know is—that nigger killed a white woman, and I'm a white man!" He shouldered his way past Charles, followed by the Chief, and left the room. Charles stood, half turned, with anger shaking him. Then he turned to Kern. "Come on." They left the room.

CHAPTER III

ANGER IN THE CITY

I

JEFF MASON was indicted by the Grand Jury on a charge of first-degree murder, and was bound over to the criminal court for trial late in September.

Immediately the pending case became "news" in Washington's press. The first hue and cry was confined to a few readers who wanted to air their points of view through letters to the editors. Their expressions of interest ran the gamut from a soberly determined abhorrence of crime to the enraged ravings of Negro haters. Sprinkled evenly between these extremes were the cries of the righteously indignant. Floundering in a period when little was newsworthy, editors plastered the story on front pages. There it stayed until the trial was over. Public sentiment, aroused, then sustained, began its rise to a fever pitch. The District Prosecutor pledged various "civic groups" that he would push the case to an early conclusion. "The trial will be," he confidently stated, "open and shut." Under the growing swell of public sentiment, a Commissioner of the District told newsmen that "an outraged law required that the most expeditious handling possible be given to the case." A Judge of the District Court hailed the crime as a "dark blot on the fair name of the Nation's Capital. Only vigorous action," the Judge continued, "can erase this stain."

Before a week had passed, the trial had become, in fact, a test of "white supremacy." As interest in it widened beyond neighboring states, a few Congressmen, viewing oncoming elections, determined to make political capital of the case. Their sonorous utterances on the matter said in substance, "To allow this perpetration to go unpunished would be the beginning of the downfall of democracy as we practice it." Thus encouraged, citizen groups in several states, and in one case the legislature of a state, gave voice to their opinions. On every hand the demand was made that Jeff Mason pay for this "national shame" with his life.

After a little probing, and with scant accuracy but unlimited imagination, the *Daily Press* carried the "Life Story of Jeff Mason." Its oft-repeated statement, "Jeff told this correspondent," must have been a surprise to Jeff as he leafed through issues of the tabloid *Press* in his cell. Therein what little of his family history the *Press* had been able to determine was colored to suit the clamor of the moment and hung out for public inspection. Much ado was made of the discovery that Jeff's brother was, at that very moment, a prisoner in a Washington jail. That he had been jailed for inability to pay a speeding fine, was not mentioned. Another tidbit of information which added to the lurid story was the revelation that while Jeff's mother lived, an inhabitant of the Old Folks' Home, most diligent efforts failed to produce the existence of a sire to legitimatize Jeff's existence. His bastard condition was linked in some indefinite way with his criminal bent.

The angry tide of feeling swung from Jeff Mason to include all Negroes. The first in a series of *Daily Press* cartoons showed Jeff Mason as a great slavering beast stalking loose through the city. It was captioned "Hydrophobia!" The last, a full-page cartoon entitled "Danger—Beware!" showed an outline map of Washington. The large Negro sections were blocked out in solid black.

Washington stood on the verge of another race riot. Whites looked askance at Negroes whom they passed in broad daylight, and at night were bound to their homes by an exaggerated fear of what might lurk in each shadow and behind each bush. A series of scare complaints, the products of imaginative minds, caused a wave of anxiety and in the Negro neighborhoods the police staff was doubled. There was, for a while, talk of placing the militia on a stand-by order to quell possible disturbances.

Actually there was no concerted violence. A few isolated Negroes, moving alone, were set upon and beaten by idle troublemakers. Four Negroes were arrested by the police for misdemeanors. One died, accidentally, from a fractured skull suffered in falling down the police-station steps. No Negro women were molested, though there were scattered complaints of insult. No white women were raped, though there were scattered complaints of insult. The evening dailies and the *Morning Clarion* treated the case in editorial and story as though Jeff Mason's guilt were already proven, and only the formalities of trial and noose remained. Though more conservative in language and style than the tabloids, their final opinion was no whit different from that of their tabloid associates.

It was never revealed in these papers that Laura Roberts had been the wife of a Negro.

The weekly Negro newspapers took up the gauntlet which had been thrown at their feet. Their first, faltering voice was weakened by an uncertainty that Jeff Mason was not in fact guilty. Their stories became more forceful and concerted when—and this was so almost immediately—it became apparent that Jeff Mason's fate was not the prime issue at hand. Once Negro editors recognized the familiar fight against a "white supremacy," they were on familiar ground and lashed out in defense of the Negro citizens in Washington, fighting to preserve the few shreds of personal dignity which they were accorded. Scathing editorials pointed out the absence of justice in this clamoring demand and the vicious publicity smear which had become injurious to all Negroes in Washington.

By the end of the second week, bolstered by the support of more than a hundred other Negro weekly newspapers throughout the nation, Washington Negroes were fighting to strip the cloak of sham from the approaching trial. Screaming headlines proclaimed that Jeff Mason had been hailed before a Grand Jury with no effort to safeguard his rights.

One banner read—"Hasty Trial Dooms Mason"—"Rush Action Seen as Sop to White Supremacy." Another, in similar vein—"Mason Never Identified." This article said, in part, "Kern Roberts, who had identified Mason, admittedly had been struck by his assailant with such force that he could neither move nor speak. How then," it questioned, "could he be certain of his assailant's identity? The streetcar operators saw two struggling figures from the height of Calvert Street Bridge in the twilight. Neither was able to give any personal identifying marks which would indicate that their identification was positive. The dead woman's son," this story held in no uncertain terms, "is not to be considered as a capable witness."

The Negro press was Nettie's gospel. On each of the three Thursday evenings which passed before the trial began, she spread the papers on the kitchen table, and with her boy friend, George Lincum Washington, at her side, traced her way by the tip of her finger through each page. After each reading she gazed more accusingly at Kern than she had before.

Charles, too, read the papers thoroughly. The white press won his bitter though most often silent condemnation for the irresponsible fashion in which it stirred up this storm of anger. Now and then a news insert, such as the statement made by a District Commissioner deploring this "injury to the fair name of the Nation's Capital," would earn a contemptuous snort. Usually he would turn away from the papers to sit in thoughtful silence. After his first questions, he was convinced that Kern was positive in his identification of Jeff Mason. He did not discuss the case with him again.

❊   ❊   ❊

In the course of this tirade against Jeff Mason—and against all Negroes in Washington—and while feeling between Negroes and whites surged dangerously, three things happened. Kern began public school. Both he and his father were subpoenaed to appear in the case of The United States *vs.* Jeff Mason. And the Freedom League took up Jeff's defense.

Kern began public school.

He left his house that late crisp September morning with a notebook and long, new pencils clutched in one hand, and less than a block from his house found himself caught in the schoolward-bound flow of children. For seven blocks after that he moved, secretly timid, with the chattering throng as newcomers from each side street swelled its number, and hurried toward school. When he was not envying the ease with which two boys were turning cartwheels for a girl just ahead of him, he was peering curiously down the alleys and courts that opened off the rough brick sidewalk. He found it hard to believe that people actually lived in the shabby, run-down houses that lined their sides. Less than a block from school, he saw the red-brick building. It was surrounded on three sides by a black dirt play yard and on the fourth by a tall wire fence that surrounded the yard into which the girls were going. Kern funneled with the boys into the open yard and through a door over which was carved the word "BOYS," to climb the worn stairs for the second time. He turned at the landing and went on to the second floor and Miss Washburn's office.

His initiation to school was harsh. Four times in one day his schoolmates, voicing things they had heard at home, called him a "tattletale" and ran from him when he would have played with them. He stopped trying to join them.

Kern and Charles were subpoenaed.

Five days after Kern began school, Charles received a subpoena requiring him to present Kern in Criminal Court in ten days as a witness for the prosecution of Jeff Mason.

The Freedom League sponsored the defense of Jeff Mason.

Kern sat at the head of the stairs and wondered why they had

63

come tonight. This was Friday and the League met only on Tuesdays. He was sure it was Friday. The school week was over. The Reverend and Miss Carey, Mr. Talley—the postman—and Miss Washburn were down there in the parlor. He could hear them talking.

"—the League is dedicated to help any move that will improve the cause of Negroes—" That was the Reverend.

"That's absolutely right." His father.

"—and to oppose any move that hurts Negroes——"

"That's right." His father again.

"Well, Charles—" the voice trailed out. Kern was not sure who was talking, "—is a crucial test. What happens to one man is not important if that man is guilty. But when the course of law becomes twisted and something that belongs to all of us is in danger, then we must——"

"I agree completely. This trial will be a mockery."

"Charles—" Kern knew at once that the precise voice belonged to Miss Washburn, "what would you suggest? We know your interest in seeing justice done in this——"

"I would have the League intervene and supply counsel. Request a change of venue——"

Kern could not understand why his father was helping these people who spoke of helping Jeff Mason. He rose stiffly and went down the hall to his mother's room. Was his father helping Jeff Mason? If he was not, what was he doing?

II

"Tell this court—!" The prosecuting attorney's voice rose higher and higher. It became a shout in Kern's ears and he pressed back in the tall witness chair, trying to escape its dinning. Before him, faces filled the seats in close files and stood against the walls. Faces that peered at him. A looming mass of curious faces. Listening and waiting for his answer.

"Tell us—" The prosecutor's cold gray eyes held him now and he could not look away.

"What was this black beast doing to your mother?"

Kern felt the quick tears press against his eyelids. He heard, dimly, a voice crying out against the low rumble of sound in the room. The voice was saying, "I object! I object!" The heat of the room pushed against Kern's face. Inside he was cold and frightened.

This was what the spectators had waited for. For ten days they

64

had waited. This was the showdown. The eyewitness story of the attack.

The first day had set the pattern and each day that followed had been charged with the same high emotion. On the first day, Kern had been ganged by two older boys on his way home from school. He had gotten his first bloody nose and a black eye, the result, he knew, of having tattled on Jeff Mason.

On that day, too, Andrew Turpeau had risen in court, squared his lean shoulders against the hostile silence, and begun the defense of Jeff Mason.

The crowded courtroom had stared at him. Curious, angry, hopeful, surly, prayerful. According to their race, each had gauged him and waited for him to speak. The antagonism in the white faces had been plain to see, and he had answered it with a thin smile. When he turned to face the first jury panel, their antagonism, too, had been plain. It had not amused him. Each step that carried him to the railing behind which the first twelve veniremen sat had tightened his concern with the task which lay before him.

Till this moment he had not looked at Jeff Mason. He did not look at him now.

His eyes ran over the jury candidates before him.

Mitchell.

Abel.

Howard.

Smith.

Smith.

Secretary.

Storekeeper.

Carpenter.

Housewife.

Retired railroad engineer.

His gaze fastened on Mitchell. At the railing he stopped and stared curiously at the man.

Mitchell looked back at the slim, cocoa-brown attorney, their eyes locking and holding. Mitchell stared easily at first, with confidence in his pale eyes. Then a hint of a flush came into his fleshy face and grew deeper at his thin hairline. His eyes wavered for a moment, then broke and looked away over the crowd, upward to the ceiling. He clasped his hands and nervously unclasped them. When his eyes came back to Andrew Turpeau, his gaze was uncertain, overdefiant.

Growing distaste twisted at his stomach. He saw a Negro of aver-

65

age height, neatly dressed in a dark-blue business suit. A Negro who stood before him, proudly, straight, head high, completely at ease. The man's head and eyes held him. The head was thin and well-modeled. It rested easily on the brown column of a neck. Its ears lay close to the crisp black hair. Its lips were narrow and sharply graven. The eyes that watched his face were a greenish-blue. They were startling in the brown face. Albert Mitchell thought he saw a prickle of amusement in those eyes. He thought, "Them ain't nigger eyes." He felt a flush of pleasure at the probability that somewhere, at some time, a white man had bedded one of this man's female ancestors. Then he recognized contempt in the eyes that watched him and in the thin lips. He raged inwardly.

This was as Andrew Turpeau had intended. He polished his gold-rimmed glasses and adjusted them carefully, high on the lean bridge of his nose. When Turpeau spoke in the dead silence, his voice was sharp, unpleasant, as if he viewed the task before him with distaste.

"Your name?" His eyes finished the question.

"Mitchell." The stain of a flush deepened in the man's already florid face. "Albert Mitchell." The man completed his statement, pushing himself erect in his chair.

"Your business?" Now the whole room felt the sharp edge of the questions.

"I'm a— I said that before." Truculence was in both voices.

"Then say it again. Say it each time I ask you!" Turpeau's cold gaze held the man, ignoring the prosecution's objection. Without taking his eyes from Mitchell's face, he addressed Judge Gowdy.

"Your Honor, the defense will justify both its line of questioning and its method of address."

Behind him a curt voice advised, "You will be sure that you do, sir."

"Your occupation, Mr. Mitchell?"

"I'm a secretary—a private secretary." Mitchell took Judge Gowdy's admonishment as support. His gaze went to the spectators who crammed the court, looking for other supporters.

"How long have you been a resident of Washington, Mr. Mitchell?"

"For 'most ten years, off and on." The answer was given in a deliberate, drawling voice.

"You say 'off and on.' Do you maintain a permanent legal residence in the District?"

"Yes, I do."

"Then you will explain to the court what you mean by 'off and on.'"

66

"Well, when Congress adjourns, I generally go back home for a month or two."

"Where is 'back home,' Mr. Mitchell?" Evarts fidgeted at his table and inclined his head to listen as his associate whispered to him. His eyes followed Turpeau as he stepped away from the railing and waited for an answer.

"Mississippi." The core of Negro spectators fidgeted visibly.

"You are a private secretary, Mr. Mitchell. Who is your employer?" Evarts was on his feet again as he offered objection.

"Your Honor, this line of examination is highly irregular. No elimination of a juryman should be based on the attitudes of an employer. The Court should advise——"

Judge Gowdy's gavel rapped sharply.

"This Court does not propose to be instructed in its conduct of this case, Mr. Evarts. I have heard no statements concerning the attitudes of any employer. If I entertain any such evidence, should it be forthcoming, it will certainly be in a connected fashion. Mr. Mitchell will answer the question." The Judge looked down at Mitchell in the jury box.

"Senator McCarrol." Mitchell's voice was low. The name he spoke sounded clearly in the room. Andrew turned to smile at Evarts as he crossed and recrossed his legs angrily.

"You have said that you hold no opinion in this case, Mr. Mitchell. Do you still maintain that position?"

"I do!" Mitchell's voice was thick with incrowding emotion. He glared at Andrew Turpeau's back as he moved away from the railing, then at his face as he turned to face the jury box.

"Amazing, Mr. Mitchell." Turpeau's precise voice was gently sarcastic. "Amazing." He continued to look at Mitchell, smiling thinly, shaking his head in a slow, barely noticeable negative. "Do you really expect this Court to believe that you hold no opinion in this case?"

Mitchell swayed forward in his chair.

"I said that I didn't have no opinion an' I don't intend to be made out no liar." His face darkened to an angry scowl.

"Humph! We shall see." Turpeau's smile was gone. "Tell me, Mr. Mitchell, do you share the Senator's beliefs about Negroes?"

"Object! This effort to involve the name of a United States Senator is slanderous. It has no bearing in the matter at hand."

"Sustained." Judge Gowdy's eyes studied Andrew Turpeau.

"I withdraw the question. Are you the only private secretary in the Senator's office?"

"I am."

"Mr. Mitchell, in what way do your duties as a private secretary differ from those of any other secretary in that office?"

"Well—I'm a *private* secretary." A smirk was on his face as he turned to the courtroom. "I thought everyone knew what a private secretary did." His sally won a thin ripple of laughter.

"Exactly, Mr. Mitchell." Turpeau smiled at him. "Everyone does know. But for the sake of the record, let us enumerate some of your duties." He counted each duty on a separate finger.

"You reply to the Senator's personal correspondence, of course?"

"I do."

"You maintain his calendar of appointments?" Two fingers.

"I do." Mitchell settled more easily in his chair.

"You accompany the Senator on his speaking engagements?" Three fingers.

"I do."

"I may suppose, then, may I not, that you are familiar with his policies?" Four fingers.

"I—I reckon I am." Turpeau turned from his counsel table with a ragged newspaper clipping in his hand. He ran his eyes over it quickly.

MISSISSIPPI'S SENIOR SENATOR BRANDS JEFF MASON CRIME

LAYS BLAME FOR NEGRO'S CRIME "AT FEET OF NATIONAL INTELLIGENCE!"

BY WILLIAM KINNAN
PRESS Reporter

Lashing out bitterly at Jeff Mason, Washington negro awaiting trial for murder next week in the District's Criminal Court, the Magnolia State Senator labelled Mason's alleged crime as "an indictment of our national intelligence." Said the Senator in an exclusive telegraphic story given to THE PRESS by Mr. Albert Mitchell, his private secretary, "If you go through the Government departments up there in Washington, you see so many niggers it's like a black cloud all around you. Now any sensible man or woman'll tell you you can't 'low wild animals to roam 'round free because if you do someone's sure to be hurt. That's exactly what happened here."

68

Declaring that "nigras ain't really to blame," McCarrol's message continued, "they jes' act like they know how. These things are instinctive with 'em. It's jes like a dog liftin' his leg. We know that down here. We guard against it."

The Senator's secretary explained this remark by saying, "We don't have no trouble out of our blacks down home because we look facts in the face. That's why," Mitchell averred, "the Senator really faults white folks for this crime. They should know by now that there ain't nothin' to this idea of equality. The Senator's solution," he explained, "is to clamp down on the niggers and we won't have these disgraces in our National Capitol."

Mitchell said that he expected the Senator to return to Washington in time to be present for the trial.

"Mr. Mitchell, I have here a clipping from the *Evening Daily Press* of twelve days ago. Will you read it and tell me if you are familiar with its contents?"

Everyone in the room waited. Judge Gowdy, Jeff Mason, Evarts and Turpeau, bailiffs and reporters, the close-packed spectators and the panel of jurymen waited. They all saw the slow flush that crept upward over his half-bent face.

"Have you seen that before, Mr. Mitchell?"

Mitchell's heavy breathing could be heard now.

"Did you not release that statement to the *Press?*" He hurried on without waiting for an answer as Mitchell looked up slowly. "It states specifically that you did, Mr. Mitchell."

"I was ordered to transmit the Senator's feeling in the matter. These thoughts are his." Turpeau's brown hand reached across the space between them to take the clipping from his hand.

"You do not subscribe to this policy of the Senator's? This is truly interesting." His laugh was unpleasant. Evarts shouted furious objection.

"No policy has been stated, therefore no commitment may be made. We must again object to this line of questioning."

"Your Honor," Turpeau turned to the bench, "at the suggestion of the Prosecuting Attorney, and in fairness to Mr. Mitchell, I would like to read this brief statement."

Judge Gowdy beckoned him closer to the bench and waited until Evarts joined them. When they were shoulder to shoulder, he spoke to them in a low voice.

"Attorney Turpeau, I believe you are seeking to disqualify this venireman for cause of prejudice. Is that so?" He accepted the nodded assent.

"Humph! Both of you gentlemen must be conscious of the tinderbox we are sitting on. I am going to ask you to refrain wherever possible from the employment of inflammatory tactics. Mr. Turpeau, you will agree, I am sure, that it will be an unusual instance in which you will discover veniremen with no opinion in this matter. I would like for you—for both of you—to bear that in mind in your jury selection. In addition, please consider my determination to insure that this will be a fair and impartial proceeding." He paused in thought, as though about to continue, then dismissed them.

"You may proceed, Attorney Turpeau."

The spectators had become curiously quiet in the interval. Now they watched with new interest as Attorney Turpeau stood in front of the jury box.

"Mr. Mitchell, you are familiar with the contents of the statement you just read?" He accepted the nod of agreement.

"Does that statement express your opinion?"

"No, it doesn't."

"Am I to understand that you disagree with it completely?" His low voice barely carried to the bench.

"Well, not exactly."

"What is your opinion on Negroes?"

Mitchell pondered his reply.

"I haven't got anything against you—you nigras, you understand. I think you're all right—in your place——"

"Oh?" Turpeau's dark brows rose sharply as he went to stand before the bench. He rocked on his toes and his voice was deceptively smooth.

"Take me, for example. You don't think that I'm in a Negro's place, questioning you here in court, do you, Mitchell?" Deliberately he snapped out the name, omitting the "Mister," smiling as he watched the flood of anger that came over the man.

"I do not, an' I'm here to tell you the Senator's goin' to hear 'bout this!" Turpeau turned and faced the Judge, laughing. Evarts, irritated, rose.

"I submit that this would be a hostile jury servant, your Honor."

"Step down," Judge Gowdy looked to where Mitchell had risen to stand in the jury box, his face mottled under the pressure of blood, running a finger between his collar and neck, glaring at the slender Negro.

70

"By God—ain't no nigger in the world goin' to talk to me like that!" He raised a leg across the railing and pandemonium broke loose as the spectators surged to their feet trying to see clearly. Turpeau turned from the counsel table with a sheaf of papers in his hands. He watched coldly as the bailiff overtook the angry Mississippian and wrestled him to a halt. He replaced the papers on his desk and aligned them carefully. For an instant he studied the wild alarm which showed in Jeff Mason's face as he stared at the struggling men, then he faced the bench.

Judge Gowdy's gavel banged again and again until the uproar was stilled.

"Silence—silence!" The old Judge towered on his bench and his voice was raging. "Silence!" He sat, regaining his judicial dignity.

"If I hear another outcry, I shall order this courtroom cleared for the duration of this trial." The silence was complete. "I find you," he lifted his gavel and pointed to where Mitchell stood, clenched fists pinned to his sides in the bailiff's grasp, "in contempt and I fine you in the amount of one hundred dollars."

"But I—" Mitchell twisted helplessly.

"But me no 'buts,'" the irate voice permitted no interruption. "This is a Court of the United States of America and I am its presiding judge. I find you palpably in contempt. Your conduct and lack of restraint are a disgrace. You may repeat that as a fact to whomsoever you wish." His words were pointed. He motioned to the bailiff. "Take him away." Shaking the sleeves of his robe loose where they caught at his wrists, he leaned forward on his table, resting his weight on his forearms. "You may proceed." He studied the now silent courtroom.

Franklin Abel. Storekeeper.

"I do not believe in capital punishment."

"You are excused."

Fred Howard. Carpenter.

"I didn't say he *had* done it. I said he probably did."

"Step down."

Mary Ellen Smith. Housewife.

"No. No, I'm not sure he could even have been the man. What? No, I'm not sure. Of course all Negroes think about—about, you know what. What? Well! I must say—I never!"

"Step down, Mrs. Smith."

"Well! A body hardly knows what to expect!"

"You are excused, Mrs. Smith."

71

Thomas L. Smith. Retired railroad engineer.

"I think I am open-minded enough to reserve judgment until you have presented your case, Mr. Turpeau."

"The prosecution excuses Mr. Smith."

That was the story of the first day. And of the second and third days.

III

For two weeks and two days thereafter, exclusive only of Sundays, Andrew Turpeau held the center of the stage. During fourteen additional days between eight in the morning and sundown, he examined more than two hundred members of the jury panel. During fourteen additional days of eight to ten hours each, broken only by brief intermissions and late-called evening recesses, he pursued his relentless course.

Old men and old women.

The young.

The scholar.

The teacher.

The avowedly anti-Negro and the self-professed sympathizer. White supremacist. Jew. Dark-faced Syrian. White progressive and Negro.

He examined them all in succession. Each in turn.

He pleaded and cajoled. His voice laughed and caressed. He wrought to anger, deliberately and savagely. His voice picked and probed, slurred and cut. He reached to the innermost secret prejudice and tore it viciously from its hiding place. He was director and actor in a living drama. He was master of his stage. He fawned, the perfect sycophant. He wheedled and soothed and opened each reluctant door of admission. And in each venireman, when he reached the last door, and opened it, he took prejudice by the hand and led it stumbling into the cold light of scrutiny.

Now and then the owner looked with startled interest, in unpretended surprise, at this newly discovered part of himself. Surprised men and women looked for a moment at this part of themselves and for a moment knew shame, then felt the wave of anger that came striding out, a bulwark emotion, determined to justify the exposed prejudice.

This with each white face.

And with the handful of Negroes he was no different. No different with the government clerk than with the retired porter. The same with the college professor as with the housewife. With the dignified he was uncouth, abruptly sarcastic. With the laborer and the domestic he was humble, seeking a favor. He confused and confounded. He led them all to open professions of partiality.

"'Course I'd give one of my own folks a better chance."

"Well, if you put it that way, I guess I do. I do hate white folks."

"How you gonna blame him—she jes' a sign of what done twisted him inside."

He examined them carefully, then turned to hear Judge Gowdy's voice.

"Step down."

With some he spent minutes. With others, he questioned for hours, picking, probing, finding an opening for attack, and always showing the fearful depths to which prejudice ran.

This was his unalterable line of questioning.

"Are you prejudiced against Negroes?"

"Do you consider the Negro to be your equal as an American?"

"Do you believe that you could give him as fair a trial as you would give a white man?"

He did this too during those two weeks and six days. He held a course of instruction on the American Negro, thrust against his will into a way of life which required his presence yet refused to accept him as a part of itself. Vividly he drew a picture of that man, battered each day by the psychic forces of inferiority, consigned to the lowliest of tasks, stripped of the pride which goes hand in hand with the soul's hope and ambition. He showed that man standing at the closed doors of halls of learning clamoring for entrance. Searching for a job by which to earn his daily bread. Made the daily, the hourly subject of fear. From the gathered panels he showed the structure of prejudice and its dark, hidden beginnings.

Each day and word of those three weeks was grist for the newspaper mill. Before the end of the first week, two New York correspondents had joined the Washington reporters at the press table. In the middle of the second week more reporters came from New York. Another table was added to accommodate these arrivals and four others, a Chicagoan, a feature writer from the Indiana *Sentinel* and two Philadelphia representatives.

There was grim drama in the fight which Andrew Turpeau waged. His goal was known only to himself as he went about examining the jury panel before him.

In the middle of the second week, too, a hurricane twisted its way in to shore from the Gulf of Mexico. It ripped across the Southwest of Florida, swept diagonally through Georgia and died out in Alabama. Along its path were ruined crops, crushed homes, a broom handle driven through the engine block of an automobile, and fifty-six dead. Among these latter was one radium scientist of international repute.

On that single day, Washington editors grudgingly pushed the story of Jeff Mason's trial to one side of the front page and recounted the news of disaster. On the following day, the story of the hurricane was buried on page three.

Before the third week began, press tables extended in a solid row across the breadth of the room. The gathered reporters, press and wire services represented among them every section of the country.

The *Daily Press* fought for the end which its columns had ordained. It was committed and determined that Jeff Mason would die for the crime of murder. Seldom did its editorial pages have less than two commentaries on the case. Each day it ran a new feature story on the trial and the principals involved.

First target was Andrew Turpeau. The city editor of the *Press* drew up a quick outline of a story designed to discredit him, "slugged" it "Negro shyster" and put three men to work on it. Each of them reported that the slim attorney's background was impeccable.

"Honor graduate of Syracuse. Honor grad, Harvard Law. President of a national legal society."

"No spots on this guy, chief, damn him!"

"The Freedom League is sponsoring this defense. There's a good target. A new organization. All Negro. Dedicated to, let's see,— 'assisting the American Negro in securing the rights and privileges denied him because of color'—slug that "dedicated to change American Way of Life.'"

"A touch of Communism. Cry 'Red.' Good!"

"This—and the tarbrush—should do it."

The Washington *Daily Press* ran the story first. In one hundred and seventeen major cities throughout the country the following day the story broke on front pages. That was Friday of the second week. Three days later, on Monday, a deluge of donations and requests for membership from Negroes and progressive white groups throughout the nation launched the Freedom League on its career of national prominence. The *Daily Press* hastily drew in its horns.

Next to be attacked was Judge Gowdy. His forthright handling of the case was termed "timorous." He was sharply criticized for permitting a "Negro shyster" to harangue the respectable citizens of Washington in his court. His refusal to limit counsel for the defense in choosing his jury caused the *Daily Press* to "wonder" whether he had not reached the span of his usefulness and to question whether retirement might not be in order. In this instance the *Press* felt it more desirable to have another, less liberal, more determined judge on the bench. Judge Growdy was charged with irresponsibility, senility, and with being a "nigger lover." If he read these things, if they came to his ears—and they must have—he gave no sign. From his tall bench, day after day, he ruled the court with an iron hand.

He grew weary. He sagged under the strain. He tired of the unrelenting storm of emotion. He visibly sagged as the days wore on. Twice he cited the prosecuting attorney for contempt. Once he cited Andrew Turpeau. One hundred and seventy-one times he excused jury servants from further attendance. His monotonous refrain caused the spectators and the papers to dub him "Step down" Gowdy.

Each day, as tempers wore thin and angers flared, the stark drama of the case became more clear.

From the first day to the last, the courtroom was packed.

Each day, before daylight, in the cold half-light of dawn, the first arrivals came to the courthouse grounds. They came in groups, in small groups, in threes and fours, feeling security in numbers, as they found warmth in the upturned coat collars that covered their faces against the biting chill of early fall. Later each morning, they came in twos and singly, not feeling in daylight the need for numbers.

They stood apart, white man and black, the current of their emotions serving to put a gulf between them. By mutual agreement they stood apart, queueing up in separate lines before separate doors. They stood apart and stamped their feet and swung their arms against the cold and glanced covertly at each other and were secretly ashamed.

Between them, and across the front of the broad entranceway, as the days came of age, a tripled force of guards and police maintained a restless watch. When the wide bronze doors opened each morning at eight, the lines surged up the narrow staircases and down the main corridor of the second floor to the courtroom.

IV

The fingers of one hand drummed against his desk in even tattoo, disturbing the flaring sleeve of his judge's robe. Propped on an elbow, the palm of his other hand held his bent head. The fingers of that hand moved against closed eyelids in a tired, reflective motion.

The voice before him rose, becoming more shrill. An angry voice, insistent and angry, rising to disturb him.

"This routine has been going on for almost three weeks. This buffoonery, this comedy, this eternal nagging and intimidation. Why, this man has even disqualified men and women who were favorable to his client. He has disqualified one hundred and seventy-one jury men."

Andrew went from where he stood against the rail before the press tables and sat slowly at his counsel table. He opened a brief case and took a slip of paper from it. He glanced at it briefly, then he put it aside and tilted his head to look at the ceiling. His eyes were closed.

"What is he trying to do, your Honor—is he trying to incite to riot? Is he trying to use legal shenanigans to avoid bringing this ravening beast to trial? What is he trying to do?" Evarts faced Andrew Turpeau. His leveled finger quivered with rage. His voice soared almost hysterically. He screamed.

"What are you trying to do?" After his words had become a part of silence he stood there, arm outstretched. Pointing, trembling, staring. The breath went out of the courtroom in an audible rush.

Judge Gowdy looked down at Andrew Turpeau. He saw his closed eyes, his relaxed face. Quietly, though he suddenly knew what the answer would be, he said:

"What are you attempting to do, Mr. Turpeau?" The Negro's eyes opened and looked up at him. "Tell me clearly, at whatever length you wish, what you are trying to do."

Everyone sat slack in his seat. Emotion had for days bellied in them—stretched them taut to the snapping point by the unending tension of each day's events. Now, in this moment, emotions sagged, loose, free of strain. They flopped and stirred idly. As unpredictable as a sail in a gusty wind. As dangerous.

The Negro at the defense table stood. He was tired. That much was plain. The strain of days gone had marked him. He seemed a little thinner, a little more bent. Tiredness was in the lines of his face, deeper now and darker. It was in the slow, deliberate walk to the front of the court. He stood in the quiet and looked around him. He looked over his shoulder at the great golden eagle sharp against a backdrop of wine-red wall, and at Judge Gowdy, patiently waiting. In his face, only his eyes seemed alive. He looked past the bailiffs to where Jeff Mason slumped in his chair between two ever-watchful guards, to the lone juryman not yet disqualified, sitting alone in the jury box. He looked at the crowded courtroom with its quarter section of dark faces.

There was no anger in his face. His eyes were thoughtful and calm. If there was feeling in his eyes, it was sadness.

Jeff Mason saw his eyes and felt a cold unexplainable chill pass through him.

"Your Honor—" Turpeau's low voice compelled attention, won silence from the whispering.

Every eye followed his pointing finger. "Jeff Mason, the defendant in this case, is accused of the crime of murder in the first degree. That much is contained in the bill against him. He has also been accused in the public mind of two more grievous criminal offenses, neither of which are contained in his indictment. Jeff Mason is suspected of attempting, on two separate occasions, the crime of rape. Living and dead, the plaintiffs were white women." He paused in the tightening quiet of the room.

"We all know this. The case of the Government of the United States against Jeff Mason has been tried and tried again during the past weeks. There is not a paper in the city which has not devoted column after column to every aspect of the case. The trial of Jeff Mason has been hashed and rehashed in the most inflammatory manner possible. Mindless of their responsibility to the maintenance of good order and a peaceful community, guided only by a starveling desire to mint pennies at the rate of three per copy, the editors of our fair city have deliberately singled out the most susceptible emotions of their readers and fanned them to fever heat. And they have not been without followers. Their kinsfolk, the radio, has rallied to their side. From the most conservative pulpits, have been delivered sermons, special pleas, for heavenly anger to be delivered upon the heads of those not on trial—innocent Negroes. Congressmen, caught in the tide of public opinion, with their fingers on the pulse of their home districts, have added their voices to the babel. Though no one has determined what is to be reformed, several reform movements have been born out of the furious publicity which

77

has attended this case. The issue has long since become larger than Jeff Mason. Thanks to the newspapers, the radio, the public now sees every Negro as Jeff Mason. Jeff Mason has become a symbol.

"For weeks, Washington has teetered on the brink of another race riot. The fury of pent-up emotions has threatened to burst forth with a terrible violence which would outstrip in sheer savagery the race riot which rocked Washington four years ago. God must bless the cool heads who have remembered the terror of that riot and stayed the hands of hotter bloods.

"That danger is not past. We still stand on the ragged edge to-day. The night streets, bare of travelers, are proof of that. The tripled guards who patrol these grounds about us, this building, the tripled force of police who walk beats through the Negro district, are proof of that. The stand-by order which is even now holding a regiment of troops on twenty-four-hour call at a nearby fort, under full arms, is proof of that fact.

"We come to trial in this court under those conditions.

"Washington is a ward of the Federal Government. For criminal offenses, for felonies against the people of Washington and against the Federal Government, there is but one court of justice—this court —your Honor. Were this a state, there would be several district courts which would be suited to handle this trial. The normal procedure in such an instance as this would be to request a change of venue, to remove the trial from the emotional hysteria of one district to another not affected by that hysteria. There is no change of venue which may be attained in Washington.

"Every expression of public opinion in this town, except a few faltering voices, has found this defendant guilty. More than that, the penalties which he should pay to expiate his crime have been described in detail, in shocking detail, in our daily papers. Concern with this case has not been limited to Washington. It has spread outward to the most distant States.

"Look about this courtroom, your Honor. There is not even standing room left. Long before daybreak, queues of human beings stood in the cold beyond the doors of this court. Before those doors opened, those lines extended from sight in the darkness. Their ranks accounted for the space in this room times over. And yet they stayed and waited. There were black men of my race and white men of yours in separate lines. They are sitting here now listening to me. They crowd the halls outside that door so thickly that it is almost impossible to move along the corridor. They are waiting on

78

the stairs in this building for any chance word of the progress of this case, hoping that in the next recess they will be able to get seats in the courtroom.

"Why are they here? These are plain, honest, everyday people, average citizens.

"Why are these housewives and civil servants, these teachers and domestics and these well-to-do gathered here, jam-packed, uncomplaining? Why do they leave the ordered paths of their everyday lives to wait hours on end for a chance to sit in silence in this courtroom?

"Is it murder alone that has brought them here day after day?

"Can the allegation of an attempted crime account for the seething passions of this whole city? I think not. Unforgivable as murder is, as revolting as the suspicion alone of rape must always be, these crimes are not new. Times without number, the well-ordered machinery of law and order has gone into gear to cope with such cases—the laws and customs of our times meet these situations with an almost mechanical dispatch. It is not fear that the law will be inadequate. No! Something deeper lies at the root of this turmoil. The issue is wider than the trial of one man, wider even than the whole race at which the slander of the press has been aimed.

"This trial has become a contest of racial superiority. That is the issue, hinted at many times these past weeks, almost, but never quite spoken. That is the fire which has been hidden under these billowing clouds of smoke.

"The problem which we face here is a grave one.

"The law provides that an accused shall have the right to a fair and impartial trial by a jury of his fellows. Further, the law provides that the rights of an accused shall be protected and that he shall be held innocent of an offense until he is proven guilty beyond a reasonable doubt by a jury of his peers.

"I have asked myself time and again if I can possibly find such a jury to hear the case of Jeff Mason. Can I find such men and women in this city? Are there men and women without prejudice, without opinion, not responsive to the tide of feeling which runs about us? No, I think not. I sincerely believe that there are no such men and women in Washington. Prejudice, your Honor, as it applies to matters of racial difference, is a curious thing. Prejudice of this sort is imbedded in us from the moment of our birth, in one way or another. It seeps into black men and white without regard for the color of their skins. Our reactions to it, yours and mine, are in a way

79

duplicates of one another. It is made up completely of the substance of emotions. Having attained the proportions of folklore in our times, it will nevertheless not withstand the scrutiny of reason. Before the inexorable necessities of logic, prejudice will retreat, break apart and scatter. Then it will rejoin itself, determined, violently determined, to resist.

"Prejudice has crowded this courtroom day after day with these usually workaday folk. These spectators are here for a reason. They may not even be conscious of its existence. But they are here in the expectation that their mandate of superiority will be fulfilled. The pressure of their presence, of their gazes, of their watchfulness, will find response in any jury servant in whom there is a seed of prejudice. These are the men and women, your Honor, with whom even the most fair minded jury servant must live. Therefore I have examined each prospective juror with exceeding care. I shall continue to do so until I have exhausted every resource at my command, until I am able to impanel a jury which will not bend to the muckrake pressure of public prejudice, or until there is not a prospective juryman in the District of Columbia whom I have not disqualified for cause.

"I do this not out of malice for this court. I do not conceive what the prosecution has termed an avenue of escape through legal shenanigans.

"I know that my course of action imposes a weighty responsibility upon the bench. Were I not utterly convinced of the merit of my course, I would weeks ago have relented in my examination.

"I did not call this turn of events. They were decided days ago at the hands of irresponsible organs of public opinion—and at the hands of the magpie public which loaned its voice to an unreasoning clamor.

"We stand here today at an impasse. We are involved in a situation which our system of courts and jurisprudence is impotent to control. There is no law in this land which can assure Jeff Mason—or any other Negro under these circumstances—a fair and impartial trial."

His voice fell from thunder. His eyes, fixed upon some inner thought beyond the four walls about him, came slowly back to the faces which stared at him. Three deep about the walls, and kneeling in a fringe along the aisles, they watched. Four squares of faces with aisles between them looked at him, waited for his words. Three-quarters of the faces white. One-quarter black to white, with all the mixed bloods of Negro veins. They waited. Black man, white man and an Indian. Thirty-seven Jews waited. One white Jew waited. One expectant mother stilled the movement within her with a whispered word. Without knowing why, at that moment, a nun began to quickly say her rosary. A prostitute popped her gum loudly in the silence. Then she defiantly looked about her. Finding herself unnoticed, she lowered her head. And waited. They saw Andrew Turpeau's dark face soften. The strange green eyes were gentle.

"So long as we pass in the streets, in the places of work and play; so long as eyes meet and are wrenched away; so long as smiles die on the lips; as hard stares are used to cloak the sudden sickening sense of shame, the confused guilt, the awareness that, somehow, something is terribly wrong——"

The tragedy of the ages was in his voice.

"So long as we persist in being strangers to the little inner hopes of our fellow men, just so long will we be without any law of man which will secure to men such as this the certainty of a fair trial."

In the silence, a green fly beat against the window pane of the far wall, trying to comfort itself in the thin warmth that was to be found in the streaming sunlight.

No one spoke. Evarts sat at his table, silent, staring at the floor. Slowly he stirred. Then quickly rose.

V

The fight was lost.

Andrew Turpeau felt it that night. Charles Roberts too.

On the Monday after that week end, they were certain of it. They knew, as did all of Washington, that the Freedom League had lost its fight. As did black men and white in each of the Union's forty-eight States and beyond. The fight for a principle was lost. The bold insistent attack upon the greatest frailty of American justice was lost.

The fight for Jeff Mason's life went on.

By Wednesday a jury was chosen. How it was done was not too important. At long last, twelve good men and true and a thirteenth, an alternate, sat in the juror's box. Eleven white men and one Negro —the alternate, white. A jury chosen according to law, sworn to do justice under that law. A jury without prejudice, or with prejudice deeply hidden. It had been, suddenly, important that this jury be chosen. A nation's name demanded it. How—why—nothing else was important. Not important, the flood of phone calls and visitors, Congressional and judicial, that week end long, from Friday to Monday, besieged Judge Gowdy's Wisconsin Avenue home. Not important, the flood of news stories and editorials, radio revues, the Saturday shoppers brought in from crowded downtown streets and Sunday churchgoers, to "have their say" about Jeff Mason's trial before unfamiliar radio microphones.

By Wednesday, the bickering and questioning were done and on Thursday, in the restive, spectator-packed courtroom, the bailiff's traditional cry began the trial of the United States *vs.* Jeff Mason.

"Hear ye—hear ye!"

The beginning of the end.

There was a simmering intensity of feeling then. The indictment was read. The plea was made. The prosecution rose to address the court and begin the case for the nation. Then, in a measurable fashion, degree after degree, witness after witness, the temper of each spectator in the room and of the city out beyond the courthouse square swelled and surged. Rose higher and higher, boiling upward.

The opening statement was hate-filled, venomous. Evarts' voice was taut-charged with anger out of the three weeks' delay. Witness followed witness and Friday followed Thursday.

"Perry Schwartz. Raise your right hand."

"I do."

"I am a streetcar motorman."

"Sure it's him. We was——"

"Go right ahead, Mr. Schwartz. Tell us in your own words just what happened."

"Lee Mandel."

"Do you solemnly swear——"

"What is your occupation?"

"—and like Perry, uh . . . Mr. Schwartz, says, we was waitin' to start our run when——"

"Paul Henry."

"I chased him."

"That is the man."

"Richard Green."

"He stumbled and I almost caught him."

"There—sitting there. He's the one."

"Paul Keech."

"He's the same one."

"Sure it's him. Look, mister, I know nigras."

"Jon Dzombrowski."

"Naw. Jes' don't try to say the "Z" and the "W"—Dombroski. That's right."

"No doubt about it. I'm sure.

"Look, I swore, didn't I? Okay then. I'm a Catholic."

There were thirteen in all. Each one eager to testify. Each one positive that Jeff Mason was the man they had seen or pursued as he ran through the park the day Laura had been attacked. The simple facts of testimony given by each one remained unshaken under Andrew Turpeau's cross-examination.

For he did fight.

Each witness he cross-examined with infinite patience, searching for little discrepancies, for the uncertainties that would create a reasonable shadow of doubt in their stories—for something that would reveal the testimony of one or the other to have been dictated by the racial frenzy which held the city in its grasp. Though it was there, the determination of each witness to have a part in the finding of "Guilty," though it could be felt in each one, no single word gave it away. No single witness was discredited. With each one the final answer was the same.

"I am sure——"

The thing which was being done was plain for all to see. Each witness was determined to have a hand in settling this issue which was no longer Jeff Mason or the matter of a felonious crime but which was "the issue." The shapeless, shifting issue which was a thing of feeling, larger than words and facts. These witnesses were the people, come to see that their will be done at trial. Come to have a hand in the doing. They came in turn, willingly, eagerly.

"Mrs. Anna Kelter."

"Hold up your right hand, Mrs. Kelter," Andrew Turpeau was on his feet.

"Do you solemnly swear——"

"I object. This witness cannot be sworn in this case. She is obviously prejudiced and biased. Any effort to introduce testimony by her is an unbelievable attempt on the part of the prosecution to undermine the rights of the accused. Her presence in this court is inflammatory and places my client in undeserved jeopardy."

"Your Honor—" Judge Gowdy turned a questioning gaze to where Evarts stood smiling faintly as he examined his nails.

"Your Honor, we will connect the testimony of this witness with the charge at hand in the most relevant manner possible. As I have been reminded by the defense, I am obliged to remember the rights of the accused as well as my responsibility to the people of this District. I can assure the bench and the defense that through this witness I will introduce only the most conclusive sort of evidence. I think he will agree with me when Mrs. Kelter and her daughter have testified." Judge Gowdy weighed the question briefly.

"Examination will be permitted pending connection. You may proceed, Mr. Evarts." The entire room hung on her words.

Anna Kelter sat forward tensely in her chair. In her lap she clutched a worn black handbag. Her tense white hands were vivid against the dead black of her dress. Her face was flushed with the heat of excitement and her eyes, fixed on Jeff Mason, were bright. Now and then she would look away toward the jury and toward the room beyond her. Her head turned quickly and her birdlike gaze gave the impression of fear. Always her eyes would return to Jeff Mason. He caught and held her gaze to where he sat, deep in his seat, shoulders crowding beyond the arms of the chair, staring at her with an unblinking gaze. She cringed against the hatred that was in his eyes, and her fear went to the jury almost as a whimper. When this happened, eleven jurymen shifted in their chairs, feeling a protective urge and first dull anger that a white woman should sit before them, afraid because of a Negro's glare. One Negro sat in the jurors' box and was unmoved.

At that moment, if it had not been before, Jeff Mason's fate was decided.

They hung on her words. The jury and the court and Judge Gowdy and Andrew Turpeau. And Jeff Mason.

"Now, Mrs. Kelter, let me recapitulate briefly." Evarts leaned forward, one foot on the second step above the witness stand. "You have told us—check me if I make a misstatement, Mr. Court Reporter—you have told us that on the evening in question you and your daughter were proceeding along the street toward the District Line car stop. It was dark. The street was dimly lit. You were almost in sight of the station when a man stepped from the shadows and halted you with a pistol in his hand. The man was a Negro. Is that right?" She nodded her head without speaking.

"Why did you not scream?"

"Well—we were so frightened—I don't know. And besides——"

"Besides?"

"He said he would kill us if we made a sound."

"Then you were both stricken with fright. What did you do then?"

"He backed us off the pavement to the edge of a brushy clearing," her words began to come in a flood and her voice rose as she stared at Jeff Mason. "He took our handbags and emptied them. He tried to count the money but I guess he couldn't see. It was only about thirty dollars and some change. He got mad because he couldn't count it and watch us too. Then he began to curse us. Our eyes got used to the dark and we could see him better. Mary whispered to me, 'Mama, that's the man who killed the woman in Rock Creek Park.' I could feel her holding on to my arm and trembling and I hoped she wouldn't faint because I felt like I was going to faint myself." She gathered herself and dabbed at her nose with a handkerchief.

"What then, Mrs. Kelter?" Sympathetically Evarts led her on.

"I suppose he must have heard her because he fumbled in his pocket and took out a knife."

Evarts interrupted her quickly, "Then what did he do, Mrs. Kelter? Tell us exactly."

"He stepped toward us and said," her eyes fixed on Jeff Mason in a malicious, determined stare, "'Yes, I killed her an' I'm going to kill you, too. You first, then I'll take her—'" She began to sob.

Judge Gowdy leaned suddenly forward. The muscles in his neck corded and his eyes widened as though he found it difficult to believe what he was hearing. His right hand reached toward his gavel and stopped. His hand remained there in plain view, clenched.

Andrew Turpeau's face mirrored disbelief. He sat frozen and stared at the woman's face.

Evarts faced the jury and righteous indignation was in his voice. "Take her? What did he mean by that?"

Turpeau rose out of the trance that had held him as he listened to the stream of words, and lunged forward.

"This sort of evidence is not permissible. The whole line of examination is out of order. I move it be stricken from the record. If this defendant is the man, and there is no evidence that he is, the witness is still not competent to interpret admittedly unexpressed intentions."

"This is a material witness, your Honor, a principal, and as such she can certainly tell what her impressions were. Intent may be determined as much by visible gesture or movement as by spoken word."

"Overruled. Mr. Prosecutor, I must remind you that this is entirely unconnected testimony." Evarts' nod held a hint of mockery.

"Tell us, Mrs. Kelter, what did his actions lead you to feel he was going to do?"

"I don't know. I was afraid he meant he was going to— You know." Her eyes sought the jury. They knew. "I hoped that he would kill her first." She began to sob again, quietly. "I felt her hand slip on my arm and then she crumpled to the ground. I screamed and then I guess I fainted. When I come to there was a crowd about us and he was gone."

The hubbub of sound rose and quickly lowered as Judge Gowdy frowned down from his bench. An undercurrent of low mutters remained.

"Now, Mrs. Kelter, I am going to ask you a question. I know I do not need to remind you that you are under oath. You must answer me. In answering, I want you to remember that what you say may decide the fate of a man's life." Evarts paused for emphasis. "I want you to look about this courtroom and tell the jury and the judge if you see the man who said 'Yes, I killed her an' I'm going to kill you, too'—if you see him, point him out."

Mrs. Kelter wrested her eyes from Jeff Mason's face. Slowly she looked over the courtroom, her eyes flickering from face to face— if indeed she saw separate faces in the crowded room—then, deliberately, she brought her gaze back to Jeff Mason. She stared at him. He returned her gaze. The muscles about his jaw knotted in tight lumps, broke and knotted again. His eyes dropped and came back to her face and fell. They stayed in his lap, fixed on his tightly gripped hands.

"There—that is the man. He is the one." Her voice was almost a scream and her head fell forward into her hands. The bailiff and Evarts moved quickly toward her. After that Evarts stepped back and smiled at Andrew Turpeau.

"Your witness." The slender defense attorney looked at him for a moment.

"No questions."

The mutters in the courtroom grew and became a roar. The first scattered handful of spectators who had half risen to see Jeff Mason were joined by the others who rose with them. For a moment Judge Gowdy was motionless as the seething grew, then he stood furiously banging his gavel.

"Clear the courtroom. Clear the court." The bailiff stared at him as if not believing his ears. "Clear the court, I say!"

The last spectators filed out, grumbling their displeasure as the guards closed the wide double doors on their heels. Judge Gowdy sat considering the upturned palms of his hands. When he spoke it was to no one in particular.

"I will not allow perjury in my court." Without noticing Evarts' effort to speak, he said simply, "I will not have perjury in my court. I know perjury when I hear and see it."

Dorcas testified, and the doctor who had attended Laura when she was taken to Dorcas' house. Three other doctors swore that, in their professional judgment, Jeff Mason was a sane but brutal menace. They gave their testimony, and when they had finished it was Friday morning.

✿   ✿   ✿

Court was open again. Judge Gowdy admonished the spectators against outbursts, warning them that if he had to clear court again in the course of the trial, it would remain closed. Thus it was that the chastened rows of spectators held their silence throughout the morning of the tenth day, staring in a curious mixture of pity and wonder at the little boy who sat in the wide witness chair.

VI

Kern stared back at the crowded courtroom and felt the heavy, damp heat of the place washing against his face. Dimly he recognized the spattering sound of rain driven against the windows of the room. He recognized, too, the odor of rain-wet clothing. Step by step the man with the hard gray eyes had led him through each moment of that evening until now it was alive for him again. Now it was so real that he could feel fear in him like coldness as he tried to find words with which to answer the question that was being driven at him.

"Tell this court—what was this—this black beast doing to your mother? Tell us!" The words would not come. Kern's eyes saw Jeff Mason. Saw the man's lowered head, his sagging body. Saw his hands motionless in their lap and the glint of manacles on his wrists. Not once since he had sat down had the man looked at him. Kern hoped that he would not.

Then the thing he had tried to forget came alive for him. He saw it all, clearly, as he had not since those first, frightening nights alone in the darkness of his room. His mother, twisting in the man's arms; crying him away from danger. Tasted salty sweat in his mouth again, lay against the wall of bushes and saw the knife driven home. Saw the face that turned to stare at him—heard himself scream.

His stomach twisted inside of him. The heat in the room was stifling. The faces before him were a shifting blur.

"Tell us, son—" Evarts' voice seemed to come from a distance. Questions. Pleading now and quiet, feeling his strength as it had been gauged from the first question. Questions that deliberately tore at wounds just begun to heal.

"Tell us—stand up and tell us." The voice became strident—broke through the daze which held him. "Tell us—is the man who killed your mother in this room? Is he? Stand up and point to him!"

Without warning, Kern saw the faces before him freeze in stillness. A compulsion he did not understand brought him to his feet. Kern stood, trembling, as he shouted.

"Him!"

"Him!"

"Him!"

He knew that he was pointing.

Then he recognized his father coming toward him to hold him upright and to lead him behind the bailiff through a door into a room where it was cool and quiet. Behind him the courtroom was in an uproar.

Two women testified for Jeff Mason. Two women swore that he could not have been at the scene of the crime. Two women left the witness stand, sobbing and tearful in the empty, silent room. Two women. A mother and a wife. Two women. And the testimony of each, obviously sprung out of loyalty, could not shake the weight of the record.

*　*　*

Charles took Kern back to that courtroom. Though he begged and cried not to be taken, he went, and stood beside his father and heard the words that meant the end of a life.

They seared themselves into the consciousness of the crowded place like a branding iron. Words. Their measured, deliberate cadence smashing hate and anger into fragments of shame and an

88

instant of sick regret. Words. Spoken quietly. With no human inflection. Merciless. Automatic. Relentless. As the wheels of justice ground toward their ponderous end.

The court stood and Jeff Mason stood with Andrew Turpeau at his side as the words were spoken. The cry for vengeance was still. The public will was done. Vengeance was certain. No anger now. Only a slow, deliberate effort to comprehend the fearful vastness of the words—the extent of the deed which had been done. And in the middle of it all, a thread of doubt. A wire-thin finger of wonder——

"Suppose——?"

"What if——?"

Doubt. And in that wondering moment the words.

"—and on the night of November sixteenth in this year of our Lord, you will be taken from that Asylum to the place prepared for your execution. And there, between the hours of ten o'clock post meridian and eleven o'clock post meridian, you will be hanged by the neck until you are dead. And may God have mercy on your soul."

The bailiff stood at his side.

There. It was done, with no malice, in fair and impartial trial, with due consideration for the rights of the accused. Done and over.

And in the silence, only the sobbing of those two who in a fortnight would be women without a son, without a husband. These things. The sagging, slow-comprehending face of the man to die. The memory of a boy, marked beyond forgetting.

CHAPTER IV

SCHOOL—FOR COLORED

I

IT WAS ten minutes past three o'clock in the afternoon and the bare schoolyard was quiet.

Kern edged quietly to the open school door and stepped inside. Before him a boy stood in the shadows staring intently through a low, narrow window that looked out on the play yard, watching two creeping "Cops" as they searched for hidden "Robbers." He did not know that his foot and stockinged leg, protruding beyond the corner of the doorway, had given him away.

It was "Blondie"! Kern felt a sudden panic. Burly, overgrown "Blondie" was a Sixth-Grader and a bully. "Blondie" was almost ready to go to "the Annex" with the older boys and girls. Ebony-skinned "Blondie" had been among the first to seek him out and taunt him when he had begun school, reminding him scornfully of the part which he had played in Jeff Mason's trial. Without humor, Kern thought that "Blondie's" nickname would never have been given him had the public school been mixed rather than all-Negro. Here, he knew, among Negroes, the title became a laughing tribute to "Blondie's" unbroken dusky color. Kern hardly dared breathe. Even Charles Ridgeway and Calvin, his classmates, had finally stopped picking at him when he had refused to answer their gibes. But not "Blondie." And not Mrs. Peterson either. Even after a year, neither of them ever gave him a chance to forget. Mrs. Peterson was his new Fifth Grade teacher and she always preached careful little sermons about letting "he who was without sin cast the first stone." And she was never too busy to explain to her class the real meaning of the slogan that hung high on the blackboard behind her desk.

"There is so much good in the worst of us——"

Kern never was quite convinced that she meant the things she said. He knew as did the rest of the class that she was talking to him—at him.

90

"Blondie" was just like Mrs. Peterson. Only his words were not the slogans Mrs. Peterson used. "Blondie's" words were raw and hard. Most often they were dirty words. They were always blunt with the threat of "Blondie's" fists behind them. Because of this they went unanswered.

Kern stood in the doorway and quaked, wishing that "Blondie" had passed to the Seventh Grade with his class and gone to the Annex instead of remaining in the Old Building to bully the younger kids.

Kern edged backwards to the door. What excuse could he use for not finding "Blondie"? Hiding in the building was "no fair." That was it! He wouldn't have to catch "Blondie." He would simply back out of the building and pretend that he had never seen him. When the doorstep grated against his heel, he knew that he was trapped, he would have to "catch" him. "Blondie" froze. There was no time to turn and run. He'd been seen. "Blondie's" shaven bullet-head was already turning toward him. Kern felt the schoolbooks slip a bit in his suddenly sweaty palm. Quickly he pointed a finger, pistol-like, and stood looking at "Blondie."

"C'mon out. I gotcha." Disgust showed in "Blondie's" face as he remained motionless, staring at Kern. Kern's nerve grew stronger. He gestured toward the door with his finger.

"C'mon out, nigger. I caught you." He used his toughest voice. "Blondie" did not move. The rules of "Cops and Robbers" said that when a Cop caught a Robber, he was caught. They didn't say anything, Kern realized, about how to take an unwilling captive. He knew that "Blondie" was going to be an unwilling captive.

"I caught you, nigger. C'mon out."

"Blondie" came out. With fists flying, he lunged at Kern, scattering his books to the ground and driving him backwards through the open door. Kern stumbled under the sudden onslaught and felt his stomach crawl as it always did in a fight. A licking was in store for him. He knew that and wondered dimly what it was for this time. The rough brick wall of the vestibule was at his back and he twisted away as "Blondie" lunged at him again, turning into the open yard. The fist that banged at the side of his head was hard and it hurt. It brought the taste of blood to his mouth as it struck again. His ears rang and tears of anger came to his eyes. He shook his head and then lowered it. He set his eyes on the feet in front of him and moved toward them, swinging blindly as "Blondie" straightened and danced toward him, fists poised. Don't run! Don't cry? He remembered the lessons of the playground. The fists were on his head again, hurting. He heard voices in the whirling distance and knew that the boys were gathering in a ring about them. He felt his fists hitting something and felt the fists that were hitting him. His breath came in short gasps as the fists stopped hitting him and "Blondie's" arms wrapped around him. "Blondie's" breath was in his ear as they strained and twisted at each other.

A foot behind his leg jerked suddenly and he felt himself falling. The black cinder dirt of the yard grated under his head and scraped against the back of his coat as he and "Blondie" rolled on the ground. He felt "Blondie's" knees reaching for his arms as they tried to roll each other to the bottom. Then the shouting was confused in his ears as "Blondie" sat astride him. Kern knew that the fist snapping down toward his face would be hard. It was. He wrenched his head aside and the fist slid along his head, burning his ear sharply. He made no noise as he twisted and writhed, trying to pull his arms out from under the knees that held them. His throat was dry. Then "Blondie" was pulled backward and off him.

He sat up dazed. The circle had broken and widened and Rollie stood in front of "Blondie." He was not as large as "Blondie." Larger than Kern, but not as large as "Blondie." His fists were cocked. Kern rose slowly and "Blondie's" eyes flickered between him and Rollie.

"Let him alone."

"Who says so?"

"I says."

"Who you to tell me what to do, nigger? Mebbe you want trouble?"

"Start dishin', nigger. I likes trouble." Rollie backed off a half step and raised his fists higher.

"He called me a nigger." "Blondie" turned his face to Kern. Rollie's laugh was short and contemptuous.

"You is a nigger. He's one too. Put up or shut up."

"He called me nigger." Obstinately "Blondie" stuck to the one thin thread, truculence uncertain in his voice and fading before the threat of Rollie.

"Ain't nothin'. I called you nigger too."

"You's different. You *is* a nigger."

"He is too." "Blondie" stepped out of the circle. Stooping, he picked up a short stick and struck it against his leg, looking back and forth between Kern and Rollie. He turned to Kern again.

"You's too white to call me 'nigger,' nigger. I don' mess with no

92

'no-nation niggers.'" Kern looked at him. He turned and walked away. Rollie jeered after him.

"Aw crap nigger. G'wan home." The boys broke into scattered groups and minutes later the schoolyard was empty. Kern picked up his scattered books. Rollie brushed the grit from the back of his leather coat and together they studied the elbows where the smooth finish was scraped. Kern smeared away the last tear-dampness on his face with the back of his hands. Rollie watched him indecisively.

"I s'pose you'd rather go on home and get cleaned up than to come for dinner." He hesitated. "Mom'll understand." Kern was grateful to him. Grateful and relieved that he would not have to go to Key's Alley. Rollie swung his books back and forth at the end of his strap.

"C'mon, I'll walk part of the way with you. That 'Blondie's' a mean nigger. But," he hastily added, "he ain't goin' to bother you no more." They went down the steps that led to Fourth Street.

It was a cold, late-January day, with a trifle of wind and a flat colorless sky that reminded them evening and darkness were not far away. Their faces tightened against the cold and Kern shivered as the chill air struck him. He rounded his shoulders against its touch, and when he looked at Rollie he saw that he, too, was cold. He walked beside Kern, carefully matching his steps, bowed against the chill, the turtle neck of his sweater seeming to reach upward to his face and head. One leg, where the stocking had fallen to his shoe-top, showed as an ashy-gray slit in the cold air. Kern raised the fleece collar of his coat higher about his neck, and felt the raw grit that sifted down his back.

"'Blondie,' the sonofabitch, the black—" The thought went unfinished, as a quick twinge of guilt made him look sidewise at his friend. Rollie was dark, too. Not black. But very dark. They stopped at the corner of Fourth and Elm Streets, and stood looking at each other, saying nothing. Rollie spoke first.

"Sure was a good scrap you was giving 'Blondie.'"

Kern smiled. "Well—guess I'd better get on home. Got a couple of sacks of coal to get 'fore my ol' man comes." They still stood uncertainly. Kern swallowed.

"Thanks . . ." he started—Rollie hit him solidly high on his arm, then ran, laughing over his shoulder. Kern followed him a few steps, then stopped. He called after Rollie.

"See you tomorrow." Rollie stopped running and waved back over his shoulder.

93

"Okay, see you tomorrow." He went out of sight behind the streetcar at the corner. Kern stared after him. Good old Rollie. Seemed as if Rollie was always on the spot, whenever he got in a fight. He crossed Elm Street, and quickened his steps toward home. Eyes cast down, he saw the snag in his knicker leg for the first time and the dark patch of dirt that was ground into the knee. Nettie'll see it sure, he thought. Nettie saw everything. He knew that. Nettie told everything. He knew that also.

✿ ✿ ✿

Arms akimbo, Nettie stood in the doorway; her eyes went directly to the tear in his knickers and to the dirt, and saw the tear streaks on his face.

"So—you been fightin' again? An' what for this time?" He stood in the vestibule, waiting for her to stand aside.

"I haven't either been fighting. We were wrestling."

"Humph! Likely story. How 'bout them tear stains—guess you got 'em playin'?" She stood aside and Kern went into the hallway and laid his books on the table at the door.

"Take them books on up to your room where they belong. Don't be cluttering up my hall with no dirty books." Kern took the books, dull resentment at Nettie flaring as it always did when she ordered him about. Her hall! She only worked here. Someday he would tell her that.

"Go 'long upstairs and wash your han's. Then come on to dinner. I don' feel like stayin' in the kitchen all night waitin' on you. Your Pa's going to be in St. Louie another night. He called today." She went off toward the kitchen, muttered words about the Freedom League trailing after her.

✿ ✿ ✿

He closed the book and pushed it aside on the desk. *Nick Carter in the Arms of Danger*. It was almost eight o'clock and he still had to write "I will pay attention in class" one hundred times. It seemed that he never did anything right. Mrs. Peterson found fault with him in everything. Tomorrow she'd know about the fight and take him to task in front of the class. He could hear her now, lecturing about "getting along with our neighbors" and looking right at him all of the time. Every fight he had been in she had learned about, even those he'd had when he was in the Fourth Grade with Miss Parker. Every time he took his eyes from a book she scolded. He

94

didn't like Mrs. Peterson. He began to write. Mrs. Peterson took place in his mind with Nettie and the Freedom League and "Blondie."

One sheet, two and three sheets. Near the foot of the fourth, he sighed.

"Oh, well—school will soon be over."

And it was! After the Fifth Grade came the Sixth and Mr. Haley. In another short year he'd move to the Annex.

II

He heard his father's voice.

"Kern." He looked at the wall above his desk and at the pigeon-holes arranged in a precise row before him. He heard his name again and noted an edge of anger in the voice. He thought, "If I wait, maybe he won't call again——"

Ever so often this happened. His father came home from the almost continuous Freedom League trips and was intensely interested in his schoolwork and his grades. His grades never satisfied his father. He closed his notebook with a slap that fluttered the pages.

"Kern." This time the voice came from the foot of the stairs and left no doubt that it intended to be heard and answered.

"Yes, sir."

"Come down here." He rose and started down the hall. What could he tell him? What had he been doing all evening long? It was dark now. Great Scott! He'd read the whole evening. Not a bit of schoolwork done since dinner. He had thought of no excuse for the report card he'd left on the dining-room table. Gee whiz!—he had never had any of this trouble with Miss Parker. With Mrs. Peterson it had been different. His trouble had started then. Now, with Mr. Haley, he never got anything right, at all.

On the landing, he came into the light from the dining-room lamp. His father looked up as he approached and went back to the outspread evening paper before him. Kern stood beside the table as he laid aside the paper and opened the yellow envelope containing his report card. Deliberately, as if for the first time, Charles Roberts studied the card, pursing his lips thoughtfully. Kern felt as if he were shrinking in height, and would soon be no taller than the table-top.

"Well?" What could he say? His father waited for some answer. "Well?" Nervously, Kern licked his lips and waited. Nettie moved slowly on the other side of the table, scraping away a few imaginary crumbs from the cloth, one ear cocked for what Kern was going to say.

"What have you got to say about this?" The card was held open in front of him. He saw the marks on it.

English: Excellent. Mathematics: Fair. Geography: Good. History: Good. Those weren't too important. What he was going to catch heck about were the others. Deportment: Average. Cooperation: Poor. Attention: Poor.

What could he say? He couldn't tell his father why. He didn't know himself. Day after day his thoughts went out beyond the wide squares of the schoolroom windows—went miles and years away and would not return. He was never at ease with Mr. Haley. He could not describe the shapeless antagonism which he felt in the man's every move. Mr. Haley was the same as Mrs. Peterson. Slighting references to the Jeff Mason trial; rebukes for fights he had not started. It seemed to Kern that they were picking on him. There were no words to tell his father this.

He wished that the man before him would stay away from home —that the Freedom League would keep him away. If only his mother had been there to help him. If he just didn't have to come home to an empty house and to Nettie. He felt the lump of self-pity that rose in his throat and twisted restlessly as he looked at the card. Kern did not know what to say. He felt Nettie sliding around the table to face him squarely. He knew that if he looked at her he would see pleasure and "I told you so" in her eyes. He waited. And his father began.

Kern was on familiar ground. He had heard this lecture before.

He had no character. He was irresponsible. He was stupid not to be able to make excellent grades in school. Rollie, with no advantages, who lived in an alley, made better grades. What was his father going to do with him? His work demanded that he be away from the house and from Washington. He had no time to watch Kern do his lessons each night. Kern never made any friends. He was always in fights. When that happened, there must be something wrong with him, not with the boys he fought. No one was ever all right or all wrong. The cold eyes watched him without expression.

He held his eyes to his father's face and half of his attention accepted his words, recognizing the halfway point of the tirade and knowing by experience when it neared an end. Gosh, why doesn't he hurry up? Was Nick Carter going to escape? The free part of his mind went back to the paper-backed detective story on his desk. A tiny corner of Kern's mind heard his father's next words as he stood gazing at his inturned toes.

"And Nettie says that you never do as you are told. I am here to tell you that this conduct must stop or I will take measures to see that it does." Inside of his mind a description of Nettie took quick shape. It was made up of four-lettered words taken from the washroom walls at school, from the language of the playground. Some of it was the tongue of the barbershop and the language which Gertie, the whore who lived next door to Rollie, used.

Kern felt Nettie looking at him. His eyes came up to meet hers and found smiling satisfaction in them. He tried to warn himself against the anger that rose in him. What was she saying?

"Don't do nothin' but read 'em books all time. Finds 'em everywhere. Hid under his mattress, in corners, in his desk. Trash. Tells him to study. Don't ever get nothin' but sass, sass, sass, all da time."

"Nothing but—" His father looked at Nettie with quick concern. Kern glared. He saw the mole with the two long twisted hairs that curled against her jawline and fixed his hate on it.

"Tells him like my granny allus tol' me—get your learnin'."

"God damn your granny and you, too, you bitch." Kern heard each separate word of the thought as it moved in the prison of his throat, as it formed in his mind. When it was complete and violent it went in anger through his eyes to hers. He said nothing.

"Drop your eyes, you young pup. How dare you glower at a grown woman in that manner? Drop your eyes." His father's voice was rough and his hands jerked against the edge of the table as he pushed his chair back.

"Drop your eyes." The words cracked like a whip.

It was done. There was no recalling it now. It was brought into the open. Kern did not know the substance of it, nor the volume. He knew, without knowing its name, that it was there. Nettie knew—it was hate.

"You insufferable pup. Ignorance and laziness I can forgive, but not this insolent disobedience." His belt slithered out of the loops at his waist. "You've had this coming to you for a long time and, by God, you are going to learn that I mean what I say!"

A whipping is all things to a child. It is being totally alone and without hope. Unearned, undeserved, within the mind of the child, it is a bludgeon that drives the secret heart to inner hiding places. It is, or can be, the seed of hate, bitter, continuing, hidden, unforgiving. It can break a spirit or fire it to lusty, determined life.

The belt coiled over his shoulders and the tip burned sharply into the center of his back. He quivered. His first licking. More than a belt across shirt-clad shoulders. Something that cut and hurt deep inside. He bit his tongue to halt the whimper that crowded against his hips. Blood was in his mouth. Whistling. Arcing. Striking.

Stare at her. His mind told him that. Remember her. She is the one who is doing this to you. The words came with which to curse her. You bitch. Damn you. Damn you. She relished this. She was glad. This was the comeuppance. She smiled a bit across the table. He saw and understood. Arms folded under her breasts, she nodded imperceptibly in approval. She would tell George Lincum about this. Tears came. Kern could not hold them back. They welled over and flowed. Wet on his face. Just like a fight at school. He could not stop tears. But he wouldn't cry out. His clutching hands held his knickers away from his legs. The belt rose and fell.

"Drop your eyes—drop them, I say!"

Don't cry. Don't cry. The determination not to cry out crowded out even the words which described Nettie for him. Then the blows stopped. His father dropped in his chair, breathing in gasps. Kern felt his gaze. He held his eyes to Nettie. Her tear-blurred figure became clearer. She had not moved. She had stopped smiling. He had not cried out. She could not understand that.

"Go to your room." His father's words were dull as he dropped his head against his outstretched arms on the tabletop. His voice was almost a sob. His fists closed and unclosed in the silence. Kern looked at him. He did not feel anger. He did not feel love. He felt nothing. He looked at the lowered head and the now-relaxed hands and felt nothing. He spoke and felt his voice tremble.

"You wouldn't have whipped me if Mama had been here. You wouldn't have dared. And I am going to tell her." He was dangerously near to tears again. His father looked at him. Just looked and dropped his head again. Kern looked at him. He felt nothing. Neither pity nor anger nor love. Nothing.

He walked slowly around the table, beginning to feel the burning as it crossed and recrossed his back, following the path of the belt, replacing numbness. In front of Nettie he stopped.

"I'll get you. You wait and see!" His eyes locked with hers and she looked away to his father and back again. Now Nettie knew why he had not cried. The answer was in the bright blue eyes that watched her. It was plainer than words. It was hate.

The stairs were under his feet and the long darkness of the hall was around him. The mirror reflected his body and his eyes saw the purpling lines that crossed on his back. The bed's yielding softness held his body and the darkness and the pillow quieted the sobs that shook him. His mother's picture bent a little under the weight of his cheek and he went to sleep. With a child's grief, he went to sleep. Alone and puzzled and afraid.

In the dining room his father sat, unmoving, head on his crossed arms, the belt forgotten on the floor beside him.

What have I done? What have I done?

The report card lay under his hand.

Deportment: Average.

Attention: Poor.

In the morning the picture stood in its usual place. The tear stains had been carefully wiped away.

III

The barber worked the chair's pumping arm in short thumping strokes and Kern felt himself rise. The clip-clip of Tom's scissors followed the comb as it ruffled, then smoothed the hair at the side of his head. The chair in which he sat was in the very front of the shop. Five chairs below him, by the shoeshine stand at the end of the room, a man called Harry was holding forth. Kern listened curiously.

Harry was lanky and forty and a yellowish-brown. His crushed gray felt hat was pushed back on his head as he re-enacted a scene for the benefit of three listeners named "Single Action," "Tip Toe" and "Fat Meat." They hung on his words with rapt attention. Every two or three minutes a phone rang in a little room at the rear of the shop and Harry would halt his pantomime to answer.

"Tuxedo Tonsorial Parlor. Yeah. Five." Times over he said exactly the same thing, hung up and returned to continue his story. The phone rang insistently and Harry answered with a growing reluctance at having his tale broken into.

"Five."

"Five eight."

"Five eight."

Impatiently he slammed the receiver down on its hook. The scissors behind Kern's head stopped.

"Say, boy, what you trying to do? Break that phone?" Harry stopped dead in his tracks.

"Boy! How big men grow where you come from——?"

"Boy! That's what I called you. Don't slam that phone down like that!" Tom's voice was irritated. Harry watched him narrowly. "An' don' give me that stuff about 'how big men grow.' You don' say nothing when a white man calls you boy." Harry muttered an answer as he returned to his story.

"—fresh from Gawgia, man, an' I'm tellin' you there ain't nothin' like a fresh farm gal. Whoooeee Jeeezus! What a night!" The barbershop roared with laughter and gentle derision followed "Snake's" account of his prowess.

"Gawddamn nigger, if'n you was as great as you tells it, you'd sure be decked out in some fine threads. Looky that drape you's wearin'——"

"Nigger, how in hell you gonna tell us how great you is—ain't what 'at gal down on 'O' Street tol' me."

"Yeah, boy, 'cordin' to her, you is a minuteman." Boiling laughter.

"Hell, man, that gal so wore and tore—I's just doin' her a favor." Laughter again.

"Favor my eye. You was chasin' her a year ago—so damn glad you caught up with her you didn't know what to do."

"She give you a case?"

"Hell, no! Ol' Harry's too smart for 'at. He ain't gettin' messed up with none of them things. They don' mean you no good."

"Hell, ain't nothin' wrong with a little case—ain't nowise worse'n a head cold." "Fat Meat's" high, thin voice.

"Man, you crazy—that ruin a man."

"You right there, anyhow," Tom commented dryly.

"You oughta know, 'Fat Meat.' If it was same as a head cold you'd have T.B. by now." "Fat Meat" writhed under the derisive laughter.

The phone rang again.

"Five eight zero. Yeah. Yeah. That's tough. Me, too. I had a five and a eight. That damn cipher ruint me. Yeah—sure is." The scissors snipped away with lightning speed on top of Kern's head. Harry was at it again.

"—and she retched up and stroked this fine Jesus grass—" He ran his hands lightly over his patent-leather-smooth hair and shook his

100

head lightly in a gesture of shaking his hair into place. His audience roared gleefully.

"Nigger, I got better hair'n 'at on my leg."

"You's a lie!"

"Hell, I ain't. 'N longer, too."

"Boy, you shakes you head like you the King of Jazz."

"I is, boy. That's 'zactly what I is." Laughter. Kern shrugged his head against the pleasant tickle of the comb as it ran upward through the short hair at the back of his neck. Tom's firm hand moved his head back into place, tilting it so that Kern looked down at the tips of his shoes. He did not see "Tip Toe" when he pointed in his direction.

"Boy, you should have had a head of moss like 'at. Gals would sure go for you then!" Kern did not see Harry when he ran the short three or four steps to the front of the shop. He felt his hand when it raised the heavy curls that fell forward over his brow.

"Boy!" Harry stepped back. "That ain't no nigger hair. That's white folks' hair." Kern pulled his head away from the man's hand, straining back in the big chair and gripping the white stone arms tightly. Tom pushed Harry away.

"G'on—leave this kid alone. He's Counselor Roberts' boy. Ain't no white folks 'tall."

"No-nation nigger!" Harry retired to the rear of the shop. The sport was gone from his voice. Kern felt a wave of shame at being a "no-nation nigger" in a land which held the blacker the berry the sweeter was its juice. That was what "Blondie" had said anyhow. Tom swung his chair smoothly around to face the wide window.

O D E X U T

L A I R O S N O T

R O L R A P

His eyes followed the spiral stripes of the red and blue posts that flanked the words and he squinted into the bright sun that poured through the half-lowered blinds on to the hobbyhorse before him.

Tom reached over the hobbyhorse and lowered the blind further against the sunlight which had begun to pour into the wide window.

Kern remembered when the hobbyhorse had been shiny and new. When he had been a little boy, even when his mother had been alive, he had sat astride the little pony and dreamed he was a grown-up adventurer, riding off to places far beyond the barber-

101

shop. It never seemed to take long enough for his father to have his hair cut, then.

Tom spoke behind him. "Don't you pay no 'tention to them guys, son. Don't know why they talk so trashy. Ought to run them out of here." Mac ruminated on the thought. "Times ain't like they was when you Daddy first brought you here. Used to be a gentlemen's shop, then. Too many these Southern Negroes flooded into town." Kern listened curiously to Tom's train of thought. "They just make trash of themselves. Happy to be in the 'land of liberty.' They not fit for skilled work. Domestics and laborers. Lot of 'em too lazy to work at all. Quickly find this isn't the land of milk and honey they dreamed about. Just hangs around and gets bitter. Cause trouble." The old barber turned the chair angrily, and Kern watched his frowning face and the slender brown fingers in the mirror as they went automatically about their business. "Waiting for a chance to get in some easy racket. Get some quick money. Never understand they can't get something for nothing." He gestured to Kern in the mirror with his scissors. "You gotta work in this world. Nothin's free." He smiled, suddenly conscious that he was lecturing to a young boy, and turned Kern toward the window again. He continued in a quieter voice.

"Don't know what we goin' to do. Washington's worse now than it ever was 'fore the war. Filled with po' white trash. Brought their meanness with 'em. Seems like wherever you get a lot of Negroes, you got trouble. Two go together like smoke and fire." Kern wondered whether Tom was peeved at the flood of Southern Negroes or at the 'po' whites'! He could not decide.

"Don't know what we goin' to do. Can't blame Negroes for leaving the South when they get treated like dogs. Certainly can't. But why they have to come up here and ruin what we worked for?"

This, Kern remembered, was what his father had called the Northern Negro's age-old question.

"Never had this dirty talk when this was a gentlemen's shop. Men that stood for something used to come in here. Then these others started. Live all 'round here. Just came streaming in. Wish I'd stopped 'em first off. Now they're all my trade. If I shut 'em out, I'd have to close up." Tom was thoughtfully silent as he whisked at Kern's neck with the soft, powdered brush.

"Yes, sir. Things sure have changed. Used to be like that hobby-horse. Bright and shiny and new. Now everything's all wore down."

102

Kern looked at the horse, frozen in its prancing pose during as many years as he could remember.

"Remember the first time the Counselor brought you here—how you liked to ride him?" Tom's voice held a gentle note as he looked at the little horse with its saddle seat. "Eight years old now. 'Spose in time I'll clip away all his tail tryin' to keep it smooth." Kern nodded doubtful agreement. "You sure outgrowed that horse in jig time. Purty soon you'll be goin' to high school, won't you?"

"In another two years, yes, sir."

"That's not long. You'll be there 'fore you know it. What you going to be when you grow up?"

Kern was puzzled.

"Lawyer like your Daddy?" Kern shook his head. No. He thought a while.

"I'm going to be a writer." He said it gravely, almost expecting to hear laughter. For a moment Tom said nothing.

"A writer, huh?" His scissors stopped and lay against the comb at Kern's neck. Tom mulled the thought.

"A writer, huh? That's good." His pronouncement was solemn. "We need writers. Need people to tell our story to the world. To tell the truth—tell when we right and when we wrong." The comb and scissors hurried back to work.

"Every people need that. Too few of us do it. Dunbar and Johnson and those—good enough for their time. But things are changing now and we need to tell today's story. Got a few men like Hughes and Cullen and such telling it in poems. But that ain't enough. We still need the cold facts told in writing." Kern understood that Tom meant telling the story of Negroes. He felt himself withdraw from Tom's words. Those weren't the kind of stories he wanted to write. He just wanted to tell stories about heroes like—well—like Jean Valjean and Tom Swift and Nick Carter. He didn't think that Mac would understand what he meant. It was the first time he had expressed the thought to himself even. Still, it seemed like a familiar idea. A writer. He liked the thought.

At the rear of the shop angry voices tore at "the problem," drowning out the latest race results and ball scores that blared from the radio. There was a unison in these voices, and a deadly seriousness, that Kern recognized. He flinched before it as he did from "no-nation nigger" and "you's too white," and meetings of the League. There was a sustained key of despair that he did not recognize.

To "the problem" the men brought the language of personal experience—throaty words of anger, of hope, and despair that rose to match and describe the form of the thing that stirred inside. Each tongue knew the language. Each tongue used its words. Each Negro tongue. At one time or another, every Negro tongue.

Outside the window, Saturday's crowd streamed past along the sun-hot street. Two boys about Kern's age stooped to peer into the window, their noses pressed flat against the pane until Tom scowled fiercely and waved them away. A blind man in a shiny black suit, carrying a tray laden with pencils, pins, candy and chewing gum slung about his neck, slowly tapped his way up the street through darkness. A faded, flowered gingham dress fell loosely from the thin shoulders of the little girl at his arm whose bare, brown feet minced along the hot pavement. Three women went by arm in arm, lithe bodies and full hips swinging easily above bare legs and the musical sound of feet shod in dancing shoes. Heavy with red powder and dark eye shadow and beaded lashes, their faces fascinated Kern. Two men rushed from the Smoke Shop next door to whistle after them. A gray-haired old woman in a prim, wide-brimmed black hat and a starched white dress labored slowly up the street burdened with two laden market baskets. The men bumped into her. A huckster stopped his cart and bent to help her recover her hat and her packages, glaring after the young toughs who returned to the Smoke Shop without a backward glance at the damage they had done.

An incurious crowd, they went their various ways, unaware of the passionate vendetta of words being waged behind the fly-specked window and the half-drawn blind of the Tuxedo Tonsorial Parlor.

✿   ✿

"Was just a kid, I'm tellin' you. No more'n eight or nine, 'n that cop shot him."

"It's a fact. I seen the kid. Tore all his face out where it came out."

"Shot him in the back?"

"That's what it was. Sure as fate. Murder!"

"Boy ain't done nuttin', you say, Deacon?"

"'Cause he ain't. Stole a paper 'n the cop caught him and he twis'sed free."

"Call it 'sistin' 'rest, didn't they?"

"A boy resisting arrest! Scared to death, that what he was."

104

"Brother, that boy was *shot* to death."

"What dey do wif the cop?"

"Ha? You kiddin'? I tell you what, nigger. Not uh goddamn solitary thing."

"Sons of bitches. Dirty crawling stinking——"

"Tain't no while to cuss, brother. White's right in this town."

"Dis ain't the oney place white's right, either. I come from May-belle, Alabama, mistuh. An' I know whut I says. Seen mis'able po' trash police beat er nigger half to death 'roun' last crap time. No uvvah reason 'n 'at po' nigger didn't take his hat off. That 'ere boy was already walkin' in der street. Could er bought 'n sold that 'liceman. Po' trash! Nuffin' else ter feed on but hate. I pack up an' cum 'way from dere."

"The Lawd works in mysterious ways, young man——"

"Don' you 'Der Lawd' me, nigger—eff'n He truly dere, He a mitey careless Lawd. Time He be a 'spectin' His ways."

"Son, don't let yourse'f doubt The Word——"

"I truly don' like to go agin' His word, suh, but you all tell me dis—what I goin' b'lieve in? Jes tell me——"

"Ain't only the South, feller—same thing North of here. I been to New York an' Chi an' they's just about like here. Folks tip their hats a little more. Don' call you 'nigger' so quick, but they still shuts the door in your face. Jes' don' pay to be a nigger in this world."

"What'chu s'pose niggers was made for anyhow?"

"To tote dat bar 'n lif' dat bale. Hah, hah, hah!"

"This ain't no laffin' matter, boy!"

"You jes' *think* I'm laffin'. I'm madder'n hell."

"A soft answer turneth away wrath, son. Vengeance is——"

"Soft answer! Hah! I got d'answer. I come outa Gawga after my brother was lynched. I'll go to——"

"What he git killed for?"

"I said lynched, boy. Not killed. Dem's two different things. What you s'pec' a nigger git lynched fo' down dere. I'll go to——"

"Did he?"

"Nossuh. He ain't at all. Was wif me all dat day. Every liv'long minute. I'll go to hell 'fore I'll let uh white man touch me an' I'll take me along some company. Ah purely means that."

"Uh huh! Me, too!"

"I'm 'deavorin' to raise mah fambly. Sen' mah young ones to school. Teach 'em right from wrong. Ah works hard. Mines my business. Jes' chef cooks all day. Ain't boverin' no one. Goes to work. Goes to church. Members in the League, 'n my wife, too. But I lives in mortal fear."

"What of?"

"Of the day a white man touches me—calls me nigger. 'Cause I mought surely have to kill him. An' the Lawd knows I don't want to lay a han' on no man alive."

"Things are better though. My boys tell me so. They're in college, both of them. Learnin' that the right way is reason and education."

"'At's O.K. for you, Doc, but how many of us goin' to go to college. We gotta work. Our kids gotta work if they 'spec' to eat. They *gotta* work."

"Lord knows I got more moufs now 'n I can feed."

"Tell me 'bout schools Jim Crow is all they teaches. My kids in school. Talkin' 'bout high school now. I ain't been to no school but I got dough! I knows enough to add and I runs the numbers in this town. Come home to me wif his hand outstretched sayin' 'I pledge allegiance—' I tol' him to stop that damn foolishness. Jim Crowed in the Capitol itself!"

"I know. I know. Everything you says is so but we still got to work, got to be patient. Don't matter how right we know we is, this old world ain't goin' change overnight. Got to work and pray. Got to build org'nizations like the Freedom League to help us."

"I 'gree with the Rev'end. Got to reason, got to work. Nothing worth having ever come free. But it does seem hard sometimes. Looks like a man can only take so much kicking around, then he's just got to hit back. If he's a man at all, he's got to quit turning his cheek and stand fast. It's hard to choose 'tween human nature an' reason."

Angry, turbulent, rushing words. Extravagant words. Words of hope and hurt and despair. Words that belched forth in harsh phrases of hate. One voice and many voices. Many voices—all of them Negro. All with hope, steel-wire-thin and strong. Faces and hearts turning toward God. The Rock of Ages.

Kern took his change and counted it and placed a quarter in Tom's waiting hand.

"Thank you kindly, young man. You just give me a call and I'll save space for you next time. Then you won't have to sit around the shop so long." Tom smiled at him.

"Thank you very much, sir," Tom called after him through the screen door. "Just ask for Tom. Be sure and tell your Daddy I said 'Hello.'"

"Yes, sir."

He went up the street and around the corner. Two long weeks before he would have to sit in Tom's chair again. "Tom." His father had warned him sharply against using that familiar address. Tom was to be called Dr. Thomson. Or Mr. Thomson. He was a college graduate and a dentist. Kern had wondered then—he wondered now —why was he working as a barber? The answer was simple. He made more money. Kern did not know that.

So much of what he had heard he did not understand.

Why did they say "nigger" so much? They didn't seem to mind it. In fact, Kern thought they sometimes seemed to like it. But he knew they would fly into a rage if a white man used the word. Even the kids at school would fight if a white kid used the word. He would fight himself. He wondered. From the lips of Negroes, he was much later to realize, the word fell in a thousand gradations. In a thousand separate tones that ranged from gentle reproof and ridicule to the affectionate inclusion of its object in a kindred host. Easily and carelessly it fell from the lips of Negroes. Yet, let the lips of a single white man shape the word and give it voice and an unforgivable, a mortal insult had been done.

It was hard to understand. He hated the word himself. He remembered "Blondie."

"You's too white to call me 'nigger,' nigger."

He knew that *he* could not use it.

Kern decided, as he had often before, that he did not like the barbershop.

CHAPTER V

"HALF-WHITE NIGGER!"

I

THE snow swept into their faces; small, driven flakes that slanted at them from the northwest as they bent their heads against the wind. The snow was an inch deep and more on the rough brick pavement, growing in lumps under their heels and falling away to grow again; sifting down on their necks where bent heads drew away from the warmth of their collars. Their footsteps trailed behind them in a rude new path; past the playground and the open lot where a few weedy clumps pushed up through the snow and marked deserted tennis courts; past the grim-corniced old Dental School and the long new Medical College to where the lean row of gray houses beyond Sixth Street broke the wind-driven snow until they turned at the mouth of Key's Alley.

Key's Alley wore white. Its short length was empty. The usual litter of trash that lay along its sides and about the stable doors across from Rollie's house was covered by drifting snow. The Alley was all white and rounded shapes, with nothing left of the ragged dirty look it usually wore. The house fronts and the stable stood unchanged for familiar eyes to find. These and the low rickety stoops of its other houses were the same. One irregular line of footsteps entered the alley before them, breaking the snow-smoothness and going at a lurching, striding gait through to the other end. The sweet smell of baking bread came from Corby's Bakery at the Alley's other end and mixed with the acrid, tarry odor of soft furnace coal that hung in yellow-gray blobs about the chimney tops before it broke and wisped away to nothingness in the wind.

Rollie's house was cold. The oil lamp's uncertain flame burned up and pushed the shadows back into the far corners of the room. Kern watched the heavy vapor of his breath as it jetted out into the room. Quickly Rollie laid crumpled paper and pine splints on the thin bed of ashes in the front room's round-bellied stove and struck a match and the fire began to crackle as it caught.

108

When Mrs. Burns came, the house was warm. The flat-topped coal range in the kitchen was a dull red as its banked coals burned with a purr. The kitchen table had been set for dinner. In the front room Kern and Rollie sat at the wall table, toes hooked on the rungs of their chairs. Pencil tips went alternately from thoughtful mouths to the paper before them as they struggled with algebra.

A few snowflakes sifted into the room as Mrs. Burns closed the door and went quickly to the kitchen to lay her bundles down and shake the snow from her hat. Kern hastened to take her coat and hang it in the hall closet beside the bedroom door. In his face its heavy cloth was fresh with the smell of cold, outside air.

Mrs. Burns was a gentle woman, dark and gentle with dark eyes and crisp gray hair drawn into a knot at the back of her head. Her head, it always seemed to Kern, sat proudly on her neck—even when she was tired and her shoulders sagged. She turned from the doorway to the sideboard at the sink, her hands deftly tying her apron strings, patting stray ends of hair into place, then spreading open the mouths of the paper bags. Kern and Rollie turned to watch her.

"Thought I never would get home—storm's gettin' worse. Cars movin' awful pokey." She talked on as she brought out mysterious wrapped packages each time her hands dipped down.

"Mighty glad now my folks had that party last night. Ain't never seen that place in such a mess. Lawd! Thought I never would get done cleaning." Kern saw the muscles at Rollie's jaw bunch and roll as his teeth set. He knew Rollie hated having his mother work for white folks.

"Missus tol' me, 'Louise,' she say, 'you jes' take everything you need for dinner. The cater' done left plenty.' So I jes' load up an' come on. Dinner won't take no while 'tall tonight." Water splashed and gurgled in the sink as she washed crisp celery stalks and lined them on a plate. "Good thing, too. Your Pa'll be home 'most any minute now." Kern turned back to his schoolwork, swallowing hungrily as the spicy fragrance of warming gravy and brewing coffee drifted through the house.

"Oh, Heavens!"

"Whassa matter, Mom?" Rollie turned anxiously. She rummaged in her pocketbook and took out her change purse.

"I completely forgot bread." She held out some silver to Rollie. "Here, son, run up to Corby's and get a pan of rolls."

Rollie's eyes widened, surprised.

"Rolls?" Rolls, Kern knew, weren't the usual thing in Key's Alley.

"Pan of Parker House." Mrs. Burns was determined. "Ain't goin' to spoil this dinner with no light bread. Hurry up now. Jes'll have time to pop 'em in the oven before your Pa comes." Kern watched enviously as Rollie pulled on his boots and went to the closet for his coat.

"Want me to go with you?" Before he could rise, Mrs. Burns turned from the stove where she stood stirring the pan of gravy.

"Nope. You stay here 'n get your work, Kern. You two boys get out 'n get to playin'—you make dinner late for sure." The door closed, cut off the brief gust of cold air, and Rollie was gone. Kern turned back to his books.

Algebra. He looked about him at the room. Everything he saw in the room was the same way. Worn, but clean. He knew that. Old and worn, but clean. Dull marks and old scratches on the tabletop before him were deep buried under polish, rubbed and shined until the marks of use and care had blended into one. Kern's eyes went over the flowered wallpaper to the lamp in the corner behind the chair where Mr. Burns would stretch out when he came from work. The stiff curtains before the windows fell in rigid, unnatural, starched curves. They had belonged to Mrs. Burns' mother, and he knew she trusted no other hands but her own to wash and stretch them.

Algebra! He'd have to hurry. Rollie would be back in minutes and Mr. Burns would be home. He'd have to leave after dinner.

❂   ❂   ❂

"Lan' sakes but your Pa's late tonight," she turned in the door, "Snowin' still, Rollie?"

"Yes'm—harder'n it was when we came from school."

II

Feet thumped heavily on the wooden stoop. Mrs. Burns smiled and began to place hot plates on the table as the door opened. Kern and Rollie turned to greet him.

Mr. Burns stood there swaying, silent. Kern knew immediately that something was wrong. In the dim light behind him, snow fell steadily in large flakes. Mrs. Burns turned as he swayed and caught at the doorknob to steady himself. He said nothing as the palm of his free hand rasped over his mouth and the rough stubble of his

110

beard. His head turned slowly as he looked at the boys, and beyond them to where his wife stood in the kitchen door, her potholder still in her hands. Snow settled in a thin carpet about the door as they watched him. Suddenly he slammed the door shut and stood there rocking slowly back and forth. The smell of whiskey came to them, sour and biting in the warm room. Mrs. Burns went to him, wiping her hands on her apron. Happiness had gone from her face. Kern saw that Rollie's head had dropped and turned away, embarrassed. Something, Kern knew, was seriously wrong. Mr. Burns never drank. He hated liquor. He often said how he had seen it ruin his brother. Twisting out of his short coat, Mr. Burns tossed it across the room to the armchair. Mrs. Burns took him by the arms, and looked into his face. Then she led him past Kern and Rollie to the bedroom.

"Get on with your work, boys. We'll have dinner in just a minute."

Kern wished he knew how to leave. It would have been less embarrassing, but he could think of no way to excuse himself. Rollie rose without a word and got a broom from the kitchen. Silently he opened the door and swept away the melted snow. Then, eyes still avoiding Kern, he got a cloth and wiped the floor dry. Kern pretended deep concern with his algebra when Rollie sat beside him. From the bedroom came the low sound of voices.

"Just leave me be, Louise—I don't want to lie down. Later. Let's eat dinner—we'll talk later."

"All right, Frank. Whatever you say."

Mr. Burns came out of the bedroom and walked steadily to the armchair where his coat lay. From the corner of his eye, Kern watched him fumble in the pocket and take out a bottle and turned to stare in spite of himself as the man twisted the cork from the bottle and turned, raising it to his mouth. His yellow eyes fell on Kern and the bottle stopped halfway to his mouth. A slow, sneering smile touched his lips and he spoke thickly.

" 'Scuse me, I'm sure. Must mind my manners. Don't drink from bottles front of company. Get a glass. Be tony." He lumbered to the kitchen and they heard him take a glass from the cabinet shelf and heard the splash of liquid as he poured into the glass. Kern half rose from his chair, intending to go when Rollie took him by the elbow.

"Don't, Kern. He'll be all right—he's just troubled."

"Sure, Rollie. I wasn't going to." Kern smiled at his friend anxiously. He knew Rollie was trying to make the best of a bad situation—that he wished Kern had not seen his father like this. He knew that Rollie didn't want to apologize for his father.

Mrs. Burns called them. "Dinner, boys. You ready, Pa?"

❊ ❊ ❊

Dinner was tasteless. The colorful, rich food, the expensive food —food to which that table was a stranger—was tasteless. It lay on their plates hot and savory and grew cold as they toyed at it, insisting at Mrs. Burns' concern that they were ravenous, forcing themselves to chew mouthfuls that were dry as chaff. They swallowed with difficulty and forced brief spurts of conversation. Mr. Burns was completely silent, eating slowly and deliberately. His eyes focused on something beyond the center of the table and he began to talk in slow phrases, almost to himself. As he talked, one work-hardened, knotted hand clutched the glass of whiskey.

"Don't never get a chance. Don't matter how steady 'n honest a man is, don't get a fair chance."

"What happened, Pa?"

"Always the last to get hired—first to get fired."

"What happened, Pa? You didn'!" Sharp worry fretted Mrs. Burns' face.

"I got fired." Flat words in the silence. Silence—except for Mrs. Burns' intake of breath as if she had been struck a blow.

Mr. Burns leaned his head forward and propped it on one hand, his elbow on the table, still clutching the glass.

"I got fired." A dull monotone.

None of them ate now. This was tragedy.

"I been working that job for ten year. I go to face the boss down —fin' out why. Big boss won't see me. I hear him say to my foreman—'Tell him we gotta have white man. Time's hard. We gotta look out for white men.' My foreman, he turn to me and put his han's on my shoulders. He almost ready to cry. Say, 'I can't help it, Frank. Honest to God! I hate to see this happen. You one good man. Honest to God! I'm sorry, Frank.' I look at him, I know he mean it. He's one good man himself. But what can I say? I gotta hate someone. I gotta hate him! He's white." His head twisted in his hand and Kern saw the man's grizzled gray hair tufting through his blunt fingers.

"I gotta hate!"

112

Mrs. Burns stood beside her husband, her arms about his shoulders.

"Oh, Pa!" Her grief was in her face as she spoke to the boys. "Eat your dinners, boys. Hurry and eat and get your work done."

"I'm—I'm not very hungry, Mrs. Burns."

"Oh, Kern, you must be hungry. Both you boys are hungry. Youngsters need food. Come on, eat—there's plenty." Mr. Burns stared up at Kern.

"Don't force him—more for us. We need it—or we will."

"Pa!" He dropped his eyes and Mrs. Burns caught at her lip with her teeth. Frank Burns sobbed and sobbed again. He twisted away from his wife and from the table, pulling the tablecloth awry as he rose, glass of whiskey still in his hand. He looked at the glass as though he wondered how it had gotten there. Then he threw it, full force, against the door and lurched into the bedroom. Mrs. Burns followed him quickly, closing the door behind them. Kern heard the heavy thud as he dropped on the bed.

A minute longer he stared at his plate before he stood up and went to gather his books. Rollie made no effort to stop him as he climbed into his coat and took up his books. He stopped with his hand on the door and turned to look at Rollie.

"I—" he could not meet the hot-eyed gaze with which Rollie watched him. "I'm sorry."

"Oh, don't worry 'bout it, Kern. Isn't anything." Rollie made light of the incident. "I know lot of people who got fired. Niggers get used to it!" The bitterness in his voice was hard and old, and Kern knew that this was a different Rollie, a Rollie whom he had not known before. He stepped through the door into the Alley carefully, extremely careful not to knock down the ledge of snow that had drifted against the door. The door closed behind him and Kern stepped into the Alley and walked along it to the mouth of the street.

He would never go back again. He knew that.

III

Kern stood at the corner in the warm, late-evening dusk and opened the letter again, his eyes going straight to the words he wanted. "Frank Richards," they said, "at 142 Adams Street, N.W., Washington, D.C." He read the paragraph quickly.

"We are happy to welcome you to the ranks of Scott Home Salesmen."

"If you will take this letter to Mr. Frank Richards, your area agent, he will complete the details necessary to starting your career as a Scott Home salesman."

The house on the corner was numbered 158. Kern walked down the block, subtracting two numbers for each house he passed. It would be the eighth house down—five white people on the porch, six, seven, more people. He passed the last houses and turned in at a concrete walk between two rows of thick hedges. The shiny number plate on a pillar of the porch said 142.

Almost holding his breath, Kern went slowly up the steps. The floor boards creaked under his feet as he crossed the dark-shadowed porch and rang the bell. The hallway was dark and he heard no movement inside the house. He rang again and heard the bell peal loudly. Gee whiz! he hoped Mr. Richards was at home.

A stirring from the deep shadows at the end of the porch startled him and he turned quickly to see a man on a couch rising on one elbow, rubbing sleepily at his eyes. Holding his letter forward, Kern stepped toward the couch. The man sat upright, still rubbing his eyes.

"Whatcha want, kid?"

"Mr. Richards—I'm looking for a Mr. Richards."

"Well, I reckon that's me. What can I do for you?" He bent to fumble under the couch and drag out a pair of slippers into which he pushed his bare feet.

"I have a letter from the Scott—"

"Oh-ho, a route—is that it? Well, young feller, we'll see what we can do." He rose stretching and yawning tremendously, before settling flat on his feet. Then he shuffled across the porch to the screen door and led Kern down the dark hallway, pushing on a light button as he went. In a small, cluttered room at the end of the hall, he motioned Kern to a chair beside a disarranged desk. Drawing up another chair, he sat down, scratching his head. The letter still held tightly in his hand, Kern watched him as he sat and pushed aside the tied piles of magazines and papers that littered the desk before finding what he wanted.

"Ah, here we are," he riffled through the packet of papers, selecting several and holding them out to Kern.

"This stuff will give you some idea of what you have to do. It's

114

got some pretty swell tips for setting up a route. You got any prospects?"

Kern gulped and nodded uncertainly. "Well, let me give you a few tips."

He listened intently as Frank Richards talked about subscribers and gave him advice about setting up his route. "—keep your territory compact—" Richards warmed to his topic and rambled on to explain percentages.

"Guess we can start you with fifty copies. Think you can get rid of them?" Kern nodded happily. "You'll get three and a half cents for each copy you sell—"

Kern busied himself with the arithmetic of three and one half times fifty. One dollar and seventy-five cents! The total surprised him. Almost two dollars a week. He began to plan what he would do with it.

"Where do you live—uh—Kern?" Kern answered, his eyes still on a picture booklet showing a model Scott Home Salesman standing at a door, hat in hand, as he talked to a customer. He did not notice that Frank Richards had stopped writing.

"You mean North*east*, don't you?" He had looked up at Kern.

"No, sir, I mean—" Kern realized what the man meant. "I mean Northwest." He held tightly to the booklet and hoped it wouldn't happen.

Sick and suddenly miserable, inside, he hoped it wouldn't happen.

It did.

"I thought white folks had all moved out from there—"

"They ha—" Kern cut himself off. Too late now to cut himself off—to say that a few families still lived there.

"What are you, boy?" Frank Richards dropped his pen on the desk and turned in his chair to face Kern. Kern looked back at him, saying nothing.

"You a white boy?"

Kern shook his head slowly. "No."

Richards reached forward and drew Kern's hand roughly toward the lamp on the desk. He stared at the outstretched fingers.

"Blue nails! 'Course you ain't white. A nigger! Well, I'll be damned!" He stood up and took Kern by the shoulder. "Come on, boy," he led him through the hall and out to the porch.

"Get on 'bout your business now. I ain't doin' no business with no niggers."

115

Kern stood for a moment on the top of the porch as the words pounded in his head. He felt hostile eyes from the neighboring porches fixed on him. "Get on, nigger—you hear me?" The man moved behind him. Kern went down the steps and past the hedges and up the street, his head bent, feeling the stares that followed him from the porches. He heard the words again and again. He wanted to cry and could not.

"I ain't doin' no business with no niggers."

He was something dirty.

Something to be spat on.

Something to be driven and cursed.

Not someone.

Something.

He felt that in the words—in the stares.

He felt that and was sick with anger and shame.

Sick—with the sickness of a race-old, futile despair.

Angry—with a hate that is not bred of reason.

Ashamed—with the desperate shame of a human being, stripped of dignity. Naked, pride whipped and bleeding.

❊   ❊   ❊

His father found him in his room, sitting on the edge of his bed, his face twisted with something too large for tears, the papers which Frank Richards had given him were still tightly clutched in his hand.

"Where have you been, Kern? I expected you to be doing your homework when I came—" He stopped as he saw the boy's face, the twisted, hurt look on the boy's face. "What's wrong, Kern— what's the matter?" Quick anxiety filled his voice.

Kern did not answer.

"What is it—a fight?" Kern shook his head dumbly and looked away. Charles stepped into the room and took the papers from his hand. He read through them quickly.

"What happened?"

Kern could find no words to tell him. "Were you refused because you were a Negro?"

"Yes, sir."

"What happened—were you hurt?"

Kern wished that his father would go away and leave him to think this thing out by himself.

"No, sir."

"Tell me exactly what happened."

Kern did. Reluctantly at the start, and at the finish, his hurt pouring out, word on top of word.

"Why?" he asked.

Charles sat beside him on the bed.

"I know, son, I know what you feel. It's exactly this sort of thing we are fighting in the Freedom League. You will meet it, this viciousness, in one way or another, as long as you live in America. Every Negro does. What happened to you is exactly what happened to Mr. Burns. But you can't let it make you quit." Kern twisted on the bed's edge. His father rose and stood before him. "I am very proud of you for wanting to work. Very proud." Kern looked at himself in the mirror above his dresser.

"Why don't you try to get a newspaper route like Eddie?" Eddie lived across the street. "I understand that he is going to get a *Morning Post* route. You might like that—and it will mean more money than this magazine thing. It's worth trying anyway." Charles paused and decided to say no more. He went silently down the hall.

*   *   *

That night, after the house was dark, after even the chirping of the crickets had dropped to silence, Kern lay on his bed, wide awake, staring at the ceiling.

"Why?"

The question pulsed in him. Sickness. Anger. Shame. None of these answered the question. He got up and turned on his desk lamp. Then he stood in front of the mirror and stared at his face. He ran his fingers over his face, along his jawline and through his ruffled hair. Stared at his eyes. They were blue. His nose was lean and his mouth was thin and straight.

"Why? Why am I a nigger?"

His fingers went along the tracery of veins at his temples, dull blue under the skin. He turned and bent under the lamp to peer closely at his fingers. They were not blue. They were pink. Pink except for the little half-moon at the top of each nail. And those were white. His thought became words in the room.

"Why am I a nigger?" He turned the light out and dropped on his bed.

117

IV

The school year had barely begun when it happened. It started on the first week of the school year, before even the disappointing hurt Frank Richards had given him had been forgotten. It started over nothing at all.

Kern could see that now. A passed word. A challenge. A schoolboy fight. Now he stood in the schoolyard face to face with Rollie and felt the circle of boys tighten about them. Teasing jibes were leading them to a fight. Kern's mind flashed to the last time he had left Rollie's house—the evening last winter when Mr. Burns had come home half drunk and bitter and announced that he had been fired. He had not been back since that night. He stood taller than Rollie now by almost half a head and he was as heavy. He wasn't afraid to fight Rollie. It wasn't that. The boys knew he would stand and fight. He'd even whipped cigarette-smoking, girl-chasing, playground-bully "Blondie." It wasn't that he was afraid.

He just didn't want to fight Rollie because Rollie was his friend. But the boys had made the fight. Kern knew that it had gone too far to stop now. He could not understand why Rollie seemed to want the fight. Rollie stood there, a short arm's length away, his face twisting into his fighting scowl. His eyes told Kern that this was something special.

Hands shoved at Kern's back and he lunged forward into Rollie.

The first blows were light and halfhearted and they closed quickly. He felt Rollie's shoulder and then his grappling arms as he ducked under a swing and ran into him, tackling him about the legs and throwing him to the ground. He fought back desperately, angry at the unfairness of the whole thing. They rolled back and forth on the ground, the boys shifting about them, careful not to raise a fuss that would bring the janitor out to break up the fight. Kern fought for breath as he rolled Rollie underneath and straddled him, pinning his flailing arms with his knees. He didn't hear the surprised cries of the boys as they watched the champ of the lot get wrestled down. Instead, he heard himself saying to Rollie,

"Say 'nuff 'n I'll let you up." Rollie glared up at him.

"Say 'nuff 'n I'll let you up." Rollie wrestled and struggled, trying to free his arms from the knees that pinned them down. His answer was a sob in his throat. Kern was puzzled.

"Say 'nuff 'n I'll let you up." The boys were silent, waiting to hear Rollie "beg out." He did not beg. He wrenched and twisted furiously.

"Lemme up!"

"Lemme up—you half-white nigger!"

Kern was stunned. Rollie spit up into his face. He felt the spittle against his cheek, dripping down to his jaw and dropping off. He could not believe it. He wiped his jaw with the back of one fist and it came away wet with spittle. He tried hard not to believe his eyes. He looked about the ring of boys and stared down at Rollie and felt sick in his stomach. Then, suddenly, he knew it was so. He heard Rollie hawking in his throat to spit again, and he hit the face below him. He doubled his fist and hit again and again as Rollie twisted under him and tried to spit.

"Lemme up—lemme up! You half-white nigger!"

Kern pounded at the familiar face until he was out of breath and half blinded by tears of anger. He stopped then, breath rasping in his throat. The faces of the boys about him were blank. Their eyes told him where their sympathies lay. Rollie had sounded a battle cry that bound him out. Half-white nigger! He looked down again at Rollie, struggling, and struck him in the face. Then he lurched up and thrust through the circle of boys and went across the play yard and down to the street crying.

He left his books behind him on the lot. And his cap. And his friend.

✿　✿　✿

He saw Rollie again each day, at school, but he never spoke to him again. His teacher called his father about the fight, but neither of them mentioned the affair to him. If Miss Washburn heard about it, she decided it was best ignored. Kern could not forget it.

He remembered the faces of the boys. He remembered the spittle, wet on his face and clinging in wet threads to the back of his hand. He never forgot "half-white nigger!"

NEW YORK—APRIL, 1941

OVER and over again, Kern had asked himself, "Why—why did I come?" Party noises had filled his ears and the room around him—laughter, a guitar, singing, ice in glasses, the drum of rain on the skylight—and the question had filled his mind.

"Why did I come?"

The question had started in him as he rode downtown on the subway. It had repeated itself as he walked, head lowered, through the slanting rain that washed the streets and ran in miniature torrents along the gutters. In tune to the squishing sound of his feet on the sidewalks, the question had repeated itself again and again.

"Why did I come?"

He had stood in front of the old, brownstone house, staring up at the four stories of blank, rain-silvered windows to the very top floor with its row of lights and known that this was Bill Gabel's place, and asked himself, "Why did I come?"

Part of his reluctance had been recognizable—his habit of shying away from crowds and from the possibility of being embarrassed by questions. Part of it was his natural dislike for large gatherings. To these was added newly remembered suspicions and angers that had been in him since he had started to write his story.

He had stood in front of Bill Gabel's house and felt the driving rain spatter against his cheek and against his neck and felt the drops gather and start in a slow trickle that gained speed and ran down his neck, and asked himself, "Why did I come?" He could, he reminded himself, have been at his own place, warm and comfortable, and writing on the story—

A car turning the far corner had decided him. The car had turned slowly and come down the street, playing its spotlight against the house fronts, searching for a number. The car had decided him. He realized that he would appear foolish trying to explain to a police cruiser why he was standing in the rain in front

121

of the very house to which he was going—trying to make up his mind whether to go in or not. The car made up Kern's mind.

He had bolted up the stairs and when the doorknob yielded to his frantic buzzing, had breathlessly climbed the four long, turning flights, stopping only briefly on the third landing to take off his sodden trench coat.

Some of his reluctance had disappeared when Bill Gabel greeted him with pleased surprise at the top of the stairs. More of it went when Bill introduced him to blonde, curvesome "Texas" Haggerty and barged off with the injunction to "Tex" to "Introduce him around, Tex. If I don't finish this sketch of Marianne now, Heaven knows when I'll get her to sit still again."

A bourbon left him with only shreds of reluctance, and these were lost in a rush of introductions that left him with a jumbled mixture of first names as Texas led him from one group to another. "Green," Kern learned with surprise, could sound almost like "McDonough." By the time they reached the circle of people at the rear of the long room, he had given up hope of remembering the last names and all but a few of the first names were jumbled in his mind.

Kern did not forget all of the names though. He remembered the name of the singer—Jeff Balanchine. A strange name. A name easy to remember—easier still when the owner was a Negro. Jeff Balanchine was hidden from sight of people as he and Texas approached the circle and Kern did not see the man at first. When he did, he felt his eyes go to the brown face and stay there, even though he tried to tear them away. The reluctance he had felt at coming surged up, saying, "I told you so." Anger at himself for having come filled him. And with it fear—and anger at the Negro man for having been there. Anger. Reasonless, but there.

Kern felt Texas' arm about his waist as they pushed toward the center of the circle and knew it was impossible to escape. They stood there and he felt Balanchine's eyes touch him lightly. A blade of fear ran through him with the question, "Could he know me?" Kern had often heard it said that one Negro could recognize another in a group of people. He believed it then. Not because there was any physical trait which could have exposed the pretender—himself—but because he realized in that instant, out of his own deep-rooted, denied sympathy, that there can be a psychic-pull born of many things known and suffered in common which can go between such kindred and which, when it does, will not be denied.

122

It seemed to Kern that this happened when he first saw Jeff Balanchine. If it did, there was no sign of recognition in Balanchine's eyes.

Jeff Balanchine. A Negro. Texas' hand went to Jeff's shoulder as he started to rise.

"No," she said. "Don't get up, Jeff, baby." The man stood just the same, rising with a fluid grace that gave no hint of effort. Standing, the guitar in his hand looked like a toy.

"I want you all to meet Kern Adams—Kern's a good friend of Bill's. He's writing for Dowd's WQAM now. Kern, this is—" The names began to blend again as Kern smiled automatically and accepted the introductions. That is, all of the names blended except Balanchine.

He knew the name Balanchine. Who wouldn't have? America knew Balanchine. All-American football player. Phi Beta man. Track star. Nationally known baritone. A Negro to be proud of. A man to be proud of. He was huge. Kern thought he was the biggest man he had ever seen, standing inches above them with an easiness that would not let them resent his height.

The question frayed at Kern's nerves.

Will he know me?

Will this thing I feel be felt by him too?

Suddenly, sickeningly, Kern realized that he hated the man. He hated him for the feeling of insecurity which he was experiencing —for the fear of exposure that ran along his nerves and stripped them raw. He hated Jeff Balanchine and he admired his unconscious ease and grace. Balanchine's hand took his in a firm grasp and Kern heard the man's voice saying the proper things faultlessly.

"I'm happy to know any friend of Bill's." The rich voice rumbled up like music. The eyes told him that the man had recognized his momentary reluctance to accept his hand. The eyes were filled with contempt and with pity. Kern shrank before the pity. They turned away, Texas and Kern, and went slowly across the room.

"You know," her voice was studied, "there was a time when I didn't like Negroes, either. Matter of fact—I don't suppose I like them now." Her eyes went quickly to Kern's face to judge the effect of her words, then back to the floor seam her feet were following. "But I've learned that all of them aren't what we have said they are. I know now that some of them are fine people. People I'm glad to call my friends. Like Jeff Balanchine. Jeff's different—" She bit at her lips and Kern wondered if she was going

123

to say "different from most Negroes." She did not. She went on—"Jeff's different from most people I know. He's a very unusual man." She looked up at him for agreement. He agreed. He had never met anyone else who affected him quite as Jeff Balanchine did. Not even Jake. He agreed and realized how absurd it had been for him to feel the urge to avoid Balanchine's hand. He understood that Texas was telling him Jeff Balanchine was not an outsider to them —that his color didn't matter. He nodded and Tex's voice took on its bantering tone again.

Kern tried to match her mood, but reluctance at being there was in him, and fear, and a wish that he had not come. These things knotted in him and angered him as they stopped near a small group of men at the hall door.

A short, heavy-set man with wide shoulders was talking, pounding one fist in the palm of a hand as he talked. His massive head was lowered and thrust forward. Watching, Kern thought that there was something bull-like in the man, that he would delight in smashing through an obstacle which might stand in front of him. He was speaking with angry sarcasm and it irritated Kern to find his own mood so nearly duplicated.

"Listen, Mister Professor, I hope that you don't teach that sort of hogwash to innocent collegians who sit in your classes. You mark this one thing—those men who went to Spain to fight were not troublemakers—not in the main! Years before their time, they saw where the world was going and they felt a responsibility to society to do what they could to stop it. Even if the effort meant placing their own lives in the balance. That was a great thing—but I suppose it's not fair to expect a college professor to understand that sort of motivation." He snorted. "Of course not—thinkers who can't understand that this whole dirty business started years ago when China and Ethiopia were ravaged, wouldn't quite get the subtleties of the Spanish war. Those peoples had different color skins—they are another color than the omnipotent great white father. Such a colossal difference those skins made that we wouldn't bestir ourselves to stop the mess when it started because we couldn't admit that anything involving men who weren't white could possibly spread and grow to involve us. Hah! Professors!" Kern watched him as he spun about angrily on his heel and came to stop in front of them. His neck was still corded by the violence in him and his lifted, black brows lent an almost satanic expression to his face.

124

"Where's the liquor?" The man's flashing eyes went over Kern from head to toes and went to the men behind him in a swift backward glance before coming back to Texas. She nodded toward the cubbyhole kitchen.

"What's the matter, Max?"

"College professors!" The two words were the limit of his vocabulary at the moment. "Oh, Christ! What's the use?" His eyes lit on Kern again and Kern had the feeling that Max was looking at what he was thinking rather than at his outward appearance. Tex's voice was sympathetic.

"Can't you take their brand of tripe, Max? Does it do something to your innards?"

"Listen, any time a punk like that—! Oh, the hell with it!" He shrugged his shoulders. "What's the use?" His eyes still lay on Kern. "What do you do?" Kern thought the voice said, "If you don't do anything, it won't surprise me." He felt his shoulders stiffen at the man's harsh tone.

"I write."

"Write!" The man's lip curled and Kern felt the anger that was already in him swerve to this ready target. "Write what?"

"Bilge—for old women and children who drool over comic programs." The man's eyes widened at the blunt words and Kern felt a grim satisfaction at having broken through his anger. Quickly, Max checked his surprise.

"You admit it's bilge?"

"Oh, it's not that bad, Max. He—"

"Why isn't it?" Max switched his gaze to Texas. "He said it was bilge—he should know. I suppose your program director thinks so too?" His eyes turned questioningly to Kern.

"Well—?" Max prompted him to answer.

"Well what?"

"What does your program director think about—?"

"Who said he thought?" Kern's brusque tone matched the sharpness in Max's voice. "He's typical of all the program directors I know. Keep everything in its own little groove. Don't disturb the public with anything important. Feed them crap. Program directors!"

Max's eyes glittered as he stared at Kern. He caught his breath and rose on his toes.

"There may be exceptions, you know." It was Kern's turn to snort.

"Show me one. Just one!" He half turned on his heel and stepped around Max with Texas tugging at his arm.

"Do—did you know who that was?" Irritation was still in him. Fading, but still in him. He almost snapped at Texas, then he caught himself.

"No. Should I?"

"That was Max Karns." The name didn't ring any bells for Kern. Not at first.

"Max Karns—" he said haltingly. "—of American Broadcasting?" Texas' headshake confirmed his answer. Max Karns and American Broadcasting represented the tops in radio.

"Well," Kern told himself, "you really put your foot in it then. Go and tell him that you didn't mean it." The urge ran through him and he started to turn back to where he had left Max Karns. Then he thought, "Why should I? I meant it. Not for him—maybe—but for the others." He went across the room with Texas to Bill, who stood in front of his easel sketching a girl who sat on a large red hassock.

When he looked toward the kitchen again, Max stood leaning against the doorjamb. His expressionless gaze told Kern nothing. As Kern watched, he sipped from the glass in his hand and turned back into the kitchen.

Kern forgot Max Karns. He forgot Jeff Balanchine and Texas and Bill. The girl was the only real thing in the room. He tried to remember what Bill had called her but he could not.

"Marianne—this is Kern—Kern, Marianne." As simple as that. She spoke over her shoulder.

"Hi—gotta cigarette?"

"Don't give her one. She smokes too much now." Bill squinted at her quickly over the tip of a charcoal stick.

"Your head—your head!"

"I know. I've moved the damned thing again. I can't keep it still, Bill." Kern watched Bill readjust the set of her head. He could feel Texas' eyes on him, but nothing mattered to him except to watch this girl.

Her hair was thick. Short and curly, it came to a point at the nape of her neck. Standing close to her, he could see the coppery lights that ran through it.

"What does he do?"

Texas nudged him, "She said what do you do?"

"I write."

126

"He writes."

The hair at her temples was fine—like smoke.

"What does he write—for whom?"

"You know—you tell her." He did not turn to look over his shoulder at Texas as he traced the startling upward flare of one dark brow. From where he stood, Kern could see almost three quarters of Marianne's face—the width of it and her eyes, so blue that they seemed to be violet. Her eyes were fixed on some target Bill had given her on the far wall.

"What does he look like?"

Her nose was snub and her long upper lip was thin—as though it caught at her teeth in reproof of her other lip's fullness. Her chin was rounded and determined.

"He's tall. And his hair is black—and curly. Almost as curly as yours—" Texas went on describing him to Marianne.

She wore a simple black dress. Full at the shoulders, banded tightly at her absurdly small waist by a wide gold belt, flaring at her hips. She wore thin-heeled ankle straps. Kern started at her head again.

Her hair—

"—and he looks sorta like Lincoln, only—" Tex's voice warned Kern that she was about to twit him, "he's gorgeous, Marianne." The flame ran up Kern's neck to his face. It was there when she turned, wide-eyed, to look at him. "The wise guys," Kern thought, "the wise guys say it can't happen like this. But it can." He knew it could as his heart pounded, because it was happening.

Her lips were half parted as her eyes met his. Then a curious little smile touched the corners of her mouth and she stood and came toward him. When he was to remember her later, Kern knew it would be like this—all eyes. Wide eyes—standing and coming toward him. She extended her hand casually as she stopped in front of him.

"Give me a cigarette, please." Kern took a pack from his pocket and shook it, then extended it to her. She glanced down as she drew a cigarette out and looked back at him.

"Thanks. Ol' Marse Legree won't let me smoke." Bill dropped his charcoal on the easel and scrubbed at his hands with a towel.

"C'mon, Tex." Mock resignation filled his voice. "Every time I get a model, someone comes along and steals her away."

* * *

The window corner beyond the easel was miles away from the party. In another world. There were just the two of them. Kern thought, "We couldn't be more alone if we were standing together in this downpour in the middle of Central Park." Their talk was tentative and shy and Kern learned many things about Marianne in a very short while. He learned the shape of her face and memorized the curving line of her lips. Her full name was Katharine Marianne Benson.

"—I don't use Katharine. Why? No reason. I just never liked it, I guess." Her smile was crooked and she laughed with her eyes. She had been born in Horton, Kansas. Her mother and two brothers still lived there. One brother was a high-school principal. The other was in the Navy.

"Dad died when I was a youngster." She liked Sibelius and cold beer. And being "very, very quiet." She was a mannequin and she wanted to be a model, "—but no one has discovered me—"

Without admitting it, either of them, both were sharply aware of what was happening. They moved toward love and the world and the room were a million miles away and they were the only realities—they and the drum of rain on the skylight above them.

❀ ❀ ❀

Then a strumming chord hung in the air and died away, and Jeff Balanchine's voice filled the space it had left. They looked toward where he half stood, half leaned against a table, his eyes watching his fingers as he tuned the guitar. The other sounds died out. His deep baritone voice filled the room. It filled each corner of the room and rushed up to the ceiling. It crowded against the darkness on the other side of the skylight. It silenced the rain and rebounded, in overtones that reached into their hearts. Jeff sang ballad after ballad. A waiting silence followed. Then Jeff began again.

"Swing low, sweet chariot—comin' for to carry me home—" His smile was gone. His eyes were fixed on something within himself. Kern knew a part of what he was seeing. He knew that Jeff was looking at the things that were behind the doors he had closed on his own past. Memories he had been determined to shut out of his own life—or tried to, until he had started to write the story. The torrent of memory swelled in him and he felt a hot prickle behind his eyes as they filled with tears. No one about him moved. He was fixed to the spot. At his shoulder Marianne's breathing deepened. Jeff's voice died out and gradually the rain sound came

128

into the room again. Kern could feel Marianne's eyes on his averted face. Still no one moved. Kern heard Balanchine's voice still tearing at him. He knew the things the man was feeling must be kin to his own flood of remembering—things that these people about him could never fully understand, no matter how they might try. The whole past tore at him.

Then Marianne's fingers touched his arm. And he began to hate Balanchine. To hate him for having torn open the floodgates of remembering. Marianne—standing near him, suddenly meant the things he had denied himself, the right to love—the need to have her as his own—Marianne was the emotion he had shied away from, knowing that when it came, it would bring with it the need for honesty, for facing squarely the thing he had hidden from. His whole mind protested the unfairness of remembering at this moment.

"He's tremendous!" Marianne's voice, her low words, were a salute. Kern knew that he was tremendous. He was magnificent. He was—the barrier he had taught himself, of scorn and anger at Negroes sprang to involuntary life—he was a Negro.

He answered Marianne, his voice low and grating with anger and self-scorn and despair.

"I suppose so. Coons just have more music in them." He felt her hand fall away from his arm as she spoke on a shocked outbreath.

"No—!" The word held disgust and disbelief. Kern felt his own anger rise. At himself. At Balanchine for having caused this. Marianne stood before him, her eyes searching his face, puzzled frown lines on her forehead. "How disappointing. That wasn't what I saw in your face when you were listening."

"I'm sorry—" Kern wondered what she had really seen in his eyes.

She shook her head slowly. "No, you're not really sorry."

Jeff started again.

"Go down, Moses—way down in Egypt lan'—tell ol' Pharaoh, let my people go—"

Again silence. And the waiting. And, for Kern, searching for something to say, something that could convince this girl that he wasn't, didn't . . . something that would break the wall that had risen between them. When the song was ended, when he spoke again, his regret was real. It was in his voice and on his face, filling his eyes. And Marianne saw it.

"—truly, I am sorry. It was a stupid thing to have said."

Her hand touched his arm and her eyes forgave him.

129

CHAPTER VI

PAULA—JUNE, 1930

HE COULD cope with Nettie. Nettie was bad enough, but had he to choose between Nettie and this "Aunt Paula" he would take Nettie. He knew Nettie. He could always go to his room and slam the door and shut Nettie out. But this strange Aunt Paula was someone he had never seen. He did not know what to expect of her.

"Your Aunt Paula will be here for your graduation." His father had told him that a month ago as he read from his sister's letter. "She's going to spend the whole summer here."

That night Kern had begun to imagine the first of countless pictures of his Aunt Paula. All during the month of May, he tried to imagine what she would be like, balancing her threat to his freedom against the known danger of Nettie. Most of his visions of Aunt Paula were shaped in the image of his father. In the best of them all, she was a dour old maid of uncertain age, even more of a tyrant than his father.

Paula was a surprise. She seemed to laugh all of the time. She was laughing as she swung down from the train and pressed something into the porter's hand. She was laughing when she threw her arms around Kern's father, calling him "Wobbie" to his dismay, and to Kern's utter surprise. The flowing crowd turned and craned their necks to stare and admire and be confused.

Paula, when Kern first saw her, was a willowy, tall girl, with a wealth of shining black hair worn in a heavy knot on her neck. She was a golden-brown girl with features remarkably like her brother's. They were the same features, with soft lines where his father's were hard—with rounded surfaces where his were angular planes. Paula was an unusually beautiful young woman—and with an unconscious grace, she accepted stares as her due. Kern stared in disbelief as she laughed and chatted with his father.

She turned quickly from Charles to touch a redcap on the arm, pointing out her bags.

"Yes, ma'am. Yes, ma'am!" She turned to them and took Kern's

131

hand. She studied his face with laughter still recognizable in her eyes.

"And you're Kern." Kern grinned at her shyly, his eyes level with hers, and was pleasantly confused as she put her arm around him. Paula laughed, "I'm sure we are going to be great friends."

And they were great friends from that first evening when they sat together at the dinner table and Paula chatted easily with Nettie, becoming acquainted as she went back and forth between the table and the kitchen. She rattled along at a rapid pace with Charles about Valley View and her job and about the League. For the first time he could remember, Kern heard a Negro talk about "the problem" without desperate hopelessness and a voice of anger. He relaxed.

Kern shared secret after secret with Paula and she was quick to feel his need for companionship. She became a buffer between him and his father and Nettie. She bought him his first long-pants suit, chiding Charles for his insistence that Kern would do well enough in knickers.

Kern wore the suit to his graduation exercises and listened gravely as his father spoke to his graduating class and to the assembled parents. When the ceremony was over he threaded his way through the crowd about the auditorium door and went directly to where Paula waited. They joined Charles and stood talking for a moment with Miss Washington before going out into the summer night. They walked slowly home, Paula in between them.

At home, Kern hurried upstairs to wash the program ink from his hands. He came back down the stairs to the dining room and stopped short at the door. His eyes widened with excitement. The mellow glow of the table lamp filled the room. His father stood behind his chair, watching him with a speculative gaze as he came into the room. In the soft light about the base of the lamp, twelve candles burned steadily in tiny holders. Kern stopped still staring. On the table before his chair, were four packages, tied with colorful bows and arranged in a little half circle.

"Gee!" He gulped and reached out to touch the ribbons on the packages.

"Gee!" He looked at his father. "Gee! A party. I never had a party before." He read the names on the cards beneath the ribbons. "From your Father." "Congratulations and love—Paula." Love!

132

From Paula! "Nettie." Just the name. "Good luck—Grandmother and Grandfather." His grandparents had remembered!

Nettie came into the room, smiling for once. She drew out the chair opposite Kern's father and started to sit down as Paula came into the room carrying a tray of dishes piled high with ice cream.

"Don't sit there—that's my mother's chair." The words popped from Kern's mouth as he watched Nettie. Anger flared in his father. Nettie stood between the table and chair, half stooped to sit, then slowly rising erect. "Don't sit in my mother's chair."

Paula set the tray down and came quickly around the table. Hand on his shoulder, her eyes searched his face. She spoke to him quietly.

"May I sit there—just for tonight?"

Kern looked up at her. "I'd really like to, Kern." He smiled slowly. "Nettie can sit next to your father."

Nettie, thoroughly miffed, snatched her token from the table, tossed her head with a "Well!" and marched out to the kitchen.

It was not a nice party. In spite of heaping dishes of ice cream, a four-layer cake with icing and the gifts spread on the table, it was not a nice party. His father ate in silence and Kern found difficulty in answering Paula's questions. He could feel his father's reproof.

Later, Kern and Paula sat on the front porch as the night streets became silent. In the rear of the house, the lights went out and they heard Nettie laboriously making her way up to her room on the third floor.

"Kern—it wasn't very nice of you to have hurt Nettie tonight." Gentle reprimand was in Paula's voice and Kern wanted her to understand what he felt about Nettie.

"Nettie means well, Kern. It's just—well, that she hasn't had too much experience with boys and sometimes she may not seem to understand—"

"She doesn't like me."

"Kern!" The bluntness of his statement and the deep anger in his voice surprised Paula.

"But why, Kern? You *must* be wrong!"

"I'm not. She doesn't like me—that's all."

"But Kern, you must have a reason for saying that. Why? She cooks and sews and keeps house for your father and you—she has done so for years—"

"She's paid for that." Kern knew his voice was mean. He wished he could change it.

133

"Oh, look here now, young fellow—some things can't be bought. Faithfulness, friendship—"

"She doesn't like me—I know. She didn't like mama either."

"No!"

"She didn't—she hated mama."

"Kern—you must be wrong!"

"She hated mama and she hates me. She doesn't like us because we're lighter than she is. She said mama was tony."

"Oh, your mother could never have been tony—perhaps Nettie didn't say quite that!"

"She did. She said it lots of times. Said it to me too."

"But why did you shout at her, Kern?"

"She didn't have any business sitting in mama's chair."

"But—"

"I hate her—I hate her!"

"—because she's darker than you?" Kern shook his head vaguely, not wanting to answer. "She can't help her color, Kern. Look at me." She turned his head in the dim light to face her. "I'm much darker than you—almost as dark as Nettie—You don't hate me, do you?"

"Oh, no—not you! You're different. You're—you're you."

"Kern, it isn't really important that Nettie is darker than you, is it? It is something else, isn't it?" Her eyes questioned him. "It must be that she didn't like your mother—is that the reason that you don't like her?"

He shook his head in a slow affirmative. Paula was not convinced. Other things began to fall in place in her mind, pointing the answer to Kern's reticence and his angers.

❁　❁　❁

Paula was Kern's constant companion that summer, the first real companion he had known since his mother. She was someone to whom he could pour out his heart. No dream was too fantastic to win her listening ear. None so imaginative, that she could not add some special bit. And with every dream there was a caution, a reminder that the dreamer must keep his feet on the ground. That he must work to make his dreams come true. They picnicked and shopped and went to the movies together. Paula arranged special dinners and filled the house with new life. For both Kern, and for Charles, "coming home" had a new meaning.

134

One by one, she filled the rooms in the house with color, new drapes, pictures that Kern helped her choose, a touch here and a touch there, the whole making laughter in that house a more natural thing. Vases that had long stood empty on side tables were filled with cut flowers and sunlight poured into corners that Nettie had kept shaded for years. Not all of these changes were won without struggle. Nettie's objection was often stubborn. She grumbled loudly when Paula hung new drapes and raised the parlor shades.

"Ain't goin' do nuthin' but fade them drapes—didn't need no drapes no how." Paula laughingly put her off. "It doesn't matter. Charles can get some others when these fade. They'll be bright for a year or two anyhow."

Nettie stormily protested the idea of getting summer carpets. "Jes' a was'eful 'stravagance anyhow—all this changin'."

Paula's patience wore thin. "This house needs other changes, too." Her direct gaze and pointed words put an end to Nettie's objections. Nor did she go railing to Charles to contest Paula's decision.

Paula talked to Kern for hours about Valley View, the great Negro college in faraway Alabama, at which she taught. She shared his letters from his grandmother, and now and then added a line or two of greeting to his notes of reply.

* ° °

Margaret Adams had foreseen this thing years ago.

Before summer ended, Paula too saw what was happening to Kern and took sharp issue with Charles.

"But Charles, you know as well as I that this boy can't be left to just grow—he's not another Topsy! He needs care and sympathy—"

"Nettie cares for him. I certainly *try* to provide everything he needs—many of the things he wants—"

"I know, I know, Charles." She saw irritation rise in him. "I am not saying you don't provide—I know that you do. I see that all about the house. But the most important thing, he isn't getting."

"And what is that?" Charles' obvious distaste sharpened into words.

"Now listen to me, Charles. You know I wouldn't bring these things up unless I thought in all seriousness that they were im-

135

portant. You're just getting huffy because you know this thing should have been thought out a long time ago. Now you sit back and listen to me." Charles sat back to listen. Nettie, already listening in the hall, rolled her eyes at the bossiness of this new boss and scuttled for safety.

"What Kern needs most is companionship. He isn't getting it."

"He has had plenty of chances to find companionship among the children he grew up with. But what has he done? He can't make friends—what few he does make, he loses. He has all the time any boy needs to get his work done. But does he get it? No. 'Bs' and 'Cs.' Everything he needs is provided for him, clothes, books, food—everything that I had to fight for when I was his age."

"But he isn't *you*, Charles—and he won't be. He's cut from a different cloth." She leaned forward to face him. "He's a dreamer. You can't bottle up that sort of energy. You can only try to direct it along intelligent lines. Give it a little sympathetic understanding. He can just as easily become a scientist as a writer. But he can't be driven to become anything. Try to do that and you will turn him inward on himself. You'll lose him and you will lose control of the impulses that make him tick."

"If he is going to be that irresponsible, then there is nothing I could do in the first place."

Paula's eyes widened at her brother's angry words.

"You can't mean that, Charles. It's not a question of responsible or irresponsible. Kern is a boy—a child. You are a grown man. Don't let resentment at hearing the truth make you determined to be right. You have been telling me that is one of the reasons prejudice is hard to root out. Kern is unfortunate in many ways. He met with a hard wall of resentment at school after the Jeff Mason trial. You should recognize that. He was a little boy then. He didn't know anything about the artificial responsibility of race which Negroes felt should have guided him. He was a boy whose dearest friend, his mother, had been taken from him and he simply told the truth. Even if he had known it was a racial issue, what else could he have done?"

Paula continued more slowly as Charles' face became impassive.

"Kern met with resentment at school from teachers—and from parents through their children. He has met it from Nettie right here in this house when he came home. He felt it in you when you turned away from the 'silly things' that were most important to

136

him. Remember how terribly you wanted to go to school and become an artist when you were a little boy? And how you were heartbroken when Uncle Will laughed at the idea?"

"That was just a child's fancy," Charles scoffed.

"You haven't forgotten it. And don't tell me you weren't heartbroken. I'm your sister—I remember how you cried."

"But I realized that it was impractical to be an artist."

"Why try to fit a man's afterthought to a boy's hurt? You know how much it disappointed you!"

"But this idea about writing is just foolishness." Charles held doggedly to his point.

"Maybe. Who can say? It is a child's ambition. It may outgrow itself. But try to bludgeon it with silence and scorn and you will only make it more determined to live. And Nettie—" Charles' eyebrows rose.

"Nettie will never be able to give Kern companionship and understanding. He has an unhealthy antagonism for her. No matter how it came about, it *does* exist and it *will* get *worse*. Nettie can't, and wouldn't, if she could, understand the interests he is using to fill up the most important spaces in his life. Kern needs the certainty that someone understands, that he is important to someone. He doesn't have that. Nettie is all right, I guess. Faithful, honest, she has most of the negative virtues. She keeps a fair house, according to her own lights—which are old-fashioned at best." Paula rose and stood before him.

"Just think about this. Something has got to change or that boy will do something that both of you will be sorry for." She turned to the door and then seeing his gloomy face, went around the corner of the desk to stand behind him and cross her arms around his neck.

"Dear old 'Wobbie,' don't sit there all frowned up. The world hasn't come to an end. I didn't mean to trouble you. You have enough on your mind, running the League and everything. And I know how important that is, but don't forget—Kern is important too."

❀　❀　❀

It seemed to Kern that only days had passed since Paula came and now she was gone back to Valley View and another year of teaching. Kern placed the picture she had given him on the end of his dresser, half turned to face his mother's photograph. Often, after that, he sat staring at the black-haired, laughing girl within the picture's frame.

Kern was in love—with the complete abandon of a boy of twelve —with the unforgettable sweet longing that only a boy can know for that first, unattainable woman.

CHAPTER VII

THE CONTEST—JULY, 1933

I

KERN felt a chill of apprehension as he saw the green stub of a ticket and the theater program that Nettie casually dropped on the table between him and his father. Somehow, he thought, the chill he felt and the clinking ice in his half-raised glass were very much alike. Nettie stood across the table from him, hands deep in her apron pockets, and her voice was filled with mock concern when she spoke.

"I mos' throwed that out, Kern. Jes' caught myse'f in time." Kern saw that she was looking at his father. For a scant second her eyes flickered to his and went back to his father. Kern saw the maliciousness in them and thought, "Damn you, Nettie—you've been prowling in my things again." Charles looked up from his paper with a frown on his face at the interruption.

It seemed to Kern that everything he did won his father's disfavor—just as he knew that this would win his displeasure. And Nettie's too—nothing he ever did satisfied Nettie. "Damn Nettie," he thought for the ten-thousandth time. "Damn Nettie!" No matter what he did, Nettie found fault with it and, without exception, she carried tales to his father.

"Was impudent—yes, sir, that's what he was——"

"Jes' cain't keep this here place tidy when he traipses in dirt alla time——"

"—always late——"

"—jes' ack'ed like he ain't heard me——"

"—was pryin' in my personal business an' I don' like it!"

Each time, Charles listened to Nettie's complaint before forming an opinion—then he heard Kern's side of the story. Then—without fail, it seemed to Kern—he administered rebuke. Kern had long since stopped telling his side at all. He found that it did not matter what he said. He found, too, that it did not matter to him what his father

139

said. He very seldom heard his father anyhow. Instead, he had learned to stand quietly before him, with a penitent expression on his face, moulding it to suit the need of the moment, as Charles ranged from mild scolding to harsh reprimand. Kern had learned to stand or sit like that and to let his mind focus on his hatred for Nettie or on whatever else had held his interest the moment before his father began, as Nettie put it, "to bless him out."

"Knew you'd want to keep it. Don' rightly know how it got in the trash." Satisfied that she had aroused Charles' curiosity with so much ado about a theater program, Nettie went into the kitchen, taking pains to leave the door open so that she and George Lincum could hear Kern get his "comeuppance."

Staring at the ticket, Kern gulped down the last mouthful of food on his plate. At least he wouldn't be sent from the table without being able to finish his dinner. The program! How had she found it? He knew that—by prowling. But when—how long had she had it? He had not seen it himself in months. Had not even thought of it in fact. But there it was. On the table between them. Solid block letters across the top of the program spelled out the name of the theater.

HIPPODROME

Damn Nettie!

presents
RICHARD EVANS

He knew his father was staring at the program too.

in
HAMLET
"The Melancholy Dane"

Damn Nettie! Damn George Lincum, too!

Even in the face of his father's certain anger, Kern remembered the night he had seen *Hamlet* with a magic thrill. The program twitched before his eyes, then disappeared as his father took it into his hands.

"What is this, Kern?"

"Just a theater program." Christ! Kern hoped that his father wasn't going to lecture him all day. He wanted to get back to his room and

140

finish copying the page of rules for the Evans Writing Contest which he had left on his desk.

"I know very well it is a theater program." Charles' rumbling voice warned Kern against any further flippancy. "Did you see this play?" Kern nodded his head and set his face in lines of regret that he hoped would match his father's dark scowl.

"Where did you see it?"

"At the Hippodrome."

"When?"

"Last November."

"Who went with you?"

"I went by myself."

"Did you know that Negroes are not allowed in the Hippodrome?"

"I didn't—yes, sir."

"Then why did you go there?" Charles' voice was icy and biting.

"I wanted to see Richard Evans in *Hamlet*."

"A whole race is being segregated and *you* wanted to see Richard Evans in *Hamlet!*" Irritation filled his father's indrawn breath. "You knew the policy of this theater——"

Nettie in and out of the kitchen, clearing the table, wore an expression of surprise that she could have unknowingly caused this disturbance.

Kern's eyes remained respectfully lowered to the table top. His mind was on the Evans contest rules. He had more than a half page to copy yet. He could almost remember what he had copied thus far word for word.

Contestants may submit original stories, one act plays, radio scripts or verse. All entries are limited to five thousand words or to one half-hour of playing time. No adult assistance of any kind is permissible. All entrants are required to submit an affidavit to the effect that this stipulation has been complied with. Entries will be addressed to "The Scholarship Board, Evans Academy, White Ridge, Vermont." Deadline for entries is September 1 of the year preceding the schoolyear in which a scholarship is sought."

"Did they stop you at the door—ask you any questions?"

"No, sir. I just paid for my ticket and walked in."

"So." Charles aped his words, larded them with sarcasm. "You just paid for your ticket and walked in, did you?" He leaned forward across the table, "And who are you to 'just walk in' when grown men are insulted at the door and refused entrance to a public place?" Kern made no attempt to answer. "Let me tell you this—" Kern switched his mind to the contest rules. He had promised Mr. Cameron that he would return them when class started after the week end. Rod Cameron was his Dramatics teacher. He was an Evans graduate, too, and he had told Kern and his classmates about the Evans contest. Tall, intense, likable Rod Cameron was Kern's favorite teacher. He had made Kern's second year of high school an especially happy one. Kern took two subjects under him—Dramatics and Basic Principles of Writing and Staging. Kern's eyes watched his father sit back in his chair and he switched his attention back to what he was saying.

"Kern—understand me—you are a traitor to your race. I have only contempt for traitors. You are a Negro—lighter skinned than most— but a Negro all the same. You must accept that fact. You cannot escape reality by running into hotels and theaters. You are a Negro." Charles paused. "Doesn't that mean anything to you?" His voice almost pleaded with Kern. The boy knew that Nettie and George Lincum were listening and enjoying this.

"Yes, sir. It means something to me." He bit his tongue. It would do no good to tell his father what being a Negro did mean to him. He could not tell him that each day, being a Negro was having more meaning for him in terms of frustration and despair, doubt and hurt and insecurity. In fact, Kern did not recognize the separate feelings himself.

"I wasn't trying to escape anything, sir—I just wanted to see a play. I didn't mean to pass as white. I couldn't see any reason I should not have seen the play." Impetuously, he raced on under his father's unbelieving stare, "I got my money's worth and then I came home. And I wasn't the only Negro there either." His father's eyes narrowed at this information.

"No! And who else did you see there?"

Kern sensed his disbelief. "Reverend Sharp's wife," he blurted the name and felt a triumph as his father gaped. The Reverend was an important figure in the Freedom League.

"I don't believe you," Charles contradicted him angrily. "You are not only a traitor, you are a liar too." Kern jerked erect in his chair, eyes suddenly hot and angry.

"I am not a liar. I don't lie. You told me yourself that if I had to lie to a man, then that man was not worth talking to at all."

He was then Charles' own son. So much like Charles that the man

142

recognized his own image. Angry. Determined. Charles rose and walked through the hallway. Whatever else, he knew Kern was not telling a lie.

✿　✿　✿

Damn Nettie! Kern muttered the words fervently in the closed-door quiet of his room. Then he pushed the theater incident out of mind, filing it with the other things he had done in the past that had infuriated his father. He could almost mark the passage of time by those unpleasant episodes.

The essay he had written in first-year English Composition was one stark memory. He had been assigned to write a "critical" essay about the Negro and he had done so. He had written about the complaints he had heard his father and the Reverend share—what they called "—a tragedy—" the refusal of Negroes to openly recognize their own faults and to correct them without delay; the continuous effort of Negroes to persuade themselves and others that they were blameless and rarely ever at fault; that they were "put upon."

He had written those things into his "critical" essay. Had he been anyone other than Charles Roberts' son, had his father not been the head of the Freedom League, his composition would not have won such bitter criticism. Perhaps, even, it might have won praise.

For two weeks afterward, however, to his father's extreme embarrassment, two local Negro papers carried stories on his essay. One headline said:

SCION OF LEAGUE HEAD SAYS NEGROES DISHONEST

For two weeks Kern had puzzled at the bitter criticism which Negroes visit upon themselves in secret and could not understand their refusal to ever "publicly" admit a wrong. Then he forgot the matter.

Kern sighed and dropped into the chair before his desk. Propping his feet on the drop-leaf top, he stared out of the window into space. The thin irritation he had felt at his father's parting words faded. Only five minutes old in his ears, the words might as well never have been said.

"You are a traitor to your race." Charles had said that.

Kern's eyes and his full attention swung from the space beyond the window to the desk before him. He dropped his feet to the floor and drew the sheet of contest rules to him.

✿　✿　✿

143

Fifteen months seemed like a lifetime ahead in the future. Kern checked his figures again, counting the months on his fingers. Fifteen months was right. It was August now. Kern knew that. His father had just returned from the annual July National Convention of the League. If he finished his story and submitted it before September 1, he still would not be able to go to Evans until next October. "Able to go——" Rod Cameron's words came back to him to temper his optimism.

"Evans is one of the most unusual schools in America. It specializes in training writers. To win an Evans scholarship, you have really got to be good. Thousands of boys all over the country try for those ten scholarships each year. If you win though, if you do good work at Evans, your scholarship may be extended beyond the 'prep' school stage to cover two years of Junior college."

Kern slid lower in his chair and stared at the ceiling, the tip of his pencil rotating slowly against one finger tip. "Yes, sirree—" he'd have to tell Paula and his grandmother about this.

An Evans man!

II

Kern's story grew out of a puzzling question—a question which had come to his mind often in the past two years. A question that filled his mind each time he stood in school to recite the Pledge of Allegiance—each time he looked about him in class and in the halls at school and saw only Negro faces. A question that had become centered around that part of the pledge that said, "—one Nation, indivisible, with liberty and justice for all." "—for all—" Kern had for some time entertained doubts that liberty and justice were "—for all." "Jim Crow" in Washington, the Capital of the Nation, did not seem to him to be "liberty and justice for all." But then, he supposed such things were written into the Constitution and the Bill of Rights just for white boys and girls.

White boys and girls!

Kern wondered what white boys and girls thought when they recited the Pledge. He wondered what they thought about anything.

He had tried for a long time to reason an answer to the question.

"I don't know what a white boy thinks I think."

"I don't know what he thinks but I think I know what I think

144

he thinks." He never arrived at a satisfactory conclusion and the whole thing remained a cloudy, puzzling mystery.

Kern decided to tell a story about these "strangers". He groped toward telling what life might be like if the strangers did not have to go to separate schools all of their lives—if they came to know one another, to know the hopes and fears they shared, to know the absurdity of the notions they held about one another.

The story became football and baseball and basketball for him. It took the place of dances and parties and filled his idle days.

* * *

Two weeks after Kern began his story, Paula wrote telling them that she was going to marry a man named James Caulfield, and it seemed to Kern that his entire world had come to an end. "How could she?" He asked this question time and again in the course of his short-lived heartbreak. It took more than a month for his broken heart to mend. But not much more.

In October, less than a week after school had begun, exactly one month after Kern had mailed his carefully prepared manuscript to Evans, Margaret Adams called from Northport to tell them that Caleb had died in his sleep. For the second time that Kern could remember, he saw his father shudder with a grief that brought tears to his eyes.

"A great man—a very great man." Numb with shock, Kern knew his father's murmured words were a tribute to the fiery little judge. For an instant the bond of sympathy between father and son bridged the gulf that held them apart. In the next instant it was gone and the space between them was wider than it had been before.

The gulf never closed. Instead, it grew steadily wider and deeper during Kern's third year of high school. Charles, on more than one occasion, pronounced to Kern his feeling that "it was high time" you got down to something practical and left this drama business alone. It is," he sternly said, "not a good vocational choice for Negroes. You can't make a living at it."

More and more Charles left Kern's supervision to Nettie. Thus, as Kern and his father grew apart, the boy's resentment at Nettie—and at her "boy friend" George Lincum, whom he suspected of prompting Nettie in much of her hostility—deepened to hatred. And too, in the face of his father's unexplained resistance, Kern's interest in writing became a determined ambition.

145

In January, just before the last semester of the school year began, Rod Cameron took Kern's Dramatics class to New York to attend a National High School Dramatics Association meeting. For three and a half days, almost unable to believe that his father had consented to his coming, Kern attended forums, listened to writers, producers and critics, saw two first-run plays and began to distinguish in his speech between "legitimate theater" and moving pictures. He was introduced to a star actress and went sight-seeing in New York.

When he returned to Washington, his devotion to the goal of becoming a writer had been whetted to a keenness that none of Charles' demurs could dull. For weeks, Kern basked in the delightful memories of that journey and not even the insulting words a Southern boy had spoken, when Myra Holcombe—the star of "Our Hearts Together"—had shaken hands with some of the Negro students, could detract from the pleasure of his memories.

III

Kern shifted at his desk as the bell jangled and listened for Nettie's steps in the downstairs hall. The bell pealed a second time, loud, at the foot of the stairs. No steps. Again the bell rang, insistently. A chair scraped in his father's study and Kern pushed away from his desk and went quickly down the hall. "Darn Nettie anyway. Where is she? I'll bet she's sitting in the kitchen with George Lincum with the doors closed so she couldn't hear. Damn her and damn George Lincum too."

He shivered as he stepped into the cold vestibule and twisted the door key. Below the drawn shade, the porch light showed the gray-blue trouser leg of a postman. Special Delivery. Probably something for his father. Kern was familiar with the letters and wires that so often came bringing news of "incidents," a lynching or a Klan raid, from beleaguered Negroes calling for legal aid from the League. Behind him Nettie came through the dining room patting at her hair.

"Somebody at the door?" Kern answered over her shoulder. "You know somebody was there—back there petting with that pimp."

He heard the hiss of Nettie's indrawn breath. She came closer to him.

"Don't you never talk to me like that!"

"Shut up!" Kern snarled at her as he twisted the knob and opened the door. The postman held a pad and a pencil forward.

146

"Kern Roberts live here? Special Delivery—sign here."

He scrawled his name in a rectangle of space and took the letter. The postman's feet thumped down the steps and his car door banged shut. Kern shut the storm door and the hallway door and stood under the hall light studying the crest on the envelope as the car gears rasped to life in the street.

Arms akimbo, Nettie stood before him, her anger yielding to curiosity as she eyed the letter.

"Who's it from? Lemme see." She stretched a hand forward and Kern looked down at her as he turned aside.

"It is addressed to me." He thrust the envelope under her eyes. "But you couldn't read it if it *was* for you." He saw her anger with glee and carefully opened the envelope. The folded page held two brief, typewritten paragraphs.

My dear Mr. Roberts:

It is our great pleasure to advise you that the Board of Judges has selected your story, STRANGERS, as a prize winner in the annual Evans' Scholarship Competition. I have been asked especially to congratulate you on the intensity of feeling contained in your story and the unusual manner in which you controlled it. The Judges are unanimously of the opinion that STRANGERS showed rare strength for a lad of your years.

If you care to accept the one year scholarship at Evans which we tender herewith, we shall deeply appreciate your advising us of your decision before August 1 of the forthcoming school year.

Very sincerely,
Donald H. Carstairs
Headmaster

Kern dropped into a hallway chair. He couldn't believe his eyes. But it was true! The letter, the proof, was in his hands.

Evans!

The dream he had almost been afraid to dream had come true. Puzzled by the delight on his face, Nettie watched as he reread the page. Then Kern remembered his father—he could almost see him standing in the upstairs hall, leaning against the bannister, waiting to learn what the letter was about. Kern rose and started across the hall, turning on the landing and slowing as he saw his father's feet and knew that he was waiting. The motionless, planted

147

feet were forbidding. A finger of doubt began to shape in him.
He slowed to a walk.

"Well—what was it, Kern?"

"A Special Delivery for me." Kern stopped on the uppermost step.

"From your Aunt Paula?"

"No sir," he held the envelope forward to his father.

Charles took it and stood looking down at him.

"Kern—I want you to know that I sternly disapprove of your
speaking to Nettie in the tone of voice which I heard you using."
Charles silenced his answer with a wave of his hand. "I don't know
what you were saying, but whatever it was, it was not spoken in
a tone of respect."

The flood of anger that always came with the thought of obedi-
ence to Nettie filled Kern. "What was he supposed to respect in
Nettie?" He held his peace. Too much lay in the balance of the
next few minutes to risk angering his father.

"I'm sorry, sir."

His father turned toward his room. At his desk he read the letter
through as Kern stood and watched his face for a hint of what he
was thinking.

Deliberately, his father reread the letter and turned the sheet to
inspect the blank rear side. He studied the envelope's crest, then
replaced it on the desk in front of him before turning his eyes to
the letter again. Slowly Kern realized that objection was facing
him. Questions raced through his head as he recalled each detail
of his father's resistance to his ambition to write. Would he feel
this was just an effort to get away from being a Negro? Would his
father think that he wanted to go to a New England school just to
shirk his "responsibility to the Negro race"? He tried to remember
what his "responsibility" was. He could not remember. Why is
father's face so stern? Doesn't he know that if a Negro was given
the choice of his race at the time of his birth, it was almost certain
that he would never have been a Negro—would not have knowingly
taken up the burden of trouble which came with the color of his
skin?

Please God—make him let me go. To go to Evans was suddenly
dear to Kern. His father saw the question in his eyes.

"Kern," he began slowly, spacing his words, "I have tried time
and time again to discourage you from this idea of writing—tried
to get your feet on solid ground. I have tried to show you that the
cold fact of the matter is that writing is not a vocation which offers

148

security to a Negro youth. You fail to see that. You persist in wasting time and money. I reconciled myself to your taking a mass of English and Dramatics in high school—if nothing else you may at least become a teacher, perhaps even in some college. But you persist in flying in the face of experience." This much Kern knew—he had heard it so often before. It meant "No!" He knew the word was coming.

"Another thing—you can't get along with people. You have proven that time and time again. Not even with people right here in your own home. You are a stranger to children your own age living in this very block. I can't let you go away to school—even if it costs nothing in dollars and cents—not knowing these things. Besides being a waste of your time, I'm afraid to let you go because I can't count on your stability. I can't——"

The recitation went on. Tears flooded Kern's eyes and spilled over on his face, ran down his quivering chin. He could not keep them back. He stood there, shoulders trembling, his gaze averted from his father's eyes.

"It's very nice for you to have won this little contest and I am glad you did. Glad to know that you can write fairly well. You deserve that knowledge as a reward for the effort you must have put into this story. But I want you to be man enough to accept this thing in its proper perspective—just as—well, as you got over Paula's being married." Charles sighed. He knew that he was not reaching the boy. "I must say no. I have a responsibility to see that you receive a practical, worth-while education."

Charles stood up and moved around the corner of his desk. Kern twisted aside from the hand that would have rested on his shoulder and ran down the hall to his room. He slammed his door behind him.

It wasn't fair! His father shouldn't have mentioned Paula. That was the sort of thing that men didn't talk about—even when they knew. And he had no right to take away this chance he'd won to go to a real school. Who was he to say that he shouldn't have this chance? It *wasn't* just a little school and it hadn't been just a *little* contest. It had been a national contest.

Why did he have to stay in Washington and grow up in his father's footsteps—in the footsteps of all the other Freedom Leaguers—and become a "professional hater," always fighting, eating his heart out with anger and despair and hate when he wanted to write stories?

149

He thought of the hours of work and writing and the dreams that had gone into "Strangers."

And remembered too the ambition he had felt when Rod Cameron had first told his Dramatics class about Evans. In a small, broken voice in the darkness of the room, Kern said over and over, "I will. He won't stop me. I'll show him. I hate him! I hate him!" The thought shaped on his lips in small silent words as he drifted toward sleep.

* * *

Head in hands, the tired man sat in his study, trying to convince himself that what he had done was right. Remembering another man and another school and another dream.

His own dream. He, the boy. He asked himself time after time— "Have I done the right thing—what else could I do?"

Wishing that there was some way in which he could mend the gap between his son and himself.

Wishing.

* * *

His father's denial of his chance to go to Evans rankled in Kern through the balance of the summer. In his bitterness, he neglected to correspond his intentions to the Evans authorities. He brooded on the "unfairness" of the decision and the gap between his father and himself widened until the two of them actually became strangers—going so far as to consciously try to dine at different times to avoid being thrown together any more often than was necessary.

When they were brought together, the denial lay between them— almost visible in the stiff awkwardness of question and answer. For Nettie too, Kern's anger became hot and deep. He tightened his lips against the things which he would have said had he spoken—though for Nettie the knowledge of the disappointment he was suffering had a reverse effect, clothing her words and her attitude toward him with a smugly complacent "I told you so."

Only with Rod Cameron, and in Rod's classes, did Kern remain unchanged, finding in the stage and in writing—and in the Summer Theater after school ended—the same keen delight he had known before the letter came from Evans. During that summer, the Summer Theater sobered his angers and gradually relaxed the tensions that writhed in him until, by late July, Kern was almost his old self again.

IV

"But Nettie, I've got to eat early. Rehearsal is at three 'clock and Rod Cameron says we won't be finished until after even."

"Shoulda tol' me this mornin'. I ain't got nothin' I can fix in such a little while. 'Sides it's too all-fired hot and I intends to get me a little rest." Nettie turned her back on him and faced George Lincum where he sat, leaning back against the wall, heels hooked on the rung of a chair. "Whatchu say, George L.?"

"I says if'n we goin' to that dance tonight—make up yo min'. I gotta get outa here an' git to humpin'. Gotta pick up the rest of my numbers." Nettie pondered her decision.

"Nettie!" The raw, shaky edge in Kern's voice brought her around, hands set on her hips. Truculence was in her glittering eyes.

"Yes?"

"I want something to eat and I want it now."

"Oh," she simpered, "so you wants something to eat an' you wants it now?" George Lincum leaned forward with a thump, grinning at the scene. "Well, let me tell you sumpin', Mr. High an' Mighty—you ain't goin' to get it. I'm servin' my nex' meal at five-thirty when your Pa comes home. If you ain't here—that jes' too bad!"

The long-fed anger seethed in Kern.

"I live here and this is *my* house. You're just a cook and you're supposed to do as you are told." From the corner of his eye, he saw George Lincum straighten in his chair.

An anger of long years, of school and home, of bitterness and resentment grown from a thousand trifles, surged up in him. This was the woman who had hurt his mother. This was the woman who had hurt him. This was the woman whom his father treated as if she could do no wrong. This—this——!

"You're just a cook and you're not such a hot one at that. If you can't do as you are told, we can get another one."

Anger—too great to be answered by words alone. Demanding something else—demanding violence, demanding to hit and hurt and tear, to spend its raging storm. Anger—out of multiple slights and slurs and wrongs both done and fancied—out of "—half-white nigger" and "I ain't doin' no business with no niggers"—out of a first whipping and a theater program. Out of frustration. Anger which was not a cause but a result.

151

Kern's eyes ran over Nettie's face as the violence boiled in him. He glared down at her and she backed off a step before something she had seen before and recognized and saw again, now full-grown.

What words could tell this thing? Could satisfy the malice that shook him like palsy?

"You black—" His eyes took in Nettie's openmouthed face with satisfaction as the words drove home. Perversely driven to hurt, he used the very words that on other lips would have hurt him most. He felt, without seeing, George Lincum lunge at him around the edge of the table and half spun about as a hard fist glanced against the side of his ear and drove past his face. He spun against the radiator with a wrenching force that knocked his breath from him. He saw the man. No larger than he. If anything, a little smaller. But a man—with a man's anger and his face twisted in a way Kern had seen once before. He knew that this was anger and danger. This was no schoolboy with whom he could wrestle and win. Kern saw Jeff Mason's face and remembered the crazed glaring eyes. Terror struck at him. The mouth in front of him snarled.

"You little half-white bastard—talkin' and walkin' like you think you's God! I bet I beatcha Goddamn face in. Talkin' to my woman like that——"

The man came toward him step by step and Kern's hand flashed up to the rack above his shoulder.

The knife went easily into George Lincum's shoulder as he lunged. It grated against bone as it bit deep. Nettie screamed. Shocked and suddenly wild with pain, George stumbled back. Kern's stomach jerked with sickness as he watched the contorted face and Nettie hands pressed to her mouth, flattened herself against the cabinet and the wall and stared. They both saw the man's eyes widen, then narrow to slits. Saliva flecked his loose lips as he snatched the knife free.

"I'll cut you to bits—God damn you, you half-white son of—" Kern was terrified. George Lincum meant what he said. It was in his eyes and face, in every tense muscle of him. The door at Kern's back gave way and he wondered curiously how he had gotten to it. He stepped back onto the porch and felt the railing against his back. George Lincum stepped through after him and stood between him and the steps that led to the concrete areaway below. No escape down the steep narrow steps. Behind him and below him, ten feet below him, the concrete square of areaway. Nothing there either. No turning and climbing and jumping. It would have to be faced

152

out here on the bare porch with its washtub and the stand on which it sat and the——

His hand snatched the club from the tub and he raised it higher than the level of his shoulder and waited. He knew now what he must do. He waited until the man was a scant yard from him and started to strike. His mind was very clear as he stopped the blow short. Clear, as he saw the man's arm jump upward to ward off the blow. Clear, as he saw the arm stop and clear, as he struck, deliberately, savagely, down across the upraised, useless arm to the head and the shoulder. George sagged to his knees and to the porch floor, the knife falling from his hand, his fingers clawing for the foot before him. Kern kicked at the face. His foot hit it. He kicked the face again. When blood trickled from the gasping mouth he stopped. His terrible fright was gone. Only rage remained. And shook him.

Only rage when he stepped across the man and opened the door and, club in hand, stopped in front of Nettie.

Here was the core of it all. He stood before her, taller and wider now than Nettie had ever remembered seeing him. She saw a man instead of a boy. He stood there and she saw the incarnate hate in him, in his eyes, deep. Written on his face. A boy—taunted and stretched to this breaking point. She saw him and knew that she was not without guilt in what he had done and what he now felt. She wanted to back away and could not. The wall at her back and the cabinet were unyielding. She stood there, her eyes wide, and chewed at the knuckles of the hand that pressed against her mouth.

"Damn you, Nettie Hockins!" Kern drew a deep breath, then searched his memory—probed the filth of the streets and the wall of the boys' room at school and the barbershop—for words to vent on her the rage that was in him and that would not break to blows only because she was a woman. Nettie said nothing. Her lips worked as she mumbled "Don't hit me, don't hit me!"

"Get out of this house! Get out—and don't ever come back as long as you live!" His voice trembled and became a scream. "Get out—get out—you——"

The boy fumbled for something to call her, something more terrible than anything he had said before—something that would hurt her as a fist against her mouth would hurt her—something that would express the years—long hate that was in him in a tight knot.

"Get out you—you—you!"

153

Nettie turned and ran through the house to the street. He could hear her screams as they faded out in the street.

Then anger flooded out of him and Kern stood and shook. Trembling started in him and a retching that began deep down and boiled up and over in dizzy waves that shook him and shook him and left him no strength to move.

The club slid from his limp fingers and rattled on the floor. Then was still. Only his eyes could move and they went to where George Lincum lay on the porch.

o   o   o

More quickly than Paula, though no more surely, Juvenile Court Judge Mae Benson saw the deep-rooted cause of the whole affair and moved directly to a solution. Charles' frequent, often extended, absences from home; Nettie's overbearing attitude, coupled with her resentment for Kern—the boy's loneliness and his unhealthy introversion, his smouldering resentment at Nettie, all fell into a clear pattern before her.

Officially, Judge Benson found that Kern had struck Nettie's "George Lincum" Washington in self-defense and shortly thereafter the record of the case was closed. A tidal wave of publicity in the Negro press lasted one week. However, Charles was compelled to see the wisdom of allowing Kern to accept his scholarship to Evans, an alternative which Judge Benson supported wholeheartedly after an extended conversation with Rod Cameron and a telephone call which resulted in a visit from a certain Mrs. Dorcas Kuykendahl.

NEW YORK—DECEMBER, 1941

KERN and Marianne were right for one another. They were matched as two sides of a medal are matched. Right. Meant to be. Mind matched mind. Mood matched mood. Hands fitted into hands.

They were hand in hand whenever they were together. Not ostentatiously. Not calling attention to their joined hands, but naturally, in a way that told watchers, even before they could have seen, that these two would be hand-linked together. In time, they forsook the crowd at Bill's almost entirely, having no need for crowds, and being too, reluctant to meet the necessity crowds would impose for altering their mood—too much together and too selfish to want to share their minutes with others.

Little things filled the hours when they were together. The discovery of a shop window on Madison Avenue. A walk along the East River that ended in a particular tavern. Rinaldo's where chicken was broiled in white wine. The ferry trip to Staten Island. A shared line from a book that had a completely and deeply personal meaning. The enchantment of the city's streets late at night. Shared hopes and dreams.

During those days when the sidewalk throngs numbered more and more men in khaki and navy blue, when uniforms from other lands mingled with the attire of Manhattan and the Bronx and Brooklyn, Kern and Marianne went hand in hand, sharing their secret hopes. Marianne never once mentioned the dream which was now closest to her heart. For love was a word that neither of them used, preferring to leave it implicit in their eyes and fingers' meeting. Instead, for hours, she listened to Kern as he talked about the things that he wanted to write. She came to understand and to share the feeling he held for Dan Croom—and for others like him—and his restless unwillingness to accept the fact that so great a nation could view the destruction taking place on all sides and not give itself totally to war. Very often they needed no words. A sidelong glance, a tightening pressure of their fingers, sufficed to say the things that they felt. Kern's wilful mind closed out the past. He shelved the story he had begun to write months ago. With little or no coaxing, his mind refused to even consider the unpleasantness of the past and the angers the story had begun to rouse in him. Kern knew as he did so that he was not settling the issue of his past. He knew that it would have in time to be answered. But the future was indefinite and the present was important. And how was he to know, he told himself, that some miracle would not happen and relieve him of the necessity of ever facing the issue squarely.

Kern and Marianne were in love. And they were sure, as so many other lovers had been sure before them—were sure at this very instant in time—that there could never have been a love like theirs.

* * *

Something else slowed Kern's steps when he stepped out of the elevator—something more than shyness. The elevator door slid shut behind him and he stood in the carpeted silence of the hall and saw Marianne's door at the end of the hall and stared at it. He had tried to imagine how her apartment would look ever since she had insisted——

"I can cook! Tell you what—We'll have dinner here at my place tonight instead of going out—and I'll cook!"

That had been hours ago, since just before noon. Now Kern stood in the hall outside of her door. His watch said eight. Slowly he walked down the stretch of hall toward the door with the number "22." Words such as "improper" and "the right thing to do" ran through his head. He glanced at his watch again and it said one minute after eight. He stopped at the door and started to push his thumb against the bell button. Then he stopped and struggled to gain his composure, chiding himself at his nervousness. His thumb went to the bell button and pushed. Almost at once he heard the click of Marianne's heels against the floor as she came toward the door.

* * *

For a while, at first, he wandered from the living room to the kitchen and back again, with the feeling that he was an interloper. He studied the things about him with nervous interest—the pictures on the tables, the sketch of Marianne that Bill had done, hanging on the wall above the combination, the two racks filled with books in disorderly array. Slowly the feeling of "not belonging," the

156

uncertainty which had bothered him at first, faded out and he began to pretend that he was home. That he belonged here, that this was his Marianne—"his Marianne"—his mind played with the words with pleasure, and that shortly dinner would be ready. As it should be—a man and his woman, his wife. He realized that this was the first time he had consciously admitted to himself that he wanted to marry Marianne. He pondered the knowledge and saw that many times before he had thought the same thing, though always in other words. Something deep and gnawing in his mind touched at the delight of the thought—a something that he did not understand, and because the dream of marrying Marianne was too wonderful for trifles to matter, he pushed the gnawing thought into the back of his mind.

At dinner with candlesticks on the table and wine in their glasses, they knew a slow delight and a shyness such as they had never known before. Fewer words than they had ever known before. And because this was so, each of them strained for words with which to fill this silence, and neither of them could find words.

After dinner, with a towel about his waist, Kern helped Marianne dry the dishes, taking each glass from her with exaggerated care, not to touch her fingers when she held them out to him. Time and again his eyes met hers, and when this was so, each of them found something deep and direct in the eyes of the other that held and shook them.

When Kern dropped a glass to the floor and stood, feeling like a helpless idiot, Marianne laughed a brief, tense laugh—and bent to gather up the broken pieces.

"I'm sorry for my glasses," she said. "I suppose they just aren't accustomed to male hands. This is their first experience, you see. Please forgive them if they're nervous."

Later, as they sat in the living room and listened to the radio, they relaxed and were very careful not to break the calmness which music had brought them. Kern slouched deep in his chair and Marianne sat at his feet with her cheek resting against his knee. They smoked cigarettes "one after another" and were quiet and content. Grateful that the unexplainable tension which had been in them was gone. Now and then they spoke brief words. But only a few.

The radio itself broke the spell. The music ended. The staccato voice of a news announcer replaced the quiet strains of symphony, and their tension came back to them as the man hurried through a brief of the day's news.

157

"National Guardsmen in Texas—tired of serving beyond their year of duty. Jap ambassadors have appointment to see the Secretary of State. Woman leaps to death—sixth story of—England bombed again by buzz bombs." Marianne rose quickly and snapped off the radio and sat beside Kern again. But the mood was gone. Broken. When they looked at one another, Kern had the tight feeling that they were almost strangers. He wondered if Marianne had the same feeling. He looked at his watch and slowly stood. It was past midnight—time to be going. He did not want to go. He did not want to stay. Marianne did not want him to go. She did not want him to stay. He went slowly to the door of the closet and opened it, taking his coat from its hanger as her steps sounded behind him. He stiffened and turned to face her.

"It's time to go home, I guess—" Her eyes were bright with tears as she stood in front of him. Her hands were tight against her sides.

"You are home." Her words resounded in his head. Halting steps covered the short space between them and his arms were around her and her arms were around him. Resistance was tight in them as they fought against themselves. Then it melted away. Slowly at first. More quickly. And with a rush they could not have halted had they wanted to. Kern heard her voice saying over and over, "You are home—you are home." His own voice saying, "Darling, my darling."

Her lips against his were very tender and when he said, "I love you, Marianne—" he meant it with all of his heart. And so did she when she answered him.

❈ ❈ ❈

Love can be gentle and frightened and tender—violent and aching, demanding and hurting, giving and taking, until in the end, there is only giving. And the only hurting is that even more cannot be given to the beloved. Love can be tears because nothing else so richly deserves the gift of tears as does love. These things can be love. These things were love.

❈ ❈ ❈

The room was strange. Then Kern recognized it, knew where he was and closed his eyes. Thoughts whirled through his head and he tried to sift them to understand what he was feeling. Ashamed? No! No, not ashamed. Not at all. Glad? Yes. Happy? More happy than he had ever been. He stretched, arching his body, and relaxing to contemplate this happiness. Then he opened his eyes.

158

Marianne stood in the doorway that led to the kitchen, her hair clubbed into a tall knot on her head, her face clean-scrubbed and shining from soap. She wore a print dress and sandals. She smiled at him.

"Good morning, darling." Kern felt himself smiling too and the happiness in him could scarcely be contained. He wanted to laugh, and he did laugh. A pleased, happy laugh. Marianne came from the door to sit on the side of the bed, a flour-covered mixing spoon upraised in one hand. She ran her hand playfully over his face and twined her fingers in his hair. Then the laughter in her eyes went away.

"I'm glad, darling—" Kern reached and took her hand and pressed it against his cheek. "If you had frowned or looked away when you saw me, I don't know what I would have done." He tried to follow this mood in her, to understand her words. "Dad—always said, if you can look what you have done squarely in the eye and not be ashamed of it—then you could not have gone very far wrong. Not if there was good in you from the start." Her eyes held a woman's wisdom and Kern listened as a little boy. "That's the thing—to be able to look back without regret and say—'I'd do it again'—whatever it was." Deep in her clear eyes, Kern could see the image of his face.

"There is good in us, isn't there, Kern?" Her eyes became a girl's eyes, needing to be convinced, to be told that she was right. He inclined his head in agreement.

The words came from him without warning and his hands clasped her wrists. "I love you." Marianne stiffened and forced her head back to watch him, then she went soft all over and her cheek lay against his and her words were in his ears, throaty, trembling. The splash of her tears was against his cheek, then on his neck and finally on the pillow.

"I'm glad, my dearest. I wanted to die if you didn't. I had the silly little idea that all my life has been just for this one moment. It's not really silly, is it?"

"No, darling—not silly. Not silly." Kern traced the line of her jaw with his finger tips and knew that he loved her very, very much and felt the gnawing thing that was in his mind. And did not recognize it.

Not then. Not until later. Not until the tiny clock on her dresser chimed one and then two, almost unheard in the living room. Restlessness seized him and he dropped the paper he had been reading and began to stalk restlessly about the living room with Marianne's eyes following him. He touched things, the little china vase on the bookshelves, the cloisonné bowl that served as an ash tray. The figurines atop the bookshelves. He stared at Bill's sketch and stood in front of the family picture on the hallway table. When he did that, he knew what the thought in the back of his mind was and tried to push it out of his consciousness. He could not. When Marianne came and stood beside him, he kept his eyes on the picture. He did not dare to look at her until he had hidden this just-learned knowledge from his eyes.

The stern-faced man in the picture held laughter in his eyes as though the antics of the photographer had filled him with delight and he had been hard put to it not to laugh outright. The woman, obviously, had been snapped as she gathered herself after quieting the boy at her side. She, Kern thought, would never say she liked the picture. The little girl had long plaits that hung down over her shoulders with ribbons at their ends. The other boy, oldest of the children, looked very little like either the man or the woman. Kern looked at them and understood the thing that was in the back of his head and was afraid.

Marianne stood beside him, one hand resting lightly on his arm.

"That's Dad. He and I were always closest. And Bud—he's the principal, and Brother Bill. Bill's youngest. He's in the Navy now. That is Mother and that is me." Kern knew, as he looked at the man's eyes, at the woman's frank face, that he was going to have to tell Marianne. He was going to have to tell her who he was and what he was, because there could be nothing less than honesty between himself and Marianne. No halfway measures. She mistook the expression in his eyes and quick concern filled her voice.

"Don't!" A worried frown creased her forehead as she searched his face. "Dad taught me those things I told you. You don't regret—?" That much Kern could tell her. No. No regret. Only pride and happiness.

"No regrets," he told her, and some of the concern left her face. No regrets, he thought, but this—this other thing—must be told.

The music stopped in mid-phrase, startling them. The air was blank except for the gusts of December wind that shook the window casements. A voice, rigid, tight with excitement, cut into the silence.

"Ladies and gentlemen." They recognized Bill Gabel's voice. "We interrupt this broadcast to bring you a news flash of unprecedented importance. The Japanese have just bombed Pearl Harbor! I repeat —the Japanese have just bombed Pearl Harbor! The President has announced that Congress will be called into emergency session at once."

There was a long unfilled silence during which the humming of the radio and the roughness of their breathing filled the room and they tried not to believe that this could be so.

"No—no! It couldn't be!" Marianne protested the knowledge, her eyes asking Kern to say that he too did not believe it. His eyes told her that he did believe it. And that she did too.

"You—you'll have to go—?" Bill Gabel's voice began again, but neither of them listened. It was the first time Kern had really considered the possibility that he too would have to go to war. It was not a frightening thought when he faced it. Only strange.

"I suppose so—if I am called. I will——"

Marianne's eyes went from him to the picture and she whispered, "Brother Bill—" Then she looked at Kern again and at the radio. "I hate war—I hate it!"

Bill Gabel's voice hurried on, clear, precise, excited.

✿   ✿   ✿

Two days later Kern stood in Max Karns' office holding three scripts and the draft of a fourth under his arm. He stood there and fully expected to be thrown out, just as Dan Croom had had him thrown out and had sworn to black-list him throughout the chain of Dowd stations.

"What do you want?" The massive head looked up at him from the curling program sheets that spread across the desk and scowled.

"I want a job." Max laughed as though the idea was ridiculous and Kern felt as he had the first time he had met the man. Tense. Irritated. Attracted.

"Doing what?"

"Writing." Kern's defiance sprang from the irritation the man's scoffing voice roused in him.

"Do you have any references?"

"Yes."

Max held his hand forward across the desk. "Let me have them."

Kern laughed. "None of my former employers would write letters for me. You wouldn't want to read them anyway. I can tell you what they would say if they had been written."

Max stared with interest at the young man who stood before him. An older face than his should be, Max reasoned. He set the young man's age at twenty-eight. He was almost two years younger than that. Lines about the mouth. Lines that might come from keeping the lips too tightly closed. Or from too much worry. A young man

161

given to long silences. He must, Max thought, have experienced something unusual to have made him at his age so much older than most men would ever be. He wondered what it could have been.

"The letters would all be the same. They would say, 'The bearer is a fresh kid with no respect for the experience of his elders. He worries too much about what he calls a "responsibility to the listener." He wants to write and air things that would sharply disturb our listener public. He cannot accept the great role which radio plays in assuaging the daily pains of the average man'—that," Kern smiled, "means I am not content to help the listener public escape from its responsibility to think about the things which go on about it, by feeding it detective stories and the doings of Mother Tweedle Dee."

Something was twisting at this boy. His words, the way he said them, told Max that. He sensed driving force in Kern and sensed, too, that it was a force over which he had not yet won control. A force in him, but one which was unresolved. Something restless and powerful.

"What else would the letters say?"

Kern's eyebrows lifted.

"That I told two station managers where to go and how to get there with the least trouble——"

Max's eyebrows lifted. "And the last one?"

The wide thin mouth before him grinned suddenly and then closed. "That I twisted his moustache."

Max chuckled in spite of himself before he leaned forward on his elbows and rasped, "You expect me to hire you on the basis of such references?"

"Yes, I do."

"Is it true?"

"Most of it."

"Humph!" Max sat back in his chair. "You've omitted one detail, I believe."

"Yes?" The eyebrows lifted in question.

"Can you write?"

"Of course."

Max tried to find effrontery in the simply-spoken words. He could not, even though he tried. Kern extended the scripts to him and Max took them, signaling him toward the chair beside the desk.

"Sit down. Be quiet." He looked up quickly as the boy sat and saw the smile that was at the corners of his mouth. Then he began to read from the scripts he held in his hands.

❀ ❀ ❀

162

Kern began to work for American the next day. Each day after that was filled with a driving frenzy of work from early in the morning until late at night. He wrote and rewrote and polished his work. He struggled for hours for one word to tell exactly what he had in mind. He spent hours on end with American's staff composer, Mike Kendal, working out scores and musical background. He drove his secretaries, Trixie Kinswell and Julia Means, to match his frenzied pace until they were agreed among themselves that neither had ever worked for so demanding a boss. Each day and each night Kern heard Max's words.

"—under all their faults, a great people, an honest people. Give them the truth and they'll come through." And he tried to tell what the war really meant.

Though his work demanded every energy he had, Kern came quickly to a decision about Marianne. He would have to break with her . . . to break it off before they became so deeply involved that neither could escape serious hurt.

He could not risk telling her the truth about himself. He could not chance explaining his reasons and seeing scorn and shame in her eyes. He was, and he accepted the fact, too cowardly to risk hearing her regret her love for him.

It was a simple answer, more simple than to have explained. Merely break a date. Don't call. Stay away. That was the answer.

Often, after that, in the long days that followed his decision, it seemed to Kern that his typewriter keys spelled out his decision as he worked.

Break away! Break away! Break away!

CHAPTER VIII

EVANS ACADEMY—XMAS, 1933

I

KERN stared moodily through the frost-edged panes of window to where the steam-filled sled stood behind its champing horses at the gate. The other boys were streaming down the plowed path that split the rolling snow-covered lawn into halves. Chub was in the van, shouting gleefully about something that Kern could not understand. Behind Chub was "Mitch" and Ray Hagan, Rickie and Paul, all of them burdened with the bags and paraphernalia of a holiday outing. Fannin Barker brought up the rear, carrying a heavy bag and struggling, with one hand, to control the long skis that swung askew over his shoulder. Conscious of question, Kern watched Fannin as the slender boy went toward the sled.

"Where have I seen him before? *Have* I seen him before Evans?"

"Why does he insist that he has seen *me* before?"

"Where?"

"Where could it have been?"

A flicker of doubt touched Kern's eyes as the sun disappeared behind the clouds and, a moment later, reappeared. All morning long it had been like that. One instant, the sun was so bright against the snow that it almost blinded and hurt the eyes. The next the land became somber and dark as it disappeared. Kern sighed and thrust his hands into his hip pockets. He wished he could get over his mood.

The last ten, all too short, days of Christmas holiday, had sped. They had been filled with square dances, tobogganing and skating, and a trip to Millfield for a husking bee. All of the fellows had had a swell time—Kern was pretty sure of that. He had, himself—except when the secret dread had come to mind and created this mood of his. Now it was time to go back to Evans and to the last half of the year. They had all looked forward to that half year. Event after special event crowded the calendar of the months ahead—Alumni Week, the annual Hodge-Podge production of a full three-act play, "Old

Henderson's" party for the First Form boys, the Final Prom—each month with its own special promise. The boys looked forward to those months. Kern did too—yet as he stood in front of the window, he was afraid to go back to Evans. Much as he looked forward to those crowded, busy months, Kern dreaded what they might hold for him.

From behind him, his grandmother's voice broke into his mood.

"Come sit here with me, Kern—I've hardly had time to talk to you since the boys came and now you're almost ready to leave." Kern turned from the window, widening his eyes to see in the shadowed room. His grandmother sat before the fireplace in a deep chair, its huge arms seeming to dwarf her small figure. With a pang Kern remembered that his mother's face had had those same planes, the same shape of mouth and chin. His grandmother's eyes held a question as she watched him come toward where she sat and bent to push an ottoman into place so that his back would rest against her chair when he sat.

Words with which to tell his grandmother about his dread were on the tip of his tongue. At the thought of that dread, Kern's throat tightened and he turned his head away to hide his feeling from her. The blur before his eyes cleared and he looked about him at the frost-white moulding, the mantel above the fireplace, the silver-threaded pale-green walls, remembering them from the time when he had come here with his mother.

His grandmother touched his shoulder.

"You're worried, son—what is it?" Her quick concern broke down the last restraint in Kern and he turned to her impulsively.

"Gran', I haven't done—" The hall door opened suddenly and a tall, dark-faced boy stopped in mid-stride. It was Fannin Barker. Kern felt his irritation at seeing Fannin swell inside of him until it became a part of his dread.

"Oh, Ah'm sorry. I didn't know you all were busy." Fannin started to leave and Margaret Adams called to him.

"Posh, boy—nothing of the sort. Come in and have a seat," she gestured toward a chair. "Kern and I were just having a chat before you boys leave." Fannin came toward the fireplace slowly.

"That's what I came to tell him, ma'am—the boys're 'bout ready." He stood before them, lean-faced and hungry-faced, his flashing eyes going restlessly to everything in the room. Kern watched him closely.

"You're Fannin, aren't you?" Kern's grandmother asked.

"Yes, ma'am." Fannin's busy eyes met hers for a moment and then darted back to the room. Margaret Adams smiled faintly as she watched the boy's face. Kern, watching too, noticed the long hair that grew far down on Fannin's neck, curling close to his well-shaped head, and the way his slender fingers rolled his long-billed snow cap, without stopping.

"Did you enjoy your visit, Fannin?"

Fannin smiled quickly as he answered. "Yes, ma'am, Mrs. Adams—had a right good time here." Kern noticed his grandmother's frown as she watched Fannin. Her next question was the question in Kern's mind at the moment she spoke.

"Do you like this room, Fannin?"

Fannin's answer was deliberate.

"Yes'm—Ah reckon I do. It's sorta like what gramma used to say our house in Milledgeville was fo' we moved to St. Louis."

Kern wondered where Milledgeville was. He wondered too why he was trembling inside. "Leastaways, she says it was like this fo' Gen'l Sherman dirtied it up—" Fannin's words were gritted out on a rising anger. They crackled in the quiet room—like the crackling fire. Spoken. Beyond recall. Both Kern and his grandmother knew he had no wish to recall them. That much was in his posture, in the defiance that filled his eyes.

"I'm sho' sorry, ma'am. I had no right to be discourteous." The boy faced Margaret Adams and bowed stiffly from his waist. "If you'll excuse me, ma'am," his hot eyes touched Kern, "I'll tell the fellas you'll be out in a little bit."

Kern stared after him, tight inside and trembling, as the door closed behind him. And then realizing that he was trembling, as though he were cold.

"What's the matter, Kern? What—?" The tightness in him broke and the dread became words in his mouth, something that he had to share with someone else.

"Suppose——"

"Suppose what, son?"

"Suppose they knew?" Kern's voice was dull.

"They—knew what?"

"The fellows at school—suppose they knew I was a Negro?"

"Suppose they—!" His grandmother was openmouthed, frightened at his strained, white-faced expression. The hand she had raised to touch him remained half thrust forward in an unfinished gesture of comfort. "That's absurd—why should anyone know?" Misery filled his face as she watched.

167

"Just suppose—" A chill went through Kern at the thought.

"You haven't told anyone?" Her hand grasped his arm in alarm. Kern shook his head slowly. "No one—you're sure?" she persisted.

"Should I—should I have told, Gran'? Should I have told them at the very first? If they find out now, won't they think I'm a cheat and a liar?"

"No—!" Her answer was an angry refusal. "No questions have been asked. No answers have been given. Listen to me, Kern. You can't beat this sort of thing with the truth." He turned and stared at her as she talked. "You want to be a writer. You came here to learn to write. You're doing that."

Kern stared into space and thought, "Suppose they knew——?"

His grandmother pleaded with him now, anxiously, frightened by his staring. "The boys have accepted you because you are one of them. Race hasn't mattered. They haven't asked. You have not volunteered. Don't let questions like this create a problem that will spoil what you have learned for yourself. That would be foolish——"

"Do you think it would matter to Paul?"

"Pshaw," she made light of his fear. "Of course not, Kern. Paul's a very fine young man. You couldn't have found a better roommate."

"I'd hate to let Paul down. We've planned to do so many things together."

"You won't let Paul down. The two of you boys just stick to your plans for school——"

Her easy manner relieved some of Kern's tension. But threads of worry remained even when she had finished.

"I hope nothing will—" Kern bit at his lip and abruptly changed his words. "I'd hate to have to go back to Washington for school. And I don't know how to approach my father about spending another year away." Kern ran a finger across the cap of his shoe, frowning seriously. "He's set against my writing, you know——"

"I know—but he might agree, Kern. He might." Kern doubted seriously that there was much hope of his father giving his approval. It showed in his voice when he said, "Do you really think so?"

"Well—I'm not *sure*. But I believe he might agree if he's approached in the right way."

"I wish I could be sure—but," Kern turned to her despairingly, "I guess I don't know how to approach him. Whenever we get together, there seems to be a clash about something."

"Suppose you—I know!— Let me handle this in my own way. Just leave it to me—I think I can get the answer you want. Charles may have found that he can do his work more easily without having the additional problems which go with maintaining a home, there in Washington."

Kern saw a ray of hope in her plan. A ray—but even so, more hope than he had held a minute ago. "It would work to your advantage, too. Leave it to me."

A shrill whistle from beyond the house and a clanging cowbell ended their conversation. Kern smiled up at her from the ottoman, then he stood.

"Guess they're calling me, Gran'." She nodded agreement and smiled at him. At this tall grandson who was all she had of her daughter. At her reason for living. She stood and faced him.

"Just between us two—" She pressed a finger to his lips. "Now come along. The boys are calling. You'll have just enough time to get down to the station." They walked to the door and through it to the hall. Kern turned quickly on the doorstep and faced her, his shoulder brushing against the red-ribboned garland of holly that hung from the door. He bent and kissed her good-bye. Her bright eyes held him.

"Write me—give my regards to Henderson." He waved to her again as he ran toward the sled, dodging the fusillade of snowballs that flew at him.

The question did not leave him. It kept time in his head to the jingle of sled bells and the muffled clip-clop of hooves as they slid down the snow-banked road to town.

Suppose——?

The thought grew in him as they passed the church spires that thrust up above the evergreens against the cold cloudy sky—as they passed the corner of a cemetery that showed between the trees. It stayed in him, in time—and almost in tune—to their voices as they sang Auld Lang Syne.

Suppose——?

II

It was a comfortable room, a favorite meeting place. In more than forty years, "Old Henderson" would proudly say, there had never been a night when some of "his" boys hadn't come in to sit around and talk, to hear him read or to plan some special program. Just, Kern thought, as they were doing tonight.

It was a room that brought people within it closer together. It was exactly as Rod Cameron had said it would be. Kern felt a guilty pang, remembering that he had written Rod only once since he had been at Evans. Rod and Washington seemed to be part of another life—something that was a million miles and a whole lifetime away.

It was a room with wide windows and a profusion of books, with worn comfortable chairs and an old maple rocker that had seen the making of history during the Revolution itself. At its very center a great circular table held an unrolled, yellowed parchment, marked with curious script and pinned down at its ends by stacks of books.

It was a room filled with the scent of burning pine knots and the smell of pipe smoke, a man's room, a room with a fireplace. Because it was this, Kern and his mates, all of them, came on any pretext. And on no pretext at all. Came, as the other boys had through each of those forty-odd years "Old Henderson" could remember.

Except for the long wall that looked through the windows to the lawn, books ranged solidly about the room, many of them—if, indeed, not most—written by Evans boys. Two bronze andirons guarded the hearth and the fireplace, and the mantel was bracketed by polished brass hurricane lamps.

Below the mantel and about the hearth, the headmaster sat with his boys. Known only as "Old Henderson" to generations of boys, glasses propped high on his forehead, he slouched comfortably in the flower-printed armchair at the end of the hearth. About him, two of the boys sat in chairs. The rest sprawled in loose-limbed ease on the deep-piled rug. All of them were older boys, First Formers who would soon be graduating.

Kern sat on the fourth cluster of pile-roses in the twining vine that began at the nearest edge of the hearth. He knew. Each time he had counted the clusters, it had been the same. The fourth cluster. Between him and the hearth on the second cluster of roses, and partly on the third, sat "Chub" Pierson. And on the other side of Chub, "Rickie" Colenbine hunched forward, chin in hands, listening as "Old Henderson" talked. Kern himself shifted in his cross-legged squat as a tiny cramp started in his lower leg.

"Well, boys, we have four—let me see—four, no, five ideas so far. I have these themes listed—Gay Nineties, the Folie Bergère idea, the Barbary Coast, the Flapper theme, and Working My Way Through College—I think that's all. Any others?"

"What about a minstrel show, sir?" Kern froze where he sat. A minstrel show! It was Fannin's voice.

"A minstrel show?" A minstrel show meant——!

170

"Yessir. It would be right unusual. 'Cording to the file of Hodge Podge's, there never has been a minstrel show heah–an' we could put it off. A 'Mr. Bones,' a straight man, some blackface––"

"Different indeed!" Old Henderson was wry-voiced. "What do you think, boys? Fannin has suggested a minstrel show."

"Well–" someone started to comment in a doubtful voice–"I dunno––"

Kern knew it was Mitch's voice, even though he could not see him. Rickie spoke up.

"To tell you the truth, sir, I don't think it's so–so hot." "Old Henderson's" grimace at the slang was not lost on Rickie.

"Well–I don't know 'bout that. It's better than anything we've had so far–at least it's different." Defiantly Fannin defended his idea.

"Oh, it's not that good–and there are things suggested that we haven't given yet." Chub came to Rickie's support.

"Name one–" Fannin demanded.

"Well, the Gay Nineties idea. That's one."

"Everybody's had a Gay Nineties!"

"What about the minstrel idea–what's been done any more often than that? Every vaudeville in the country's used it."

"Boys, boys–" "Old Henderson's" level voice broke in as their clamor brought Mrs. Henderson to the door. He caught her eye.

"Mother–do you think you could serve us now?"

"Why, of course–I was about ready to start anyhow. Let me see– Fannin–Rickie, come help Sue and me serve, will you?"

"Why, of course."

"Yes, ma'am–" Even Fannin's truculence faded. Mrs. Henderson's hot chocolate was something special.

"I don't think we should have a minstrel show––"

"Neither do I––"

"Now, boys–just a minute. I think we might let the discussion rest until Fannin has come back. After all it is his suggestion that is being discussed. Don't you think he should be here to defend it?"

The boys agreed reluctantly and Kern was relieved that the contention could rest for a moment.

Kern didn't move when Sue bent her blonde head close to his and whispered, "Hi!" as she handed him a plate with toasted cake and a steaming cup of chocolate. Propping the plate carefully on his knees, Kern studied the rug under his crossed legs. Carefully he counted the separate rows of woven stuff that went across each rose petal.

Had he actually seen "Old Henderson's" sudden glance flicker to him when the minstrel show was suggested? Was the headmaster looking at him now as his head bent? It seemed to Kern that he could feel that gaze touching him lightly.

He would not raise his head. He didn't recognize the whirl of thoughts through his head, nor any of the chatter around him. He heard without hearing talk of the past football season, of baseball practice started a week ago, and a spoofing story being told on Chub who sat beside him and protested with righteous indignation.

Kern forced himself to look up and found the headmaster looking full at him. The old man looked away immediately, and when Kern saw his eyes again, they were filled with laughter at the boys' joke. Kern knew the mood in his eyes had changed. Did "Old Henderson" know?

Suppose the boys found out that he was a— He looked cautiously about him as the dread he had known at his grandmother's came rushing back. Fannin returned to his place at the edge of the mantel and the boys grew quiet, waiting for "Old Henderson" to speak.

"Well, boys—what about the minstrel show—shall we consider it or shall we not?"

"I don't think so!" Rickie spoke up quietly. "It's not up to Evans' level." Kern thought the old man smiled approval. The boys waited, watching Rickie. Mitch added his approval with an emphatic nod.

"Not up to Evans' level, Rickie—why do you say that?" Kern knew he was right, approval *was* in Henderson's voice as he pressed Rickie for his reason.

"Well—" Rickie searched for words to tell what he meant. "It just hasn't got enough dignity, sir. Besides——"

Fannin laughed scornfully, "I suppose the Gay Nineties idea has dignity."

"I think so," Chub faced Fannin. "I think dignity can come from intent."

"Well—whatcha' all fussin' about? All this is in fun." Fannin scowled as Chub answered quickly:

"Sure, it's in fun—but let's keep it clean."

"Clean! How come a minstrel show's not clean—what about a Folie's cancan?" The boys waited for Chub's answer and their faces told Kern nothing at all as he glanced quickly about him. Even "Old Henderson's" face was impassive as he looked from Kern to Chub. From the corner of his eye, Kern saw that Mrs. Henderson and Sue were standing in the doorway behind them listening.

172

"Well," Chub hesitated, then spoke boldly, "well, I've got a good friend at home named Charley and he's a colored boy and I don't want to write and tell him we had a minstrel for our Hodge Podge." Kern felt a warm gratitude at Chub's earnest words, and quick anger at Fannin's derisive laugh.

"I know niggers too—known 'em all my life. They like minstrel shows—have 'em themselves." Kern felt the anger in him shaping to words. Chub spoke before he could.

"You miss the point, Fannin—we're not out to poke fun at Negroes or anyone else—not like that. Minstrel shows aren't true to life——"

"They're true of all the nigras I've ever known. Just happy-go-lucky darkies, always looking for a handout."

"If anything is plain at all, it is that you don't know what you're talking about." Kern's cold voice surprised him as it surprised the boys about him. He knew "Old Henderson" was watching him, but he could not halt the words that were in him. "The Negroes I've known are as intelligent as you are—and much better bred." He was glad the words had been said. Relieved. He wished that he said the rest of the things that were in him. He leaned forward, eyes blazing, as he watched Fannin.

"Nigger lover!" Fannin sneered, his eyes locked with Kern's.

Chub spoke quickly in the shocked silence.

"Well—that's what I think too, 'cause I'd rather have Charley's friendship than that of some broken-down Johnny Reb."

"Boys—boys!" The old man reined in the flaring young tempers. "We're letting our feelings run away with us. Paul—you haven't commented on this yet; what do you think?"

Propped on one elbow, Paul studied the palm of one hand before answering.

"Well, sir—I think we should vote on all of the suggestions on merit." He smiled thinly as he looked up. "I don't know how we got off on this business, but we can't refight the Civil War. After all, the minstrel idea is *just* a suggestion!"

The boys about him were quickly agreed and the list was closed.

"Very well, gentlemen—we shall vote as usual."

"The last shall be first."

Suppose, Kern thought, suppose they do choose—?

"Those in favor of having a minstrel show for the annual Hodge Podge will signify by raising their hands." The old man's eyes swept over the circle of boys, then carefully, without saying a word, he shaped and reshaped a "1" beside the words "minstrel show."

173

"Those in favor of using the theme, 'Working My Way Through College'——"

Kern breathed deeply. The dread was in his mind as he forced himself to pay attention to the voting.

✿　✿　✿

Fannin scowled darkly as he muttered "good night" and left Sue and Kern standing in the alcove off the hallway. For a second Kern watched him as he went toward the door and felt tight fear. Then triumph rose in him as he looked away from Fannin to the girl before him.

"You're still planning to go on the hayride with me, aren't you?"

She laughed mischievously and said, "Well—I might—if you promise me not to quarrel with Fannin. I never knew you had a temper——"

✿　✿　✿

The cool late April night wind came in at the window, bringing with it mixed sounds—a night bird's calling notes, the thin sound of rustling branches, a mournful, far-off train whistle—sounds which Kern heard and was unconscious of. Rigid, he lay in his bed and listened to Paul's measured breathing a few feet away and remembered.

And was afraid.

Kern lay in the darkness and remembered where he had seen Fannin before and was afraid that Fannin would remember too.

He could not see how Fannin could fail to remember.

He could hear Fannin's voice as memory came back to him. He could see the vaulted roof of the Palladium Theater with its balconies rising to the roof, saw the wings backstage and the curtain going down on *Heart of the Land*. Surprised at the clarity of remembering, he saw the single jagged brick in the corner of the walkway that led to a dressing-room door on which there was a star. And Myra Holcombe, greeting a group of high-school dramatics students—white and colored, as they filed past her and were introduced. The other celebrities who had been there and the angry voice——

"Where I come from, no niggers shake hands with a white woman."

The trickle of perspiration on his forehead tempted Kern to move his arms. But he did not. He held them rigidly to his sides. Why had he taken so long to remember the angry face? The scornful, unrepentant face of the boy who had stalked, head high, from Myra Hol-

174

combe's dressing room. One sharp flash of remembering. Why had he remembered at all?

"Damyankee!" Parting contempt that had matched the lash of Myra Holcombe's tongue.

"The nasty little bigot!"

Fannin! Kern knew that the boy in that dressing room had been Fannin.

"He doesn't know! He doesn't! Not yet. But he may. He may remember at any time." The thought paralyzed him with fear, as it had at his grandmother's.

"He may not remember! One week before the school year is over. He hasn't remembered in all this time. He won't remember now. He can't. He mustn't.

"He mustn't!

"But he may. Easily. I remembered. And I didn't try to. I didn't think of it. Fannin is thinking about it. He wants to remember. He doesn't know what it is he's trying to remember—but I do. All those times when he's stared at me, the times when we have clashed."

*　*　*

Two months and then three weeks. Ten days. Finally, one week.

On week of dark doubt. Of being afraid. Of expecting, each time Fannin looked at him, that it was about to happen. One week of waiting for Fannin to remember, to find the thought for which he was reaching, clear and remembered.

Four days. Three.

He was edgy even with Paul, and each day more frightened and more certain that his luck would not last the week. He counted the days and held his breath and found his own name on the tip of his tongue, as though he would prompt Fannin when he started—if he started.

Two days.

In spite of himself, Kern found himself searching for Fannin in a crowd. When he found him, he stared without being aware that he did. He held doggedly to the thin thread of hope that it would not happen. He counted the days over and over, weighing the balance of time in his favor.

He stood on the eve of the last day. Within sight of the hoped-for, prayed-for freedom from fear of exposure, and he was giddy with relief. Soon, in a day, he would not have to be afraid that the secret of his mixed bloods would be exposed. Not ashamed of those bloods

175

and angry at their being. One day would end fear and shame and anger.

III

They stood in a close circle, arms entwined, and the slither of crepe festoons sounded just above their heads. Mitch and Paul, Rickie, Chub and Ray, and Kern. Between them, Sue, Mary Ellen, Jo, Helen from town, and Myra Barker. All of them close together. In the background, low music and the sound of a song just ending. The lump in Kern's throat had nothing to do with Fannin or with fear. This was the end of a year and a hundred little things were trooping through his mind with an aching nostalgia. Paul's eyes were bright and Mitch's head was cast down. Kern felt very close to these boys.

In a clear bell-like tenor, Chub began "Girl of My Dreams" and the circle took it up. Low and sweet, with the girls humming in the background.

Low and sweet. They swayed in their circle. Arms crossed and hands clasped. Swayed slow as the melody rose and filled the place. Far away—or so it seemed—the tower clock struck the half hour. The song ended and they stood there, hands still clasped, caught by the magic their voices had made. Beyond them another circle, closer to the orchestra stand, began "Sweet Sue"——

Young voices, earnest and sincere and serious.

And now a fox trot. Now a floating waltz. Again a song.

The night went like that. It sped in spite of Kern's fear that it would pass too slowly—would offer chance for his exposure. Ten o'clock and eleven. And the tower clock told the hours and each quarter hour in between.

Sue's cheek was touching his, light as the touch of a feather. Touching, then apart.

Sue's face was turned up to his and looking away. Blue eyes, wide. Startled, misty-tender eyes.

Sue's hair, a froth in his face. Sue, whirling, floating, light as a feather. Sue's hand, tightening on his at the end of a song. Starry-eyed, light-headed—light-hearted. Caught by a witchery which they knew could never have touched another night since the start of time. God, don't let this ever end!

A night with magic woven through it.

And Fannin.

Fannin!

176

Alone.

Coming across the rapidly emptying floor, his eyes fixed on Kern. A smile on his face, a smile without laughter in it, a smile that told Kern——

He knows!

It's in his eyes. He knows! A wave of panic ran through Kern. Run! Where? How can I get away? Fear blotted out everything. Kern's mind moved as though it were on sand and could move only if he struggled.

"Is something wrong, Kern?" Sue tugged at his arm and he saw that he had stopped in the middle of the floor. Taking Sue's arm, he hurried toward where Paul and Mitch were standing with Mary Ellen and Jo. Sue almost ran, trying to keep up with him! "Maybe," he thought, "he won't dare say anything before them—maybe."

"Are you sure you're all right—your face is so white!"

"Sure. I'm O.K."

Sue's choice of words filled him with bitter humor as he realized what was coming. Strike him down, God—don't let him tell! A foolish, a mad thought, whose folly he recognized, crowded to mind. Kern knew he could not escape. He could not hide. He could hear Fannin's step behind them when they stopped beside Chub and Mary Ellen.

Kern stood there and faced his friends, cold inside, and saw the puzzled curiosity in their faces. He thought of Frank Richards and the kids he'd known at grade school. Of Rod Cameron and of the Summer Theater as his mind tried to hide from what it knew was about to happen. If only he could disappear—if only Fannin hadn't remembered. But Fannin had remembered. Fannin stood in front of him now and everything about him told Kern that he had remembered.

Fannin's voice told him.

"I knew I remembered you!"

"Say something," Kern thought, "defend yourself. Don't just stand here and stare at him. Close your mouth." He reached for words with which to deny, to tell away the truth that was on Fannin's tongue.

"I don't know where it—" The others were staring.

"I do. *I* know where." Fannin's voice was triumphant. "It was in New York."

Kern sickened.

"You were there with a delegation from Washington for the National High School Drama Convention." Fannin turned to face Sue

177

and Kern felt her hand tighten on his arm. He dropped his head. He knew that Fannin bent at the waist and he remembered the little half bow he had seen him make to his grandmother.

"You'll 'scuse me, ma'am, but I reckon you didn't know you were dancing with—" Hypnotized, Kern watched the word shape on Fannin's mouth, formed it silently himself, knowing what it would be like, knowing the shape it demanded of the lips. "You were dancing with a nigger." Fannin said the word deliberately and clearly—not loudly, but clearly, and his voice carried to curious ears and to the eyes that watched them standing there together. It slashed against Kern's face with the contempt of spittle.

A nigger! It seemed to echo in the hall. Kern felt Sue's hand go slack and leave his arm. Fannin ignored him.

"May I have the pleasure——"

Paul stood unbelieving, staring first at Fannin and then at Kern. Kern's lowered head told them all it was the truth.

"I don't believe it—Kern a Negro—! Not a——"

The girls stared, Jo's outstretched fingers pressed to either cheek, mouth still open as it had been when she gasped. And Mitch. Frowning, watching him. Quiet-voiced.

"Well, I'll be durned."

Free from the hand that had been on his arm, free from the magic he had known. Free to leave. Kern walked stiffly through the group of them, past Mitch's soft, repeated, "Well, I'll be durned," toward the door and the hallway and to the outside. He walked slowly, forcing his head erect, in a daze, feeling that all eyes were turned on him. As he had walked along a street, at night, somewhere in the past. He walked until the night shadows beyond the building had closed in on him. Then he ran. Blindly, headlong, he ran from something shapeless and terrifying. Empty inside. Not hurting. Not yet. Not aware of any thought. Not thinking. Only empty inside.

* ° °

The dark room was a shield. It hid him from himself. The dull silver face of the mirror told him nothing. It hid his face. He did not want to see his face. He did not want to look into his eyes. He was afraid to stand face to face with the shame he felt.

Nigger nigger nigger!

The words hammered at his brain, pulsed along the fibers of nerve and the channels of blood—torturing him.

178

The sudden coldness of their eyes, the widening stares had told him that he was suddenly no longer Kern. He had become a curiosity. A Negro who had not been "like a Negro." A curiosity. And unreasoning hate in the glittering eyes of the boy who had stood in front of him.

Nigger nigger nigger!

Why?

Why suddenly, with a word, was he something to be stared at and hurt?

Why?

Why do I have to be what I am—and what am I?

The darkness was quiet. The quiet of the room was dark. He walked restlessly back and forth. His steps sure in the dark. One by one he saw simply, and with sharp pain, the pennants on the walls above his mirror, miniature skis from a week end at Mt. Manchester, a sprig of holly and twined mistletoe, and against a wall, below the window, a square board on which was mounted a photo of the opening curtain of the last "Hodge Podge."

Nigger nigger nigger!

Hostile eyes will search for little things that will make me different. All at once—different. Purple fingernails which I have never found. A "different" odor about my body. A kinkiness that must be hidden somewhere, deep, near the roots perhaps, of my hair. Heavy, black wavy hair.

Nigger nigger nigger!

Pulsing in my blood. In plain sight, through the thin blue network of veins above my temples, lining the backs of my hands. Curious, unaccountable. Something never found. Something that is—and yet which is not and because it is, makes me of another, a scorned, people.

Nigger nigger nigger!

Does God let this happen? How can He? A just God? "—To the least of these—" Not God—! Not the God Mama taught me about! The Golden Rule. Not a merciful God! But who else? "Do unto others—my brother's keeper—" Who else hears prayer? "Whither midst falling dew while glow the Heavens—" "Now I lay me down to sleep—" The same God—the same—the same——!

Nigger nigger nigger!

This was not new—but Kern could not know that. It was an old grief and an older woe. It was heartache for one and two millions of hearts and five times that number and more besides. A personal

179

hurt. A deep hurt. A fearful hurt. A hurt that reached down to the core of him and tore cruelly at the roots of hope and dreams—stripping from their resting place these first, growing roots.

There was no reason in him to understand these things and he had a thin knowledge that reason would not be enough to turn this hurt—even if there had been reason.

Nigger nigger nigger!

Well—what are you going to do about it?

Nigger nigger nigger!

Are you going to stay here—going to face it? The faces that were once your friends will turn to you with curiosity now—with reservation. Can you stay and know that whenever you leave a room, voices will whisper? Can't you hear them now?

"I didn't know—" "I wouldn't have known—!" "He doesn't look much like one, does he?—but I guess you can never tell——"

"I remember little things he did——"

Nigger nigger nigger!

Not even your hands clasped tight against your ears, pushing inward on the drums, can shut out the words, can they? Not the dinning words from which you wanted to hide.

Nigger nigger nigger!

All right—cry! Lie on your bed and shake with sobs. Ache! Ache down to the roots of your soul. Stand aside while the dreams totter and then tumble about you. You had no right to those dreams! Haven't you heard of staying in your place? Well—you're out of your place now. You've forgotten yourself. You brought this on yourself!

Nigger nigger nigger!

Do you see the answer now? Hate! That's it. A net of hate. Wrap it around you. Draw it tight. Cover every point. Every Achilles heel. Be sure that no single chink is left for the darts to enter. Hate.

Each white face. Every white face.

Each gesture of friendship—hold it suspect. Because you know that behind each one, behind every word, every smile, is an unconscious reservation, a smug feeling of superiority. Polite condescension—so long as you stay in your place.

Nigger nigger nigger!

You lost your way.

You forgot your place.

Hurry home!

Hurry home!

180

Cry. Run back to your ghetto. Sob in the darkness. Nigger!—now do you understand the Freedom League? Do you understand now the violence and the hatred, the dull anger in the voices you've known? The hopelessness that lies under their words? They have known this thing over and over again. They could never have come here in the first place—could not have enjoyed what you have known from the start. They *look* different—they meet the barrier at every turn.

You have the money. All you have to do is pack up and leave. The things you can't take with you, they'll send after you.

Run home.—"I ain't doin' no business with niggers!"—"Half-white nigger, lemme up!" —"You're dancing with a nigger!"

Nigger nigger nigger!

✿   ✿   ✿

Kern sat in the window sill and stared up at the ceiling. He heard the rhythmic creak of the rocker and saw, reflected on the glass above him, the fading and brightening glow of Mr. Henderson's pipe. Even though he tried to shut out the old man's voice, he could not. Not for long. The first words he had shut out—he had mustered up enough anger, told himself harshly enough that a "white man" was talking to him, to have shut out the first words. But the effort had been too great for him to sustain. The tension and the anger in him had waned in spite of his determination and he listened to the old man.

"You know, Kern, this whole race problem is a strange thing—so simple, so complicated. Take Fannin for example."

Fannin! Fannin's name brought boiling anger to Kern.

"The things he feels, he has been taught by his elders—without any reason, just because they want him to feel them. In a way, he's not responsible. He's just 'white'." He drew deeply on his pipe. "Funny—a man is the first one to recognize his guilt in a wrong that he has done. He is probably more conscious of it than anyone else."

Doing wrong, Kern thought, didn't seem to matter to the white men he knew.

"Bring a man face to face with the person he is wronging—prove to him how wrong he is—and he becomes determined to be right. Guilt becomes so terrific in him that you cannot tell it from hate."

Kern did not quite follow this. Exactly what was Mr. Henderson driving at?

"This whole business of prejudice is a myth; it won't stand the

181

test of truth and reason. Over the years lies and half-truths have grown to the size of a folklore." Kern shifted his feet on the sill as a cramping pain caught his leg. "I can't say to you, 'Don't be angry,' Kern. Nothing I or anyone else could say would stop you from feeling that. It is entirely natural. But—try not to let it eat into you like a cancer. Don't let resentment pile up in you and crowd the better things out. Remember this, Kern, when you are tempted to blame this thing on race alone—it is more than that."

"How much more? How can these other things be divided from race? Wasn't it a word, one word, that had made him different—a stranger, a curiosity?"

"What do you think would happen if tomorrow morning everyone in America were to wake up and find that everyone else was white? Nordic in appearance? With blonde hair or brown or black, with blue eyes or green or gray? What would happen to the 'race problem'? It would have disappeared overnight—and a great many very confused people would be left behind. This thing is deeper, you see, than the catchword of 'race' will tell you. "Everyone white. No 'problem.' What then?"

"Man has a very short lifetime. Time enough in which to do some work, to be happy for a short while, to help his fellows. One day you are going to have to choose your way of life. You will either have to go at this game of living as your father has, and fight segregation and discrimination and against the Negro at every turn, give your whole life to that, or—you can be yourself."

Kern moved abruptly, dropping one foot to the floor.

Not a lifetime of brawling, fighting, being angry! Not that!

"I don't believe that you have the temperament to fight as your father has. You're not emotionally designed to live with the twisting pressures of being a Negro."

How can I find a way to do the thing I want to, I must do?

"Each of us must meet our need for self-realization. A man can die for the lack of self-realization just as surely as he will starve for the lack of food. Someday you will come to a crossroads in your life. When you do, you will have to choose between the road that will lead you to self-realization, and the road will be indicated by what you may feel to be your duty to your race."

The crossroads, Kern found, were difficult to visualize. The word "hate" was insistent in his mind. Hate! He looked through the window at the dark lines of trees and the thin chapel spire.

Hate!

182

"When that happens no one else will be able to choose for you. You will have to remember that your greatest responsibility is to your own self-realization."

What choice? This was cut and dried. All settled at birth. Before that even—long before. No choice now. No nothing! Run nigger! Run back to your people.

INTERLUDE IV

NEW YORK—SPRING, 1942

KERN missed Marianne at first with a sharp ache, and then with a frantic longing, and finally with a ceaseless, drumming hurt. For sixty-one endless days he did not see her. One thousand, four hundred and sixty-four hours in all. He multiplied the hours by minutes and those again by the sixty seconds that were in each minute, and contemplated the total of more than five and a quarter million seconds since he had seen her, heard her voice or called her, walked along the crowded streets with her hand in his or sat across from her at dinner.

He took a certain satisfaction in the total of the seconds as though each one was a special measure of his ability to keep his resolve never to see her again.

He stayed away from Marianne. He didn't see her. He didn't call her. He fought down impulse after impulse to go to where she was. Each night he planned exactly what he would do with tomorrow, so that no chance meeting might bring them together.

He tried to forget Marianne. He took each memory of things they had done out of its place in his heart and examined them in detail. He examined each one, remembering the way they had walked together hand in hand and the things they had promised one another. Remembering the way Marianne had looked, what she had worn, and things she had said. Then he said to himself, "These are the things I am going to forget."

Every day he took these memories out of his heart and studied them, to be quite sure that they were the right ones, and said to himself, "These things I am going to forget."

Instead of forgetting, he remembered everything they had ever done or shared or dreamed about. More than once he caught his steps taking him toward some place they had known together. More than once, he stopped himself from calling Bill Gabel to ask him how Marianne was and what she was doing. More than once he found her name on his lips and stared into the darkness of a theater toward the place where a girl's laugh, "just like Marianne's," had sounded. He knew that something was gone and there was only an emptiness inside of him.

More than anything else, did he want to see Marianne again. But he could not. He knew that. Because if he saw Marianne, he knew he would have to tell her the whole truth about himself, and he was afraid. He called to mind the instances when he had seen her flare up in angry argument against bigotry and close-mindedness. He remembered the times he had seen disgust and disappointment show in her eyes and her rigid shoulders, in her tight fists—when scorn had filled her voice, as it had the night when he first met her and she heard him call Jeff Balanchine a "coon." He remembered all of those things and tried to tell himself that she would understand if he told her. Each time he decided against telling her. He knew that she had never felt the brutal force of the Negro myth before. Nothing in her experience had toughened her to withstand the impact she would feel if it touched her as a person. He had no way of knowing what she would do or say—what would happen to her when she was told that the Negro myth had come into her most personal experience.

Kern could not risk seeing her face fill with scorn and possibly shame—as though she had been dirtied—with sick wondering how this could have happened to her. He couldn't risk having her regret that she had ever known him.

That was why he did not see her. Because there was no other way. He hated the jagged edges the rough break left—the indecision —the not knowing. He despised himself for the unfairness of it. But he could not risk the more deadly hurt. It was—at least—a break. The best that he could do. That was why he had not seen Marianne for sixty-one endless days and nights. For twenty-four times that many hours and sixty times sixty—that many seconds. That was why.

His confusion was more than missing Marianne.

The story that had been pushed out of mind when he had met Marianne was alive in him now, calling for existence, and try as he might, Kern could not find the words with which to tell it. The story was there. It spread out in front of him in minute detail, his for the remembering. Yet he could not tell it. He could not visualize the force about which he wanted to write. Day after day he struggled with the problem of putting that shapeless force into words. As he did so, remembered angers and suspicions came to new and eager life. They nurtured themselves in his subconscious and when they had grown too large for the inner recesses of thought to contain them, they pushed their tentacular fingers out into his conscious mind. Kern was dimly aware of their presence and of what they were doing to him. He knew, too, that they were responsible in some way for his decision not to see Marianne again.

His work at the office slowed down to a dribble as he wrestled with stories that would have been easy writing under other conditions. Finally his work stopped. Each day he went to the office. Each day he struggled with the stories before him. Many times he thought he saw clearly what he wanted to do—what a story needed to make it ring true. But when he turned to his typewriter, his ideas disappeared. Or, if the ideas were there, he could not find the words. The harder he tried, the worse his work became.

There came a day when he stared at the typewriter before him and damned it and damned it. Damned it in despair, because it would give him no words. Then he slumped across the keyboard and cried and wished that he could do something with his hands— something, anything, besides this business of chasing words with which he could never come to grips.

He damned the day when, with eighteen other American Broadcasting staff men, he had been commissioned by the Army as a writer in the Radio Bureau. He squirmed in his chair remembering the smugness with which he had taken salutes from enlisted men on the streets—men with ribbons on their chests, men who had actually been where the war was being fought. The very little work he had been able to do, the few radio stories he had written, seemed pitifully unimportant to him now. In fact, remembering the days on end when he had not been able to write at all, those stories seemed completely unimportant. Finally, he resolved to see Max Karns and ask for his release from American Broadcasting and from his present assignment. Perhaps, he thought, he could find something else to do, something in which his contribution would be real.

Kern did not see Max Karns. Instead he came to work and sat and stared at his typewriter and tried to work as he had each day before. Sheet after sheet of paper he tore from his typewriter roller and threw into the wastebasket before trying again. The next day he did the same thing. And the next day too. Finally, he began to write again. Only a trickle at first. Not all of it good. Then more— and better.

Max Karns gave him the answer he was looking for. One morning

187

in late 1943, he came in to work to find his office empty. A note from Trixie stood, dropped against his pencil tray. Edgy he picked up the folded piece of paper and opened it.

"Boss—I've gone downstairs with the girls for coffee. 'K' wants to see you at once. Good luck. Trixie." "K," Kern knew, meant Karns. Everyone in American knew that "K" meant Karns.

For an instant Kern wondered how he could avoid this meeting, then, just as quickly, he decided that he might as well get the thing over with. He did not relish a bawling out, and as he headed down the hall to Max's office, he was sure that was exactly what lay in store for him. In the outer office, Betty waved him into Max's sanctum with a cheerful flip of her hand. Kern thought with distaste, "We who are about to die—" She needn't be so cheerful about it. Max sat with his eyes closed, listening to a playback from a dictagraph as Kern walked in, and he motioned to his lips for silence. Kern went to the farthest chair from Max's desk and sat, fidgeting, wondering what he could say that would explain to Max the doldrum into which he had fallen.

"Sit still, damn it! I've got to get this finished. Can't finish a thing with you squirming all over hell." Kern sat still. He could almost hear Max's voice snapping at him, "You're fired." He wondered what it would be like to be fairly sacked, and smiled thinly at the thought that he would know in a short while. Max switched off the dictagraph and hung the earphones on the rack beside him. He spoke without any prelude.

"How long before you can be ready to sail for England?" Kern felt his jaw fall open and tried to force it shut. It stayed open.

"Dammit, don't sit there and gawk at me. I asked you a simple question!"

Kern swallowed. Max meant it. Sail for England. He swallowed twice again under Max's baleful glare.

"I—I don't know. Why?" Max's scowl deepened.

"What's the matter with you, Kern? I asked you 'how many'—not 'why.' How many days?" Kern began to check the things he would have to do.

"I—I——"

"Listen—you're not fired. Though you damned well should be. You haven't done a decent piece of work in the past three months. If I didn't know you could do better—well, damn it, man. Answer my question!" Kern's mind raced. Close out the work in his office.

Close the apartment. Ship some things to his grandmother. Get his kit together. He foresaw conferences.

"About a month."

"You'll be ready in nineteen days. Your orders will be cut in Washington. You will contact the people at the Fort for details, medical work, that sort of thing."

England—a chance to get away from New York. To be free of the fear of seeing Marianne—of having to stay away from her. A chance to do a real job—to be in the war.

"The folks down in Washington think it's high time people here at home know on the spot what their boys are going through on the other side."

This way, Kern thought, Marianne couldn't blame him. She could feel that they had grown apart naturally instead of—he shifted to the edge of his chair as Max's enthusiasm caught him.

"Colonel Hatchett is coming in tomorrow. He has the Department outline. We will work from that. He will also have an itinerary for you. Three staff members from our outfit will be going along with you."

A chance to be near the mix of things. To be away from the story and the fear of going mad because he couldn't write. To be so busy that he wouldn't be able to think.

"Generally, we are going to use the theme, 'A Doughboy in England.' Human interest stuff. Something that'll have a real bang and bring the war home—" Kern knew. He and Max had thrashed through the idea months ago. England. It seemed to Kern that the burden which had rested on his shoulders had already lightened.

¤   ¤   ¤

Nineteen days isn't a long time any way you look at it.

Fill those days with travel between Fort Jay and Manhattan. Budget time for medical examinations. Add the complexities of overseas equipment issues. Cut out an hour or two for sleep. Consider the need for securing such odds and ends as shaving cream and extra pencils and burlap with which to cover furniture. Give a moment of time to contracting with the charwoman to give special care to the apartment. Allot time for the writing of letters and to the final rewriting of work already begun in the office. Add a visit to the tailor, and at the last minute race back to Fort Jay for a recheck of an X-ray picture. Do these things and nineteen days isn't a long time at all.

The days passed so quickly for Kern that he found he would not be able to visit his grandmother as he had planned. On the afternoon of the nineteenth day, he had to satisfy himself with calling Northport and talking to her for minutes on end until her Yankee thrift rebelled at the cost involved. When Kern hung up, he realized that he was packed and ready to go. Suddenly, nothing remained to be done until the staff car picked him up in the morning and took him to Fort Jay from which point he would officially begin his trip overseas.

With nineteen days behind him, during every one of which he had wondered a thousand times if he would have enough time to do the things that had to be done, Kern found himself sitting in a living room with packing cases all around him. Only bare necessities lay at hand for his use. Covers draped his furniture. Tomorrow the Quartermaster would come for his bags and the landlord would get his keys. No one to call. Nothing to do. Nothing, but to wrap the manuscript on top of the large packing case and mail it to his grandmother. He began to think of Marianne—as he had not thought of her during the past nineteen days. The old bitter-sweet ache was in him, and the quick urge to call her—to go to where she was.

He reached for the phone and dialed quickly. Two letters. Five numbers. Listened for the ringing tone. When a voice at the other end of the wire answered, he gathered his breath.

"Bill Gabel?"

"He isn't—do you know where you can reach him?" The hopefulness left his face and his voice. "I see." He drew a deep breath. "He may—? Listen, would you mind taking a message for him? Yes—yes—thanks a lot. Tell him that Kern Adams called. Yes—yes, I'm the same one—yes. Tell him that I'm leaving for overseas sometime tomorrow. Ask him to give me a call at home, please. Yes, he has my number. Thanks. Be sure to leave that where he will see it, won't you? Thanks." He hung up and fell back against the chair. "Small chance," he thought, "that Bill will see that in time to give me a ring." Marianne came crowding back into his mind and he fought off the images. He didn't have too long to fight off missing Marianne now.

Only hours.

❋ ❋ ❋

Kern stalked through each room in the apartment. Carefully he went over his check list of things to be done. None had been omitted. He leafed through a book and tossed it aside. He stood at the packing case and thumbed through several pages of the unfinished manuscript he was going to mail his grandmother, then turned away quickly. He was not in the mood for the story. By four o'clock he had given up hearing from Bill Gabel. No call from him. At five he called Bill's office again and learned that he had been in and had gone back out. At five-thirty he decided to shower and go out for dinner. Maybe a theater. Anything would be better than being alone in the apartment. At two minutes of five he stood in front of his bedroom mirror tying a knot in his tie, deciding that when he returned he would certainly have to see to this business of making some friends. The past four hours had taught him that he needed companionship. He gave his tie a last touch and turned from the mirror when he heard a rapping on his door. Thought creased his brow for a moment as he went toward the door, thinking it might be Bill—or the landlord.

It was neither. It was Marianne. She was the same. She had not changed. Her eyes were the same. The same hair. The same mouth. No—the mouth was different. Kern saw that there was a wanness about her mouth. He stared at her and his first thought was, "Please, God, don't ever let us be apart again," and he was simply and completely happy because the waiting days were over. Then the hard fingers of his determination forced themselves into his mind and he knew that this was the thing that he had feared above all else. Marianne was standing before him and now he would——

He stood there and held the door and she looked at him. She said, "May I come in?" and he remembered that the room behind him was junky and disorderly. He was ashamed of its disorder, as he stepped aside and inclined his head. He said, "Hello, Marianne." Slowly she went by him toward the center of the room.

The story! Kern knew that she could not help but see the manuscript lying on the packing case behind him. Panicky, he thought, "I can get it out of sight before she can ask any questions about it," and in the same breath he knew that he was not going to move it. He *knew* what he was going to do. He turned from the door with a sense of relief. It was out of his hands now. He went past her and stood before the window.

"I'm sorry the place is so torn up. I'm going overseas——"

"I know." Her voice told him that Bill had told her. Though they held no rebuke the two words also said, "—and you were going to

191

go without letting me know." Kern peered out a window to the narrow street below.

"Do you mind if I prowl?" He shook his head. "I've always been curious about your place." Kern did not answer. He followed the sound of her heels and tightened as he felt her stand behind him.

"Match?" He held a match to Marianne's cigarette, watching the flame as she puffed quickly and moved away, looking about the room. Then he lit himself a cigarette, holding the match until it burned his fingers. Behind him, Marianne's footsteps went into the bedroom and he listened as she flipped the light on and off in the hall. Then she was in the room again, moving behind him. He waited. Beyond the window, everything seemed far away. He looked out at what he could see of the city and waited. Her steps told him she was not far from the packing case now.

"Kern, you could have called. I've wondered so many times—" He had no answer. This was what he had hoped to miss. Marianne's voice was close to tears. She moved and he counted her steps and heard them stop. She was at the trunk. He knew it. As a blind man might know the number of steps needed to gain any given point in his dark world. He knew where she stood and what she saw and he started to pray. He didn't know what words he used or even if he prayed to God. Maybe it wasn't a prayer. Maybe it was just a hope. He heard the stiff-backed folder on the manuscript flip against the packing case. It sounded like a clap of thunder.

Marianne *was* reading the manuscript when he turned. Standing there, her teeth caught at her lower lip. A thin white line against red. Her eyes ran from line to line, and as Kern watched she turned the page slowly. He waited. And he prayed. There was no doubt about it now. He was praying. Praying that her love would be strong enough. That she would understand. That what had made her flare with anger that night he had called Jeff Balanchine a "coon" would come pushing through now. He prayed and watched her lips shape the words before her. Once she looked up, then read on. Kern was fixed to the spot. He tried to moisten his lips. His throat tickled and he wanted to cough. To say something, anything, that would fill the silence.

Something filled Marianne's face. Tightened her lips and twisted at their corners. She blinked her eyelids quickly and Kern's hope died. Not enough love. Not enough to carry through this.

Her head bent and her face rested in her hand. Her shoulders shook and Kern knew she was crying. He knew that he couldn't touch her—couldn't go to her. Suddenly, he knew too that he didn't want to touch her. He didn't want to put his arms around her. He didn't want anything from her—just for her to get to hell out. He wanted her to get the hell out and leave him alone.

He wanted to cry.

He began to tremble when she stepped back from the packing case and looked at him. With last hope, he prayed that she would come toward him, but her eyes told him that she would not. Her eyes were bewildered—as though she didn't know how to take what she had read. Whether to believe what she had read or not. Whether to laugh or cry. Kern saw that she knew this was real. That this story was his own.

Her smile faltered at first, then it became bright as she forced cheeriness into her lips. Her fingers ruffled the pages of manuscript and her chin quivered.

"You'll be gone long?"

"Not too long." He spread his hands. "These things—it's hard to say." She nodded, understanding.

"Take care of yourself." Her eyes fleeting over the room told him she was eager to get out. "And when you come back—give me a call."

"Yes." His voice was heavy and he looked away because it hurt him too much to watch her. He didn't want to see her walk out the door. He looked down at the floor.

He stood there looking down at the floor long after she left. Then he sat in the chair beside the lamp and looked at the things she had just touched and tried to gather enough of her presence from the room to wrap around himself.

* * *

He did not mail the manuscript to his grandmother. Nor did he take it with him. Instead, carefully, he wrapped it and sent it by messenger to Marianne. The note he enclosed was brief.

"I love you. Please try to understand."

CHAPTER IX

LEARN TO HATE!—SUMMER, 1934

ALL SUMMER long, Kern searched for kinship between himself and the Negroes with whom he came into contact. In the barbershop, on the streets, in the theater lobbies, at meetings of the Freedom League, wherever he met Negroes, he consciously tried to widen his smile, to make his greeting warmer. At the earliest opportunity, he turned any conversation in which he was engaged to the discussion of the narrow-minded, cruel prejudice which lay behind the acts of the white man. Each white face he passed, each bigot of whom he read or heard, became the imaginary subject of minutely detailed and horrible torture. Within his own mind, Kern rehearsed many times the holy inquisition which he would like to carry on against discrimination and segregation—and against the white men who were responsible for the outrage. Whenever he expressed his views in this respect, his words were charged with hot anger and his speech itself was pungently flavored with vicious profanity. His scorn was leveled with equal impartiality upon the "po' white trash," the average white man in the streets, the wealthy and the gentry on Capitol Hill who, as he put it, made "democracy" a damned joke.

Grateful to his father for not having plied him with questions about his early return from Evans, and for not once using the "I told you so" which he had feared all through the long train ride home, Kern plied Charles at every opportunity for information about the League and its activities, read and reread books and pamphlets on "the problem" and—to Charles' everlasting surprise—began to call his father "father."

Even so Charles was puzzled and wary of Kern's interest. Knowing as he did—thanks to a long letter he received from Mr. Henderson the day after Kern returned home—the conditions under which Kern had left Evans, and knowing the intensity with which the boy wanted to write, he realized, as Kern did not, the substitute part that this anger at whites and this sudden "devotion" to "the problem" played.

195

In the very violence of Kern's anger, Charles saw the full measure of his hurt. While he did not discourage the boy's interest in the League or his discontent with the prejudice and practices to which it gave life, he did subtly and at each opportunity wean Kern away from the blind emotional hatred which filled him to a more sane and logical approach to the questions he raised.

Kern's anger flared less brightly as the summer wore on. The instances he met among Negroes of careless disregard for the final outcome of "the problem," the unwillingness of almost all to even say they would "die if need be," the absence of an acute sense of racial responsibility among Negroes, combined, one by one, to blunt his zeal. The more closely he viewed the bleak despair that marked the Negro's life, the more did hopelessness come crowding in upon him. A core of hopelessness started in him and became a despair that associated itself with the question——

"—if Negroes themselves won't—who will?"

His anger at shiftless, irresponsible Negroes who, by their very actions and bearing, served to give continued life to the symbolic Negro about whom so much of the myth of prejudice revolved was equaled only by his anger at the white man.

Kern matured that summer. Turning inward upon himself for the answer to questions which he could not—or would not—take to Charles. Twice he wrote his grandmother—each time in reply to her letters—and each time the wave of hurt that came with remembering Evans made his letters brief. Neither of them said anything about his plans for the future. Nor could they have—for Kern had willfully thrust all consideration of the future out of his mind. He reread a letter from Paul Williams, his eyes clouding at the lines——

"—Mother says to find out what you are going to do. If you are going to visit us, let me know so we can plan what we shall do.'

Both times his eyes brimmed over and an aching lump stuck in his throat. After the second time, he crumpled the letter and threw it into his wastebasket. He never answered Paul.

The summer moved in an erratic manner. One week would drag itself out almost endlessly. Another, perhaps the very next, would fly by so quickly that Kern would not be able to remember what he had done during its course. Usually his weeks were filled with the same things. He read. He went swimming. He went to the library. He met his father for dinner each evening. Now and then he visited with some of the gang in the Summer Theater. Once he saw Rod Cameron.

Once he saw Dorcas.

* * *

Outside the library door, Kern stood under the awning. Heat waves shimmered over the wide apron before him and he blinked his eyes against the glaring light. Along New York Avenue a few pedestrians moved slowly past, a woman with a parasol, a young girl trundling a baby carriage, three men engaged in garrulous, arm-waving conversation.

He usually stayed longer at the library. Today the promise of a tall pitcher of cold lemonade and his favorite window seat had decided him to draw his books and go home.

Settling his books under his arm, Kern went down the stairs and across the heat-baked apron toward the park where a few idlers sat or sprawled at full length on the benches that stood along the curving walks. His head was bent to trace the irregular path of his feet along a seam in the concrete, and he scarcely noticed the woman who passed so close to him that their arms brushed. In a quick backward look he saw her, a tall woman, wearing a wide-brimmed hat and a gay colored dress, moving away from him with an easy, swinging stride. The set of her head and the dark coils of hair against her neck struck an almost forgotten note of memory, a note that her easy stride confirmed. Kern stopped and turned full about to stare, watching her steps slow and gather speed again, then stop. Hand raised to her mouth in surprise, she turned.

"Kern!" They went toward one another slowly at first, then more quickly, and with a rush as her arms went around him.

"Dorcas!" His books tumbled to the ground unnoticed as he swayed back and forth in her grasp. When he bent to pick them up, he could feel the gaze of curious eyes on him like a hand, and wire-thin caution started in him.

"Kern Roberts!" He faced her, his eyes higher than hers and smiled self-consciously. She held him off at arm's length, her hands on his shoulders.

"Why, Kern—you've grown. Look at you. You're a man now. I do believe you are going to be handsome." He remembered the warm pleasure that seeing Dorcas had always brought and gulped down his confusion.

"How long has it been, Kern? Let me see—seven, eight? Oh, no! It couldn't be—not eight years!" Kern nodded.

"Yes. I'm fifteen now. Almost sixteen." Something in him drew

197

back, and he felt vaguely uneasy as Dorcas surveyed him from head to toe.

"Where are you going now? Home?"

"Uh-huh." He wanted to get away. Actually wanted to. The realization surprised him.

"You don't have to rush, do you?"

"Well—" He cast about for some excuse.

"You don't, do you?" She seized upon his hesitation as a reply. "Good. I do want to talk to you so much." Kern felt a prickle of irritation as her eyes left his face and looked about them. He wondered what they had to talk about.

"I've got it—you'll come and have lunch with me, and we can have a long chat." Dorcas turned and took his arm and they went down Ninth Street and across "F" to Bromley's, Dorcas chatting on easily.

❁　❁　❁

"A party of two."

"Yes. Two, thank you—where it's most quiet."

"I'll seat you in an alcove." They threaded their way across the main floor and followed the hostess up five steps to a corner table. Kern surrendered his books and sat across from Dorcas. Quick to sense that he was ill at ease, Dorcas kept up a flow of small talk until a voice spoke beside them.

"Your order, please?" It was an impersonal voice, carefully modulated. Kern looked up. The girl was a Negro with skin the color of smoky honey, and a mass of auburn hair that was piled atop her head. Pencil poised above her pad, she was all courteous efficiency. "What," Kern wondered, "if she knew I was a Negro?" His eyes wandered over the floor below him. "What if all of them knew?" An urge came in him to rise and shout out his identity, to cry out:

"Look—look! I'm a Negro. Look at me, sitting here among you. You don't want to believe me, do you?" To shout that out. To watch the expressions change on their faces. As he had seen them change at Evans. He knew what they would look like.

Dorcas broke into the unruly train of his thoughts.

"Do you mind if I order for you, Kern?" He shook his head.

"Hungry?"

"No, not especially." The pencil above him moved quickly back and forth in response to Dorcas' voice.

"—and I'll have iced coffee."

198

"The young man?" The girl's dark eyes looked directly at Kern and the thought was in him again. "What if she knew?"

"Milk, I think. That's right, isn't it, Kern? A tall glass—very cold."

The waitress was gone. Dorcas took his hand across the table and held it, then seeing his constraint, began again to fill the silence with chitchat.

Before luncheon was done, Kern had relaxed under her banter, and was telling Dorcas about the years which had passed since he had seen her last. He told her about Paula, about Nettie and Rod Cameron and Evans. About Rollie. She laughed and was sober-faced. She laughed again. And at just the right things. He forgot his early reluctance to talk.

What became of Rollie?"

"I don't know, Dorcas. We drifted apart. I haven't seen him in a long time." He realized that he was talked out. Kern knew that he couldn't tell her why he and Rollie had fought. He couldn't bring himself to say the word "nigger" before her. Not—"nigger." The silence grew strained.

"You've changed, Kern." Dorcas' voice was worried. "Don't let them change you too much." Irritation flowered in him at her remark. "Them"! What did she know about "them"? What did she know about who caused the changing—who was responsible for the everyday hurts that made Negroes change?

"Don't forget the goal you had and the things we promised." Kern knew she meant the things he and his mother had dreamed about. Her eyes told him that, and he knew he should not have doubted her concern for him. A prickle of tears behind his eyes matched the brightness of her eyes and he regretted his moment of angry resentment at her words.

They parted outside of Bromley's. Dorcas kissed him on the cheek, squeezed his shoulder, and then she was gone, her wide hat swinging from her hand as she disappeared in the crowd that swirled along the street. Kern watched her until she was gone, then, squaring his books away, walked west to catch the streetcar home.

All the way home and evening long, he went over that meeting in his mind. For the first time he had seen Dorcas as a white woman. He had not seen her as a dear friend. He did not understand his resentment immediately.

He had seen and talked to a white face and the lessons of eight years had bridled his tongue. Many things were not for her ears.

199

Neither the Freedom League, nor the Association of First Families. Neither the Negroes who hung their hopes on "Yaller money, yaller women and yaller cars," nor the heartbreaking agony of Negroes. Nor the grasping shabbiness in some Negro leaders. These things were not for her ears. They were not for the ears of any white person. Not these things nor a knowledge of the quivering, pain-shot quick to which the word "nigger" struck. Instead, for a white face, disinterest, laughter, or a blinding flash of anger. These things he knew.

Kern had, without realizing it, come to think as Negroes do.

But if he was hurt and ashamed at having misunderstood Dorcas' concern for him, he found pleasure in the thought that he had pulled the wool over the eyes of every white person in Bromley's. The thought stayed with him all evening. It pleased him to think that it had been within his power to strike them aghast with a single word.

He did not tell his father that he had seen Dorcas.

☼ ☼ ☼

And he went to a Freedom League Convention with his father.

He went to the Convention, and for the first time he began to see what the Freedom League meant to Negroes—what it really was.

The rest of his life, Kern would remember this.

They came to Cincinnati from the North and South, the East and West. By train and car they poured into the town that Negroes called the "jumpin'-off place" for southbound travelers. By train and bus and private car, they came.

From each state in the United States, they came. From towns called Hesitation, Pauling and Luling; from New York, Swift Creek, Seattle and Atlanta. They came from Tecumseh, and Baton Rouge and Indian Spoon, from Tupelo and Hartford. From the way stops and great cities of forty-eight states and one District, from the territories of Alaska and Hawaii, from the Virgin Islands and from Cuba, they made their way to Ohio and to Cincinnati. They came in a common hope, though not in a completely common voice. And not all of them were Negroes.

Black man and white. Brown, yellow, cinnamon and ginger. Blue eyes and brown and black, green and tawny tan. Broad lips, shapeless lips, thin lips, full lips, sharp, graven mouths. Flat noses and broad, pug, aquiline and lean, high-bridged Roman noses. Noses with wide flaring nostrils. Hair brown and auburn, gray and white

200

and Nordic blond. Hair curling close to the scalp, hair pressed and freshly rolled, waved, short and kinky and long in satin waves that were obedient to the touch of fingers and a breath of air.

Black man and white. Farmer, lawyer, merchant, laborer. Druggist, teacher, philanthropist, and doctor. Streetcar operator, postal clerk and one-crop farmer. Porter and redcap and Doctor of Science. They came with one child or with two or three. Or they came alone. Chapter representatives and members at large. With meager belongings or burdened with luggage. With the only, the best, the Sunday suit or dress worn upon the back. With a change of shirt or underclothing, with fresh-made lye soap and a brush, roped in cardboard boxes that crumpled and threatened, if they had not already done so, to break at the corners. With the hoarded, many-times-counted few dollars pinned or sewn or worn close against the body, its lumpy presence verified a thousand times again by conscious fingers, they came to the Convention.

By first-class rail with first-class hotel reservations, with bonded liquors and fat purses, they came to the Convention.

There was at first only a handful of them. Then there were hundreds. And a thousand. Two thousand and, finally, more than three.

They moved into convention.

They met and sat in conference. Black men and white from every station and every walk of life. And while there were forty Negroes and more for every white man there, the handful of white men came and sat. And spoke their thoughts. Stayed, and faced the deathless animosity, the involuntary suspicion which the mere presence of their faces aroused in many of the Negroes about them. Stayed in spite of this, and did their bit to give new strength to the Freedom League. Mingled together in Emory Hall they sat, not all of them familiar with convention proceedings. Though they did not always follow the procedures of order, they attended. Attended faithfully, missing none of the long, tedious sessions, enduring sweltering heat with a patience that would not be denied.

They were the sensate spirit of the Convention. When they rose to speak in halting, unskilled words, when they strained forward, hand cupped at ear, to catch a word that might otherwise be lost, their words and their faces reflected the conviction which had brought them to the Convention. And their conviction became a felt thing. One felt the roots from which it rose, and knew that the unswerving belief of these people in the Freedom League made it the biggest and best hope of Negroes in the history of man. And

201

one knew that this hope which they brought with them would die slowly, if ever, and that if it did die, its death would be stark tragedy. The League was, for Negroes, a desperate hope, born of hopelessness and the eternal human need for at least one inviolate hope.

Throughout three or four days a handful of selfish men struggled to use the Convention as a means of advancing their personal stature as leaders. For selfish gain they would have stripped away the promise of democracy within the League.

Time and again Charles Roberts came to the platform to explain in simple language the issues at hand, the things involved, to lash out at the would-be "bosses" and to declare that above all, if the League was to live and prosper, it must remain of the people, by the people, and for that people. With each word he spoke in defense of their hope, with every effort to give the League to the people, to make it plain that it was theirs and theirs alone to choose their leaders by common voice, he became in their eyes and thoughts and hearts the symbol of the League itself.

Time after time under his leadership, the people sensed that the hope which the League held was in grave danger, and their rumbling, assembled "No!" was given in answer to the selfish men.

To each man Charles gave dignity. For each he had a kind word, a personal word. A word that warmed and gave hope and reached always to the personal problem. He gave a word and the willingness to listen.

❅   ❅   ❅

On the last day the Freedom League mass meeting was held in University Stadium. On the last day—after the business of the convention was finished, after Charles had been re-elected as National President of the League—the mass meeting was held.

More than three thousand strong, members of the Freedom League sat, tiered upward in curving rows at the stadium's lower end. With them under the burnished, fleckless sky, sat more than their number again of native Cincinnatians, gathered to witness the final mass meeting of this Freedom League which had invaded their city.

A choral group presented two numbers and a minister invoked the grace of God upon the gathering. Telegrams of greeting from the President of the United States, from a National Jewish Conference, and from a National Council of Churches were read. The

Mayor of the City of Cincinnati addressed the gathering briefly.

Charles walked slowly to the center of the speakers' platform. The silence which came with his raised hand was as thunderous as the applause which greeted him when he stood. Briefly, plainly, his voice rose on the microphones and went on the air in a national hookup. He dedicated the Freedom League to continuous concern with the problems which arose from the denial of democracy to Negro citizens of the United States because of race or creed.

"However," his words rang out, "the League must and will work on a wider canvas than that outlined by racial interests alone. It was not our intent," the silent listeners hung on his words, "to deal with a series of small things, however attractive the yield of sensational publicity may have been or may yet be. We are not troublemakers as some of our reactionary fellow Americans have painted us. Neither are we 'Reds.' We are American to the core. And we shall continue to be just that. Right or wrong, America is ours. Right or wrong, we belong to America. We shall do all within our power to be right, and in clear conscience—because we cannot do less, to help America to be also right. We have an unlimited faith in the final end to which the essential goodness of Americans will bring us. One final thought. The fruit is, as the Bible says, of the seed. If the Freedom League is to urge the cause of democracy, it must be in the deepest and purest sense, a democracy itself. The Freedom League is a body of the people. It shall continue to be of the people. And you members here assembled must bear in mind that no small group of men, however well intentioned they may be, should ever be permitted to hold the destiny of the League in their hands. You must choose your leaders year after year by the process of open election."

In the silence after Charles had sat down the editor of the *New York Graph* rose and belittled his ability to add to what had already been said.

"I shall write in my paper that in my entire life I have never before experienced anything which has been so filled with hope and faith in the ultimate goodness of mankind as has this convention. I believe that in your hands and in your hearts the Freedom League will do much to wake a sleeping nation to its responsibility in meeting the problem of racial discrimination.

A great contralto stood poised on the dying thunder of applause and when the scraping feet of the rising throng had stilled, her voice rose in the words of *America*, and after a chorus the voice of the stadium joined hers and shared the sky with the first parading clouds of evening.

Minutes later the Convention ended on a note of prayer. In another year the Freedom League would hold its annual Convention in the nation's capital.

❀   ❀   ❀

The train slid smoothly north toward Washington. Now and then its rocking motion made itself felt in the diner as silver jingled on the tables and cautious waiters caught their balance. Kern and his father waited for their dinner and idly noticed the small towns that rushed past their windows. The screaming sirens and the police escort which had sped them from the stadium to the terminal were behind them. Too, there was the staring crowd, the final hurried shakes in the hustling terminal building. Their conversation was idle. They were both tired after a week of nothing but the Convention and talk came to them in fragments.

"I had a letter from Paula just before we left." Kern's face expressed nothing beyond pleasure and mild curiosity.

"What did she say?"

"Oh—nothing in particular. She wanted to know if you were going to the Convention. Wondered what you would think of going to college at Valley View this fall." Charles waited, studying the boy's serious face.

For the first time in weeks, Kern thought of Paul's letter that had gone unanswered.

"She thought that if you did, you might live with her—with Jake." He wanted Kern to say yes—to want to go. He did not urge him. He said nothing to decide his mind for him. He did not know, really, how hungry Kern was for the happiness he had known at Evans. He did not know Kern would say yes because he was torn by a complicated mixture of anger and hurt and perverse defiance.

"I think I would like that."

Charles was pleased when the two of them rose and walked along the swaying diner and made their way back to their compartment.

It was as simple as that. Kern would go to Valley View in the fall—in little more than a month.

CHAPTER X

FIRST JOURNEY SOUTH

1

Kern went South as a Negro traveler.

The Negro traveler, if he goes by coach—and most of them do—rides southward from Cincinnati by Jim Crow car. He leaves the easy-riding Pullman which has brought him through the night from Northern, Eastern and Central states and crosses the station to the line of gates that lead to what Negroes call the "jumpin'-off place." He goes through one of these gates and flows with the crowd down a dusty ramp to the long shed beside which trains stand waiting. He walks past long gray cars with curious names and a double diner he will not use later unless he sits at a solitary table shrouded by a green drape, until he reaches the cars that have numbers only. "Forward!" A conductor jerks his thumb and signals him forward, and another does the same until he curiously notes that HIS fellow travelers have dwindled and now there are only dark faces about him. Dusky faces who climb aboard the coach—under rare conditions, two—which is reserved for them. The traveler, Negro, is now "in his place," and if his spirit feels the vise of shame drawing in upon it it is helpless. For in a trice the clicking wheels will cross the Ohio's swirling flotsam to Covington in Kentucky where he will see the first sign "For Colored." From Covington, the wheels race southward through Kentucky to Tennessee and beyond, and all along the way, the sign "For Colored."

In mid-September the Negro traveler is most likely to find two cars for his use. For in September of each year, caravans of Negoes travel along this way, from the Far West, and the Central states, from the East, and join at Cincinnati, flow down the ramps and board the cars that will take them into an alien land. Alien—they to it, and it to them. And deep in the dark heart of the land are the colleges—Louisville Municipal in Louisville, Fisk University and Tennessee Agricultural and Industrial College in Nashville.

Talladega and Tuskegee in Alabama. Dillard, Xavier and Southern in Louisiana. These and others. Below Nashville only the *Dixie Flyer* and the *Comet* carry two Jim Crow cars, and that but rarely, for most of the students will have gotten off at Louisville and at Nashville, having either arrived at their destinations, or changed to other trains that furrow out at angles from these central points, reaching to the less trafficked way stops.

II

Coal smoke choked the yards at Nashville, palled the late-afternoon sky and could be tasted in the throat with a biting, tar-like flavor. Its fallen flakes lay in dusty film on the sluggish Cumberland backwaters as the *Dixie Flyer* rounded the long curve that led into the station. When it was pointed out to him, Kern could barely see the thin spire of Fisk's Jubilee Hall pushing up above the low ragged skyline to the west.

In Nashville, for the last time, Kern changed trains and boarded the *Comet*. He found himself sharing a double seat with a silver-haired, elderly man who had boarded the *Dixie Flyer* at Louisville. His name, Kern remembered, was Dr. Gray. Excited screeches of delight had marked his arrival on the *Flyer* and Kern had been drawn to him at once for the ready, infectious smile with which he had greeted separate members of the Valley View student group. Dr. Gray was a Chem prof at Valley View. He was, in fact, the Dean of the Chemistry Department. He was, too, the senior advisor for freshmen. He had a way of addressing the male students as "old boy," leaving no doubt when he did, that you were included in the inner circle of his confidence. Kern had liked him from the start and he had been drawn even closer to him while he had regaled them with "tall tales" as the train clicked away the seemingly endless miles. He liked both his laughter and the way with which he handled the minor crises which appeared among the students—for example, the way in which he had dismissed the frightening tales which the older boys had been telling about Bill Noble, the sheriff of the town of Valley View.

Kern chatted easily with Dr. Gray as the car quieted and the train slid out of the Nashville station. Then the breaks in their conversation became more frequent and more lengthy until, finally, they fell silent and Dr. Gray dozed with his pipe still held easily in his mouth. Kern stared out of the window.

206

The *Comet* slid out of the yards, and whistled its way past the radio towers to the south of the city, raced for a moment on equal terms with the cars along the Franklin Turnpike, then gathered speed for its long journey south to the Gulf and rushed away, leaving the cars, and finally the road, behind.

Beyond Nashville the land took on a subtle change. The rolling, green hills gave way to a broken, rutted land on the face of which long, ragged, narrowing gashes showing red earth, ran upward and out of sight into the hillsides. Where there were no hills, where the roadbed clashed through embankments, blank red faces of earth slanted steeply up from the tracks, heavily marked with cinder dust and with the brush that crept to the edge of the tracks.

There was only one Jim Crow car on the *Comet*, one car that was comfortably filled. Enough filled to give its riders the feeling of security that comes with numbers. There were some twenty students, identifiable by their bags and by the tight groups in which they sat. There were, too, a sprinkling of older men and women, obviously working people, whose faces declared that they were natives of the land. These were passengers who boarded the train and rode for short distances to the next stop or to the one beyond and then got off. These the conductor would greet with familiar words and a laugh—with "boy" and "Aunty." His easy familiarity won grins from these folk and a quick gratitude to him as a white man for having recognized them and in a measure salved their prides and allowed them to sit apart and stare at the clustered students with a feeling of "I'm better'n you—white folks jokes with me." Kern listened tight-lipped and gazed out of the window. He said nothing until a dining-car waiter came into their car to take their dinner orders.

"Take a little time, suh—but," the man confided quickly, "we'd sooner serve you here'n behin' 'at curtain." He jerked his head toward the dining car somewhere behind them. Kern ordered and lapsed into silence again. Across from him Dr. Gray ordered, and with a brief smile at Kern went back to dozing.

Kern's mood changed with the land. It had begun to change with the first "For Colored" sign he had seen in Covington. The change had been a tight waiting that was handmaiden to the knowledge that the land through which he rode was alien and hating. The car was quiet now. The students who remained were tired. Their chatter had run down to silence. As evening came on, Kern's mood settled on him heavily.

Lights showed in one town after another. Indistinct in the early dusk, they came up to his window out of nothing and swirled backward out of sight. Propping his chin in one hand, Kern set his elbow on the window edge and stared out intently until their dinners came. Two waiters came first, close together. Minutes later, a third waiter followed them, his tray disarranged and his white coat spotted with coffee stains. He placed his tray on an empty seat and held a muttered conference with the other waiters, then, smiling, he came back and began to arrange the tray.

"I think this is yours, suh." His gleaming smile was forced, Kern felt.

"Mine and his—" Kern leaned forward to the man who shared his double seat and touched his arm.

"Dr. Gray—Dr. Gray. Dinner's here."

"Hum-um. What—oh!" He straightened in his seat with a friendly grin. "Guess I was pretty done in." He raised his arms as the waiter settled the tray on their knees. "I guess the train's pretty jerky." He looked at the coffee stains on the waiter's jacket.

"Aw, nossuh—not that." The suggestion slighted the waiter's professional ability.

"No? What happened?" Kern could not translate the man's grunted answer.

"I'll bring you some more coffee." His eyes flashed toward the two waiters who stood waiting at the door.

"Oh, no. Don't bother." Kern stared curiously at the man's face as he counted out change.

"Any trouble?" Dr. Gray watched him too.

"Nothing serious——"

"What was it then?" Kern insisted.

"Some 'peckers in the nex' car back said they didn't want no food comin' up here for no niggers. Tried to mess my tray up. Bastards!" Shame flushed the man's face and Kern was sorry that he had pressed for a reply. It would have been better not to have seen the shame in the man's face. He and Dr. Gray ate slowly from the shared tray. When they spoke, it was mincingly and their words were chosen with care.

"Is this your first time away at school, old boy?"

"No, sir. I went away to school last year."

"To college?"

"Well, no, sir. Not exactly. It was Evans Academy. Sort of a prep school for writing and drama."

"Evans? In Vermont?" Kern nodded.

"How did you like it?"

"Oh, lots. It's—" Words failed Kern.

"This is your first time to go South, isn't it?"

"Yes, sir." Kern puzzled for a moment. "How did you know?"

"Oh, I don't know. There's something about a Negro when he travels South for the first time." Kern did not quite understand. "—as if he were a little leery of what he was going to find. As though all the tales he had ever heard about the South were piling through his head." He understood this. Those stories were running through his head now. The youngsters in the car had told fantastic stories for him to add to those he already knew. Dr. Gray's face twisted into a wry smile.

"South's pretty bad, I suppose. 'Specially for Negroes. It's not too good for whites." Kern speculated on the stories he had heard.

"Dr. Gray, Bill Noble," the old man's eyes narrowed, "is he as bad as the fellows say he is?"

"Well—" Dr. Gray rubbed his cheeks reflectively, "I suppose they may have made Bill Noble a little worse than he really is." As an afterthought, "Not much worse, though." He leaned forward resting his arms on his knees. "We don't have much contact with him or with the city of Valley View either, for that matter. Almost everything we need is right on the campus. So we seldom go to town. Bill Noble usually stays in town where the mill hands and the Negroes from The Gut congregate." His words were more blunt as he turned his attention to the tray between them. Kern tugged his watch from his waist pocket and looked at it, turning it toward Dr. Gray. It said 6:20.

"Due in at 11:45." Dr. Gray stretched a little and leaned back in his seat, yawning widely. "Just time for a good snooze." His eyes closed. "I seem to get sleepy about this time every trip. It's gotten to be a habit, I guess. It helps these last few hours to pass."

Kern took their tray back and placed it with the others where the waiters could get them. When he came back, Dr. Gray was comfortably settled in his seat, eyes closed, drawing contentedly at the ever-present pipe that slanted from his mouth. Kern inched into his seat beside the window and placed his feet on the unused half seat before him.

Over the back of the seat before him, along the aisle, he saw other students, sleeping or smoking. Talking quietly. Two men and a woman who had boarded the train at a town called Pulaski sat in the seat behind Dr. Gray. They had lapsed into silence almost immediately after giving their tickets to the conductor.

Adoriah, the girl from Lansing whom he'd helped with her bags at Louisville, sat on an outside seat two rows down. The lashes of her closed eyes made vivid dark lines against her olive skin. Her hair was thrown back from the sides of her face and fell over her shoulders, her arms were crossed in front of her. The high, Indianlike bones of her cheeks held his gaze. As he watched, she opened her eyes and looked at him, then she closed her eyes. The smile stayed on her lips.

At grade crossings and hamlets, the train whistle split the silence with a distant shriek that broke over their car and quickly faded behind them. The train was running on a long, gentle downgrade through dark, rolling country that was fast losing shape in the darkness.

At intervals the lights of hamlets and towns flickered by and were gone, and once they came headlong up against the shape of a long freight train on a siding. The blurred shapes of freight car, stockcar, flatcar, coal car, hurtled by them, in pell-mell backward flight out of sight. With a slam they were in the clear again, and the horizon showed like a faint blue line in the distance.

Kern closed his eyes. When he opened them, a trainman came in and turned on dim ceiling lights. Southward—into the lion's den. Defiance out of the bitterness which he had learned that summer faltered at the thought. He was hours and miles apart from the things he knew and from the feeling of safety they offered. He tried to put down the fear of what the South might hold—and each minute took him deeper into the land about which he had heard so many tales.

He pressed his forehead against the window and stared into the darkness. He saw nothing to remind him of the New England hills and Northport. From what he had heard, he knew Valley View would be nothing like Evans. The sharpness of the difference cut him. All summer he had gathered resolve, defiance, anger, trying to set himself for this trip. Evans was salt in his mouth, a dream he knew he'd best forget, and he had tried to deepen his anger against the white man. All summer he had done that. June, July, August, and now September, he'd manufactured hate. He didn't hate Dorcas, though. Nor his grandmother—nor "Old Henderson." He didn't hate Paul. He could not manufacture that much hate. But all the others. He had written Paul. "So I guess it will be better if I go with my people and you go with yours. It was swell knowing you, Paul, and I didn't intend to deceive you."

He hoped Paul had understood. If only— He drew away from the thought.

The signs were in his mind as he dozed.

For Colored.

He twisted in his half sleep as the train rocked its way through the night, announcing its passing to hamlets and grade crossings with shrill hoots.

III

"Valley View—Valley View. All out fo' Valley View." The porter went through the coach taking down bags from the luggage racks. "All out fo' Valley View." He touched sleeping passengers on the shoulder and stirred them awake. Kern stretched widely. Dr. Gray was already awake. The two men and the woman who had boarded the *Comet* at Pulaski had detrained somewhere in the night. Their seat was held now by a frail little man who wore an overcoat in spite of the car's stifling heat. Kern's image in the window prompted him to straighten his tie. He wiped at the dirt streaks on his face without noticeable improvement and hastily stuffed his handkerchief back into his pocket as the train jerked to a halt. The gate slammed back and the door opened.

Outside the night air held a soft, strange scent. That was Kern's first impression of the South as he stepped down from the car. The Valley View students were laughing on the platform, gathering their bags and handing them up to the bus driver who was to take them out to the college. A cluster of students who were going through to Talladega stood in the open train door calling, "Goodbye!" and promising "See you at Homecoming."

The orange-yellow globe above the platform washed the station's dull-red front in a rough circle of light that folded where the station and platform met and extended to the sides of the train coaches. Orange letters on a red board below the light spelled the words "Valley View." Near the fringe of light at the far end of the platform, the stationmaster talked with the conductor while baggage and freight were loaded and unloaded.

Kern looked about him uncertainly, trying to find Paula. Beyond the dim light he could see only shapes. Dr. Gray came toward him.

211

"Paula is meeting you, isn't she?"

"I think so, sir." He still did not see her as he searched the platform and the darkness. And then they came, hurrying across the end of the platform. Paula and Jake. Jake Caulfield was exactly what his father had said he would be. A towering man, so tall in the shadows, so straight and tall, that it seemed to Kern that he reached out of sight. He saw him plainly as they came toward him. Paula was unchanged. Laughter was still in her eyes and on her lips.

"Kern, oh darling!" She embraced him quickly, standing on tiptoe to squeeze him to her.

"Well, now, wait a minute." Jake laughed playfully beside them. "I'm not sure I like that." He looked to Dr. Gray for agreement. "Paula tol' me he was a boy. Why," he looked down at Kern, "this's most a man growed."

"Kern, this is Jake," Paula turned to him, "the big idiot. You'll have to get used to him. He talks such foolishness all the time. And Dr. Gray! Oh, how are you? It's seemed as though summer would never pass. I'm so glad you're back."

"Well, I am pretty glad to get back. Can't seem to want to stay away from here. I'm sort of like Jake, though," he teased her, "I am a bit jealous of this youngster." He bent and turned his cheek to receive her friendly peck.

"Can we drop you off, Doc? Be glad to," Jake took his hand in a firm grasp.

"Oh, I don't think so—I guess I'll go along on the school bus. It's not very crowded and you folks won't have to go out of your way."

"Oh, it's no trouble," Jake assured him. "We got nothing but time right now."

"Well, I certainly thank you, but I'll go along with the crowd." He motioned toward the students with his bag.

Three whistle blasts split the night, and the chuff of the engine jerked the train couplings tight behind them as the train began to slide away.

Kern looked curiously about him. He saw the bulked shapes of trees and the outlined forms of several houses grouped together. The gray outline of a road pushed out from the platform to a darker, shiny band along which the taillight of a car disappeared in the distance. At the far end of the platform, three white men were talking. As he looked, they laughed loudly and turned away.

The stationmaster turned and tugged the lead tongue of a baggage cart into line and then disappeared into the station. For the first time close at hand, on a door of the weathered frame building, Kern saw the words:

FOR COLORED.

He wanted to walk over to the door and touch the sign with his fingers. Instead, he grew tight inside and stood there staring. He did not hear Jake's first questions until Paula touched his arm.

"Is this all the baggage you have, young feller?"

"Oh, yes, sir. The rest of my things were shipped on my ticket."

"Well," Jake looked doubtfully at the cluster of baggage on the end of the platform, "s'pose we pick it up in the morning? No reason why you must have it tonight, is there?"

"Oh, no. I can unpack the stuff any time. I have enough in my bag for a day or so."

"All right. Let's make tracks for home." Jake bent and took his bag and they walked slowly toward the little coupé parked on the edge of darkness. The school bus chugged away, the words of a song trailing behind it.

"Alma Mater, sweet beloved, we raise our arms to you. . . ."

They stopped and waited until they could not hear the words any longer. At the moment, remembering Evans brought only a faint pang. Perhaps, Kern thought, it might not be so bad at Valley View. The softness of the night, the edged shapes about him, the voices in song and the sweet scent that filled the air were different and intoxicating, and they drugged away part of his earlier fear. This first glimpse of Valley View was not as foreboding as he had imagined. Not even the sign, "FOR COLORED."

The short grayish strip of road was, he found, deeply rutted. The little car pitched back and forth as Jake inched along, throwing him against Paula and Paula in turn against Jake. Past the three houses that huddled together at the road's edge where a brief high-pitched laugh and the arcing glow of a thrown cigarette were the only signs of life, and out to the paved highway road that turned and ran with easy curves beside the railroad tracks finally to cross them, they came to a steep hill. All the while, Paula chatted on.

". . . been expecting you. Your room's all ready. Jake insisted on getting everything spic and span." Jake laughed in the dark.

"Don't you let her fool you, young feller. She's fussy as a settin' hen. Always keeps things like that." Pride filled his voice and Kern was quick to recognize the bond of affection between them.

"How's 'Wobbie'?" They rumbled across the tracks and climbed the steep hill, then turned sharply to the left. Ahead of them was a cluster of lights.

"Valley View." Jake motioned with his hand. Kern leaned forward. There wasn't much to see. Only the cluster of lights drawing closer and widening beyond the first small group.

"We'll come through town in the mornin' when we get the trunk. Isn't much to see—not like Washington or Cincinnati. Just a small country town." Paula tugged at Jake and pointed.

"Here—here, Jake. You're going to take the Selma Road, remember?"

Jake turned sharply. "Almost overran my turn." The steering wheel spun back under his hand. "This is the Selma Road. Off there," Jake pointed toward pale-blue lights arranged in three regular tiers, "is Millville." Paula mumbled indistinctly as Kern strained his eyes trying to see Millville more clearly.

"They're 'bout the first mills to come to this part of the State. Help keep some money here. Used to be, all the money went out with the cotton. Now some of it stays here."

"Little enough," Paula snipped. Jake did not pursue his praise of Millville.

"And th' other lights off there in the middle come from The Gut."

The Gut? Dr. Gray had mentioned "The Gut," Kern remembered. He thought it was a strange name to give a place. The faint clatter of spindle looms came to them as they passed Millville.

"What's The Gut?" Kern still wondered at the strange name.

"That's where the city Negroes live. Lies in a pocket of ground sort of, between Millville and Valley View. That's why it's called The Gut."

"And over there," Paula pointed across him into the dark, "is the college. The lights are hidden. In the daytime you can see the top of Tubman Hall."

Beyond the lights of Millville they drove in silence, and the road was a shiny strip under the bright moonlight. The fields rolled easily back from the Selma Road, and here and there Kern saw spatterings of white as if a giant hand had scattered snow over the fields. He pointed into the darkness.

"What's—what's that?" Jake, and Paula too, followed his finger to see what he meant.

"What, Kern? I don't see anything." Paula looked harder.

"I mean the white."

"Oh," Jake laughed deep in this throat, rocking with laughter, and Paula joined him. She broke through her laughing. "Why, that's cotton, Kern. You've never seen cotton before, have you?" Kern shook his head.

"No? At least not lying out in fields." Jake's laughter subsided to a chuckle.

"Kern, we uns take cotton so for granted. We live with it from the time we're little tads. Reckon it's hard for us to understand how other folks could live without knowing about it."

"The same way I might think it was funny if somebody didn't understand about subways?"

"Yep, that's it," Jake agreed, "just the same way."

The pines closed in about them, now close to the road and suddenly thinning to dark open spaces, then tight again in dark shadows. The air cooled with their closeness and their pungent aroma mingled with the other sweetness. It was different from the air at Evans. Not even the pines were the same. The air was not as hard or as clean. It seemed to Kern to be softer and filled with something strange.

❂ ❂ ❂

White, two-storied, trimmed in blue, the house sat back from the road behind a cleared, grass-grown yard, and a neat, white-paled fence. Jake opened the gate and drove through.

Kern stood, stretching, on the little graveled drive as Jake closed the car doors and then led the way up the three wide stairs to the screened-in porch and opened the front door. He snapped on the light and they stood inside. Kern set his bag on the floor and looked about him. Jake stood behind him and watched his face as Paula went ahead of them to the kitchen.

"Come on back here, Kern—you can wash your hands here in the kitchen. When we go upstairs we'll be up for the night."

"Come on, young fellow." Jake put his bag at the foot of the stairs and followed him into the kitchen where Paula had set out a plate of sandwiches and some milk, and was taking glasses down from the wall cabinet.

"We'll eat a bite and then sit a while on the porch and talk. You'll sleep better that way. Give you time to relax."

"Bossy, bossy," Jake chided her jokingly.

"You sit down there." She sternly pointed to a chair and Jake sat. He laughed up at Kern.

"She'll boss you, young feller. If there was ever a woman with a min' of her own, it's Paula."

"Oh, pshaw, Jake." She grinned at Kern. "How about some cold milk with those sandwiches?" Kern grinned back and sat down.

"Sounds awfully good to me, Paula."

"You'll learn quickly enough that when she says do something— just as well do it, then argue after." Kern felt Jake's eyes appraising him as he sat. He wondered what the big man thought of him.

"Now hurry, boys, so we can finish and sit on the porch for a while."

* * *

It was almost two o'clock when Jake finally stood up and stretched.

"You folks can stay up all night if you wanna. I'm a working man, and I got to get up in the morning." He sidled toward the door.

"You come back here, Jake Caulfield. What do you mean by going off without kissing me good night?" Jake chuckled delightedly as he turned to Paula.

"Jes' wanted to see if you'd mind, honey."

"Of course, I mind." He bent and kissed her.

"Good night, Kern. We'll pick the trunk up in the morning."

Kern sat and talked to Paula until he grew sleepy. He told her about Nettie and George Lincum; about Evans and his grandmother and the fun he had known until Fannin. He told her about Dorcas and the Convention and the whole summer of trying to whet his hate.

It was the first chance he'd had really to talk about those things and Paula listened as closely as she had years ago when she had come to Washington for his graduation. Almost at once he began to feel better.

He could not explain to her how the signs he had seen had affected him, though he wanted to describe his fear of the South. All he knew of the South was the soft night air about them. Nothing else. He was afraid that if he tried to tell her about the fear that was in him, she would be disappointed in him. After all, she and Jake were living a normal, happy life here. He could feel Paula gazing at him through the dark. He yawned widely, catching himself midway and covering his mouth.

"Well," she rose abruptly. "That's that. Time to go to bed." He trooped upstairs after her, to the front room in the corner of the house that he was to have as his own.

The linen on the bed was cool against his bare arms and legs, and he drifted off to sleep in the night, hearing only the crickets and the distant barking of a dog as it began and suddenly stopped.

CHAPTER XI

VALLEY VIEW, ALABAMA

I

KERN signed the release slip and handed the pencil and board to the stationmaster.

"Want some help with this thing, Jake—it's purty heavy?"

"I don't think so, Mister Hawkins—I'll jest heft it a mite—maybe I'll be able to get away with it." Jake turned his back to the low counter and reached over his shoulder, fumbling for the trunk handle. His back bulged and stretched under the faded blue shirt as he shrugged his shoulders and settled the trunk into place. Then, hand on his hip for balance, he walked slowly and easily to where the coupé stood with its back cover raised. He turned and lowered the trunk to the bumper, then slid it into the compartment. "Sure would hate to have Jake mad with me—reckon he mus' be 'bout the strongest man in Valley View." Mr. Hawkins' face reddened suddenly at having "'lowed" so much for a white man and he looked covertly at Kern to see if his words had been heard. Then he disappeared into the station office.

Jake came back and took the larger bag. Kern carried the other and they piled them into the back of the car. Jake dug into his pocket and pulled out a handkerchief to mop at the beads of perspiration that glistened on his forehead.

"Pretty hot, isn't it?" Kern squinted into the glaring, cloudless sky that curved overhead about them. The first heat waves of the day were beginning to shimmer up from the pavement and the land.

"Yep, pretty hot, but just you wait 'til this afternoon. Give old man sun time to get up a little higher. He's just beginning to feel his self now."

Jake eased his bulk in under the wheel and ground on the starter button. "Yes, sir, this summer's been nigh as bad as '21. That summer, cotton didn't get no higher'n a foot tall—'n where the cotton was s'posed to be, there was nothing but little blossoms."

"Was it a drought?"

"Young fella, that was a drought to end all droughts." Jake hitched at his belt and straightened his shirt about the waist. "Yes, sir, that sure was a drought." He took a list from his shirt pocket and studied it.

"Let's see. We've got to do some shopping for Paula, gotta go by the Harleys' and gotta see Mary Jennings."

"We have got to meet Paula too, haven't we?"

"Yep, that we do." Jake pursed his lips as he read. "Reckon the shortest way is to shop first—then take the back road past the farms and come in to school from the Union Road— All set, young fella, we'll get started. Like to get this business finished before it gets too all-fired hot."

He let the clutch out and they edged slowly forward, lurching along the short deep-rutted road that Kern remembered from last night. It was different now. Not gray but red, sandy and like clay. Distinct. Everything was like that. Last night everything had been all shadows and shapes and outlines—no details. Today the details were there. Brush, sedgelike, dry and brown, grew uneven and ragged to the very edge of the rutty road. Kern stared at the low cabins that stood side by side between the station and the Selma Road. Gaping slits were visible in their weathered gray planking. The chimney of one was crumbled and smoke-blackened bricks lay at odd angles along the rusting tin roof. The others had no chimney at all, though a thin streamer of smoke that rose slowly through the gaping roof of one stood straight in the hot air. In the bare, littered yard of the middle house, ringed by brush, almost a dozen children in all states of dress and undress were tumbling and shouting. Two were without a stitch of clothing. Kern watched them, openmouthed. Brown, brown, dusky black and two yellow. One was creamy pale. Almost, Kern thought, as light as I am. They turned and stared at the car as it crept past. Recognizing Jake, they set up a furious clamor, jabbering and calling after him in words that Kern could hardly understand. Only "Jake! Jake!" was clear.

"Those are the Barker kids. Lord only knows their names. I think two of 'em belongs to Miz Barker's daughter Mary. She got squatted 'n went off and left 'em with her maw. Rest of 'em is hers. Dunno how she feeds 'em with no man in the house. But she's carried on for 'most ten years since ol' man Barker up and left."

"But—" Kern choked off the question on his lips. He wouldn't have thought those kids were ten years old. One or two of them maybe—maybe three—but surely not the rest. And if Miz Barker wasn't——

The winding macadam strip of the Selma Road stretched out in front of them, glistening as though it were wet in spots. The clearing where the cabins stood ended where they turned in to the road, and the land began to stretch away out of sight in rolling hills. Jake speeded up and they rolled along smoothly, grateful for the fresh breeze on their faces. Kern looked obliquely at Jake as he started to hum a low tune. He tried to catch the melody and could not. Jake's great hands lay carelessly on the bottom of the wheel, his coppery forearms swelling into huge upper arms that cooled in the breeze and showed small white grains where the salt of sweat was left. Cooling and brown, the arms disappeared under the stretched blue cloth of his thin short-sleeved cotton shirt. Jake's eyes were thoughtful as they approached a man walking toward them. Head bent, his curling wide-brimmed straw hat pushed back, he plodded on and barely looked up as they approached him, lifting his hand as though the half wave of recognition he gave them were an effort. Kern twisted around in his seat to stare back at the man's overalled figure as it dwindled in the distance.

"That's Hez——"

"Hez? Hez who?" Kern turned around to hear Jake's explanation.

"Don't know as Hez has any other name. Man an' boy, I've only knowed him as Hez." Jake grinned broadly. "Never knowed a man so slow-paced—so easy in his ways. Don't believe nothing short of a hurricane could speed Hez up. Good farmer, though. Gets his crops out. Never misses." They turned and crossed the boarded train tracks and gathered speed as they neared the front of a long steep hill.

"We are almost to town, aren't we, Jake? Isn't this the hill we climbed last night?"

"Sure is, young feller—right up the top of that hill and a little ways on, we turn left and you'll be able to see town right dead ahead of you." Near the top, Jake slowed his speed and pointed off to the right beyond the car.

"There's a sight for Yankee eyes—see there!" Kern gave a low whistle of pleasure when he saw it. "That's a real, old Southern mansion."

Through the trees and wearing a cloak of mystery lent by distance, the house was something out of a storybook. High on a hill-side, it glinted in the sunlight, notched between huge trees. Kern could make out the tall columns about its face, the thin lines of its upper gallery and, with greater difficulty, the thread of a driveway. The woods beside them pushed close to the road and blotted the house from sight. Jake slowed his speed.

"No sense in getting picked up for speeding." He jerked his thumb back over his shoulder. "Used to be the Jennings house—big plantation owners; two, three generations back." Kern drew pictures of faithful old retainers sending up songs about the "Big House" in the dusk.

"Are they still there—the Jenningses, I mean?"

"Nope. Ol' Missus Jennings was the las' to leave. She went away 'bout two years ago. Kids had already pulled stakes for the North. Seven families of mill hands live there now. Ol' place only looks good from a distance."

They rolled slowly along the tree-lined road, past the beginning of a sidewalk and the first houses set back from the walk, on to the fringe of the business section, and turned into a wide street that split and joined again about an open square that lay lifeless and sun-baked under the eagle-eyed gaze of General Jeb Stuart. Horse and man looked frowningly northward and down upon them as they approached.

The streets were almost empty. Beyond the square, past the courthouse, a handful of cars slanted in toward the pavement, their noses hidden in the shade of the corrugated roof that slanted out from the row of buildings to cover the sidewalk. A single lounger leaned against the wall of the drugstore, paring at his nails. He did not raise his head as they drove past. At the end of the long block, by a gas station, they turned to a side street. By the side of a blacksmith's shop, two Negroes hunkered on their heels in the shade, propped against the wall. In the middle of this block, Jake pulled in before a wide-windowed store front and turned his motor off. He dug in his shirt pocket for Paula's list and stepped out into the street. A post office and a grocery store. A drugstore and a restaurant. Kern looked at the row of stores.

"Want to come in!"

"Sure!" Kern clambered out eagerly and came around the front of the car to meet Jake. Together they went into the grocery store.

In one corner, sacks of flour were piled almost to the ceiling. Slabs of a strange-looking meat were racked in a rough line across a far counter. In the center of the store, a large square display stand held bright-colored boxes of soap flakes, corn meal and breakfast cereals in tall tiers. Kern trailed Jake toward a counter where an old Negro woman was turning away with a paper bag clutched in her hand.

"Come again, Aunty—come again." The storekeeper bent his head as he counted pennies and nickels from the counter with one finger, guiding them to where his palm waited beneath the counter's edge. He raised his eyes as they approached.

"Why, hello there, Jake— What can I do for you?" A smile twisted his mouth under its yellowed moustache and showed blackened, ruined teeth. Jake smiled back.

"Well, I reckon not too much today, Mister Porter." He glanced at Paula's list. "Just need four or five things."

Mr. Porter looked curiously at Kern, as he stared into the showcases with their jumbled horde of lipsticks, chewing tobacco, penny candies, thread and licorice sticks.

"You want anything, Mister?" Kern looked up at the man and at Jake.

"Oh, no—I'm just waiting on Jake." The man's eyes widened.

"My wife's brother's boy, Mr. Porter." Jake offered explanation as he began to read from his list. Mr. Porter scurried back and forth behind the counter reaching up to loaded shelves for tea and coffee and sugar. Midway between armloads, he snatched a piece of licorice from the candy showcase as he passed and jammed it into his mouth.

"Cain't sell the durned stuff—dunno why I ever let that feller talk me into buying it. You don't want to buy any lic'rish, do you?" He peered up at Jake as he figured his prices on the back of a paper bag. A slattern woman came into the store and stood in front of the meat counter looking up at the rackful of slabs.

"Haouw much's fat back this week, Johnny?" Fat back? Kern had never eaten fat back. Rollie had, he knew. He looked at the racked meat with new interest. The storekeeper kept on totting his figures without answer. Kern heard impatience in her voice when she spoke a second time. He turned away. A coke would be nice now. Circling the large center display stand, he went toward the red and white ice cooler against the wall. High-piled fresh ice pushed its lids up and the necks of bottles poked out, dewy with cold. His mouth watered as he started to raise the cover, imagining the cold liquid already in his throat. His hand stopped. On the wall above the cabinet he saw the sign:

FOR WHITE ONLY!

Underneath, lettered in a scrawling hand with the "N" made backwards, was a penciled line:

THESE BOTTLES HAVE TO BE USED AGAIN.

Kern's throat tightened and dried. He withdrew his hand cautiously, hoping that neither Jake nor Johnny had seen him, and turned to stare through the flyspecked window at the street outside.

"Johnny!" The woman's voice was sharp. "Do I hev to stand heah all day long while you wait on a nigger?" He heard Johnny mumble something to Jake, as he turned away. Kern stood frozen at the window. Behind him the querulous voice went on, "Don't see why colored folks don't buy at they own store anyhaow." In infinite detail, not wanting to hear all, Kern heard and was sharply aware of everything that happened behind him. In the window, he could see Johnny groping among the slabs of fat back on his rack until the woman chose one small piece. He watched as Johnny took the slab from its hook and weighed it. Kern could see the woman's half-turned face. Her hair was hanked low on her neck and her dress fell loose from her shoulders. Run-over shoes and the worn cotton stockings on her legs were telltale of poverty. The slow, distrustful look of "po' trash come to trade" was on her face as she watched Johnny reading the price from his scales.

"Uh dollar eighty-two."

Johnny looked over the counter wiping his hands on his already greasy apron.

"Dolluh eighty-two! Why, you read them scales again. Ain't no way in thuh worl' fo' that little ol' slab of fat back to weigh no dolluh eighty-two worth."

"Does weigh that, though—smallest piece I got, too." The man's voice sounded weary, as though he had gone through this routine of haggling more often than he cared to remember.

"Well—I guess if'n I mus', I mus'. Wrap it up." She twisted at a knotted handkerchief.

"Anything else?"

"Nope—write it on my slip, 'll you?" Johnny stopped midway of dropping the meat into a bag and spoke sharply:

"Yo' slip ain't no good, Miz Breckman. Reckon Pete musta tol' you that las' week."

"Ain't no good? But that was las' week." Her mouth was open in blank amazement.

"I know—an' ain't nothing been paid on your bill since."

"How much my bill stand at?" Johnny read from a list tacked on the shelves behind him.

"Certon, Davis, Breckman—Owe nine dollars sixteen cents." Mrs. Breckman whirled out of the store, swinging the screen door shut behind her with a bang. Johnny came back to the corner counter where Jake was waiting silently. Kern moved closer to them, the woman's face still clear before him. He wanted to get home and write a description of her. Of a woman who had nothing—only the feeling that the color of her skin made her better than niggers. He thought with satisfaction, "She can't buy a cheap piece of fat back, not even the smallest piece, with her white face." And the thought came back to him: "With all of your money you can't buy a five-cent drink."

FOR WHITE ONLY. He studied the knotted worn floor and scuffed at the sawdust with his toe.

"Sorry, Jake—you know how it is. Po' trash—don't buy nothin'—want to credit that. But I still got to live here, 'n white folks would raise hell if'n they heard I rather wait on a n—Negro—than to wait on a white woman like her. Don' know what they does with their money. Four 'n five workin' in the mill in same house—twenty, thirty dollars a week each. Still they're always broke. Boozing. Making trouble with the Negroes in The Gut."

"Three eighty-two." He pushed the bag with its column of figures toward Jake, who counted the money from his pocket and laid it on the counter. Mister Johnny counted with him. Three—fifty—sixty—seventy, eighty, one and two. His hand scooped up the money.

"Yo'hs truly." He pushed the cash-register keys, cranked the handle, and the drawer jerked open. He stood ruffling his gray-black hair, eyeing the cash drawer as Jake picked up the large bag. Kern followed him out of the door into the hot street and got into the car.

"Do believe it's getting hotter."

"Uh huh." Jake sensed his disturbed feeling. "Well, that's an introduction to our South. I don't imagine you think very much of it." Kern grunted a reply. His thoughts went beyond the rolling hills that hemmed in the horizon to faraway Evans. "Suppose we stop here at the gas station. I need to tank up, and maybe we can get us a cold soda pop or something." Kern nodded gratefully.

❀   ❀   ❀

"That's the mill." Jake pointed to a tall three-story brick building that rose above gathered rows of uniform frame houses. "Central Mill Corp. No. 17." The name was blazoned in graying white paint across the upper windows. "Call the whole thing Millville. Actually it's all part of Valley View. An' The Gut too." He spoke with an expression of wry distaste. "The mill folk work there. Most of them live in those houses. Some of 'em are scattered around though." Kern stared at the houses. They were identical; all one-story bungalow style with red roofs, all painted gray and the paint on all, like the letters of Central Mill Corp. No. 17, was cracked and peeling.

"Did all of the workers come from around here?"

"Reckon most of them did."

"Then who works on the farms?" Jake laughed shortly.

"Reckon that's a good question, young feller. There aren't many left now to work on the farms. Most of them come here to work. Same thing in other towns. They get real hard cash and it's lots easier than working on the farms when they can't tell whether the crops will turn out good or bad."

"But the man in the store said that they didn't make more than twenty or thirty dollars." Kern didn't think that was much.

"That isn't much money, I'll agree. But there's three to five of them working in every family. You multiply twenty or thirty dollars that many times and you'll have more money than most of these folk ever dared dream of." Slowly Kern began to understand.

"What about Negroes, Jake—do they work in the mill?"

"Not on your life—not in there!"

"Oh." Why didn't Negroes work in the mill? "Don't they even work as porters?"

"Negroes ain't working in them mills in no kind of jobs. Fact is, crops got so bad these last couple of years, mos' all the whites have come to live in town. Here and in Selma and Union. All over they're job-hungry. They're even taking jobs that used to belong to Negroes. Elevator operators, waiters, everything." They drove past the mill

225

with its clatter and the gathered rows of identical houses above and below the sluggish brown strip called the Collatchee River, past a brief wooded strip where the road bent in to a helter-skelter group of houses, poorer even than the cabins near the train station. They seemed to Kern to be little more than shacks. Poorer than anything he had seen, their walls a patchwork of rough lumber and metal scraps and odd sign plates, with stovepipe chimneys, they leaned against the road and one another, cheek by jowl with Millville; as Millville stood by the city proper. They were, Kern thought, an odd trinity.

One large brick building housed a grocery store, a beer parlor and a billiard parlor. Loungers leaned about the doorway of the billiard parlor, careless of its moulding damp wall.

"Is this the——?"

"This here's The Gut." Jake's scorn was obvious. "Most of these people do housework and piece work in Valley View."

"Is this part of Valley View?"

"Well—yes and no. Sort of depends on how you look at it." Jake waved from the window to a woman coming out of the grocery. "They pay taxes—such as they are—so they must be a part of Valley View." Kern thought if Jake smiled that wry smile again, he'd be able to describe it perfectly. "Other hand, the City Council don't spend any money to improve The Gut, so I guess that they aren't a part of Valley View after all. I guess it does depend on how you look at it." Frankly puzzled, Kern had little more to say as they left The Gut behind them. "These city Negroes, they look down on us country folk."

"But how can they look down on anybody—living like they are?"

"Don't have to *have* anything to look down on the other feller, young feller—you just need to *think* you have something the other feller hasn't got and wants. That's all."

They were out in the country again, where the road rolled with the land, up and down, up and down. Everywhere, wherever the eye went, it found either cotton or brush or pine. Kern saw that though the natives boasted cotton as their staple, little of the land had been cleared to make way for crops. The cleared plots would stretch away for a while, and then always they would be hemmed in by brush or scrawny stands of pine. Great ruts sloped down the hills where the gush of rain, of wind and dry sun had cut away the top-soil and left red clay. The land bespoke its barrenness. It complained that it had been used and used again until now it was tired and would yield little more than brush, and that reluctantly. Here and there on the slopes, high up near the tops, were cabins, all of them seeming to Kern to be alike. Now and then a tin roof gave sign that its tenant enjoyed more prosperity than his neighbors. Kern's face grew sober as he looked about him.

"What do you think of our dear old Southland?"

Kern could think of nothing to say. "Dear old Southland"! He did not miss the biting tone of Jake's voice.

"You're looking at all's left of the plantation days, young feller. It strangles the Negroes of Valley View. This is our heritage—at its worst civilization's been shut out. White and colored, our way of life comes from a bygone day. Habits like a blight. They hang low on the land. You can see and feel 'em everywhere." Kern was surprised at Jake's eloquence.

"These folks live jes' like their grandparents lived—they haven't advanced in modern ways at all." Kern sensed his depressed mood. Jake slowed to a stop where junction arrows pointed southwest to Selma and north toward Union. Quickly surveying the junction, he turned right onto the Union Road and a short distance turned again from the soft tarred highway to a narrow, rutted road that climbed along the side of a low hill, pushing farther back into the hill country.

"We'll be up by the Hartleys' in a little bit."

"The Hartleys'?" The name was strange to Kern.

"They live on a little piece of land my daddy left me. Farm it on shares."

"Oh—on shares?"

"Yup—shares are just about what they say. The land is paid for. All Mart does is farm. Sell the crops. Then he gives me shares 'nough to pay the taxes, with a little something left over. Out of the rest, he pays his bills, keeps up his tools, buys a little stock. Any that's left, he puts it in the bank."

"Are the people living in those houses we saw sharecroppers?" Jake's head jerked scornfully.

"Yep. Most of 'em working for whites. Never get much out of their land." He edged the car wheels into a deep rut and relaxed his grasp on the steering wheel. "We got two kinds of colored folks down here. There's colored folks and white folks' colored folks. The colored folks got some ambition. Try to save money, send their kids to school. Mind their own business and don't get in no trouble. The white folks' colored folks are in the main. They rent and they sharecrop and they just manage to keep body and soul together 'til they die." He spoke these last words with a sharp bitterness as they rounded a bend and dropped down a hill toward where a man worked at a flight of wooden steps that slanted up to a house. The man straightened from his work to watch them as they stopped. Jake leaned from the car.

"Hi, Mart!" The tall man called over his shoulder to the house and came toward the car. "My'! Hey, My'— Jake's come with company! Howdy Jake, light down, an' stay a while." Jake and Kern got out and walked toward the stairs.

"Mart—like for you to know my nephew by marriage—Kern Roberts. Kern, this here is Mart Hartley." Kern extended his hand.

"Glad to know you, sir."

Mart was a tall man, taller even than Jake, with a string-bean lankiness about him, deceptively heavy with his lean, lanky height. Mrs. Hartley appeared at the door of the cabin above them. Hands on her hips, calling down with a laugh on her face.

"Well—howdydo, Mister Jake—been a coon's age since you was las' 'round here. Wheah you been keepin' yourse'f?" Jake laughed happily.

"Oh, hasn't been that long. My! What's in the pot for dinner?"

"Oh, Lawdy—I didn't spec' you here. Guess I'll have to slaughter uh— Who that wif' you down there?"

"Name's Kern," Jake pulled at Kern's shoulder drawing him in beside him. "My nephew by marriage from Washington——"

"Washington! Well, dew tell! He come a mighty far piece, ain't he?"

"Here for school—didn't Paula tell you?"

"I spec' she did—I done forgot it." She leaned forward on the porch rail above them, seeming to hang in the air. She looked down closely at Kern. "Boy's mighty like uh albino, ain't he?"

"Shesh yo' mouf, gal," Mart reproved her acidly. "Ain't no way be talkin' to no company. He's fren' of Jake's— He's fren' uh ours." Kern reddened at Myra Hartley's words but they were spoken in such a light, matter-of-fact voice that he could not be offended. Kern grinned as he called up to her, "How do you do, Mrs. Hartley!" He stood back then and listened as the men talked.

"Expect you'll be startin' to turn under soon, won't you, Mart?"

" 'Bout 'nother week, Jake. Got a mite to do on the house an' a few things to set right about the place. Ah'll turn under for sure 'fore frost sets in. Then it'll be 'bout stickin' time and I've got to slaughter." He counted to himself, "Cutting three porkers this fall— an' got to stab that ol' boar. He got mighty mean pas' few months.

228

Reckon I'll take some of the orneriness outen him 'fore fall." The men laughed heartily.

"Got to set a nail or two 'fore I quit here." Mart turned to his work taking several spikes from a bag on the bottom step and sticking them in his mouth. He braced the handhold that ran along the steps, pushing it into place. "Here," he spoke indistinctly with the nails in his mouth, "hol' onto this a minute, Jake, an' I'll get this done in a jiffy." Kern watched as the railing was tightened in place, then clumped up the steps behind Jake and Mart. Mrs. Hartley brought a pitcher of cold water out to the porch.

"Here—have some Adam's ale, Jake—you young un—the bes' drink in the worl'."

"Ain't got a long time to light, Myra—want to stop past the Jennings' on the way, and got to get on up on the campus to see Paula. Young feller here's got to see some of his teachers today." He squinted up at the sun. "Got 'bout time to drink an' run." Mart disappeared in the house and came back holding a rough piece of paper marked with a row of figures and a small roll of bills.

"Got the balance added on this sheet heah, Jake. Reckon you can make head 'n tails of it?" He pointed to the figures. "This is what we cleared. Not so bad, huh?" He clapped an arm around Jake's shoulders as he studied the list. Mrs. Hartley watched them with a wide smile.

"Wish our other farmers would do near as well—we'd all be better off."

"Folks still plants too much by signs," Myra scoffed.

"An' here's your share." Mart counted the money into Jake's hand. "One hundred—and one dollar and twenty cents." He dropped the two dimes into Jake's hand with a flourish.

"Reckoned we'd break jes' 'bout this way, Mart." Jake counted off two of the ten-dollar bills. "How 'bout putting this against that harrow we 'tended to get this fall, Mart?"

"Oh, naw, Jake—I cain't—" Mart pushed Jake's hand away.

"'Cain't' ain't in your lessons, son—sure you can. We talked 'bout it already. It's just a good investment."

"Well——"

"Ain't no 'well' either—you know's well as I do that harrow will more'n pay for itse'f in the next crops."

"Well—" Jake pushed the money into Mart's hand.

"If'n you break ahead, you can make me a tenth share more—" He turned and started down the steps leaving Mart to stare after

229

him, the money in his hand. "C'mon, Kern—we'd better get a shake on." Kern started down the steps.

"Stick with Jake, son—you won't go far wrong," Mrs. Hartley advised him, " 'an tell Paula we ain't seen her in uh age."

They waved to the Hartleys and headed off down the rutted road toward where the top of the Jennings place showed behind a hill. Kern was more cheerful than he had been when they had driven out of Valley View.

"Mart Hartley's about the best man to be found hereabouts. Goes about things with some reason. Got three kids, too—all 'em raised an' off to school. They're workin' their way through—all 'cept Ellen. She's the brat of the family. It's folks like that we need—not The Gut crowd and the shif'less folks that don't do nothin' but borrow." He shifted his position under the steering wheel and settled against the back cushions, his hands resting on the wheel lightly.

The Jennings place slanted sidewise on a rising slope of a "highland." It was surrounded by a bare, hard-packed yard in which one scrawny chicken picked hopelessly for feed. Ringing the yard and the cabin was the eternal brush. Behind the cabin, cornstalks slanted at awkward angles in a small crazy-quilt patch. Higher than the corn and the house, beyond the brush, were the pines. Two boys wrestled in the dirt yard. Another boy, smaller than either of these, sat on the upper step of the narrow porch and watched, dividing his attention between the chicken, the wrestling boys and Kern and Jake as they approached the cabin. He spoke over his shoulder and a woman came and stood in the open door.

The path to the cabin followed a set of rough steps, hewn out of the hard clay, through the brush to the yard. Twice Kern slipped in the narrow toeholds the steps afforded as he followed Jake up the incline toward where the woman stood in the door watching. As they entered the clearing and started across it, the boys stopped their wrestling to stare at them. They disengaged themselves and Kern could hear the flat slap of their bare feet behind him. He saw with a sickening feeling that the little boy on the porch step was not a little boy. She was a little girl with two clumsy clubbed feet which were turned inward and drawn under the hanging hem of her dress. Her dark sensitive face looked outward at the yard and the chicken, and when she turned her sad eyes full on him in a quick glance, Kern felt an ache. Jake stopped to pat her on the shoulder.

"Howdy, Miss Idy Mae— You're lookin' mighty purty today." Idy

Mae did not even smile. She kept her eyes on the chicken and her brothers as they stood behind Kern, looking at him from head to foot. Now and then she rubbed at a wide gray patch on her right cheek with the knuckles of one hand. Mrs. Jennings greeted them with a careless flip of her hand and a loud "Hello there! This mus' be the young man Paula said she was 'spectin' to come." Her keen little eyes covered Kern from head to toe.

"Howdy, Mary—Kern, this is Mrs. Jennings." Kern reached forward and Mrs. Jennings took his hand in hers as she shooed the boys away. "You boys g'on an' play—ain't no cause to be stan'in' 'roun' heah gawpin'!" She came across the porch to the steps and folded the little girl in her arms. "Chilly, Idy Mae—why don' you move over into the sunlight?" Idy Mae murmured some answer that pleased Mrs. Jennings and stayed where she was. A hissing sound from inside the cabin turned Mrs. Jennings away from Idy Mae. She hurriedly went inside, calling over her shoulder, "C'mon in, Jake—great Heabens! Pot's b'ilin' over!" They followed her inside and Kern stopped short at the door to watch her swing the iron pothook out from the fireplace and peer into the contents of the pot. He stared in amazement as she dropped her holding cloth on the kitchen table and picked up the baby that had been lying there. "Laid this down when I come to the door—" She placed the baby in the center of the nearest of the two beds.

"Maybelle's chile," she commented in an offhand fashion. "Maybelle done got squatted by one uh them wuthless Johnson boys an' went off an' lef' it. Says she be back—humph! Mus' think I'm uh fool. I knows right well she ain't 'tendin' come back heah."

"Baby all right? Paula told me to stop and pass the time of day. See if there's anything we could do." Kern looked about him. The musty odor that came through cracks in the floor from the ground underneath reminded him of Rollie's house. The rough splintered floor was grease-spotted and littered, its worn surface patched here and there with strips of tin cans that had been hammered flat. Two beds crowded against a far wall. A cut-down barrel and a backless chair stood close by a rough wooden table. The walls were papered with newspapers and scraps of cardboard in a helter-skelter design of pictures and print and colored letters. Faded blue cloths hung drapelike across the two open window spaces. Above them, the sunlight came through where the tin roof buckled along its seams. Under the scorching sun, the roof baked the inside of the cabin to oven heat. Mrs. Jennings' voice interrupted his intent survey.

"No 'count nigger didn't hol' with hep'pin take keer of the baby."
She shrugged her shoulders philosophically. "Ain't nothin' you can
do," and turned toward the door with Jake. "An' Herbert—Gawd
know he ain't no man to speak of—don't hardly know how I come to
marry up wif him less'n it 'cause he's so helpless. Spec' anytime to
wake up an fin' he gone too." She sighed deeply. "Well, won't be no
loss to mention—he ain't never here an don't do no work when he is.
Mos'ly hangs 'roun' that pool place in The Gut. Got that Jennings
blood in him, you know—ol' man Jennings an' his pappy spread that
rakehell blood uh ther'n all 'roun' an' it done bore bad fruit eve'where
it go." Jake nodded his head in solemn agreement.

"Idy Mae there don't look so sprightly, Mary—how 'bout them
gray splotches on her face? Looks like pellagra——"

"Das 'zactly what 'tis. One uh them ridin' nurses come through
here uh while pas', she says dat's it. Can't git no food to set right wif
her. Jes' don' seem to thrive on potlicker and hoecake like the boys."

"Why don't you send her to the school—she could get free lunches
there anyhow?"

"Would that—but Idy Mae cain't walk an' I ain't got the time to
take an' git her m'se'f—" Mary looked despairingly at Idy Mae's
hunched back. Kern saw that Mary was as tall as Jake, even with her
shoulders slumped as they were now. He killed an urge to whistle.
And she wasn't fat. She must weigh at least two hundred pounds.
Crinkly brown hair rimmed her light brown face in tight rings. She
walked down the yard with them to where the brush began, carelessly upending a hand plow that lay in her way. At the clearing she
stopped, arms akimbo, and looked about her at the slanting stalks
of corn.

"Got to get thet stuff plowed under one uh these days—'n come a
dark night, might be able to get me in some winter peas—'cose, a
body only got two han's." She stretched out her hands, flexing the
fingers slowly in front of her and turning them slowly to study the
work-hardened palms.

"Min' you'se'f, youngster," she cautioned Kern, "don't slip on them
steps. Jake, you tell Paula I'm holdin' body an' soul together well as
might be 'spected. She gets a chance—come an' talk with me. Gets
mighty lonesome outchere." Jake waved back at her and Kern swallowed his good-bye. Not even in Key's Alley did people live like the
Jenningses lived.

❈   ❈   ❈

232

Kern craned his neck curiously as they rode slowly along the street. Beyond the far side of the open stretch of green lawn, another street ran parallel to theirs. Valley View College lay within, scattered along the outer edges of this long rectangle, enclosed at either end by shorter cross streets.

With an easy familiarity, Jake called out the names of the buildings as they passed. Tubman Hall, where the girls lived, was a tall four-story building of dull-red brick peaked at one corner with a tower. The building was trimmed in a gray stone. An oval drive led up to its main entrance and curved away to the street again. Newest of all the buildings on the campus was Douglass Hall, the main classroom building. Three levels of new brick. Backgrounding Douglass Hall was the spiring library, its terraces of brown stone shot with leaded windows. The sprawling frame Playhouse, the gymnasium in which Valley View had begun years ago as a college; Chemistry Building, the row of red-brick houses on the far street that housed the Music School—Stone Hall, the men's dorm and, below, at the far end of the campus, in ancient Bender Hall, the School of Social Science. There were others whose names Kern could not remember, they came so quickly together. Here and there he saw groups of students standing about the doors of buildings or walking together through the campus. Jake turned and drove along the end of Stone Hall and then went north again, passing close by the Faculty Club and the Music School, the Chapel, and came to Heritage House. There he stopped in front of the long magnolia-lined walk that led to the house.

"Paula's supposed to meet you here," he pointed, "she should be here now. That's Dr. Johnson's house."

"Dr. Johnson—the president?" Kern stared at the house.

"Yep! Now you go on. I think you'll like him. He's a pretty fine man. Sort of stern, but most of it's cover-up." Kern climbed out and stood uncertainly at the edge of the walk. Jake started away.

"Tell Paula I'll be home when you all get there." Kern started up the walk toward the house with the feeling that he was being stared at.

* ○ ✱

Three days later, wearing the traditional green frosh beanie, Kern began his first year—and his last—of classes at Valley View College.

CHAPTER XII

A SOUTHERN GENTLEMAN—NOV. 1934

THE sweet dry-leaf smell of late October was pungent in the crisp fall air. The land drew in upon itself. Browning cotton stalks lay in dry, disordered rows in the fields, while in town and on the campus, the summer-thick foliage of the trees began to thin with each passing breath of wind.

The acrid, sweet tang of burning leaves drifted downwind from the basket fire on the lawn and sifted through the windows and the screened door of Jake's workshop. It caught at Kern's throat as he sat on a tall drawing-board stool watching Jake. Almost noon. He slowly pocketed his watch. It would be dinnertime in a few minutes, and after dinner he had to mow the front lawn. Jake said this would be the last time it would have to be mown before winter. Then he had to study for Monday's mid-term exam in English. He jerked about as the door beside him opened and slammed shut.

"Howdy, boy?" The man stood in the middle of the workshop, swayed back on his heels, one thumb hooked through the single strap that held his sagging overalls. Bleached, strawlike, blond hair pushed out from under the band of his bent hat.

A white man! Kern's stomach tightened and drew away from his belt. The man's jovial tone did not ring true. Meanness was in his face as he stood there swaying, waiting for Jake to turn from where he bent over a whirring polisher. He had not seen Kern. A leering grin tugged at his mouth, and he spoke again, more loudly.

"Seed your pretty wife as I come up. Disappeared 'round the corner of the house. Reckon she didn't see me." The man laughed shortly, and Kern saw Jake's hand tighten on the piece of wood he held. Kern felt quick anger at hearing this man talk about Paula. He knew that the man was different from the others he had seen in Jake's workshop. The others had been white too, but none had the poor meanness that lay close to the surface in this man. Jake straightened and turned, switching off the polisher.

"Why, howdy, Mr. Meeker." He laid the piece of wood on the table

234

and came slowly forward, brushing the dust from his hands and shirt front. The man turned as Kern slipped from the stool at the drawing board and stood by the door. Surprise showed in his face.

"Who's this yere boy, Jake?" Half twisted about in his tracks, he stared over his shoulder at Kern.

"That's my wife's nephew, Mr. Meeker. Kern, this is Mr. Tom Meeker." Kern moved his lips in a soundless answer as Tom Meeker looked at him.

"Well, I dew declare!" His eyes ran over Kern from head to foot. "Some mighty funny things kin happen in uh lifetime—cain't they now? Woulda hardly thought he was——"

"Can I he'p you, sir?" Jake cut in on his statement. Kern stared, swallowing his distaste, at the thin, miserable face and saw the grimed hands and the imbedded dark lines of dirt that pocked the creases of his neck.

"Well, I reckon so. Had a thought about fixin' the ol' lady up with uh wall cabinet for Christmus, an' I couldn't think nothin' else but 'Jake's the boy to do thet chore for you.'" Jake waited, his face impassive. Tom Meeker's voice became more brusque. He took a folded piece of paper from his pocket and held it out to Jake.

"Now that there's what I want." Jake studied the sketch and walked thoughtfully to his drawing board. Tom Meeker followed him, bending over his shoulder.

"I don't reckon we can fix it for you quite like that, Mr. Meeker." Jake's pencil slashed through the drawing. "There ain't no way to tie the frame together like that."

Tom Meeker bridled. "Don't tell me, boy. I know it can be done! I know what I'm talkin' 'bout. I drawed that m'se'f." He straightened pugnaciously. Jake stayed bent over the drawing.

"S'pose we say I can't do it, Mr. Meeker. Now I *can* do it this way." He sketched quickly at the paper as Tom Meeker watched. "An' we could put in an extra shelf here, an' use that space." Jake smiled a small smile and Tom Meeker dug at the back of his head.

"Waal, ain't 'zactly what I wanted, but I reckon it'll do. Now when'll you have it done—'fore Christmus?" Furrows of doubt lined Jake's forehead as he stared down at the sketch.

"I don't rightly know 'bout 'fore Christmus, Mr. Meeker. I got uh order promised for a furniture shop in Montgomery, 'n there's two others——"

Tom Meeker's mouth set in an ugly, thin line.

"Now looky here, boy. I'm home folks an' I'm set on havin' thet cabinet for the Missus on Christmus." There was a hardness in his voice. It said, "To hell with an order from Montgomery. You have to live here with us." Jake understood that part of it. His face tightened.

"I'll do my best on it—but I won't promise you, Mr. Meeker. 'Fore the end of December, that's certain. 'Fore Christmas—I don't know." He shook his head doubtfully. Kern thought Tom Meeker was going to say something else. He didn't. He wheeled about abruptly and started toward the door. Kern jumped to one side and pressed against the wall, staring at him.

"Mr. Meeker—" Jake's voice stopped him. "What kind of wood do you want this made out of?" Tom Meeker turned, flushing.

"What you say?" He came back toward Jake.

"White pine would make a right pretty cabinet when it's finished off."

"Don't make much difference to me what kind of lumber——"

"Well, sir, I think we should have an understanding about it. For example, walnut costs 'bout twice as much as pine——"

"Are you indicatin' that I cain't pay for this cabinet?" Kern saw an angry red flush run into the man's neck and fill the sunken pockets of his face. Tom Meeker hitched at his overall straps and braced himself, wanting to look down on Jake. He was, instead, forced to look up at him.

"Of course not, sir—nothin' like that. Most important difference the kind of wood makes is in the time it'll take to get this finished. Seasoned walnut, for example, I would have to send to Decatur for. Wouldn't get it less'n two weeks an' I wouldn't be able to finish no way at all." Tom Meeker was mollified.

"Waal, if'n thet's it—" Jake shook a clean piece of paper and stood at the drawing board.

"Way I see it, the cabinet could be made sorta like this." His pencil slid easily back and forth. "An' it sure would be a pretty thing to hang on your kitchen wall." He continued to sketch and Tom Meeker gazed over his shoulder. Kern stared out through the door, bewildered by the tightness in him. He pressed his hands against his belly, hoping to still the trembling inside.

"Kern! Kern! Dinner!" That was Paula calling. Kern twisted out of the door and ran to the house. He knew one thing for sure—he didn't like Tom Meeker. With a thud and a jump, he crossed the porch between the breezeway and the storage house and burst into the kitchen. Paula turned from the range.

"Lord, Kern! What's after you?"

236

"Nothing!" He started to laugh at her surprise. Remembering Tom Meeker, he stopped short. Paula bustled about behind him as he soaped his hands and rinsed them, watching the running water in deep thought.

"Where's Jake? He's never late for a meal. What's keeping him?"

"He'll be right in. He's busy with a man who wants a cabinet made by Christmas."

"By Christmas!" Paula laughed. "Why, he's so tied up with orders now, he'll hardly be able to get them finished."

"That's what he said—but the man insisted. He was kind of angry too."

"Angry?" Paula stood beside him. "What did the man look like?"

He faced Paula as he dried his hands. "He's po' trash!" His eyes dropped before her reproving gaze. "He doesn't look like much. Tall and lanky, kind of worn-out face, gray-eyed. Name's Meeker."

"Meeker! What on earth is Tom Meeker doing buying a cabinet? Is Jake going to do it?"

"I don't know. He was making sketches when I left."

"Humph! Tom Meeker's bad pay even for whites. How does he think he can pay Jake for a cabinet?" She placed a dish on the table and plumped indignantly in her chair.

Jake was quiet when he came through the door and went to wash his hands. Paula's eyes stayed on him as he stood at the sink and Kern wondered if he should have said anything to Paula about Tom Meeker. Jake sat down and lowered his head to say grace. Absently Kern followed the familiar words.

"Heavenly Father, we thank Thee for the right to eat your bread and for the goodnesses which Thou have given us this day. Your humble servants. Amen."

Without a word, Jake raised his head. Carefully, he unfolded his napkin and spread it across his knees. Then his eyes met Paula's.

"Tom Meeker. What'd he want?" Contempt filled Paula's voice.

"Wanted a cabinet. Pine. By Christmas."

"You can't finish it by then. What's he going to pay for it with anyhow?"

"I'm going to try. Money—I suppose—I hope. Says he'll pay me before Christmas." His effort to joke fell flat.

"Meeker's nothing but poor trash!"

"Paula!"

"It's the truth, and you know it and I'm not sorry I said it. Trash—trying to lord it over Negroes because he's white. You don't think that deadbeat intends to pay you, do you?" Her scornful snort reminded Kern of his father.

"Paula!"

"I mean it. I wish that you wouldn't have anything to do with him— He won't bring any good."

"I've never had any dealings with the man 'fore this, Paula. But he is a man. I can't go on hearsay about him. He is a human being to me, and I will give him the same respect and attention that I give to anybody else until he proves that he is not to be trusted where I am concerned. I demand that for myself—I must give it to others." Kern listened to the precise, calm words.

"But Jake, you know as well as I that Tom Meeker's bad pay even for the white folks. He never has any money. The merchants in town won't credit him for anything. They even let Negroes know it." Jake watched her without a word. "Oh, Jake, you are impossible! You know you can't change a zebra's stripes." Jake waited until she was quite through and when she was, he answered with finality in his voice.

"My father and his before him and old Mister Bryant who gave 'em their start—all of them believed like I do. The best thing on earth is the human spirit. Given a square chance, it will do the right thing. My pa an' his pa lived here in peace. They didn't 'yassuh' an' bow and scrape. They was fair an' thoughtful. They didn't have no trouble neither."

He started to serve the plates in front of him, passing them to Paula as he did, and Kern saw the frowning gaze with which Paula watched him. They ate silently, and almost cleared their plates before Paula broke the silence.

"The postman brought a letter from your father this morning, Kern." Kern barely turned his head as he handed his plate to Jake for another helping.

"What did he say?" Both Paula and Jake frowned at his unconcern.

"Oh, nothing much. A little about the Freedom League. He says it keeps him on the run. He hopes that he'll be able to stop over here for Thanksgiving. He wasn't sure."

"Where was he when he wrote?"

"In Los Angeles— He's trying a case against restrictive covenants."

"Restrictive covenants?"

"Yes. You know—the agreements that keep Negroes from living in certain neighborhoods."

"Oh."

"He plans to stop in Kansas City on the way East for a meeting with the League's Kansas State Committee, and he may be able to come through here on his way to or from a November meeting in Atlanta." Irritation grew in Kern as he ate. Why did they have to talk about the Freedom League? Every time he heard "The League —the League!" it was like a shouted battle cry. He was sick of it! He wondered whether he was sick of the League or the continual "battle cries." He felt ashamed of the thought and recognized the pattern of his reaction. Always when these fervid discussions started he was irritated. Always ashamed afterward. He was never really sorry. The nearest he came to that was the feeling that he should be sorry. But he never was actually sorry.

"One of the best things ever happened to Negroes—that League," Jake's heavy voice entered the conversation.

"Charles feels that they are going to get some cases before the Supreme Court in Washington soon. He says then that we'll see what real justice is."

"Mebbe—mebbe—" Jake wasn't too sure. "Only to be expected that the outland courts will mostly do like the land in which they find themselves. Not right that they do—but it's natural. Segregatin' Negroes in America is natural. Mebbe the Supreme Court'll see it like that."

Kern kept his eyes to his plate and half heard their words as he tried to find a logical explanation for his feelings. The League is good. I know that. I don't like to hear talk about the League. It is right that we should fight "the problem." I am tired and sick of angry fighting voices. I am ashamed of my feelings—but not enough to do anything about them. I have tried to change them but I can't. Why does talk about the League and "the problem" affect me like this?

Why?

Why?

Jake noticed his strained face first and stopped talking, touching Paula on the arm.

"What's the matter, young feller—what's wrong?"

Kern looked up at Jake and past him, blankly.

"Why am I like this?" His question was dull-toned.

"Is it Tom Meeker?" Jake's voice was as anxious as Kern's. Kern shook his head absently.

"The Freedom League—isn't it, Kern?" Paula divined the reason before he could tell them. He dropped his eyes and felt the shame, more strongly than he had ever felt it before.

239

"The League!" Jake was aghast. "But why, Kern?" This was beyond him. Jake couldn't understand why any Negro would not be wholeheartedly for the League.

"I don't know—" Kern shook his head miserably. "I can't explain it, Jake." He looked at Jake and his words tumbled out. He hoped that they could find an answer. "I just can't listen to talk about fighting 'the problem' and the League without feeling like this. Like I'm getting ready to get in a fight. I never have been able to talk about it like—like other people. You remember—don't you, Paula?" His eyes pleaded with Paula to confirm his words.

"I remember. We won't talk about it any more, will we, Jake?" Kern knew that she meant they wouldn't talk about it any more when he was around. Suddenly he felt like an outsider, alone. Next to church, he knew that Jake placed greatest stock in the Freedom League.

Why was he feeling ashamed? Why was he afraid?

His felt resentment at the League was strong in him at the moment. There was anger at whites, contempt and hate for men like Tom Meeker. Dull resentment at the sort of Negroes who by their careless "the hell with it" attitude gave whites targets for their race hatred—at Negroes who thus, indirectly, added to his own burden. Anger, too, at the whites who were too blind to see that there was a difference between him and these Negroes—who simply lumped all Negroes in the same boat.

Doctor, lawyer and Seventh Street hanger-on—professor from the University and troublemaker from The Gut—all in the same boat.

Anger, bright and crackling, equally and impartially, for the user of "nigger" as well as for him who cried "half-white nigger."

Kern was confused—it showed on his face.

"It's not that bad, young feller." He grinned at Jake with a stiff face. "Why, why?"

CHAPTER XIII

MEEKER'S CABINET

"Here it is, Paula—right here in the paper!" The charged feeling in Jake's voice drew their attention. Paula looked up from her sewing, on the other side of the table. Redmon? Redmon? Kern came across the room as if drawn by a magnet. He bent over Jake's shoulder. The kids at school had been talking about the Redmon incident all week. He had heard them and it had even been broadcast over the radio on some news reviews. The lamplight fell on the opened green paper before him.

THE DISPATCH
Southern Edition

He remembered *The Dispatch* all right! How could he forget the solid green wrapper pages and the headline—"Son of League Head Scores Negroes—" Kern read the glaring two-line head that ran across the top of the green sheet.

7 NEGROES, 11 WHITES DEAD IN RIOT——
FREEDOM LEAGUE HEAD WILL DEFEND

There was his father's picture, unusually clear, hard, wearing what Rollie would have called his fighting face, staring at him from the center of the page. "Charles Roberts . . . Freedom League Chief"— Paula listened intently as Jake started to read, the shirt in her lap forgotten, and Kern, standing behind him, followed his finger quickly as it went from one side of the column to the other, keeping time with his lips.

"Redmon, December 12—Messengers of death, wearing the blue uniforms of State Troopers, struck seven times last week in this usually quiet hamlet town and claimed the lives of Negroes who resisted police efforts to enter their homes with neither search nor arrest warrants.

241

"Negroes dead in the battle were:
   Roger Williams, 28, son of
   Jeany Williams, 70, also dead.
   Goldwin Bush, 24.
   Tansy Perry, 19, wife of
   Macon Perry, 37, also dead."

Paula gasped.
"Isn't that Mart Hartley's cousin on his mother's side?"
Jake's nod said "Yes."

   "John Lucy King, 41, and
   Herman Bayless, 50.
   "Eyewitnesses to the start of the incident state that Roger Williams resented insulting remarks which a Redmon storekeeper, Augustus Greene, white, directed at aged Jeany Williams, his mother. Not satisfied with having sworn at Mrs. Williams, the shopkeeper struck the old woman with his fist and knocked her down. He was about to kick her when her son flew to her defense. Striking Greene with a piece of wood, he knocked him to the floor unconscious. Williams and his mother immediately fled the scene and took refuge in near-by Donaldson with friends.
   "Mob groups supported by police moved into 'The Slide,' the Negro area north of Redmon, and started to search the homes of residents for Roger and his mother. In an unparalleled violation of basic human rights, they forced their way into every home and severely beat Negroes who resisted their entry."

Kern felt an involuntary shudder of fright. Could this actually have happened? To people they, at least Jake and Paula, knew? One State away?
   "Twenty-four-year-old Goldwin Bush, Negro student at Northern University, Michigan, home for the funeral of his grandmother, answered the door of his home when the police came. When the peace officers started to batter the door down with a section of railroad tie without knocking to determine if the house was occupied, young Bush suddenly opened the door and volleyed shot after shot into the ranks of the housebreakers, killing three of them on the spot. Fatally wounded was Hyram King, State Trooper, who died en route to the Donaldson hospital. Also shot by Bush before he was killed in a fusillade of gunfire were white civilians Martin Hives and Bechard Wil-

liams, the latter reputedly a half-brother of Negro Roger Williams whom the police were seeking.

"Hidden witnesses state that the remaining police officers 'deputized' all white men on the scene into a posse and legalized them to carry weapons. The activity that followed immediately thereafter lost all semblance of being a search for Roger Williams and his mother and turned into what peace officers themselves were heard to call a 'coon hunt.'

"Negro residents fled in terror through the woods. Those remaining behind were fired on indiscriminately. Several barricaded themselves in a large barn and concentrated their fire on the posse as it advanced, fatally wounding five and critically wounding at least three others. Four Negroes were killed in their fearless defense of the last stronghold left to a man—his home.

"For years since the development of Old English Common Law, a man's home has been regarded as his castle, inviolate from invasion even by officers of the law unless a—Jake slid rapidly over the words —"just and sufficient reason exists." He looked up at Paula before going on.

"Ought to be on the editorial page." Kern agreed silently, his eyes racing ahead a line or two before Jake's hand blocked out the words.

"Caught as they attempted to board a northbound train at Donaldson were Roger Williams and his mother. State officers say that both Williams and his mother made 'threatening gestures' that indicated they were armed. Both were shot to death on the station platform." Jake's teeth gritted with rage. Kern felt sick in his stomach. A woman, 70 years old! Paula, he saw, was wide-eyed, shocked with unbelief. "A train porter, whose name is withheld for obvious reasons, says that neither of the Williamses was armed and, further, that both of them pleaded with Troopers to spare their lives. Their bodies were paraded through the Negro section of town before being thrown into the street where they lay for eight hours before Negro residents felt it safe to remove them."

Kern's mind protested the facts, so illogical, so senseless. This was murder. The man and his mother were guiltless. At the worst, Roger Williams was guilty of provoked assault. Or had they broken some other law? The unwritten law of the South?

"Charles Roberts, fearless leader of the militant Freedom League, when reached in Kansas City, Kansas, where he was appearing in a speaking engagement, stated that the League would throw every ounce of its resources into a fight to protect the ten Negroes now

243

being held in Redmon on charges of first-degree murder." Kern could imagine his father's cold anger, remembering nights when a wire or a jangling phone had brought messages which he realized now must have been like this. His hatred now matched the remembered image of his father's anger.

"Said Roberts—'This is the most shocking case I have heard of since a race riot shook the capital of the nation itself. No quarter can be given in this fight. The actions of the men against whose depraved bigotry we must fight clearly tell that they are sunk to the level of animals who will stop at nothing to secure themselves against the results of their own evil-doing.' " He would say that! Kern could see his father speaking with cold contempt that held its target up to scorn. But did these people care whether the nation, the world even, laughed at them or not?

" 'I will leave here for Washington and will proceed to the State capital to secure writs of habeas corpus and begin the defense of these citizens of the United States.'

"Redmon attorneys stated at press time that members of the families of the ten men now held have not been permitted to visit at the jail. Held incommunicado, the men are being further denied their basic rights."

Jake leaned his head back against the pillow of his chair and stared up at the ceiling in silence. Wordlessly, Paula began to slowly fold the shirt on her lap, and one by one took her needles and thimble and spools of thread and placed them in their proper places in her sewing basket. Silently, too, Kern stared down at his father's picture and the headline, at the long column that they had just read, and saw them all as an indistinct blur. He stared at them until Jake's voice startled him.

"The seed of hate in this thing is deep buried—God alone knows when it will be unearthed." Jake sighed a tired, despairing sigh and straightened in his chair, shuffled the pages of the paper into place and folded it carefully. Paula felt his need for understanding.

"There is so much that must be done, Jake—so much for both sides to do. Much has been done—yes! But much remains." Jake raised the paper and gestured with it.

"Same thing could easy happen here. Even be worse with The Gut and Millville side by side. 'Course this is just one side of the picture —yet the truth is there. We know the pattern. It's happened before. Only then there was no Freedom League to help." Kern was startled to hear Jake's voice tremble. It was the first time he had ever seen

244

or heard Jake stirred from his usual calm. His voice was the same now that he had heard so many other Negroes use when talking about the Freedom League and "the problem." Paula set her basket on the table and came to stand beside Jake and put her arm around his shoulder. He took her hand and held it. She bent and kissed him lightly on the cheek before going to the kitchen. Her mood was suddenly different, light and airy.

"My baby's growling—he must be hungry. Got to feed my baby——"

* * *

They could hear her moving in the kitchen, opening and closing the cabinet doors. Jake dropped the paper to the floor beside him and stretched prodigiously.

"Going to—" he gaped, mouth wide, "Montgomery—'scuse me, please," he finished his yawn and settled in the chair, "tomorrow. Have you decided what you want me to get for you?"

"For Christmas, you mean?"

"Yep—s'pose you better get your shopping done now—might not be able to get the things you want if you wait too late."

"I have my list upstairs." Kern started to leave the room. "I'll get it."

"Not now." Jake reached for his arm. "Paula would be back before you. We'll keep it hush-hush from her. Jes' leave it on your desk in the morning. I'll pick it up first thing." Suddenly, he spoke more seriously, "I won't get back 'til late tomorrow night, Kern. Paula's going to visit up on the campus. I want you two to come home together. Don't let her come alone." Kern saw that Jake's eyes were dead serious and there was no laughter in his face. He could not understand the seriousness, but he did know that Jake meant he was to come home at the same time Paula did. He was not fooling either. The tight grasp on his arm told him that. He wasn't sure, but he thought there was a worried look in Jake's eyes. Paula came back with a tray that held a teapot, sugar, cream, cups and saucers, small wafers and —a shopping list. She placed the tray in front of Jake.

Jake eyed the list skeptically as he sipped the steaming tea. "What's hooping?"

"You just tell the salesgirl you want hooping—she'll know just exactly what you mean." He shook his head in mock fright.

"An' all these numbers behind these patterns—what're they for?"

"They'll tell the girl— Oh! Jake, you know what they're for, you've bought patterns before." She stamped her foot in mock exasperation. Jake laughed gleefully.

"Say, Kern—I don't see anything on here that looks like either of us could be getting a Christmas present. Do you suppose Paula intends to send her shopping list to Santa Claus?" They laughed.

"All right, Mr. Smarty, I'll do my own shopping for Christmas sometime next week. I've already ordered my things."

"Who'd you order from? What are you getting, Paula?"

"Never you mind what I'm getting—you'll see in good time. C'mon," she gathered the teacups, "it's past time this house was in bed. Kern's got classes in the morning and you have—" A thought struck her.

"Are you going to see Tom Meeker in the morning before you go?"

She stood in the doorway with the tray in her hands. Jake was slow to answer and his clouded face told them both the answer before he spoke.

"I saw him today—when I took the cabinet."

Paula waited and Kern shifted his eyes between the two of them. "He said he wouldn't be able to pay 'til early in the spring—around first-crop time." Kern thought that would be about May. Paula went into the kitchen. Her unspoken "I told you so" was obvious in her refusal to say the words themselves.

❊   ❊   ❊

Kern tossed restlessly in his sleep. He saw pictures of the riot in Redmon and imaginary faces of the men and women who had been so brutally killed. The faces were strangely like those of people he knew. He saw Tom Meeker standing in Jake's workshop and he heard his voice clearly.

"Are you indicatin' that I cain't pay for this cabinet?"

246

CHAPTER XIV

THE LONG ARM OF THE LAW

I

"Ssh! Here they come!"

A hush started at the rear of the chapel and ran outward and down to the very front seats stilling the chattering voices in mid-sentence, leaving heads and eyes turned, with mouths not all closed, to stare toward the entrance at the rear of the building. Dr. Johnson walked quickly down the center aisle. With him were Dr. Gray and Mac Rodgers. Serious-faced they mounted the rostrum together. Dr. Gray and Mac sat side by side while Dr. Johnson placed his hat on one of the high-backed maroon leather chairs and stood gripping the lectern before him. For a moment he waited, as though trying to find exactly the word he wanted before starting. The crowded auditorium waited in dead silence.

"I won't beat about the bush with you. The purpose of this assembly may be simply stated. As of now, you students are denied the privilege of going into the city of Valley View." A patter of surprised voices rose and quieted abruptly. "Off-campus students are cautioned to exercise the utmost care in going through Valley View— Use the most direct route between your homes and the campus. Only in the most unusual cases will permission to visit the city be given to resident students." He paused. "Under *no* circumstances are women students to visit Valley View."

What is this? The gathered heads and eyes turned to look at their neighbors in frowning silent question. What is this? This must be bad! Kern shifted his books in his lap and edged forward on his seat.

"Those of you with normal shopping errands to perform may convey your needs to your deans. They will be consolidated, and a faculty representative will shop for you. I believe that the theater, the snack shop, the 'candy wagon,' our other facilities should take care of your recreational needs. For those scholars among you, the library will continue to operate." No laughter greeted what would ordinarily

247

have been an uproariously funny twist from usually stern Dr. Johnson.

"This unusual regulation is not made with disregard for your judgment as mature young men and women. Nor is it meant to deprive you of any slight pleasure you may have found in being able to go to Valley View.

"This morning three of your young women, while walking along Harrison Street in front of this Chapel, were molested and insulted by a carful of men—white men." The hush deepened. No one moved. No one spoke. "I will not call the names of these young women at this time. You will find out for yourselves who they are quickly enough. The important thing is that this incident did occur. I want you all to know exactly what happened so that you will have no false impressions—so that in writing to your parents and friends, or in discussions among yourselves, you will be acquainted with the facts.

"The young ladies concerned were walking down Harrison Street shortly after ten-o'clock class break. They had delayed leaving the Social Science Building for a few minutes, and as a consequence, the streets and the campus were practically deserted. Just as they reached the corner of Richardson and Harrison Streets and were about to cross and go up the Oval to Tubman Hall, a car came up behind them, turned the corner, and stopped in their path. There were five white men in that car. The only one who was positively identified was Sheriff Bill Noble. He was the driver. These men insulted these three young ladies with their proposals. They swore at them. They tried to pull one of the women into their car. When she and the others screamed, they drove away. The University has lodged a complaint against the known offender with the town council. I doubt," he acidly added, "that any redress will be given."

A low mutter of anger grew into a rumble of angry sound and filled the chapel. Dr. Johnson listened to its swelling before he raised his hand. When he spoke, anger had replaced his usual calm.

"I feel just as you do. I, too, would like to go out and put my hands on these men and tear them limb from limb. But I know so well that violence is not the answer. It is simply not wisdom to pull the lion's tail in the lion's den. We must counsel ourselves against that unwise course."

Mutters of anger could still be heard in the chapel.

Who? Kern wondered. Who? Hate and the twisting filled his stomach. His whole being. Softly, he began to curse.

"Valley View is one of the oldest of Negro universities. We were

248

founded in a great ambition. We have served that ambition well. We have sent out graduates into the world equipped to take their places and to serve creditably and well. For almost eighty-two years, they have done that. The name of your university is known in far corners of the world. Our choristers have received audience in the courts of the world. We are supported by men and women who know the work we have been doing and who have faith in its worth. Had I been one of the founders of this college, I would never have put it here in the South. But I was not one of those founders. Originally, Valley View was built for young men and women who lived in this section of the South. During the years it has grown so that now you typical students come to us from Oregon and Washington and Massachusetts as well as from Florida, Mississippi and Alabama. We cannot move the University. No more can we change the pattern of the community in which we find ourselves. We must assume a reasonable, cool-headed approach to the situation. We must reckon the fact that we do good against the obvious evil.

"I have given you the facts. I hope that you will bear them in mind in your discussions of this matter. If there should be any students who for any reason whatsoever were unable to attend this meeting, I ask you to pass on these suggestions and directions to them. I shall be compelled to deal in summary fashion with anyone who disobeys this request until I, personally, have lifted the ban."

They filed slowly out of the chapel and trooped in buzzing knots along the bricked sidewalk to Tubman Hall and the dining room. Kern knew he would not have time to get home and back before time to start his one-o'clock class. He called Paula from a phone booth in Tubman Hall, then ate in the cafeteria. He did not mention "the thing" to her, though she sensed his excitement and pressed him with questions. Wary, he decided that Valley View operators might be listening in on his call, on any call from the school.

II

When Kern walked into the Playhouse for three o'clock rehearsal, a clamorous discussion of the episode greeted him at the door. He had heard nothing else during the past two class periods. Teachers and pupils had joined in "fighting the problem." Nobody knew who had been involved. Everyone was guessing. Clawing fear and hate had grown in him. Damn the South! Damn white men!

"All right. All right—break it up!" He tried to imitate Mac Rodgers' gruff voice and failed. The circle of heads barely turned in his direction and closed again tightly. Kern pushed forward curiously.

"Hey, what gives? Why so hush-hush?" The circle widened to include him.

"'Doriah!" With a sudden, sickening feeling he understood why he had not seen Adoriah. She had been one of the girls.

'Doriah was sitting on one of the bench seats, dark shadows below her eyes marking her usually clear olive skin. Sammy Thompson was sitting beside her.

"Go ahead, 'Doriah. What happened then?"

"Well, they said some nasty things and—" she hid her face, "and then they finally drove off laughing." There was a letdown in the listening group.

"But what did they say?"

"Well, damn it, if she won't tell, I will!" Sammy straightened angrily in her seat.

"But Dr. Johnson said no good was to be gained by telling, Sammy. You know that." Adoriah protested any more discussion. Kern's eyes were riveted to her bent head. Anger started in him. 'Doriah, his steady date, had been one of the three girls! How dared they? His anger deepened.

"Damn Dr. Johnson—and this college, too!" Samuella Thompson spoke her mind clearly and distinctly.

"But he might expel——"

"Expel who! Not if I don't want to be expelled he won't. My daddy's a trustee of this—this—!" She gazed ceilingward for a descriptive word. "Anyhow, this child of Hagar is leaving here as soon as money comes by wire. I don't intend to spend another day in this hole. I called Mama and told her to get me out of here right away. Must have been crazy to come here anyway."

"What happened, Sammy?" The circle was eager for details.

"What did they say?"

"Was anyone hurt?" Impatient curiosity filled their voices. Sammy, Kern saw, was plenty hot under the collar.

"You want the horrible facts? Okay, here they are." Pushing her flaming red hair angrily back from her ears, green eyes flashing, her

250

full figure tense with excitement and anger, she seemed older and more mature than her listeners—as mature as she actually was.

"—then this rattletrap pulled around the corner and stopped. We stopped too, thinking they were strangers looking for directions. Then we saw they were ragged peckerwoods—Bill Noble among 'em. One of the men in the back stuck his head out and said, 'C'mon, gals, let's go for a little ride!'" A voice on the outer edge of the circle swore.

"Goddam bastards!"

"You're damned right, Bud," Sammy added. "That's exactly what I say. I suppose we were so shocked it didn't occur to us to run. That sort of thing happening right in broad daylight—you just don't expect it. These bums said a lot of things—I don't remember exactly what, about who'd take which one of us first and when. Then Bill Noble, and I know him by sight, hooked his finger at me. He said, 'C'mon, baby, be sweet to ol' Bill and give him a little stuff—I'll show you how to do a good job.' Him—the fat son of a—" She flailed about for a substitute word. Kern found her thought complete without the word. So did the others as they tightened their circle.

"I suppose I told him to go to hell!" There was an appreciative nervous giggle. If they knew Sammy, she had certainly told him to go to hell—and she had probably given him explicit directions.

"Anyhow, he jumped out of the car, grabbed my arm and tried to drag me toward the car. There were two cars coming down the street, and we screamed for help and he cussed me. He told me if I ever came into town again, he'd take me and break my head in the bargain. Then he drove away laughing something about 'nigger bitches.'" She finished almost breathless. Beside her 'Doriah kept her eyes in her lap as if ashamed. Kern stood paralyzed, looking at her bent head.

"Terry broke down. Nurse has her in the dispensary now." Sammy's face blazed. She stood and pushed her way through the circle and stood tall on her slim, high heels.

"And I'll tell you what I am going to do. I am going home to my daddy's lumber company, and every goddam Southerner he has working there is going to get the boot or my name isn't Samuella." She pressed her clenched fists tight against her hips, her breasts rising and falling with her deep stormy breathing.

"Serve 'em right."

"No better for them."

"Wish it was me."

Her vow received approval from her audience. She drew her hair away from her head with nervous hands, flouncing it wide and letting it fall on her shoulders. Arching her body, she set her hands at her waist.

"Can you imagine that poor bastard, that trashy scum thinking I'd look a second time at him? Why, my daddy hires bums like that to do our dirty work and they like it. Down here, with a pistol at his side, he's God."

None of them heard Mac Rodgers come in as she spoke. He came forward from the door quickly. Not until he spoke and they jerked about, did they know.

"Here, what gives? What sort of talk is that for a lady, Sammy? I'm surprised!" She faced him, but she wasn't contrite.

"Normally I'd be ashamed too, Mac—but this isn't normally. Little Sammy blames nobody but herself. If I had owned an ounce of sense, I would have stayed at home where I am just 'Sammy' and make my own complete little life. But not me. Oh, no! I read books. I am intelligent. I have a sense of responsibility!" Her posture and her voice dramatized her words. "When I discovered that Hagar has contributed to Sammy's blood, nothing would satisfy me but to come here and find out how 'my people,'" she spoke with faint derision, "live." They stared at her aghast as they began to realize what she was saying.

"Well, now I know. And when I think about it, I want to vomit." Her voice softened in the shocked silence though sarcasm still gave it a razor edge. "One of my finest memories will be to have known all of you, my brethren. I wouldn't have missed it for anything. Not even at the cost of being insulted by those dogs today. But now I'm through." She turned and started to the door. Mac Rodgers called her.

"Wait a minute, Sammy!" She turned about and stood watching him.

"Sammy, you can't run away like this!" A little frown creased her forehead, at odds with the smile that touched the corners of her lips.

"Oh, come now, Mac. We're not going to ham it up with emoting, are we?"

"But running won't answer this, kid. You know that." His spread hands were despairing.

"Who said anything about running, Mac? One 'runs' involun-

252

tarily, without premeditation—out of fear." She came a step nearer to him—to them. "I'm a big girl. Remember? I know what I want. I know what I won't take. This is one of the things I won't take. I never let anything tie a cord to me that I can't break when *I* get ready. Nothing. So, please—no sentimentality, Mac. Save it for the kids."

"Okay, Sammy—I guess I understand." He dropped his arms wearily. She came to him quickly, in affection, and threw her arms about him.

"Too bad, Mac! I thought I could make a go of it. I find I don't like the tune well enough to pay the piper." She swayed back to look into his face and they saw her hands tighten on his arms.

"Thanks. Thanks for everything." She turned and ran up the slanting floor to the door. It banged shut behind her and she was gone.

* * *

"Well," Mac faced them, hands thrust in his pockets. "I guess you know." He stared at their faces. "Once upon a time, the natives tell me, University people were treated with respect in Valley View. They say that the white folks almost tipped their hats and said, 'Thank you, sir,' when you went to buy. Then the mill came along and all that changed. When our dollar value went, there was no longer any reason for the white folks to put aside their prejudices. Curtain." He drew a chair and sat down. His eyes stayed on the door as if he expected Sammy to come back.

"Let's read through these lines once and we'll call it a day. Oh, yes—the town council said that since none of the girls was harmed, there is no ground for complaint."

It was a flat rehearsal. Mac stopped them halfway through the first act.

* * *

As he started home across The Gut, Kern wondered how he would tell Paula and Jake about the thing. The tightness in him was stretching him like a drumhead. And Sammy— "One runs—out of fear." He could see the house now, through the bare limbs of the last trees. He ran the last few yards to safety.

253

CHAPTER XV

XMAS, 1934

THE ORNAMENTS on the Christmas tree nodded in slow pattern, tiny bells, long glittering tinsel streamer icicles, and glistening balls, catching the light and breaking it to gobbets of light that flashed for a moment and died. The flashing caught his eye and Kern lowered his book to his updrawn knees and turned his head on its pillow rest to watch the shimmering. A good Christmas, he thought, it had been a good Christmas. Even remembering Boston and Evans and his grandmother's last Christmas—it had been a good Christmas.

He turned his book outwards to read the gold letters of its title. "TECHNIQUES OF PLOTTING by James Varden." The small square letters stood out boldly against the dull maroon binding. He fingered his way to the flyleaf. A bold, decisive hand had written, "To Kern from his father—Xmas 1935."

If anything had surprised him more than seeing his father in the kitchen talking to Paula and Jake when he came downstairs that morning, it had been finding this book among his presents. Least of all would he have expected his father to give him a book on writing. The plush davenport creaked as he shifted his position and, wiggling his stockinged toes comfortably, returned to his book.

Their voices rose and reached him distinctly and he lowered his book to stare across the room to the loose half circle where they sat, Mac Rodgers and Dr. Gray, Jake and his father. Paula sat on the fringe of the circle, her eyes going from one to the other as they talked. Kern recognized the rumbling undertone of their voices before he understood what they were staying. His father's cold, controlled voice was deliberately scathing.

"We use their blind conceit to our advantage. In fact, one of the main props of our defense rests on that conceit." Charles' eyes flashed as he leaned forward.

"Monumental conceit possesses the Southern white man. He is controlled by it, not it by him—" Kern saw his face in full view and remembered what his grandmother had said, "Charles is like high-voltage electricity. They touch him and they are hurt by his fierceness but they are unable to cry out or draw away." Mac, Dr. Gray, Jake and Paula leaned in about him like that now.

"Conceit is almost born in him—almost a part of heredity—as the color of his skin or eyes or hair. Not even to their innermost selves will Southerners admit that a Negro could possibly be as intelligent as they. The most illiterate of them will admit that there *are* educated, intelligent Negroes. But the most intelligent Negro, they will hold, is not as intelligent as they. Proving by the knowledge of their subconscious minds that they are wrong. They struggle to reject totally the idea that any Negro could be more intelligent than they. Very well!" he clapped his hands on his knees, "give them the sop their infantile minds demand. They have committed one grave procedural error in this Redmon trial. I would fail any senior law student who could not immediately spot the error. It's just that obvious. They know it, but I don't want to make an issue of it now. I want this case to go to the Supreme Court of the United States for decision—to set a precedent—and so long as we leave this reversible error alone, we shall win in the Supreme Court." They listened, nodding at this strategy. "Up there in Redmon they are going around with their tongues in their cheeks, patting themselves on the back, laughing up their sleeves. You can almost hear them say—'How dumb can those niggers be?—We're really pulling the wool over their eyes this time.'" His laugh was brief and sardonic. It chilled Kern. It was not a laugh. It was almost a snarl.

"Let them laugh. When we are good and ready—we will drop the trap and leave them dangling by their necks. I shall then be interested to hear the sound of their laughter." His precise, emotionless words were more violent than a convulsion of madness. The calm words from thin lips left a gallows in the room before their eyes, and before them too figures dangling in payment for their conceit. Charles leaned back in his chair, out of sight, and Kern stared at the space where his face had been. Dr. Gray broke the silence first.

"Understand that the State Troopers have made it pretty hot for you, Roberts— Any truth in that?"

"Well—yes and no. The Governor personally assigned a pair of Troopers to us for what he called 'protection.' They meet us in the mornings when we leave Asheville and take us down to Redmon. In the evenings they escort us back to Asheville."

255

"You mean to say you go back and forth between Redmon and Asheville every day?"

"We have to—there's no place we could stay at Redmon without the risk of being molested—and if we stayed with a Negro family there, it's almost a certainty that the townspeople would take it out on them after we left. So to avoid trouble, we stay in Asheville. But——"

Mac was incredulous. "But man, that's almost seventy miles away. What time do you get up in the morning in order to reach Redmon?"

"Oh, about five-thirty——"

"Then you spend a day in court and go back to Asheville at night?"

Charles nodded.

"By George, man—how do you stand up under it?" Mac shook his head as Charles shrugged his shoulders.

"It's not so bad—I'm generally in Asheville by midnight." Charles laughed wryly. "Our biggest trouble is with the Troopers who are supposed to escort us. Here's an example of what I mean. The first morning we started very early, about five, in order to be on time for court. The Troopers met us outside of Asheville and we clipped the trip off in about an hour and forty minutes—really moved along at a good pace behind a motorcycle escort. Two mornings later, we started a little late. We could have made it easily if the Troopers had speeded up a bit. Instead, they slowed along at forty miles an hour. When we asked them if there wasn't a chance of speeding up, they simply laughed and said, 'It's a forty-mile speed limit.' We reached Redmon more than a half hour late. That wasn't the pay-off. Oh, no! The presiding judge found us in contempt of court and placed a $100 fine. On another day, we swerved to avoid a cart on the highway. The Troopers pulled us over and wrote out tickets for driving on the wrong side of the road. Then they proceeded to escort us on into Redmon. Instead of being defense lawyers at trial that morning, we were charged and fined for reckless driving."

His listeners were incredulous.

"Child's play," Charles murmured, "child's play. Children with firearms— They're just that dangerous. You know," he reflected, "the prosecution laughed when it heard we would fight the case to the Supreme Court if necessary. They actually think we meant the State Supreme Court. I don't believe they've once thought that we might mean the Supreme Court of the nation." Jake watched and

256

listened to Charles, his face serious with thought. He began to shape each word slowly, carefully. "What if the lower court decision is in your favor, Charles? What then?"

"It must go against us!" For the first time Charles let go his restrained calm. His words were almost explosive. "We must lose! This must go to the Supreme Court— We must have a national precedent. Fundamental liberties have been invaded here——"

Jake smiled, understanding his tactics now. Lose here. Win in Washington.

"Is there a chance the State Supreme Court would reverse an unfavorable decision by the Redmon court?"

"The odds are in our favor. Our whole case depends on their upholding the lower court. It's the only way we can get to the Supreme Court."

Dr. Gray sighed heavily. "It's bad I know, Roberts—but something is happening in this South. It's better now than it has been——"

Jake nodded in slow agreement. "There are new faces in the large cities, new ideas. The progressive centers of the nation are only hours away by air. Men are realizing a responsibility for the South. They are doing something about it. The change is slow, but it is a change. There was a time not long ago, remember, when violence like this Redmon thing would not have won more than passing notice in the nation's press. This—this has been in newspapers all over the nation."

"I think you're right, Dr. Gray." Jake measured his words. "I think the rest of the country's coming aware of its responsibility for the South's condition. It's beginning to realize that we can't be drained year after year of our strength and our manpower and still be 'spected to be a healthy, needed part of the nation. Men don't change their ways of thinking easy, and for generations the whole country has made the South sort of an economic slave. That's hurt us all—white and black. But there is a change. Maybe the mill-owners ain't really interested in helping out—but they do. They're interested in cutting their operating expenses, but now they're keeping in the South some of the money that has been taken away in the past. More money means more chance to learn. That's the thing that makes for change." He stopped short, abashed at his positive tone, and looked about him. "Leastways," he added shyly, "I see it that way." Paula smiled happily at their approval and Kern saw the pride with which she watched Jake.

"I see meanness though," Mack stirred, "meanness of the spirit.

A poor, thwarted spirit that has grown inward on itself until it festers on hate and its own miserable poverty of goodness. Look at these people—look on every side. Gutted land, too poor to grow decent weeds. Gullied fields with no crops. Tumble-down shacks for white men and black—ugly, burned-out towns, worried ignorant faces. The pitifully few who have managed to wrest a living from the land are so twisted by what they have gone through that they will never be normal again."

"Well—I don't know, Mac." Jake took calm issue with him. "I sort of think any victory is worth something. The South has a struggle on its hands. We got more children here than any other part of the country. We spend less for education.

"Lots is said about that. But we spend more for education out of what we has than any other section, and at the same time we're fighting to live through a slavery we don't want. We're fighting under great odds." There was a note of pride in his voice.

"Well, Jake, you're a Southerner. I'm not. I'm just a dramatics teacher. A writer. I don't like ugliness. I don't like Southerners—neither the things they stand for nor the things they do. I don't believe praise is due a man for doing what is right. No matter what the material gain, unless there is also an increased goodness of spirit, unless there is something richer in the soul than makes itself felt in the faces and in the eyes, in simple acts of human kindness, you have nothing. That's the commodity—simple human kindness. The South—!" Mac's scorn was withering.

"It's the Negro," Dr. Gray broke into Mac's tense words. "It's the Negro who is hardest hit. I know men who live in the hope that each year will be better than the one that went before. They do without food and clothing. They know nothing about books, they move from place to place, always struggling to break even. They face landlords who refuse to wait even a little while. Injunctions are placed against their property, poor as it is. Their farm implements, everything except a few household goods, are sold. They struggle to get other implements, to start again, sinking a little deeper into debt each year, moving stealthily at night, hoping that the sheriff won't come. Fighting on——"

"There is right and wrong on both sides, I guess." Kern sat upright to see his father's face. "I see a parallel between the Negro and the soldier in combat. Just as soldiers in war who are subjected to shelling hour after hour become 'shell shocked,' so too is the Negro 'shocked.' He is shelled with abuse, ridicule, denial, in one form or another, every day he lives. I wonder if there is in this whole nation one Negro, just one, who is 'normal'—who has lived through this 'shelling' without damage to his heart or mind or soul. Just one—!" He sat far forward in his chair now, voice low, arms heavy on his knees, looking at them and past them. Past Kern and beyond the house, his glittering eyes intent on something they could not see.

Kern felt the familiar hard-wound tightness inside of him and he felt as if he were teetering on the brink of a chasm with nothing above or below him but an infinity of space without a handhold.

❆   ❆   ❆

Long after Mac and Doc Gray had gone, after the house had grown quiet and his father had fallen asleep beside him, Kern lay staring up at the ceiling, sleepy but afraid of the dreams that the past weeks had taught him would come with sleep. Finally he slept and dreamed. His dream started with the Christmas tree in the living room with Paula's Dresden doll from Jake standing in the center of their gifts spread about its base. It ended with 'Doriah's face, and in between were Sammy's blunt-worded "Good-bye," Tom Meeker's face, and Rollie squirming under him years ago on a playground. Somewhere along its course, on a summer night, a man led him by the arm to a door and shoved him roughly through it. He saw a face and drew away from it in suspicion because it was a white face. He did not recognize Dorcas.

❆   ❆   ❆

He dreamed that night and he dreamed the next night, too.

❆   ❆   ❆

The same faces filled his dreams that night after Christmas night and with them were other, more recent pictures. He watched his father straighten in the living-room chair and stare at Jake, his eyes filled with disbelief.

"When did you first hear about this?"

"Heard about it yesterday." Jake's head was bent and Kern was unable to see his face in his dream—just as he had not been able to see it from where he had stood at the foot of the stairs. Dreaming,

259

he stood there on the stairs, holding the balustrade, hearing their words clearly.

"Just try to keep her out of town as much as possible."

"Uh-huh," Jake agreed. "What I got was gossip. I don't credit the source too much, but I know these people an' this country, so I can't disregard it completely. Missus Jennings' man Herbert tol' her he heard Bill Noble talking to some of his cronies down at the store. I wasn't too surprised. I knew he'd stared at Paula before. Saw it myself. But I didn't think nothing of it. Men just seem to look at her a second time. I didn't say anything to Paula, 'cause she thinks she can protect herself—but there ain't no protection she could offer from that sort of thing. I don't want trouble 'bout her being insulted or molested, so I try to do the shopping myself. Don't leave her here alone any more'n I can help."

So that was it! When Jake had gone to Montgomery why he had insisted that Kern be sure and come home with Paula. He had been thinking of Bill Noble. The name filled Kern with dread and he turned restlessly in his sleep. He could see his father's face and savage anger was in it.

"You see, Charles, I wouldn't want to kill a man—not even Bill Noble. I'd have to do that if he bothered Paula."

"Why don't you leave the South, Jake? You don't have to stay here. You could go to Washington—to any one of a dozen places—and make a better living than you do here. You are a craftsman and you can sell your handiwork."

"I know, Charles." Jake shook his head slowly, looking at first one palm and then the other of his work-hardened hands. "I have thought about it a hundred times since this started." He spoke hesitantly, considering his words. "I can't leave." Charles' eyes widened. He started to say "But why—" and stopped, waiting for Jake to continue.

"I don't know whether I can make you understand this or not. But I'll try. I want you to know. In the event anything ever happens—" He broke off his words. "My father owned this land and his father before him—clean back to the times when there was slavery, it's been ours. Ol' man Bryant, who bought my grandpa as a slave, had seen some of the things grandpa had made with his hands. He bought him, and the minute the papers were signed and grandpa was paid for he set him free. Grandpa used to talk about his 'manumission.'" He smiled at a memory and went on. "Ol' man Bryant told him—'You are an artist, Frederick. An artist must be free if he

260

is to create. You are a free man from this day. And so long as any of my family shall live, or until this damnable slavery is ended, you and your family shall be free. I ask one thing of you!'—these were ol' man Bryant's words—'I ask only that you spend as much of your life as you can in creating some small bit of beauty, and that you pass that gift on to your sons.' Those were his words. Well," he turned to stare directly at Charles, going on in his low reflective voice, "that was the beginning of our heritage. Freedom and a devotion to the creation of beauty. Grandpa taught my daddy to work wood with his hands, taught him how to be a craftsman, and he taught me. Some day, I pray God, I'll teach my own son these lessons. I have a responsibility to this ground and to this house to keep them both free of bondage, whether it be free from a bond of taxes —free from being gullied and ruined until it is too poor to bear harvest. I must be as honest with my fellow man as I try to be with—with a piece of wood. I haven't done too badly. I've made enough to be able to help some others less fortunate. You might say I'm sort of pledged to stay and see something through. Can you understand that?"

He saw his father lean forward and wordlessly grip Jake's shoulder. There was a gap of silence and he swirled through dream space pursued by something he could not see and could not fight and, fascinated, watched himself run out of sight into nothingness.

✿   ✿   ✿

He awoke more than once that night, came jerkily from sleep, and lay rigid in the bed, afraid to move for fear he would arouse the man sleeping next to him and have to explain the troubled thoughts that caused him to dream. He was glad the next day when Charles waved good-bye to them from his car and drove out of sight down the road that passed the turn to Valley View and bent sharply northward on its way to the Franklin Pike and to Asheville. But his tension didn't leave with Charles' departure. It stayed in him in a tight knot that he couldn't reach. He tried to read and could not focus his attention on the page before him. He stared aimlessly out of the window thinking of many things he should do and deciding, one by one, to do none of them. Finally he went out of the door and around the corner of the house toward Jake's workshop. His mood as gray as the dark overcast sky, he went in and sat on the tall stool beside the drawing board and watched Jake without a word.

He watched Jake take a long slender piece of wood from the rack above his bench and run his hands fondly up and down its grain. He watched him mark its surface carefully and heard the first whine of the lathe as it bit into the wood. Then he saw Jake's hands turning and shaping the wood until it began to take on the soft curves of a chair leg and saw Jake's hands brush over it in a caress that wiped away the soft, powdered dust from its surface. Then, as he had known he would, he heard Jake begin to hum a low melody. He thought it was " 'Zekiel Saw the Wheel," but he wasn't sure. Tension loosened in him though he was sharply aware that it did not go away entirely. In one way and another, it seemed to him now that tension had been in him since that June at Evans.

"I seem to think better when I am working—sort of eases me." Jake didn't look up. He hummed another song. Kern had known he would say that. He had known too that he wouldn't look up and that he would, in a moment, hum another song.

"Roll Jordan Roll."

CHAPTER XVI

"—WORSHIP GOD"

I

THEY pulled into the churchyard and edged their way between a mud-spattered pick-up truck and a wagon whose un-
hitched team, a few feet away, tossed their heads fretfully at the
ends of their tethers while suspiciously eyeing a mule hitched to
the far side of their holding rail. Jake switched off his motor with
a pleased sigh. Church. He was glad to be there.

"Right on time! Sunday school's just about out." He chuckled
and pointed. "See old Elder George there moppin' his face. Can
always tell when that man's just finished tellin' the Lord's word,
hasn't had time to cool off." His chuckle faded out as he lowered
his head to look up at the cross atop the steeple. Every fourth
Sunday since Kern had come to Valley View, he had reminded
them that it was "Church Sunday—ought to be goin' to the Lawd,"
but something had always cropped up to stop them. They knew
the urge in him to come to God was rooted deep. So, though Paula
confided to Kern that she could get as close to God by simply
stepping out on the porch and having a talk with Him, and though
Kern himself had no special desire to go to church, they had
bundled up this crisp February morning, piled in the coupé and
come along with him. There had been no escaping it.

"Golly, Paula, it's coming Church Sunday again, an' if I don't
go I'll bust!" All week long he said that and they had believed him.
His irrepressible spirit bubbled over and caught them, and before
they reached the Union Road Baptist Methodist Church they were
looking forward to services and to meeting the churchgoers as
much as he.

Kern looked curiously out of the window. The unusually chill
air reached inside the car and nipped the tips of their fingers and
toes. A handful of small, cotton-puff clouds hung almost motionless
in the curving sky.

Drawn as by a magnet the Negroes from Valley View and

Union, from the surrounding countryside, came to church. Walking, on horseback and in trucks, they came. By horse-drawn wagons, in a few model T's, here and there in a Chevrolet, they gathered to worship God. Along the roads and across the fields they came, for this "Fourth Sunday." Church Sunday. "Gettin'-together time." Time to swap tales and rumors and see old friends. The Union Baptist Methodist Church opened its doors to them all, to Methodists, Baptists and Congregationalists, to those of any faith, or none, to all who wanted to go to church. Kern saw them standing about the yard and in the doorway in small groups, groups that were all men and some all women. One or two that were mixed. They got out of the car and waited until Paula flounced her skirt into place and satisfactorily settled her bonnet on her head. Then they walked around the car and past the bare ground about the hitching posts where the horses and mules chopped at the circle of bare earth with their shod hooves. Two small boys, squatting on the bare ground beyond the tethering posts, were playing mumblety-peg, so intent on their game that neither of them looked up as Kern, Jake and Paula went on toward the crowded yard. Jake knew everyone.

"Mornin', Deacon——"

"Mornin', Brother Hobbs——"

"You're lookin' mighty fine this mornin', Sister Kent—mighty fine——"

"Well! Missus Jennings—mighty glad to see you—an' Ida Mae—well now!" Only with Paula, Kern saw, did the haunting sadness leave Ida Mae's eyes. She came to Paula as quickly as her crutches would carry her, outdistancing her mother.

"Oh! Aunt Paula—you look so pretty!"

Paula bent and hugged the little girl tightly.

"Darling, darling— My, Ida Mae's walking so well——"

"Wanna thank you for them crutches, Jake—touched a body fit to cry. Idy Mae's done changed overnight."

"Oh, shucks. It weren't nothin'! Should've thought about it long ago." He drew away, embarrassed by Mary Jennings' thanks, and they went into the churchyard proper. A huge woman called to them across the lawn. All wobbly, bulging fat, it seemed to Kern that she was larger than even Mrs. Jennings as she rushed toward them breathlessly.

"Lord save me—" Jake started to pull away but Paula held on to his arm tightly.

264

"No, you don't—just you stay right here with me. I don't want to be talked to death either." Jake's face showed the effort it cost him to face the descending avalanche.

"Mornin', Missus Friendly— How you this fine morning?"

"Oh middlin', Jake, middlin'—jes' trying to get erlong. Howdy do, Miss Paula—an' you, young suh." She caught her breath in deep gasps. "Don't see how I goin' to make it though. Try as I may, I cain't never get 'head at all." Kern surveyed her from one side as she rattled on with Jake. Short gray hair bristled from under the edges of a faded blue head rag and a man's coat bulged tightly about her shoulders and spread open at one seam. A dark-brown dress hung loose from under her coat and covered her legs leaving only a thin gap of ashy brown skin to show above the broken men's shoes which she wore. Kern almost laughed as Jake tried for the third time to move around her. With half an ear he listened to her complaint and at the same time heard plainly the group of older boys who leaned against the picket fence and teased the girls who switched back and forth without their parents, grinning delightedly at the madrigals which greeted them. This one, for a bright-skinned girl whose manner was more aloof and disdainful than that of the others——

> Yella gal, yella gal,
> You can't shine,
> Got uh black gal
> Kin beat your time.

Cackling laughter greeted the angry toss of her head as she saucily rolled her hips and passed on.

"Looky ol' hincty, mariney nigger. She think she too good——"

"Man, I bet she get her tell-off un' these time."

"Ho, ha! Yeah man!"

"Half-white nigger!"

Like the sound of a gong breaking on its peak, numbing his eardrums. Numbing more than his eardrums. Here it is again! The words awakened memory. Are the eyes watching me—hostile eyes? Yes! Are these hostile people? The stares seemed curious. What was Missus Friendly saying?

"Doin' the bes' I can though. Mah house sops up all thuh rain water in thuh county. Jes' fas' as it come from Heaven, it run through mah roof. Cain't pay up on mah loan from the bank no

265

way I tries. Thet ol' ten-percent int'res' eats me up wuss'n the weevils. Gotta buy seed, an' a body cain't grow nuthin' 'tall roun' heah wifout no fertilize. Got uh bale uh cotton outen mah craps, an' it all went fer rent. Had me 'bout uh hundred poun's er lint which was nowheres near 'nuff to score off my bills, an' I ain't got nary dime lef' in the end. Hed two chicks, but the houn' et them. My hawg done et my corn, an' the white folks done shot thuh hawg fo' I could eat um. Gals got squatted an' birfed kids, then run away an' lef' 'em wif me. Man! I'se havin' it turrible."

Kern thought from her booming laugh that it didn't seem to matter too much to her. Jake slipped around her and as she stood there laughing, arms akimbo, her head thrown far back, they passed Sister Lucille Friendly and went toward the church.

"Lord, that's the talkinest woman in Alabama." Paula laughed at his relief.

Outside of Jake's house and the Hartleys' house, the church was the best-built building for Negroes Kern had seen in the county.

It was painted white all over, Jake's yearly gift, and the cross that topped its steeple held his eye. Kern saw it caught Jake's eye, too. A cross against the sky, a cross to which Jake turned for prayer. Beyond the church was a graveyard, almost choked by brush that hid the cinder-block headpieces which, in leaning confusion, marked the final resting places of former inhabitants of Valley View and Union. In a far corner, and in the center of the cemetery, two "real" headstones, simple and straight, stood above the brush-hidden graves of two who had once had more of worldly goods than their fellows. Behind the cemetery, a wavering path led through tall brush to where a frame blind hid the entrance of a common privy from view.

Kern looked at the cemetery plot and blinked quickly against the stinging prickle that came with memory. In reality, he thought, there was little resemblance between the two, scarcely enough to cause him to remember. This one here, untended and weedy with brush, and that other one in Vermont. So much difference between them. He felt a sudden longing to be in Vermont.

They went up the low wooden steps and into the church. Above them, in its loft, the bell began to toll off its call to worship.

He would do it this very evening—he settled it in his mind. He should have written his grandmother months ago, during the summer, instead of the short note in which he had said he would not come back to Northport again. He would write her today, this evening, right after dinner. His grandmother.

266

They walked forward to the very front bench and sat down. Jake leaned across Paula to tell him in a low whisper that this bench was reserved for deacons and deaconesses and some of the elder brothers. Behind them the faithful flocked in from the yard and took their places amid a shuffle of feet and a murmur of voices. Kern could hear mothers and grownups hushing their youngsters. Somewhere behind him a baby began to cry in a high-pitched, jerky fashion. Kern looked about him cautiously, unable to restrain his curiosity. A plain, raised stand at the front of the church made up the rostrum. Four chairs provided the choir with seats. A lectern stood on the forward edge of the platform, its leaning top draped with a blue velvetlike material.

The Laws of God.

The letters were spelled out in rude Old English characters, announcing that the ten groups of words below it were, in fact, the Ten Commandments. The words were almost illegible from where Kern sat. This placard flanked the left-hand wall of the church. To the right of the pulpit, a simple two-line sign said:

> Help Valley View College
> Give Whatever You Can

For minutes, off and on, Kern looked at the clock above the rostrum and looked away. Each time he looked back the clock hands remained unmoved. He decided, finally, that it was not running. It was not. Behind him the churchgoers filled the benches solidly except for an irregular circle around the rumbling potbellied stove where heat held them away. The gray-painted walls were somber, the more so for the dull light that sifted down through the buff-colored paint that covered the windows.

"Roll, Jordan, Roll!" The throaty song went up loud and clear to the roof of the church. Its rolling sound had scarcely died out before a dark heavy man with a smooth-shaven head leaped to the pulpit and began to chant a phrase which Kern could not understand. He listened, mystified, as the church members caught it up.

II

Oh ooooom mmmmmmmmmm um

Ah mmmmmmmmm mmmmmmmmmm. The members of the church chanted in time with the leader, their voices rising and falling, now dirgelike, now swift and almost unrecognizable.

267

mmmmmmmmmm mmmmmmmmmm um
Ah mmmmmmm mmmmmmmmmm fallin' inter thuh bloody sea
Ain't no mo' foes to fight . . . mmmmmmmmmmm
Ah uh mmmmmmmmm this is a mmmmmmmmm mmmmmmmmm
Ah uh mighty fine worl' mmmmmmmmmm mmmmmmmmmmm
A mighty fine worl' mmmmmmmmmmmmm
mmmmmmmmm Thank you, Gawd mmmmmmmmmm
mmmmmmmmm this is a mighty fine worl' mmmmmmmmm
mmmmmm oh ah to be friendly with a
man like Gawd mmmmmmmmm mmmmmmmmmm

The chanting chorus ended and the leader raised his hands and bowed his head. He quickly began a slow moaning chant of a prayer and the congregation bent their heads and began to sway slowly from side to side in time to his words.

"Oh, Gawd—duh Favah of the worl', hallowed be dy name—an' 'low your kingdom to 'give us of our sins—'cause they mighty little white things, Gawd—an' give us some of dy mercy like you done them that walks on yo' brother like he dirt on da groun'——"

The audience caught the spirit of the prayer with moans and humming. One man behind Kern, in a shiny black suit, fell from his seat and rolled rapturously on the ground, kicking at the ground with his heels. Kern was surprised that no one paid any attention to him. He looked obliquely to Jake to see what he was doing. Jake sat motionless, his head bent and his eyes closed. He felt Paula watching him, but when he turned to look at her she was staring down at her gloved hands. Neither of them had joined in the chanting supplication. The woman beyond Paula was quiet, too. She sat stiffly upright on her bench, her shoulders not touching the back of the seat at all. With one gnarled hand she clutched a gray woolen scarf tight about her head and shoulders. The other was busily engaged in stuffing some brown substance into a pocket of her lower lip. Kern watched her with interest, trying to decide what the brown stuff could be, staring at her lower lip as it began to twitch back and forth with a slow regular motion. The woman seemed unconscious of the clamorous noise. Her masklike face did not change expression. Her hooded eyes were fixed on a spot in space above the rostrum and below the clock. Kern almost jumped with surprise when something spurted out of her mouth. Quick as a striking snake, before he could see where it had hit on the floor, one of her feet darted out and struck the spot, turned slowly, wiping it from sight, and returned to the cover of her long skirt.

268

"Snuff!" Paula's whisper was filled with distaste.

At the first amen in the prayer, a tall lean man on the far end of his bench stood and raised his hands calling for silence. The prayer leader looked down at him reproachfully for having cut such a good prayin' short, then, reluctantly, came down from the platform. The deacon went on without a break.

"We's late startin' this mornin', neighbors, an' we gotta get on wif c'lection an' get started wif de sermon. Bruvver Harris got to move erlong today. He gwine to preach a spiritual meetin' tonight down at 'Pelika. So le's us give all we can to Gawd an' send Reverend Harris on his way. Bruvver Johnson an' Elder Hawknis'll pass among you fer c'lection." The tin cans passed among the benches as the choir started to sing "Rock of Ages—clef' for me—" The congregation entered in almost at once, drowning out the choir. At the end of the second verse, the money was counted. The tall Deacon stood again, this time with a frown on his face.

"Lock de do', Sister Jennings." There was a bustle of feet as Sister Jennings pushed along her row of seats and stood at the door.

"Jes' you go 'head, deacon. I'll stan' here. Reckon I'm good as er lock."

"Folks, we's short. Cain't 'ford to be chinchy wif Gawd. Now who gonna give two cents mo' to make dis come even—" His eyes roamed over the church. "Jus' two cents mo' of der Lawd's money make dis right." Jake signaled to Brother Johnson to bring him the can. He looked embarrassed when the pieces of change clinked into the can. Kern could not understand why Jake was so reluctant to be seen doing good.

The sermon started. A little bent man with a white head was lifted bodily to the platform by two of the deacons. He made his way unsteadily to the rostrum and stood wiping his glasses as he looked down at the congregation. He looked at each one of them with his bright little eyes, from front to rear, from side to side. He settled his glasses far down on his nose and braced his hands on the leaning lectern.

"Gwine talk 'bout our troubles today. Here's a mighty powerful subject, brethren. Could maybe talk erbout it all night an' not get finished, maybe not even get started—but whut I want to say is dis. Trouble don't just happen—somebody gotta make trouble. Takes people to keep trouble going. An' Gawd, the great Gawd himself, ain't gwine come down here an' stop it alla sudden. He ain't never comin' less'n we hoomings do somethin' ourselves ter stop makin' trouble. We done just prayed long an' mighty to the great Gawd an' He hear us for shure. We knows that. He hear everythin', everywhere. But hez He come down an' stopped them things we was prayin' 'bout? No! He ain't. An' is He? No! He ain't. An' why ain't He?" Fire leaped in the little man's eye. His pointed finger jabbed toward the center of the church. "Sit up there, brother. Don't go sleepin' an' fallin' off'n your chair like at'll hep you. Ain't no fallin' down'll hep you. It's walkin'll do it. Walkin' an' talkin' spite of you'self. Rightchere lemme make dis plain. There's good cullud folks an' bad uns. Jes' same as there is white folks. An' I'm talkin' to the bad uns. Now the shoe fit or don't it, sit deah. I ain't wantin' no hollin' an' goin' on. Jes' y'all lissen to me——"

Kern looked with sharper interest at the little, bent old man as he clutched the sides of the lectern and began to talk in earnest. He forgot to look about him and listened. Ungrammatical? Yes. Understandable? Yes. He thought his father would like Reverend Harris.

The last prayer was interminable.

The tall deacon knelt, spread the tails of his shiny swallow-tail coat on either side of him, and prayed:

"Our Father, who libs in Hebben
    Lead us outen our evilsome ways,
  Camp yo' army 'round' us for protection.
  Bring dy Jedgment inter our days,
    Put our feet in der right road,
    An' make us strong when the evil win's blow."

The audience began to rock with the sound of his voice. The last thing was a song.

"Come and let's go to that land where I'm bound."

They moved in the slow press and eddy of people up the center aisle and through the door. The chill air on their faces was refreshing and welcome. Their good-byes were quickly said, and in minutes they were on the Union Road to home, snaking along beside the white center line that dipped and rolled as the highway yielded to the hills about it.

"It's a good day to be alive. Good people—honest people." Jake shook his head. Kern listened curiously to Jake as he spoke pensively, half aloud in time to his thoughts. Paula wiggled farther

270

down on the seat, leaning her head back comfortably. She waited without a word of reply, having heard Jake like this before.

"Don't make much money in a lifetime—not as much in a lifetime as your daddy makes in a year." His eyes flickered to Kern. "Mos' of what little they do make goes for insurance and burial association dues." He laughed shortly. Kern thought there was less bitterness in his laugh.

"Sometimes it looks to me like they work through life to ready themselves for dying. Like to hurry and get through living is an aim in itself." The idea stirred Paula to tart reply.

"But Jake, they could do better—they lock themselves up in these hills and won't come out for anything. Won't even let their youngsters out for school. I think sometimes they are opposed to accepting any help which is extended to them."

"Don't enough help come, Paula. Everything here drains outward. Send our boys and girls off to college. Do they come back to help out here?" He shook his head firmly. "Not even the whites."

"What can they be expected to do, Jake? This place stifles any young ambitious person. They want to get away. I didn't mean it that way, anyhow. What I mean was the Public Health Service, for instance. The ones that need its help the most are the very ones that don't come to it. They could be immunized against typhoid and diphtheria—even receive intensive checkups if they needed it. But will they come? No. They stay up in the hills and inbreed and crossbreed. Ten and twelve kids in a single family living in the same room."

Kern realized that this was an old disagreement between them. He held his peace. Jake stuck doggedly to his point.

"They're good folk. They come to God. Change is slow, Paula. Takes an awful long time."

"Of course they're good, Jake. I'm not saying they aren't. I don't know but one or two people in whom I could see no good. But you have to do more than just come to church. You can't rationalize change into being. You can't make it take place by explaining why it hasn't already occurred. You have to *do* something about it." Jake laughed and rumpled her bonnet with his free hand.

"All right, Paula, honey—reckon I musta got your dander up. You're right. God's good. Very good. But we have to do something ourselves." Paula took her bonnet off and laid it on her lap. She was exasperated that Jake's capitulation stripped her of her argument.

271

"Jake," Kern ventured into the silence. "Reverend Harris' grammar wasn't good, but he certainly taught a lesson. I liked him."

"One of the bes' preachers in these parts. Ol' Reverend Harris mus' be—le's see," Jake mused, "mus' be more'n ninety years old. He was preachin' up an' down this county when my daddy was a boy. He really knows the Gospel an' he's got a lot of mother wit."

"Mother wit?" Kern frowned.

"Yep, mother wit." Jake chuckled. "Good ol'-fashioned horse sense, young feller. He's gettin' a little feeble now——"

"Remember, Jake, how sprightly he was last spring?"

"Down 'Pelika way?" She nodded.

"You wouldn't believe it, Kern, but he chose me for a reel and almost danced my legs off." Her laugh was happy. "It just doesn't seem possible that some day he'll be gone."

"Mighty sad day that'll be. That ol' man's a boon to our folk. Take today, for example." He was serious, Kern saw.

"We need to have a lesson taught us ever' so often. The good and the not so good." He swerved a bit to avoid an oncoming car and straightened out again, closer to the shoulder of the road. "He really lit into the not so goods."

"I guess he doesn't care much for laziness." Thoughtfully, Kern added, "I think my father would like him."

"Well, I'm sure Charles would. As for laziness, he sure hit 'em all, didn't he?" Paula bit her lip.

"Uh huh. I wish he'd been more explicit though."

"I s'pose he would've, Kern, but he didn't have long to preach though." Jake paused. "He's right when you stop to think of it. Not much difference 'tween a lazy sharecropper always lookin' to borrow an' those folk in The Gut."

"The Gut!" Paula could not hide her distaste. "Drinking, gambling, hanging around making trouble with the lintheads——"

"You mean like the men who robbed those two boys from school —tied them up, threatened to beat them, then took them out on the highway an' left them?"

"I mean exactly that, Kern. Those are the ones. Violence is their way. 'Go to Hades with company.' Humph—they're all bluster and talk."

"No, honey—I disagree with you there. Be good if they were, but they're not. The Gut and Millville's a tinderbox. Jes' liable to go up in our faces one of these days, just like up to Redmon. No difference at all between The Slide and The Gut." The same deep despair Kern had felt in Jake once before was there now.

"What can we do, Jake?" Paula's voice was touched with fear.

Kern drew his shell about him. Violence! The possibility, the bare possibility of a riot. He turned from these things. White man, black man, fight. Always, it seemed, he had to push them out of his conscious mind. Had to force them out and close the door on them.

* * *

He'd write his grandmother. He'd do it that day, that very evening. No more delay. He saw them in his mind's eye. Two stones, two real stones, slanting up out of choking brush. Untended. Raw. Two stones in a graveyard. And one stone. One stone among many others. All carved by artists—by stonecutters. All standing above clipped, green lawns.

Our Beloved Daughter

Wife
Mother

Laura Adams Roberts
1890–1922

He'd write today. It had been a long time. It would be snow-bound in Vermont. Outside of the car, the clear thin sunlight, the blue sky. Not a snow cloud in sight. Not a smicker of cloud in sight. I'll write her today. I have so much to tell her.

"Kern! Kern!" Paula poked at his shoulder. "We're home."

"Hum-humph? Oh! Gee whiz! I must of—" Jake chuckled.

"You were a million miles away, young feller." Kern grinned sheepishly.

"I—I guess I was daydreaming." He looked away from Jake and felt guilty, as though he had done Jake and Paula an injustice. He waited as Jake opened the door, then followed Paula into the warm hall.

CHAPTER XVII

THE SHAKING WORLD

PAST the corner of the house, Kern turned into the breeze-way and went toward the kitchen. The light from the gay Japanese lanterns that bobbed on their steel-wire tether about the front yard faded out and the sound of laughter and voices became indistinct. Other voices just ahead of him coming from the kitchen. Paula's pleading and placating. Jake's angry and rumbling. Funny, Kern thought, he had not heard Jake come back. He must have been in the yard with his guests, enjoying the surprise party Paula had given for him, when Jake returned from town. That was it, he decided, as he drew nearer to the porch outside the kitchen, otherwise he would have seen Jake return. He stopped on the first low step that led to the porch. Feet away from the door, he saw Jake standing in the kitchen with his cap on, towering above Paula as she stood twisting at the tea towel in her hands, her eyes open wide as though she were afraid of something.

Jake's voice was trembling. He was angry. Kern had never seen him angry before. This must be something unusual, Kern knew as he pressed back against a pillar of the porch beyond the light and watched with a curious interest.

"Why didn't *you* tell me—why?" Paula shook her head without a word.

"Why did you let me learn this from someone else? I would rather have learned it from you!" Still Paula shook her head slowly from side to side. Jake moved closer to her, his hands spread wide, his voice trembling.

"Paula, baby, white men take my substance. They refuse to pay me. They do everything they can to make me and my brothers walk like dogs in their sight. They do everything they can to take away my right to stand up like a man. I tell myself, 'Jake, you're better than they are. What they try to do doesn't matter too much. You understand what's in their minds.' I don't lose my head. I don't fight. I know they want violence so they can beat me down—

274

so they can prove to themselves that they're right when they say they're great and strong and smart. And me—I'm just a nigger like they always thought. I don't fight." Misery was deep in his voice. Deep in his throat. Shaking him as a terrier shakes a rat. Shaking his heart and his soul. Shaking the house and the floor and the ceiling and the walls. Shaking the world. And Kern, trembling with his own anger, felt the shaking world.

"Jake, listen to me. Listen to me, Jake." Paula clutched at his arms, stood against him, gazed in fright into his face, her eyes pleading with him to listen to her.

"This land's mine. It is owned and paid for. It's been owned and paid for these years past. These folks can't understand that. A good white man did that. Three generations ago. I can't leave here. This is my house and my land. I will not leave." He drew a deep breath, and his hands took hold of the small arms that rested against his forearms.

"But when white men try to take my woman—when they put their hand out to her—when any man touch her, he robs me of something I gotta have to live. He makes me an animal. He thinks that I'll crawl an' take his leavings an' be glad—just like he done since 'fore slavery to other black men——"

"But he didn't take me, Jake. He didn't touch me. He didn't hurt me—he only said—" She pleaded against the madness that was in him.

"When he reach for my woman," his huge biceps tensed and grew like great bulging bands, spreading the grip of her fingers until it was no longer a grip and the fingers instead lay flat on his arms, pressing against them, no longer able to hold them, "when he do that, I kill him with these two hands!" She stared in horrified fascination at the two hands opened in clutching fingers in front of her. She stared helplessly and finally leaned against him in weak fright as his eyes rolled ceilingward.

"An' you, God—I believe in you these years. I say you do the right thing always—hah! You don't like my killing him? Then damn you—you come down here an' stop me. You so great—you stop these two han's." He closed his two hands, slowly, tightly, and Paula bent her head back to stare at him, shocked beyond belief at his blasphemy. Kern shuddered and was frightened at what he had heard. The thought of Jake's two hands closing on any man's throat—of Jake, cursing God!

Tears welled out of Jake's eyes and ran down his cheeks. Jake could give up no greater thing than his belief in God for the love of this woman. Paula lay against his chest and Jake did not move. He stood and gaped at the ceiling and the tears came soundlessly and ran down his face and into the corners of his mouth. Kern did not hear the steps behind him. He scarcely heard the words that were meant for him. Only when a hand took his arm and drew him away into the darkness did he see Mac Rodgers' tight face.

"Come on, Kern—" They stopped in the darkness and Kearn tried to regain control of himself as Mac comforted him.

"This isn't new, Kern— Folks in town have known for months that Bill Noble wants Paula. But there won't be any trouble. She'll just stay away. And Jake will be all right—he'll get over this. Jake gives men the benefit of the doubt. I don't—I know how much dog is in them. He won't admit it. But he'll not get into trouble. I promise you that. He is too levelheaded." Jake was so proud of his right to go to God with his troubles—with words of thanks for His goodness. Kern shook his head.

He followed Mac back to the house and, forcing themselves to laugh, they went into the kitchen where Paula stood at the cabinet board absently slicing bread for buffet sandwiches. Jake sat in a chair near the kitchen table, staring into space.

CHAPTER XVIII

JAKE'S DEATH—MAY, 1935

KERN left the edge of the Union Road just where it bent out of sight of the campus and started through The Gut. Two hundred yards to go and he would be able to see the house. His feet followed the familiar wide path without a conscious thought as he thought about what he would tell Paula. This had been a day filled with surprises. A dozen times Kern had slowed his steps to study the tiny gold key he now held in his hand, delighted by the scrolled design in scarlet enamel that was crested against the gold triangle of the key, sign of membership in the Playhouse fraternity. Now his name too would be added to the long roll of other Valley Viewers who had held membership on the Playhouse rolls as far back as 1871. From the very founding of Valley View itself, there had been a Playhouse. His election had been announced during chapel exercises that day. He searched his shirt pocket carefully for holes before letting the key fall from his fingers, and then confirmed its presence, pressing the shirt close about its outline. He'd get a chain and wear it from his waist.

But the key wasn't all. He knew Paula's eyes would light with pleasure when he told her this too. He was going to be on the first Playhouse group to go to the I.D.A. in Nashville. The newly formed Intercollegiate Drama Association would meet week after next in Nashville at Fisk University. They were going to do "Mighty Wind A-blowin'." What a kick! To be traveling for the school—to compete against other colleges.

He could hear voices calling back and forth on the Selma Road now. His mind registered the slurred, soft speech as that of Negroes. Through breaks in the trees he caught glimpses of three wagons rolling slowly along the road toward Valley View and Millville. Cotton wagons, their slanting sideboards piled high with grayish white cotton. In one a Negro sprawled on the soft, high-piled cotton, one leg hooked over the sideboard, his voice clear in a song. The drivers sat on their high seats, slumped forward, lazily

277

flicking at the rumps of the mules who plodded along indifferently below them. He was near enough to hear the squeak of the wheels, the slow grind of iron tires on the black-top road, and the laughter. Then The Gut bent into sudden, cool shade and came out again into sun-flecked space where the trees ran thin and he could see the dark-green roof of home. He slowed to a stop then, rubbing his chin in quick decision, and left the path to run across the clearing, circling the house to come upon the front porch from the far side. He knew Paula would never expect him to come from that direction.

And she did not. He came around the corner of the house and saw her sitting on the porch, her back to him as she faced toward the Selma Road and Valley View. He crept quietly around the porch and up to the steps. Then, with a sudden "Hi!" he leaped up the steps. Paula turned her head quickly and stared at him for a moment before fixing her eyes on the road again.

"Dinner's on the table." Her voice was flat and, like her face, without expression. He stood scratching his head, puzzled. This was utterly unlike Paula. What was wrong?

"Paula—" he started.

"Sssh!" As though she were irritated. "Dinner's on the table. Go eat." Her voice was brusque. Her head stayed tilted a bit to one side as though she were listening for something. As though she were waiting and listening.

Dinner was tasteless. Alone in the big, empty kitchen, Kern poked without relish at the crisp green salad and nibbled at a bit of cake. He stared out of the window at nothing in particular. The hour wore on and the shimmering quality of early twilight began to fill the air. His glad news was flat and forgotten. Paula's strange silence troubled him—and Jake's absence. He felt—he knew—that something was wrong.

At last he pushed back from the table and took his dishes to the drainboard. Then, gathering up his books, he went slowly through the hall and up the stairs to his room where he sat listlessly in the gathering dusk and tried to study. He could not concentrate and finally put his books aside. A group of O'Neill plays held his attention for a while, and he read hurriedly, trying to fill his mind with the plays until his head drooped sleepily over the book. When he awoke the house was silent. He sat rooted to his chair as fear began to take hold of him. He wanted to get up and go down the stairs to the porch where Paula was.

278

Quiet blanketed the house and it was dark outside his window. The night noises seemed to come from a long distance. His eyes gathered keenness in the dark room. It seemed, as he sat there, that the room was an island whirling alone out in space. The idea fascinated him. It frightened him and it compelled him to stand up to see if it were really so. He reached the dresser and, switching on the light, looked about him. He was alone in the room. The closet door stood open and the closet was empty. Kern felt dampness across the shoulders and on his forehead, and prickling ran along the short hair at the back of the neck, as he looked into the dark hall. If it killed him, he was going down those steps to see Paula. Down the dark steps. The thought was curious. Each of his thoughts was curious. As though each was a separate being which he had never known before and which his mind now held in the palm of its hand and considered.

He stepped into the dark hall. Went to the steps. A turn at the second step and the light was behind him and above him, a dim, distant source of companionship. The shape of his fear, the thing it was about, grew more clear in his mind. He told himself that this fear was foolish. He did not believe himself. Twelve steps below the turn was the foot of the staircase. His hand on the right-hand wall, his lips counted the steps as a part of his mind kept track of them. Four. Five. Six.

He expected at any moment to feel Jake's hand on his shoulder, to hear Jake's booming laughter making a small thing of his fear. He could not escape it. Chill certainty. Something was wrong.

Nine.

Ten.

Eleven.

He would not let the substance of fear take shape. He knew what he was afraid of and he pushed it out of his consciousness with a determined effort.

At the bottom.

Four steps on the carpeted strip that led to the screen door. Kern pushed the door open slowly and stood in it. He could see Paula, still sitting in the corner where he had left her when he came home from school. The same posture of her head, slanted on a side, her whole body listening and waiting. Under a tall moon the road to Valley View was a shiny black ribbon that disappeared from sight at the wooded turn. The white center line stood out clearly. She was still looking down that road.

For a flashing instant, not long enough to allow himself even to think, Kern knew what Paula was waiting for.

He tried to say "Good night," but the words would not come. His lips moved wordlessly. He gulped and tried again. The words came explosively this time as though they had been wrenched from him. They were almost a shout. Paula did not turn, did not take her eyes from the strip of road. He turned and stepped inside the hallway, letting the door swing quietly to behind him. The dark didn't frighten him now. Something larger was in him; a fear that made being afraid of the dark like the fear of a little child.

He turned the light off in his room and fell across the bed fully dressed.

Something had happened to Jake. There it was. Admittted at last. Kern was afraid to think what might have happened. Even in the twisting, dreaming sleep that followed, he always awoke just as he seemed about to learn what had happened to Jake.

✿   ✿   ✿

The screech of tires sliding to a halt awakened Kern and he lay rigid on the bed, staring at the ceiling. He would not let his eyes move to the door or to the window—not even beyond the rectangle of ceiling which he could see without moving his head.

He did not want to go to the window. He wanted to lie on the bed. He wanted to lie there and see nothing and know nothing— but he got up. He got up and he walked slowly to the window and, though his mind told him to stop with every step, to turn back, he did not. It told him not to look out the window. But he did. He stood at the window and bent to see more clearly. And in the moonlight he saw Paula walking, then running toward the gate and kneeling. And he saw the car, long and black, seeming to glide away down the road toward Valley View. It was almost gone before he heard the snarling mesh of gears and the scraping of tires from its lurching start—longer still before a jeering voice came to him and ended in a laugh that ended in silence. He could not move and his eyes blurred when he heard Paula scream.

A high, shrieking scream that broke on a sobbing note of pain. Sweat beaded his forehead and trickled from his armpits down his body, cold, as he listened. In terror then, in a need to be near some other human being, and not because he wanted to go to whatever it was Paula knelt by—with an unadmitted knowledge of what it was —he bolted across the room and down the steps.

From the porch he saw her clearly, kneeling near a huddled shape on the ground near the gate. He could not turn his eyes and a horrible understanding halted his headlong rush. Step by slow step he edged down the steps and went across the yard to where she was kneeling. His eyes cast over the yard and to the road beyond, over the brushy area and the looming shapes of pine trees, looking for an avenue of escape—in his hesitancy wanting to discover that this was all a nightmare from which he would awake in a moment.

The shape was Jake.

All that remained of him.

He looked down and turned away retching with sickness that bubbled in his throat and spilled over. Paula reached out and took him by the hand. He turned back under her fierce grasp, and looked at the man at full length. Forced to stare and to see.

"Look—remember. Don't forget!"

He would remember what he saw. Dumbly he knew that.

Sprawled halfway between the gate and the dusty road's edge, Jake lay in a strange, twisted posture of death. He had been tortured and burned. The perversity of not wanting to know compelled Kern's eyes to search out the tiniest details.

To see where the copper wire had cut deep into the swollen flesh of Jake's wrists, binding his hands together in an obscene gesture of supplication. To see that his legs too were bound with wire, at the knees and at the ankles. And at the knees, that the wire had broken as a spasm of pain, perhaps, had drawn his feet up behind him to almost touch the small of his back. He saw empty eye-sockets that oozed a thin trickle of blood already congealed among the hardening bubbles of tar that covered one side of his face. Almost indistinguishable from his flesh were a few charred, clinging bits of clothing. Panic filled him.

This—this stinking hulk could not be Jake! Not clear-eyed, laughing Jake! No! He tried to reject the thought and failed, knowing that this *was* Jake. All that was left of him. He did not have to force his eyes away from Jake's body. They came easily enough. They had seen their fill—had given to his brain images that it would never forget. They slid to Paula's face, turned up to his.

Kern wondered, as he watched her, if she had not known this would be the end. Had she waited, hoping against hope, knowing that her vigil would end in this?

Her eyes were dry now. Her throat was empty of screams. The screams had become knives in her heart. Paula looked away from him to Jake and her hand released his. She stayed there on her hands and knees, a keening sound in her throat, looking at Jake and remembering God only knew what.

Retching started in his stomach again, and Kern started quickly for the house. Nothing he could say or do now would help Paula. He knew that. He dragged himself up the steps to his room and turned on the light above the dresser. A crack ran slantwise down the face of the mirror, and he ran his fingers over it as though he had never seen it before. With the same feeling, he looked at his face and ran his hands over his forehead, brushing away the beads of perspiration that filmed it. As he watched, his face changed. His eyes turned brown. The veins that made a dull-blue web at his temples disappeared in a wave of brown. His hair began to kink and curl. In the swiftness of a thought, his face became Jake's face. With still another thought, was twisted, eyeless in death, his face torn by a load of small shot. He retched and was sick and went to his hands and knees on the floor, finally rolling over to lie on one side. He lay there, not moving, trying not to think, trying without success not to remember. He lay there until heavy steps on the floor announced that Paula was climbing the steps.

"Oh, Kern—oh, my darling!" She came to him with distress in her voice and helped him to get to his feet and led him to the bedside. He undressed and stretched out on the bed while she went hurriedly down the stairs. In a half daze he heard her in the kitchen and then again on the steps—and took the cool glass from her hand as his mind tried to search other days for something that had happened—something like this. Dimly, he heard her leave the room and more dimly heard the jingle of the wall phone in the hall below. With a last effort at understanding, he knew that she was grinding the phone crank. Then he slept.

❀ ❀ ❀

The last gray edges of dawn were turning to daylight when he awoke. A voice filled the hall below and came up the stairs. He knew that voice—the tone of it. It was the same voice that had come from the car. Jake!

He came wide awake. What was that voice doing here in the house? Had he dreamed?

No!

The pile of clothes on the chair—the floor before the mirror told him he had not.

What then? He crouched at the foot of the bed. Were he and Paula going to share Jake's fate? God! Of a sudden he knew how much he wanted to live. He was deathly afraid.

"Waal, git on upstairs then an' git the boy!" It was the same voice. "Get the boy?" Get *him!* No! Kern felt cold fear.

"Yessuh." Paula's voice was strangely obedient. He counted her steps on the stairs and knew when she opened the door. She stood there wordless, watching him. Her face was old. Her eyes were fever-bright and without emotion. Kern stared as though she were a stranger—an enemy who was going to tell him to dress and go down to the men who waited in the hall. He did not want to go. He wouldn't! She came to the bed and put her hand on his bare shoulder. Her hand was hot and dry, and he drew away from her touch. Her hand tightened on his shoulder and would not let go and Kern stared up at her dumbly.

"Kern, listen to me. Those men downstairs—they're going to take us both to jail." He twisted. "No, wait!" she gritted out. "We won't be in any danger. It's—it's a formal investigation—of Jake's death. Everything will be all right if you do just as I say. Remember this! No matter what you are asked—no matter what you are told—you saw nothing last night. You saw nothing!" Dumbly Kern watched her lips shape each separate word.

"You saw nothing. You understand? Nothing!" He did not understand. Paula's hand tightened until it hurt. "You saw nothing—you heard nothing. Remember that."

"Nothing!"

His mind flashed to the car roaring off through the night—he had seen that clearly. And the voice, the jeering shout—the laugh.

"But—" Desperately, vehemently, she repeated her words.

"Nothing, I tell you—there are no 'buts'—you saw and heard nothing! No matter what anyone tells you—what anyone says I said—nothing." Her dark eyes probed his.

"Paula—you Paula! Damn thet gal! Whatchu doin' up there anyways?" The voice bellowed in the hall. "Git on daown here, gal—I ain't got all day to wait on no niggers. You're 'structin' jestice." A muffled laugh followed this sally, and Paula stepped to the door.

"Yessuh, Mister Noble—I'm comin' right along." She turned back to Kern.

Bill Noble! All that he had heard and all of last night knotted in him at the name. Bill Noble!

"Hurry and get dressed and come downstairs." She crossed quickly to the bed and took his face in both hands. Looking down at him, her eyes softened. "Nothing—until I screamed and you came down— only that—nothing else." She kissed him softly. "And when you can —run. Run for your life. Get away from this tearing, twisting mean- ness—get away and do the things you dream of." She was gone. He heard her steps in her room, hers and Jake's, then he heard her on the steps. He went to the dresser and took out a clean shirt.

✿　✿　✿

Bill Noble was a tremendous man, larger about the shoulders even than Jake, and great about the belly. A wide leather belt circled his belly snugly and a holstered pistol rode high on his right hip. The bottom buttons of his shirt strained against his girth. He filled the lower hall when Kern came down the steps, crowding out the two deputies who stood behind him. When he saw Kern, his beefy face swelled with red and he whirled on Paula.

"Who's this boy?"

"He's my brother's son, suh." Paula's voice was low and placating. Her words pointed sarcasm at Kern. "He's tryin' to get learnin' at the College."

"Your brother's son—" One of the deputies stood on tiptoe to see over Bill's shoulder. Bill brushed the man back against the wall angrily.

"Waal, let's git on. Ain't you never seed a half-white nigger afore?" The two men turned and filed through the hall toward the front door. One of them took with him the tiny Dresden doll from the mantel in the living room. Forlorn, its blue hat sitting askew, it stared a sad farewell at the house from its place in his hip pocket. Between them went Paula, barely stopping to stare at the living room as though to memorize the place—then Kern and Sheriff Bill Noble bringing up the rear. Neither of them looked at the place near the gate where Jake had lain. His body was gone, taken by neighbors to be prepared for burial. At the gate they crowded into the car. Paula in the back between the two deputies, Kern in front with Bill Noble, and headed for town for the start of the investigation into the death of Jake Caul- field, age 35, Negro.

CHAPTER XIX

SOUTHERN JUSTICE—MAY, 1935

I

THE Valley View jail stood on a corner of the town square, diagonally opposite the courthouse. Below the jail, along the center street that led southward out of town, were business places—a harness maker's, the grocery store to which Kern had gone with Jake on his first trip to town, two beer taverns, a dry-goods store, and a three-story building, the tallest in Valley View. The lower windows of this "skyscraper" bore the worn gold-leaf letters of Martin Kennedy, Attorney at Law. Its upper-story windows were shared by Bill Kind, Contract Buyer, and Dr. Charles Tinker, Specialist in Painless Dentistry. Behind these, and almost hidden from sight, were the huddled dwellings of the town dwellers thinning quickly and ending in the brush-grown wilderness that marked in irregular fashion the outer limits of the town.

The buildings stood alike under the blistering sun, burdened by the incessant weight of scorching sun, aged and streaked with dirt.

Shadeless windows made blank faces in the ancient red-brick walls of the jail itself and the traffic of countless feet had hollowed the stone steps that mounted to its door from the street. A handful of men turned to stare as they drove up, gawking in unconcealed curiosity as they got out of the car and stood uncertainly on the pavement waiting for Bill Noble to come around the car and lead them into the jail. All of the men were white and Kern could not muster enough courage to return their bold stares. He looked at them in quick flickering gazes. One tall, thin-necked man, whose Adam's apple bobbed constantly in his throat, appeared to be their leader. He leaned lazily against the street lamp, carelessly cradling a shotgun under his arm. And nodded when Bill came around the car and stopped in front of him.

"Howdy, Bill—got the boys. There ain't goin' to be no nigger uprisin' to fret 'bout." His eyes ran over Paula in an insolent stare that deliberately moved from head to foot. He spat and scuffed at the mark with his toe.

Bill pushed the barrel of his shotgun aside and grunted approval as he went up the stairs. Side by side Kern and Paula followed him.

The square front room of the jail was filled with the throat-biting odor of disinfectant. Through a door at the back, the jail bars of the cell area could be seen. A stench sifted through the half-open door and mingled with the harsh disinfectant. The door to the left-hand side of the room was marked by a sign that said: "SHERIFF'S OFFICE." On the opposite side of the room, a closed door made the only break in an otherwise solid wall. The back wall was lined all the way across with benches, except where the door led to the cell block. A tattered calendar hung askew on the wall, its half-torn page turned to December. There was no year. There were no other pages. The top part, obviously the reason for its hanging on the wall, bore the picture of a lush young woman provocatively posed in a scanty, fur-trimmed bathing suit. Kern looked away. The girl was white. A heavy black sludge of dirt and oil lay like tar on the floor and dragged at their feet.

Bill Noble turned into the room marked "SHERIFF'S OFFICE." Kern followed him. He could feel Paula standing at his side as he watched Bill uncertainly. Sheriff Noble dropped his bulk heavily into a complaining chair and tossed his hat on the desk. Pulling a large blue spotted handkerchief from his hip pocket, he popped it at the flies that buzzed about his head. Mopping his face, he dropped the handkerchief on the desk and leaned back to open his desk drawer. He took a dog-eared ledger and laid it on the desk alternately licking his fingers and shuffling through its pages. The binding of the book cracked as he found his page and pressed the book open with the heel of his hand and threshed in the jumbled drawer to find a pencil. Licking the stubby point, he wrote in the date, June 7th, talking as he wrote.

"I'm goin' to book you two for questionin' in this yere case. C'ose you understan'," he looked up at Paula, "this is jes' a fo'mality." Paula said nothing. Kern wondered if this was exactly right. He had never heard of being booked for questioning in such a case. There had been no charge made. How did Bill Noble know officially that Jake had been murdered? He had not even stated the case in which they were being held. Like Paula, Kern said nothing.

"What's your name, boy?"

"Kern Roberts."

Bill's brows gathered in a furious scowl. "Now by Gawd——!"

"He means Kern, Mister Noble, suh. Roberts is his las' name, suh." Paula cut her eyes sharply at Kern. Call him Mister, the glance said, even if it kills you—'cause if you don't, he may do just that.

"Humph!" Kern watched the man write his name, Kern Roberts.

"How ol' are you?"

"Eighteen, sir—in September."

"Race?" The pencil stub poised above the page. Bill looked from under his brows. "What are you, boy?"

Kern didn't know what to say. "You ain't no white man, an' you sure don't look like no nigger——"

"He's a nigger, suh—jes' like me." Paula's voice soothed him.

"You're damn right he's a nigger!" Negro, Bill wrote. One of the deputies hurried in and whispered something in Bill's ear, looking from Paula to Bill as he whispered. Kern thought he heard the words "telegraph office." Bill slammed the book shut and stood up, looking at Paula closely.

"I'm goin' to hol' you two—" he puzzled for a moment, "in protective custody. That's it—in protective custody." He hesitated. "Your brother's son, is he? Lock him up in the bullcage." He jerked his thumb at Paula. "Put her in the room across the way—an' don' none uh you bastards tech her neither." He snatched his hat up and stormed out of the room muttering something to the men at the door as he went out. They roared with laughter and turned to stare at Paula.

✻　✻　✻

There was a four-sided bullcage at the rear of the jail, a cell of bars that ran without a break from floor to ceiling. Two double tiers of bunks lined the sides of the block and the farther edges of the cage, their wooden surfaces bare of cover. The stink Kern had smelled in the outer room came from a filthy black galvanized can in the center of the pen. Across the top of the cell, five pipes, inches apart, made a rack a foot or two below the ceiling. On one of the bottom bunks at the far side of the cell, a huge black man lay, half in, half out of the bunk. He snored raspingly through his open mouth, one leg dangling carelessly to the floor. The guard looked at him in disgust.

"Drunken bastard!" His key grated in the lock and he swung the gate wide. "All right—git in." Kern heard the lock click behind him and stood looking about him. Two white men slept in the double

287

bunks of one of the smaller cells that ringed the bullcage in. The rest of the cells were empty. Kern dropped to the nearest bunk. Even in jail—white and colored. Colored and white. His thoughts raced. He stretched out on the bunk and stared at the ceiling, his eyes following the pipes across the cell and coming back again. He forced himself to look at the heavy bands that tied the pipes, like a rack, to the ceiling. He looked, too, at the questions that ran through his head.

How will we get out of this?

How will it all end?

Where had Bill Noble gone in such a rush?

Will Jake's death be avenged?

Am I right—is that what Paula meant by "Nothing!"?

He knew what Paula meant by "Nothing!" He was as sure of what she had meant as he was sure of who had been in that car. The certainty surged through his mind. With it came a destructive urge to cry out his knowledge. Bill Noble! He could almost feel the words on the tip of his tongue. Fear stopped them there.

The hours dragged by and the shift of shadows on the floor told him that noon had come and gone. Kern licked at his dry lips and wished he had enough nerve to call and ask the guard to bring him some water. He wondered about that simple problem. He gave all of his attention to it.

How did a nigger boy in jail in Valley View ask a white man to get him a drink of water? The answer was—he did not. He knew that to ask a white man to do a personal favor for him would be to offer him personal insult. He twisted on the hard boards and found a less uncomfortable position. Swallowing down his thirst, he fell asleep.

*　*　*

Someone was near him. He knew it as he awoke. He did not move. The heavy breathing was close to him, heavy, quick, excited breathing. He opened his eyes carefully and looked straight up at the ceiling. A face—a dark face—withdrew quickly from before his eyes. Footsteps scuffed against the floor as he turned his head. It was the man who had fallen asleep on the far side of the cell. The man cringed against the back side of his bunk, deep in the shadows of early evening, gripping the bars. He stared at Kern and said nothing. Then, without warning, he jumped up and ran to the cell gate.

"Hey, boss—Cap'n! Oh, Cap'n, hurry, fo' Gawd's sake! Cap'n." His

288

voice rose to a call of fright. Yet it held a comic quality. A comic quality was in both his voice and his tense body as he swayed backwards from the bars. The startled guard rushed through the door looking back and forth over the cell block. The white men in the outer cell came awake, sleepily knuckling their eyes as they stared in the direction of his calls.

"What'n hell you yellin' 'bout, nigger?" The guard hitched his fingers into his waistband and stood a foot or so away from the bars. The Negro shrank back from his gaze.

"Didn' mean no trouble, suh—hones' to Gawd, Cap'n, didn' mean no harm. You knows Tige's a good nigger, boss." His voice whined and his eyes rolled wide. "Jes' drinks a leetle mite too much now'n then—an' his ol' lady's sure goin' to whale hell out'n him if you puts him out'n this yere jail house." His rolling eyes and his pantomime said that *his* wife was a *worse* fate than being here in *jail*. In spite of himself, Kern laughed shortly and Tige looked away.

"But boss—y'all musta made a 'stake," he chided the guard gently, "you knows Tige cain't stay in no cell wiffun dis yere young white gempmums." The men in the outer cell chorused loud agreement.

"Gol durn yo' hide, Mel'—you know better'n to put him in there with that there nigger——"

The jailer's eyes squinted shrewdly. He looked at Kern and laughed.

"Hell, Tige—I orta whale hell outa yo' black hide. This yere boy's a nigger." He remembered his morning's lesson. "Ain't you never seed uh half-white nigger afore?" Tige tensed against the bars. The laughter went out of his eyes before a rush of hate. He turned to look at Kern.

"Laugh at me, will you, nigger?" The words were deadly and vicious. "I'll slit your gullet or my name ain't Tige." Kern twisted upright on his bunk. Tige meant what he said. There could be no doubt of that. He felt the silence as the men in the outer cell pressed against the bars, forgetful of their own plight, hoping to see some excitement—perhaps some bloodletting. He looked at the guard. No help there either. There was no mercy in the guard's eyes.

"Jes' play with him a little, Tige—don't hurt him—not much, anyway—" The guard egged him on. "He thinks he's better'n you, Tige, 'cause he yaller an' you ain't."

Tige's answer was a growl in his throat. The injury Kern had done him was taking form in his mind. Yellow-brown eyes slitted, lips drawn back from his teeth, he moved toward Kern and Kern watched him, step by step. He saw the great hands dangling loose at the ends of his arms. The man's breath came in heaving, labored gusts. Big as he was and as strong for a boy, he knew he was no match for this man. Tige could and would tear the life out of him before these men would do anything about it. He waited until the man towered over him and slipped quickly under the reaching arms and ran to the other side of the cell, clambering frantically up to the topmost bunk. Tige spun about unsteadily and stalked slowly toward him. He was satisfied. Kern could not escape from the cell. He would get him. Kern swung out to the rack of pipes, praying as they sagged that they would hold his weight. He inched backwards toward the center of the floor and watched as Tige raised himself to the top bunk and reached out to get a handhold on the pipes. He waited until Tige was in mid-air, then he swung his foot desperately at the man's head. Tige pitched backwards, his head rattling on the edge of the bunks as he fell to the floor and lay still. The guard was stunned. The cell block was silent.

"Gawd damn!" The oath was long-drawn and fervent as the guard hurriedly opened the gate and came in. Kern watched as he bent over Tige and peeled back his eyelids. He looked up at Kern and the waiting men.

"Ain't dead nohow—Joe! Joe!" He raised his head to Kern again. "Come down from there—come down, I say!" Kern was paralyzed. He did not move. He leaned forward, holding tightly to the pipes, staring at the upturned face. "Joe—dammit! Where are you, Joe?—Oh, c'mere an' drag this boy out front an' call the Doc—wait a minute—better not call the Doc—try a pail of water first." Joe grabbed one of Tige's legs and backed toward the gate dragging him. "If he comes roun', turn him loose. He's 'bout due anyhow." He looked up at Kern thoughtfully. "You'd better hope that nigger don't die, boy. He's Mr. Collins' favorite nigger, an' there'll be hell to pay—" He left the threat of his words unfinished.

Kern crouched forward on the pipes all night, afraid for his very life. Even after nightfall, after the men in the outside cell had lost interest in taunting him and had gone back to sleep, he crouched there in sheer fright. On the floor of the bullcage, near the cell door, the contents of his dinner plate became a soggy mass that made a feast for a swarm of roaches. One shining, large roach held his attention as time after time it tried to scale the height of the cup. Kern watched it, fascinated. Each time it fell back to the floor. Kern wondered if Jake had tried to escape torture and death as determinedly as the roach tried to climb the cup. He wondered if the jailors would come back to get him—if Tige had been seriously hurt. He recalled the swift vengeance which legend said could come in the South for injuring a "white man's nigger" and wondered if it was to come to him for having hurt Tige. He wondered about Paula. Many times, as the pain in his cramped limbs crept into his upper body, he wondered about Paula. He recalled that Paula was a "white man's woman." That was the thing Jake had been afraid of. He wondered if she would be harmed—if, perhaps at that very moment, she was being molested. In his mind, he thought through the detailed torture which he would visit on anyone who touched her. The complete helplessness of his position mocked him. Twice he awoke from the half doze into which he had slipped to strain his ears into the silence, trying to be certain that he had not, as he had thought he had on awakening, heard Paula crying for help. The second time, he cried himself slowly and quietly back to his half doze. Once, late at night, brief laughter and the sound of muttered voices awakened him, as the white men were let out of their cell. He did not move. Even when the guard's flashlight found him in the darkness, he did not move. He closed his eyes and listened to the voices and to the laughter.

"Nigger still up there, Joe?"

"Shine the light up—yup!" The yellow glow of light touched him then and he lay stiff and unmoving. "There he is." The light winked off and shortly the jail became quiet again. The mocking last words of the men stayed in Kern's ears after they had gone.

"D'ya ever see uh nigger as white as thet, Joe?"

"Hell—he's a nigger jes' thuh same."

Kern was too tired and too heartsick to care. Paula. Jake. Jail. Who was to help him? Again he cried as helpless anger ran through him.

Kern awoke in the early morning, chilled and drawn with pain. Each pipe cut into his legs and straddling thighs like fire. His body protested when he tried to straighten up. Cramped and stiff, he started to edge forward on the pipes. Time and again he stopped and bit his lips against the urge to cry out, then inched forward again. The edge of the bunks seemed to move away from him.

Two things were certain in his mind. He must climb either down off his perch or fall. He could not hold on any longer. Too, he knew that life was precious—*something* to be preserved at any cost. When the time came, he would be another Tige, he would bow and scrape and simper. He would leave no doubt in the minds of his jailors that he knew his place. He would let them know he understood that he was "just another nigger" in spite of going to college and not looking like the Negroes they knew. He crouched against the pipes, panting with exertion, aching in every muscle, trying to muster up enough strength to creep forward again. He had to reach the edge of the bunk. That came first. When he did, he would have to span the gap between bunk and pipes. The space had grown terrifyingly wide. He would have to cross it——

II

A key grated in the lock and the gate scraped open. He twisted his head slowly to see Bill Noble squinting up through the bands of sunlight that rayed down through the high windows. He wondered if Bill could tell how frightened he was. He knew his fear must be showing in his face. Looking down, Bill Noble seemed wide and short, swaying on the balls of his feet as he peered at Kern.

"Jes' like a treed coon—come on down from there, nigger." Kern wanted to move. He wanted to obey the harsh command. But try as he might, he could not force his muscles to move. Quivers ran through his legs. His arms gripped the pipes even more tightly.

"You hear me! Git down offen them pipes—git I say!" Bill reached toward the pistol on his hip and Kern gulped as cottony fuzz gathered in his parched throat. His mouth fell open and he could not shut it. Bill Noble was going to shoot him!

"Nigger, don't you know the penalty for resistin' 'rest?" Terror lent words to his tongue, a babble of words that tripped over one another seeking to find shape on his tongue.

"Please, suh, Mistuh Noble, I wants to get down! Honest, I do, suh. But, fo' Gawd, I cain't move. Honest, I cain't!"

Bill Noble laughed as though the fright that twisted his face was the most comical thing he had ever seen.

"Hell! Fall down, boy—you ain't goin' to hurt yourself. Fall on yo' haid. Cain't hurt a nigger's head noways." He broke into loud laughter. "You git down from there an' come on in my office." Turning on his heel, he went out of the cell, leaving the gate wide behind him. Kern felt hopeful, as he inched along the pipes. Bill had not been angry. He was sure of that. Tige must not have been seriously hurt or Bill would not have been so full of laughter. Perhaps they would get out of this without any harm. Paula! Was she all right? For the thousandth time he thought about her. He wanted to see her.

The gap between the pipes and the edge of the top bunk was an

292

agony of reaching and finally slipping, falling, grasping for a hand-hold, as he banged against the edges of the bunks and dropped to the floor. He sat and nursed his scraped arm briefly before struggling to his feet. He gulped greedy swallows of brackish water from the water can and lurched toward the gate. He stopped at the fetid can in the center of the floor, then gathering himself, went slowly out of the cell block into the glaring light of the outer room, blinking his eyes and rubbing them against the brightness. A bench, he saw, had been drawn across the door of the room where the Sheriff had told the men to put Paula and a man stretched on it asleep. There was no sign of Paula. Two men lounged against the sides of the front door, blocking out any view of the street. They turned to stare at him curiously, as he went into Bill Noble's door.

Sheriff Noble sat at his desk. Two men were with him. One of them was the tall, seedy man who had stood outside of the jail yesterday morning with the shotgun in his arm—the one who had stared so at Paula. The second man was one of the deputies who had come to the house with Bill Noble to get them.

"Come on in an' set there, boy." Noble made an effort at pleasantness as he twisted a chair toward his desk. Kern sat down and the sunlight struck him full in the face. The man against the wall, "Mister Shotgun," leveled his chair to the floor with a thump. Bill Noble leaned across the edge of his desk, bringing his face close to Kern's.

"Now we ain't goin' to hurt you, boy—ain't nothin' to be afeared of. You mighta heard tell that Bill Noble is hard on niggers. Ain't a word of truth in it. Ain't any man in this here town is any fonder uh his niggers than I am—ain't that so, boys?" He looked about him at his deputies as they inclined their heads in agreement. Kern hoped that his thoughts were hidden. He was going to be one of Bill Noble's niggers. That much was certain. The sour smell of chewing tobacco filled the man's breath.

"All we wants you to do is tell us what you know 'bout this horrible crime."

"About Jake, sir?"

"Yep—'bout Jake—everything you know or think." His little eyes fixed sharply on Kern.

"Well, sir—I just know he was dead and laying at the gate when I heard Paula scream and came down the stairs."

"Who done it?"

"I don't rightly know, sir—I surely don't."

"You don't know! Now looky here, boy—your aunt tol' us everything you seen and heard." Paula's warning sounded like a clanging bell in his ears. He could even see her face without closing his eyes. "Nothing—you saw and heard nothing!" He knew that Paula had not told them anything like that.

"Nawsuh—I ain't seen nothing, sir. I don't see how she could have told you that, suh—I really don't."

It went like that. Thrust and parry, and always, without change, he stuck to the one statement—"I saw and heard nothing." Kern was determined. Not by word or glance would he show that he had any idea of the identity of the men who had killed Jake. Jake's murderers sat before him. He was sure of that—at least he was sure of Bill Noble. He was sure, too, that if he admitted his certainty, he would die.

The sun rode up to the top of the window sash and for a short time Kern was free of the glare that bit into his eyes and drew great running rivulets of sweat to his forehead. A solitary fly buzzed in the room, apart from his fellows who clustered almost motionless on the ceiling. From the street came the occasional sound of a passing car and the scuff of feet against the sidewalk below the window. Suddenly the line of questioning changed. He felt that a danger point had been passed.

"What do you do, boy—whatchu doin' here in Valley View?"

"I goes to school, suh." Deliberately he slurred his speech, drawing on the remembered phrases of the natives, not forgetting the respectful "sir."

"School!" Bill Noble bellowed as he lunged across the corner of his desk. Kern shrank away from the face, a bare inch or two away from his own, in fear. He did not have to pretend. He was afraid.

"Let me tell you something, nigger! School ain't for niggers. Jes' gives 'em a lotta dam' fool notions an' ruins 'em. What you needs is to get a good job workin' for some good white man an' raise you a passel uh little coons to take keer uh you when you gets ol'." Having dispatched himself of his sage advice, the sheriff settled himself back in his chair. Kern nodded respectful agreement with his words, feeling a silly grin come over his face.

"You damned right—that's what you oughta do—jes' like Bill says."

It started again. When one grew tired, another took up the chase, trying to wear down his resistance, determined to know if he shared any part of their secret. Smoke lay across the room in shifting blue bands. Kern felt that if they didn't stop, he would have to tell them

294

his suspicions, what little he knew and felt. The words kept pushing into his mind, more clearly each time he tried to put them down. Anything to get this over with.

What if they did know—wasn't this America?

They wouldn't dare do anything to him—or would they?

As he had the thought, he knew he was wrong. This was the Southland—a nation apart. Tears welled up and over and streamed down his face, desperate, exhausted tears. He felt his stomach twist with a gnawing pain and realized that he was hungry. He hadn't eaten for almost two days.

"Truly, Mister Noble, sir, I don't know anything—if I did I would tell you an' help you solve this crime."

Disgusted, "Mister Shotgun" slammed his cigar butt at the spittoon against the far wall. His voice was testy and angry.

"Aw hell, Bill, he don't know uh damn thing! Let's git this over with." Bill's eyes narrowed. He sat forward and took a typed sheet from his desk drawer. He ran his eyes over it and handed it to Kern.

"Read this, boy."

"I do solemnly swear that I have no knowledge of Jake Caulfield's death. The sheriff and deputies of Valley View have tried in all ways possible to find out who killed Jake Caulfield and I have given them all the assistance I can in this case."

It rambled on in loose phraseology, a legal attempt to void any future testimony he might ever try to give about Jake's murder. In any other city, in other courts and other cities, he knew it would be laughed at. But this was not any other city or was its court any other court. It was Valley View—and this was justice, Southern style. The blind goddess of justice flashed across his mind as he read. He thought that the statue did not tell the whole story—that for the Negro in the South, justice was not blind. For him, brought into its places of law, Southern justice reserved its most jaundiced and cruel eyes. He lowered his eyes, afraid that his anger would show on his face. He was surprised that he could feel anger. When he felt more calm, he looked at Bill Noble.

"Is them the facts?"

"Yes, suh—they's right."

"Then sign it." Bill handed him the stub of pencil. Kern slowly signed his name, fighting down the wave of excitement that came over him. Free! He was almost free—almost free.

III

"Did you know that your pappy was coming to town?" The words shocked Kern like a dash of icy water. He jerked erect. He had not known. But he should have. Paula telephoning in the hall. His surprise was genuine—there could be no doubt about that. He held his eyes to the signature he was slowly writing.

Tear it up.

Deny the whole thing. Your father will get you out of this. He can use the things you know.

No. He knew better. His father would only heap coals on the anger of these men. He would not be able to do anything here in Valley View. According to the common law of the land, lynching was not a crime. Not unless the lynchers were caught red-handed. Then they would be committing a misdemeanor.

Not guilty! These men were not guilty of a crime. The thought sickened him. Carefully, slowly, he raised his eyes.

"Here, Mister Noble." He finished signing the paper and Bill Noble reached out and took it from him. Bill's eyes narrowed again for a crucial moment as he studied Kern's face. He was satisfied with what he saw. Kern sat half slumped in his chair. He was beaten. He had put everything he had into the effort. The rest lay with the man before him. Bill Noble was satisfied. Kern looked just like a hundred Negroes he had brought to heel. He laughed shortly and handed the paper to "Mister Shotgun."

"Get thet entered into the records at the Co'thouse, Pete—by person or persons unknown." A trickle of tears came to Kern's eyes again. Not anger. Not grief. Only sickness, that the life of a man could be so cheap, so worthless. The dignity Jake had believed in—for himself and for others—as the best way of life, hadn't worked out for him. His homespun philosophy hadn't been enough. In the end, at the very last, Jake must have realized the futility of reason when it comes face to face with emotion. No time for thoughts. Just time to play the part out—be a nigger, listen——

"Looky here, nigger—jes' you 'member what you done signed. Now git outen here. I still got to question thet Paula. You too, Jack—get on over to thuh Co'thouse 'n see if Pete's doin' thet job right or wrong."

"Yessuh—thank you, sir." Kern stood up shakily, and went to the door, eyes cast down, shoulders slumped. Bill's voice called out behind him.

"Manny—bring thet Paula gal in here." Laughter filled the office.
"Okay, Jack, get thuh hell outen here. Sheriff wants to be alone."
Outside the door Kern bent to retie a shoelace, stalling for time to get a glimpse of Paula.
She crossed the room with an expressionless face—taller than he could remember having seen her—her head high and proud. For an instant her eyes swept over his face as he straightened. Satisfied with what she saw, she raised her head even higher and went into Bill Noble's office.
"Sit down, gal—sho am sorry to have inconvenienced you thisaways. Ah'll try to make it up—" The door shut, closing off his words.
Kern stood for a moment in the glaring light of the street. Mechanically his feet took him to the corner of the jail where he cut across the street, angling toward the harness maker's shop and the path that would lead him above The Gut to the campus.
When he reached the path, he broke into a run and ran until scorching, burning lungs and legs that turned to lead weights stopped him, left him gasping for breath. He held to his lurching, unsteady gait until the booming thud of his feet on the wooden planking of the bridge that spanned the Calahootchie spurred him to run again. He did not stop until he reached the edge of the campus. There he stopped to regain his breath, looking over his shoulder to see if he were being followed, and going on, heedless of tradition that confined underclassmen to the paved walks, across the wide open lawn, heading toward Heritage House.
Dr. Gray saw him first, as he passed the front of the Chemistry Building, and ran from his laboratory to meet him. Kern saw him and stopped, swaying, wide-legged, until the man reached him before letting go and leaning heavily on his supporting shoulder. Curious students watched as he passed, half walking, half carried by Dr. Gray, to Heritage House and the instantaneous oblivion of cool sheets and sleep.
The die was cast. Even before he slept, before he could have talked with his father or the news of Paula could have reached them, before he could have consciously thought through the problem which faced him, he had arrived at his decision. Some time much earlier, the decision had been made. When he awoke, he was determined. He had chosen the path he would follow.

CHAPTER XX

FLIGHT FROM THE SOUTH—MAY, 1935

I

THE decision that had been deep-bedded and growing in his subconscious mind pushed through to the very forefront of his consciousness as he rode north from Valley View.

The roots of decision were set in rock-hard earth. His mind was made up. Never again would he undergo the humiliation that was heaped on a Negro—nor experience the fears and hatreds which shredded his feelings to tatters.

He fled from the bestiality that had twisted men in Valley View—from the cruelty that had killed Jake and from the thing that had been strong enough to bring Paula from laughter to the final acts of her life.

Kern changed trains for the second time in Washington. Tired and travel-worn, he walked along the lower level where traffic came and went to and from the South—where almost six years ago he had come with his father to meet Paula—and slowly climbed the long, narrow staircase that led to the station's upper level. At the top of the stairs he stopped rested his bags, turning to look behind him. There was nothing following him—nothing he could see that resembled the thing from which he had fled. Slowly, timidly, he began to realize that he was free. He had escaped from the South with his life. He had escaped the tearing brutality that he knew now was real and not just angry, distorted words on the lips of Negroes.

He had done that much.

The realization brought a swift, heady relief from the tensions that had knotted tightly in him as he had stood in the hallway at Heritage House and listened to his father's raging voice.

Last night.

❀   ❀   ❀

No matter what his father said, he was going to leave Valley View. His mind was made up to that.

"Only a yellow dog will run away!" The words did not touch him.

He was invulnerable to contempt. The nerves and muscles that lay under the skin of his frozen white face were already taut. Each separate sense was stretched to the breaking point. If a force were to touch him now, it would have to be stronger than contempt, stronger than any of the things he had experienced.

Strange, he thought, I see my father's face. I know he is talking because I can see his lips move, but I can't hear him. I hear Paula. I hear Paula and Jake.

"You won't be running away, Kern." Paula must have foreseen this moment and armed him against it. "You are going to face life on different ground—on firmer ground. That is the only important thing—face life and see it out—" Paula understood. And Jake. He somehow thought that Jake would agree with him. "Shell shock," his father had called it.

The tearing, numbing day-after-day shocks that gave never an instant of relief; that were always alive and beyond control in the subconscious mind; that were often a part of the conscious mind—shocks that were a way of life, their damage even worse than the changes wrought in a soldier under continued shelling. That was the substance of what his father had said. And Jake had agreed.

Jake, who had gone to collect from Tom Meeker and been refused his money. Jake, for whom Tom Meeker and Mrs. Meeker who had called Bill Noble saying, "Take keer of this yeer troublesome nigger." Bill Noble goading Jake about Paula. Bill Noble and his deputies—the men who had "taken keer" of Jake.

Kern could not recognize grief in his feelings. Grief, he reasoned, would be something different from this wild, stampeding, animal fright that filled him. Grief would have come naturally for death at a bedside where loved ones had gathered for the final ministrations that always preceded its coming. There had been none of these for Jake.

This—this murder didn't bring grief. Not at first. Maybe later, but not now. Now he knew horror and fright.

Grief was for the dearly loved, familiar forms of those just passed. The twisted, stinking thing he had seen with hardening tar bubbles on its face and body brought only horror and fright.

His father was shaking him. The fierce, tight-fingered grasp on his shoulders hurt and the hurt cut through his clouded mind. He came back to reality. Dr. Gray stood anxiously by his father, his face filled with concern. Mac and Dr. Johnson were wordless, standing at the door.

"Then get out—get out!" He had never heard his father's voice raised as it was now, tight, almost hysterical. High and quavering. The hands turned him and almost shoved him toward the door. He lurched forward a stumbling step and caught himself. Mac and Dr. Johnson stared at him as he bent and picked his bags up and stepped through the open door. At the end of the long walkway, a jitney cab waited in the Oval. The first stars were showing. He would, he realized, have barely enough time to get to the station and catch the train. Mac stood beside him at the cab. "Good luck, good luck." He could not answer.

II

That was behind him now. The long train ride too was behind him. Yet each detail was clear in his mind. From the time he had changed trains in Atlanta in the dim light of early morning and gotten on the Jim Crow coach till now, it was plain in his mind.

❊   ❊   ❊

"You're on the wrong car, young man. This car's for nigras."

The conductor stooped and half whispered as though he were ashamed of what he said. The other passengers in the car were either engaged with their own thoughts or pretended not to hear. At any rate none of them turned to look.

"No," he raised his eyes, "no, sir, I'm in the right car. I'm a Negro." The man's eyes widened and he stared at Kern closely.

"Uh what—c'ose you are!" He looked over his shoulder at the dim ceiling lights. Irritation was heavy in his voice. "Body cain't hardly see these tickets even in this light." Kern had a grim delight in knowing that the man had thought he was not a Negro, a grim delight in destroying his certainty that Negroes could not look like he did.

"Whatchu goin' Nawth for, boy?"

Kern smiled inwardly and answered in a low voice.

"Got to visit my a'nt, suh—she's ailin' an' I'm goin' to bring her home." He drew on remembered words and inflections as he had with Bill Noble. He told the lie without conscious thought. Now the only important thing was to get out of the South—safely. One night of riding and he would be out— He thought, "If you only knew, you peckerwood bastard, if you only knew." The man laughed brittly as he unfolded Kern's ticket.

"Whassa matter—she got lung fever or sumpin'?"

Kern agreed. Whatever the man thought he would agree to. If he had been told to get off the coach and wallow in the dirt, he would

300

have done it. He would do anything he was told to do until he was safely out of the South. The train wheels gathered speed under him and he wondered if he could count the revolutions that would take him to safety. The door opened and the sound of the wheels against the tracks came to him on the rush of air and was dulled again as the door shut behind the conductor.

He dreamed during that night-long ride—dreamed fitful, tumbled dreams. Time and again he awakened. At one time it was to hear the steady click-click of trucks against the joints of the rails and to see the sleeping figures unmoving in their seats or shifting in sleep. At another, he woke with a start to find the train motionless at a way station and sat stiff and afraid until the voices on the platform outside his window slid away in the darkness behind them. Always he awoke hoping he would find it was all a dream, part of a nightmare. It never was. The train was real. His cramped, aching body was real. When he came full awake, he remembered and knew that the ghastliness itself had been real too.

Jake's death was not a dream. Neither was what had happened to Paula a dream. Kern shrank from the thought. Violence in one way or another was natural with men. Not with women. Not with Paula who had laughed so easily. Who had lived the small joys of life so deeply. Everything in him protested what had happened to Paula.

Kern did not have to dream about Paula. One after another, in his waking moments, he took the words which described what had happened to her and made pictures of them. In fascinated horror he focused his mind's eye on each picture and studied it in each tiny detail.

Bill Noble had made good his boast to the hangers-on in Valley View—almost. He took Paula and made her a white man's woman. In his last living moments he had done that. He had known the satisfaction of making good his pledged word. In those last shocked moments of understanding—as life jetted out of him beyond the power of man to staunch its flow—he knew that he had kept his vow to have her. He knew, too, that he was, or in moments would be, no longer a man and thus no longer required to keep a pledge of this sort. For he could never be a man again, even if he had lived.

But he could not have lived—and he knew that too in those soul-shaking moments as darkness closed in and he struggled to draw his pistol and did draw it. Drew his pistol and pressed it against the side of the girl in his arms and squeezed. He had known, too, as she laughed and taunted him with the price of his victory, that she had intended even the pistol. Even that.

Kern stared long at each picture and was fascinated.

But it was over.

Paula and Jake. The Negroes of Valley View would gather the latest crime against them to their bosoms. Anger would flare for a short while, would be voiced in angry threats. But in the end nothing would be done. The crime would never be punished, as this last one had not been punished, and as the next one, too, would go unpunished.

Over. All done and over.

Paula.

Jake.

His father.

"The problem."

The Freedom League.

'Doriah.

Valley View.

Seventeen and almost eighteen years. Done and over. Finished. Only terror was left. Terror and a resolve that no matter what the price, it would never happen to him again.

✿   ✿   ✿

Kern stared down the stairs and remembered these things. They were in him and on his face, marking his lips and darkening his eyes. The man and woman who pushed past him where he stood could not have understood. They saw only a tall young man with slumped shoulders and a strangely old face.

They looked back curiously as they passed and went on. Kern picked up his bags and followed them slowly across the concourse, past the magazine stand, threading his way automatically toward the central waiting room and the Western Union desk.

The marble counter was cool against the flat of his hand as he wrote:

Mrs. Margaret Adams
Northport, Vermont
            Coming home.   Kern.

He started toward the closest bench and saw a Negro couple sitting, asleep, leaning against one another's shoulders, next to the empty space in front of him. He stopped abruptly, his eyes searching the waiting room. There was another bench beyond him with an empty space. On either side of the space were white faces.

He walked slowly and deliberately toward the space.

302

INTERLUDE V

WAR YEARS, 1942-1944

KERN spent almost two years overseas.

He went from England to North Africa. From North Africa he went to Sicily and on to Italy. Then he returned to England. Months after, when the program series, "A Yank in England," had been completed, he went on to Omaha Beach on the heels of combat troops. There he saw the war from close up. From closer than he wanted to. He learned what a Jerry "88" could do and what the sky was like when there were so many bombers in it that he could hardly hear his own voice for the thunder of their passage. He saw men die. He saw men dead. And he sickened and wearied of what he was seeing. He saw courage. Rich and fine and tattered after years of holding on. He saw courage in England and in France, where the will to live had not died, even though the Nazi had tried to crush it out with every cruelty he could devise.

Kern saw these things and tried to write them into the scripts which his team was preparing. Tried to pack into them the meaning of a bomb blast and of starvation—of living with hope when one should reasonably have been dead long ago.

The battle-front scripts which he developed did what he and Max wanted them to. They carried a part of the war to America. They were authentic. They were real and powerful. They were listened to—which was Kern's major interest—and they won him a continued spattering of applause in the trade magazines and gathered a larger listening public to American Broadcasting which, by his express desire, never "by-lined" him on any program.

From France Kern returned to America. For three and one half days he stayed in New York, pleading with Max to use his influence to cut the red tape which threatened to keep him from going to the Pacific.

Even better than Max Karns did his grandmother understand the urge which drove him, in spite of his weariness, to the Pacific. She offered no objection, did not insist that he had seen enough slaughter in Europe—when he told her that it would be several months before he would be free to spend an extended leave with her. She simply wished him Godspeed and good luck, understanding that he must go at once, before the full horror of what lay behind him—and ahead—sapped his resolve.

Reluctantly, Max pulled the wires necessary to clear his early departure, and on the fourth day after he had landed in New York, Captain Kern Adams, shiny new bars on his worn, stained tunic, was on his way to the West Coast and the first leg of his long journey down through the Pacific to join the island-hopping fleets and armies as they fought northward through the endless miles of sea and the everlasting islands.

Kern was dead tired. But he had to go. The things that made it necessary for him to go were tightly sealed behind his lips. Not even with Max could he talk about them in detail. Not even though he tried. As the miles slid away behind him, Kern looked forward to his arrival in the theater with relief, knowing that he would find kindred spirits there as he had not found them in the States.

In the Pacific, Kern found loneliness and fever and strange diseases about which medical science knew little or nothing. He found the fetid, steaming jungle and poisonous insects—waiting and slow movement. He found desolation that made him recall the European theater as a civilized battleground. Each island was an assault. Each assault meant waiting. Each assault preceded by an hours-long bombardment by cruisers and bombers and then the last, silent moment when the bombardment stopped. When both enemy and attacker knew that this was the time when they would move in. And almost always there was but one direction from which they could make their assault. Always into the face of concentrated fire. Each assault another Normandy.

Once, without orders, Kern went ashore in an assault wave. Just once. He splashed through the warm, waist-high water toward the faraway shore and wished to God he had had enough sense to have stayed on shipboard. He learned the whisper of a bullet when it passes close by and understood what the men in his boat had meant by "keeping a 'tight holt' on himself." He lay face down in the dry lava ash of the beach and wished that he could push even further out of sight. He began to shake, and when the first boat started to take off the wounded, he helped to load it. Not because he was a hero. Because he was scared. Because the quickest way to get off that beach was to help load that boat. He was sick with fear, and he pitied the men who stayed behind him.

304

He never went ashore in an assault wave again.

He never forgot the sour taste of fear in his mouth.

Five weeks later, he moved south and east through the islands to Australia. From there he went north and east toward Hawaii and the States.

He was tired and sick to the core. He was sick of fighting and of the horrible toll it took. Above all else, he remembered the dreadful lonesomeness of the Pacific—the absence of civilization— of the things to which the European GI would turn when he was out of the lines. Not that he felt death was any less final in Europe than it was in the Pacific. Not that—but there was something cleaner about the war in Europe.

One thing else he brought back from the Pacific with him— understanding of the force he had wanted to write about when he had started his story that last time when he had gone to Harlem.

His longing for Marianne began the moment he returned to the States. It pushed in about him as he reopened his apartment. It grew when he met Bill Gabel for dinner. It stayed in him through-out the month of leave he spent with his grandmother in North-port. It was as strong as it had been before he had left New York for England. But it had deepened and matured. The first sharp, almost unbearable pain had been tempered. Longing was in him, but bearable. At times that longing seemed unimportant in the face of the things he had seen and remembered.

Max Karns sensed the new depths in Kern, saw that the fire in him, the restless drive that had made him high-strung and taut, had been replaced by a self-contained, determined force that burned no less brightly than the other force had, but which was now under stern control.

Kern's story occupied him now, filling the blank space of time when his office work was over. Kern saw his first story on a larger canvas. It was not now a matter of telling about the unkindness of one race in America to its largest minority. He saw, or thought he saw, that at the root of the world-wide turmoil which he had wit-nessed was the need for simple, human kindness among men. Kern thought of his story now in those terms—as a story for all men and all creeds and all races, for he was completely convinced that the need for understanding and love among all men extended just so far as that.

In the office, he worked as he never had before. There were now no spurts of work followed by idle days. No times when Trixie and

Julia could wonder whether there would be work or not. There was always work. A steady stream of it, work to be done on a schedule which Kern would not allow himself, or them, to break. The backlog of projects built up rapidly in the first month of 1945. Special assignments came from the War Department and from the Office of War Information. American found its work load doubled and almost tripled. When Kern went to Max to tell him that it would be "impossible" to accept another special assignment, Max knew that the maximum burden had been reached. That same day, at Kern's suggestion, he telephoned Hollywood for Carson Newman, a radio and movie script writer whose work Kern had heard.

※　※　※

Carson Newman was a Negro.

The surprise that marked his arrival in Kern's office lasted five minutes. Then the office settled back to its normal routine. It took him no longer than that to begin work. He was a tall, deceptively broad-shouldered man with a face whose planes and hollows reminded Kern of his father's face done in brown. He had the same calm, self-assured poise which had set Charles off from most men.

Newman walked into the office on a bright, cold Monday morning five days after Max had telephoned him. He stood, just inside the door, looking about him. He met Trixie's polite smile of greeting with a pleasant nod and walked toward Kern's desk, stretching his hand out.

"Adams?"

Kern nodded.

"I'm Newman, Carson Newman." There was no note of apology.

Kern realized that he had automatically thought Newman would be a white man. His first thin reluctance for Newman yielded immediately to the press of work. After the first two days, when he had a breathing spell and time to think, Kern found that there was no tightness in him, no reluctance to work with the man. In fact, he found that he worked better with Newman than he had with anyone since he had come to American. The two of them made a team. They clicked. Newman was professionally sound. He assumed the share of work allotted to him and finished it on schedule. When other tasks appeared and needed doing, he stepped in and did them without fanfare. He asked for no praise. He never called attention to the extra work he did. The staff accepted his orders without question and gave him the same ready support they gave to Kern.

The office moved smoothly through January and into February. Then everything went haywire.

Neither of them could write. Their minds would not meet. Minor delays exasperated them. Work piled high on both of their desks. The higher it piled, the less they could do. Their major assignment, a script for use when the Germans surrendered in Europe— the war was reaching that point—dragged to a scraping halt as deadline time stared them in the face. Each day they kept hourly track on the news bulletins, always afraid that surrender would come and the script would not be ready for use on the air.

The story simply would not jell! There were too many interruptions. Light bulbs needed changing just as the germ of an idea seemed in their grasp. A door banged shut and broke a train of thought. A typewriter carriage slammed against its stop and was maddening. Pencil points deliberately broke under their fingers and typewriter keys purposely made strike-overs.

"Nothing, goddam it—nothing would work! Nothing would work."

Irritation exceeded irritation. Tempers raveled and frayed. Carson, who never permitted himself less than complete self-control, finally broke. Hands planted in his hip pockets, he stood in front of the window and looked out and down at the swirling specks of people and fervently murmured. "God damn it! God damn it!" His utterance had the effect of a bombshell. Kern, Trixie and Julia gaped as he walked back to his desk and dropped into his chair. "I wish we could go to China for about a week—just a little peace and quiet. We might get this thing finished." Kern moodily contemplated the wall before him and the suddenly fading object of his irritation. In his haste to scramble upright he almost tilted his chair over.

"Holy cow!" he shouted. "Why didn't I think of that before? We can go up to my grandmother's place and get this thing polished off."

"Your grandmother's place?" Carson's eyes rolled ceiling-ward. "Now don't tell me it's really in China."

"Hell no, man! It's in Vermont. Hills—tall, green, quiet. Can't you see it—a house against a hill—?" Kern spun the dial of his phone quickly and waited, his fingers playing against the top of his desk, until the operator took his call.

"Mrs. Margaret Adams—yes. That's right. Northport, Vermont.

P-O-R-T, that's it—port." He grinned up at the ceiling through the cloud of smoke. Vermont was the place—they'd finish it there. Quickly—on time, Kern was sure of it.

❋ ❋ ❋

"We can leave tomorrow," Carson nodded agreement from across the room and Kern relaxed, looking about him at the walls and the polished furniture that filled the room. This room had been his grandfather's favorite retreat.

"I shall be sorry to leave." Carson's voice was thoughtful. "In a way, a part of this house shall always belong to me."

Kern thought that he understood Carson's meaning. Standing he stretched on tiptoe. "Think I'll get a breath of air while you wrap that stuff up, Carson."

Newman nodded. "I'll join you—this won't take me but a minute or so." He bent at the table arranging the sheets before him while Kern moved toward the door, shrugging a pull-over sweater over his head.

Outside, Kern bowed his shoulders against the first numbing cold. Broken clouds from the morning's storm still marked the sky. The wind had died down completely and an immense calm surrounded the house. Tall, blue-black pines spired against the sky, launching up from the smooth white snow. Kern's eyes went to the mountains. They were, he thought, as immovable as the will of God. Carefully, slowly he drew in a deep breath, finding that the air, icy and clean, stabbed at his chest with sharp little fingers. The air was heady with pine scent. Kern thought of the Pacific islands.

"Beautiful!" Carson's word and the way in which he said it were almost a prayer. Kern wondered how long he had been standing there behind him. He felt the man's eyes on him and knew before he spoke that he was going to ask a question.

"What are you thinking?" Kern wondered how to answer him.

"The ultimate beauty—untouched—ready to be possessed by those who can see and feel." The dull cold bit at Kern and he felt the thump of his heart. "I always find a challenge here. Something stronger than the strongest effort I can make, than my best hope. I see things more clearly here." He could not see Carson's face when he questioned him in turn.

"You?"

"The final loneliness!"

"Loneliness?"

"Yes—the reminder that there must come a time when a man must face himself——"

"You mean face his God——?"

"No—I mean himself. When man must account to his own consciousness—the one thing to which he cannot lie—" Kern ruminated on the words. Shrugging his shoulders against the cold, Carson turned toward the door. He stood staring at the sky for a moment as Kern went through the door, then he followed.

They slouched on the floor in front of the fireplace, grateful for its warmth. Kern spoke first.

"You say 'final loneliness'—isn't that when man meets his Maker?" Newman's sardonic smile said "No!"

"I mean when man faces himself—when his sands are running out and he can no longer avoid asking himself, 'Have I done the best with what was given to me of time—of potential for good or bad?'" Carson spoke almost to himself. "That's the question to answer. Have you realized your responsibility to yourself?"

Kern swallowed. Those words—they were the same as his old Headmaster had used. The night, the room at Evans—the hurt—were very clear.

"That's when he may remember that he has not been faithful to the goal he set when he started out—when he bargained with his ambition. When he stopped and might have gone on to win. That is important too—man must have set his own goal and fought everlastingly to reach it." Newman straightened and sat hunched over his knees, staring into the fire. He was oblivious of Kern's presence, and did not notice when Margaret Adams tiptoed in and sat behind them.

"I had to be a competent writer. Not a competent 'Negro writer.' But a 'competent writer.'" Kern knew that his grandmother was listening too. "It seems to me that I have always known what I want. But I had things much differently from you. I was miserably poor in a way which you could never understand. In a way which I could never describe to you. Spiritual poverty. Negroes know it well. I hungered all of my life for a house such as this one—and for the dignity that goes with it. For a simple, everyday existence without hating and brawling." A knife twisted inside Kern as he recalled the years when he had not had this house—or the things it stood for—when he had had only a terrible driving hunger such as Carson's.

"But what happened to me isn't important—the main thing is that with what little I had to offer, I have—I hope—been able to help my fellow men—all of them." He turned then to look at Kern and his grandmother. "I think, sometimes, that must be the final question we can ask of ourselves."

Margaret Adams' voice was low and warm.

"You're right, Carson, very right." She came and stood between them, holding out her hands. "Dinner, boys—my boys." They went with her.

        ❋   ❋   ❋

Kern turned from the bookcases to find his grandmother watching him with a speculative gaze. He smiled at her.

"Looks like another storm is brewing in the northeast. Might blow around though."

She smiled. "Might." And Kern noted for the thousandth time the taciturnity of speech for which he had always remembered this house and the people of the land. "Been nice having you and Carson here——"

"You like Carson, don't you?"

"I certainly do. I admire and respect him."

"Do you admire and respect me, Gran'?" Kern asked impulsively.

Margaret Adams thought at first he was joking. His level, waiting eyes expressed his seriousness as he drew a chair up to face hers.

"Yes, I do, Kern. I admire you a great deal. As much as I did your grandfather." That, Kern knew, was the highest accolade she could give him.

"You've grown a great deal, Kern. More than you may know. You've overcome the handicap you had at the start, the angers and fears you felt. You made a preliminary adjustment to life when you began to grow after college. But most of all have you grown in this war. You've matured and, I think, you've learned the greatest lesson of all—humility—the need for kindness." She smiled a little grimly. "You didn't have that before you went overseas, you know."

"Kindness is important, isn't it, Gran'?"

"Very—" She reached to touch his knee, in an affectionate gesture. "It's about the most important thing in the world. That and love for one's fellows——"

Kern nodded, cradling his chin on his knees. "I believe that too, Gran'. I started a story once in which I wanted to tell about the absence of human kindness that drives the Negro to despair in

America. But now I think that it isn't only America—it isn't only the Negro—it's the world that needs to learn that lesson. I wish that you could have seen the start of that story," he said reflectively, "it——"

"I have," she spoke in a low voice that Kern did not at first hear as he went on:

"I guess it must have been pretty stormy. I was— You *have!*" He twisted about to face her as her words sifted into his consciousness. "Seen it where?"

"Here—I have it here."

"*You* have— But how—how could you? I——"

"I know."

"Marianne?" The long-denied swirl of emotion—of missing and longing—came to him.

"Yes—Marianne brought it with her."

"When?" Marianne had been here—here—in this house?

"Months ago—more than a year. Not long after you left for the Pacific."

"What did she say—did she ask——?"

"Kern—" her hand tightened on his shoulder, "don't you suppose that she should tell you herself what she said?" He lowered his head under her direct gaze.

"Yes—I suppose so."

"Kern—listen to me. Marianne is a very fine girl. An unusual girl. But you must remember—don't judge her too harshly. No matter how liberal one may claim to be about this sort of thing, or how opposed one may be to bigotry." Kern heard her even, spaced words and thought that she had withdrawn to memory. "The first time one is brought into personal contact with it, it is something to reckon with. Until then, we never know how deeply the taboos and myths have become rooted in us. We can never realize it until the thing they represent actually affects us. When Marianne learned that you were a Negro, in spite of herself, she was confronted with every myth and taboo that the word 'Negro' has come to represent. She couldn't help that. Nothing in all her experience had prepared her for the shock." Kern listened and understood. Part of this he had thought of before. Even before Marianne learned.

"I love her a very great deal, Gran'."

Her hand tightened on his shoulder. "I know, son—she loves you, too."

311

"Gran'," he turned his face up toward hers, searching her eyes for an answer, "will she—have me——?"

"Kern—that one question I cannot answer for you. If I could I would not. I believe you should ask Marianne that."

* * *

He did not get through to New York on the first try. Nor on the second. The third time he tried, he got through to the New York operator, and though the connection was poor, he recognized Marianne's voice at once.

"Marianne——?"

"Yes." Nothing in her voice. Merely a word, telling him nothing.

"Marianne—this is Kern."

"Yes, Kern—I know." That was what he had heard—her voice was tired.

"Marianne—" he took a sweet delight in pronouncing her name, "I'm coming down to New York tomorrow."

"Yes——"

"Marianne—can—would—can I see you tomorrow—for dinner?"

"Yes, Kern."

"Thank God," he murmured to himself.

"What did you say, Kern? I can't hear you clearly."

"Nothing—nothing." His heart sang. He would see Marianne again. If nothing more came of it, he would at least see her. "The connection is bad. I can't hear you very well either."

"You'll call when you get in?"

"Yes—yes, I'll call."

"I'll wait for your call."

"Good night, Marianne."

"Good night, Kern." He heard the click on the other end of the line and then the operator's voice cut in:

"Are you finished with your call?"

"Yes—thank you. I'm finished." He replaced the receiver in its cradle.

312

EPILOGUE

FALL, 1948

THE tree shapes were large. Now dark. Now somber. Now silvery. Matching the mood of the sky. Marking the path of the rolling clouds as they went, wind-driven, across the moon. The shadows and the light played on the carriage windows. Outside the hansom, the even clip-clop of shod hooves sounded on the roadbed.

The road dipped and bent to the northern end of the Park and climbed again, turning to run beside the distant line of lights that marked 110th Street. Then it left the far-off lights and bent southward. Here the hooves gave forth a clear metallic ring, and their beat on the pavement seemed to quicken as though their owner sensed the approaching end of labor.

His gathering arm drew her closer and his free fingers followed the line of her cheek and cautiously stirred the hair at her temples. Her head tilted back and he knew the ripe softness of her mouth. Then she drew away from him, went into the corner of the seat, and the quickened pulse at her throat was her only sign of feeling as she peered through the carriage window.

"Kern—I am—sure." He waited, afraid to prompt her deliberate words. "You believe that, don't you?"

"Yes." He could not help her, could not find words for her. She would have to find words herself, to tell the thing that was in her mind. There could be no tomorrow when either of them would look back on this moment and find confusion in it, feel, the one, that the other had prompted with words that had not been the right words. Through the window the moonlight was bright on her face.

"I never knew before what panic was like." She spoke slowly as if she were uncertain that each next word would have the meaning she wanted it to have. "When I saw that one word—'Negro'—on the page before me, when I saw you standing there so stiff at the window, all the pieces fell together. Your silence. The strained way you'd met me at the door. The months when we'd been apart—no

313

word, no explanation. I knew that I was looking at your own story. Remember those first words?"

Those blunt words—Kern remembered them.

"I was once a Negro."

"When you turned around and looked at me, I was sure it was your story. That was when I felt the panic come to me. Way down inside of me, something said, 'It doesn't matter.' But I don't believe I ever really heard the words. Not my mind anyway." Marianne frowned as she looked out the window. Finally she began again.

"About the only thing I know that can describe that panic is a dream I had when I was a little girl. I was standing in a valley where three mountains rose up about me and three rivers converged. I saw floods come rushing down each valley toward where I stood. I couldn't move. I wanted to. But I couldn't."

Kern remembered that kind of dream—when he had run from a hand that clutched a knife and there had been only blind alleys. He wanted to put his arm around Marianne, but he had to wait. Had to listen and wait.

"It was a panic like that. I remember that I did remember everything I had ever heard about Negroes. Things I have argued against myself. Things that I *knew* couldn't possibly be true. But in my panic I could not question them. Because the words on that page told me that you were a Negro—all of those things meant you."

For others, Kern thought, it was like that too. The unthinking transference of the entire myth to all Negroes—without exception.

"I wanted to run, but I was afraid to. You were suddenly a total stranger, and I didn't know what you would do if I tried to run. I was afraid——"

Kern's heart twisted in him. Marianne afraid—of him! She turned with a faint crooked smile, then looked back out the window.

"The nights and days after that were like some hideous nightmare. I was afraid that someone else would discover my—my sin, and I would become an outcast. I promised myself that I would guard my secret very carefully. I was very casual about the whole thing when Bill and the gang asked about you—your being away made it easier." Her words came more easily, and Kern could sense the decision in her.

"Then the panic began to wear off. It did not go in a day. Not for months. It was a long time before wanting you broke through. When it did, I was sure I had lost you. Bit by bit, I found that a

314

single word couldn't describe you. A word hadn't changed you. It hadn't stopped me from missing you. I did miss you." She turned as she repeated herself, her words more emphatic. He had missed her too, for days and weeks, more than years—on beaches and during curtain time, on empty streets. He'd missed her too.

"You were gone so long. I had time to inspect the things I had thought I believed, and I found that I did believe in them. I couldn't see how I had lost my hold on the belief. I don't know whether I'm making much sense." She pushed into the corner of the cab and her face, white, wan, was almost lost in the shadows. "I am trying to tell you that nothing matters so long as you are Kern—so long as we can make a life for ourselves as decent human beings."

Kern waited. Not yet the words he wanted. Not yet. The two large tears that formed at the corners of her eyes took ages to fall along her cheeks and he felt his arms gathering her and bringing her to him.

"I love you, darling. Please forgive me—for what I couldn't help." She was in his arms and nothing else mattered.

* * *

This hushed place was the Supreme Court of the land. And the seal upon the wall was the Great Seal of the nation. That long bench was where the robed Justices sat in judgment. This was the final place of recourse under law for Americans. A strong feeling of awe filled Kern. Seated about him were Negroes. And white men. Waiting faces, representing both sides of the issue at hand. Here in this high court.

And his own father would shortly stand before them all to present his argument. Almost nine years had passed since Kern had seen him last. Angry then and bitter. Today he was to argue against covenants. Contracts that shut men out from dwelling places because of race and religion. Contracts that condemned them to a lifetime of owning and living in second-class homes.

Tomorrow, Kern knew, he would be in Northport. Home with Marianne and four-year-old Margaret. Tomorrow, Northport—but today, this.

"Honorable Justices—" Kern exulted at his father's voice. That voice, the instrument on which his father had for years played with the skill of a virtuoso, had not been touched by the reedy tones of age. There was no treble in it. No falsetto.

The crowded room was without motion. Save for Charles Roberts' voice—without sound.

"Law is a thing of the spirit. It is the guardian of hope. It is, in its finest sense, a living, growing reality. It may, in its purest form, be recognized as the child of the spirit which gave it birth. Often the realities of life and growth are so far apart from the concept of original origin as to defy description——"

So much had happened to this man. So much in a single lifetime. So much pain. So much fighting. Kern wondered if his father had been lonely—and knew that he had.

"A child may plant an acorn in a flower box and carefully nurture it from day to day, dreaming of the roses that may, in time, bloom. For just so has he seen his mother set out plants that in time grew to be roses. In the same way do men conceive their dreams and hopes and nourish them and secure them with law.

"The acorn springs to life, and the child, not understanding that this is the natural, the ultimate, shape of creation to which he contributed, still envisions the rose and is puzzled and dissatisfied and cannot imagine the towering wonder of a full-grown oak as the seed he has planted springs to life.

"So too with men and their hopes—with society and law. When the limits of original intent are unchanging, when the dream of tomorrow today is measured by the inflexible yardstick of yesterday's facts, law becomes static and it inexorably strangles the society which has fostered it."

Charles' voice gathered resonance. Hands clasped behind his back in the manner of an old and capable schoolteacher, he moved easily before the bench, back and forth, and all eyes followed him.

"The law of contracts, under which the matter of restrictive covenants comes before this court, is not a cause. It is, instead, an effect, a result. And as such it requires most careful inspection to determine the causes which have rendered it inadequate as a law. For any law which causes prolonged controversy is an inadequate law. The fundamental question is this— Is the theory of these laws of contracts, as applied to restrictive covenants, now insufficient to our present need?"

"In all the world, Kern, there is only one thing I wish I could know—" His grandmother had said that when spring came last year—in the few moments before she had left them. Kern's sorrow was sharp and deep. Three tall headstones in the cemetery now. Caleb Adams. His daughter, Laura Elizabeth. And now, Margaret

316

Mary, beloved wife. "That in some way you could make peace with your father. He'll understand now, Kern. He's a fine man." Kern felt his heart tighten.

"And like all liberties of men, privilege is valid only so long as it does not, by any device, interfere with the fundamental liberties of other men. That is the moral foundation which is contravened in this case."

Melancholy came into his voice. Melancholy and a yearning that was hunger, expressed in words, in tone, in the simple gestures of his hands.

"Side by side—in peace and contentment." His voice was low and reflective. "That is the thing. Was it—or was it not—the intent of our Constitution that this should be?" Kern followed his words closely, acutely conscious of the quality of silence that was in the room. The silence was almost audible. He followed his father's words, a part of his mind racing on ahead to the inevitable conclusion the words were pointing.

"It is for the members of this Court, for you who more than any other body are the guardian of our national conscience, to determine the answer to this question. Do the guarantees of our Constitution *really* mean that, because of race or creed, no man in America is to be penalized? Is it true that *all* men are guaranteed the inalienable rights of life, liberty and the pursuit of happiness? You must determine what the shape of that original intent may have been. If you determine that these things were not truly intended by the founding fathers—if, in the light of common usage and of our future promise, you find this not so—then I beg you, say to this enjoinder——

"'This was not the intent of the founding fathers. This is not the end to which America is being wrought.' Say that 'It is your considered opinion that America was meant to be a nation for men of one race and one creed.' Say then, 'That men of other races and other creeds may live here—but under certain specified conditions.' Say these things in the firm knowledge that you will be doing an immeasurable kindness to millions of men and women. You will be making their lives, for the first time, livable and understandable. You will have stripped away from their everyday existence the fearful cloak of misapprehension under which they now live. You will, once and for all, have outlined their position in American society. You will have forever removed from them any reason for false hope and for misconceived opinion. Do this and you will have

317

struck to the canker of discontent which today—and for many years past—has riven the lives of these millions with despair and with puzzling, unanswered discontent.

"If this be not the case—and I pray Almighty God that it be not —then so find, and in doing so you will affirm that which has through the years made America the beacon of hope in a world all too familiar with the hand of tyrants—with the harshness of rulers without obligation to the ruled.

"Simple human kindness—" Charles' voice lowered even more. The words drummed in Kern's mind, rousing up pictures from memory. Pictures of Jake and Paula. Of Jeff Balanchine. Of his grandmother. Of the twisting, billowing shape of fear that had been in him that night, years ago now, when he had fled the South in fear and desperation. Pictures that included Jerry behind his bar in Harlem. And Max Karns. Pictures among which were the tight, listening faces of Negroes sitting about him at this instant. Waiting faces. Faces marked with tiredness and hope. His father's voice became clearer.

"I believe that the law of this land should be a testament of human kindness—that now, as never before in our life as a nation, must we declare to the peoples of the world what we are and what we are determined to safeguard for all men in all ages. This is not a case of interest to Negroes alone. It is, I conceive, of interest to Americans everywhere—of importance to freedom-loving men wherever they may be on the face of this earth." His last words came slowly, were widely spaced. He raised his shaggy head and looked into the faces of the Justices ranged before him. "That is the case of the plaintiffs."

❁   ❁   ❁

There was only a little time left after the spectators had pushed out into the hall. Time enough for Kern to make his way through the shifting, forming groups, and grasp his father's hand as he stood among the host of well-wishers, the merely curious, who clustered about him. Their hands met in the press of the crowd, and their eyes, and recognition struck instantly between them, spanning the years that had passed as though they were nothing. Their hands held and their eyes held as Charles drew Kern aside to the quiet of an alcove.

"Kern!" Their hands were still clasped as Charles looked at his watch. "Dinner. I don't suppose you'd have time enough—?" His

318

question went unfinished. Kern winced that this man should wonder if he could spare time to have dinner with him.

"I stayed over today just to hear your argument—" the one word with which he had never addressed Charles surged up to his lips, "Dad." He felt his father's hand tighten on his own in a sudden, hurting grasp, and was glad he had used the word. Somehow Charles managed to get away from the horde that waited for him, and, arm in arm, they hurried down the long steps and across the wide marble entrance to the street and hailed a cab. There was time enough for dinner in Union Station before Charles caught a train for the Midwest.

"Of course," he laughed, "I'm running off on another case—" For the first time in their lives they were relaxed and able to say to one another the things that they would once never have been able to mention. Charles hurriedly recounted the years, touching on Jake and Paula, on Washington, lightly mentioning himself and, of course, running on at length about the Freedom League. Mostly he plied Kern with questions about himself and his grandmother —about college and the war and his job. They raced through his first book and went as far as Kern himself had gone into his second book. The clock hand on the wall before Kern had moved close to the time when Charles would have to catch his train before Kern took out his wallet and extracted a snapshot which he held out to his father. He watched Charles' face as he looked at the picture and waited until his eyes rose to look at him.

"That's Marianne." Kern leaned across the table to point her out and to launch into the tale of how he and Marianne had parted and of how they had come together again. Charles pointed to the little girl standing beside Marianne.

"And that is?" Kern could not mask his delight when he answered.

"That's your granddaughter, Margaret."

"My granddaughter—why wasn't I—?" Charles subsided sheepishly. "Well, I'll be doggoned." He asserted twice again that he would be "doggoned," as he tilted the photo and leaned back in his chair, as though to see his granddaughter more clearly.

"Well, I'll be doggoned!"

Then their time ran out. They stood together at the station gate, hands clasped, before Charles went through the open gate.

"I can count on your coming, Dad?"

"You're quite sure, boy, that it won't embarrass——"

Kern cut him short.

"There is no way you could embarrass me. Nor Marianne. She'll be looking forward to your visit and to meeting you. As much as I." So often he had heard Marianne express the wish that she could know his father. Charles smiled a shy, pleased smile—as Kern had never seen him smile before.

"Tell—my granddaughter—'Hello!'—" Kern's arm went around his shoulders.

"I will—I won't forget." Then Charles was gone through the gate, hurrying along beside the waiting train. Hurrying away, but looking back and waving his hand. Kern watched until he was out of sight. His own steps were light when he turned and went through the station to the front to hail a cab. Tomorrow he would be in Northport. Home with Marianne and Margaret. Next month his father would be with them.

But now, at this instant, there was the warm knowledge that the ends had been joined. That his father understood and there was no more bitterness. He could forget the angry words in the hallway of Heritage House—the first steps that had brought him to flight and to a new life.

He still felt his father's hand in his. Still felt Charles' understanding as he had sat and nodded his head in agreement as Kern had covered the years between them.

For a moment, as he stood in the late-afternoon sunlight, before a taxi stopped, Kern wondered what it might have been like had he stood and fought. Had he been one with that tiny band of men —the Whites and Washingtons, DuBois and Wilkins and Douglass— men who gave their whole lives to the fight for a race. The moment passed, and he felt calm assurance that for himself the bargain with Life had been a good one—a fair one. His father knew that.